PRAISE

"I don't just read about these people, I am living their lives with them. Gail doesn't keep you on the sidelines, she plunges you into the heart and soul of the Tanner family and everyone who comes in contact with them. Never more so than in Triad."

— READER REVIEW

"I have to say this is one of the best, if not THE best, books in the 'Phoenix' series. The themes of love/hate, family, slavery/freedom, faith, self-sacrifice, and humanity shine through on every page. I seriously could not stop reading. Once the action started it never stopped and the tension kept ratcheting right up until the surprising cliffhanger. Ms Delaney definitely leaves you wanting more."

— AMAZON REVIEW — 5 STARS

Phoenix Rising
Book Two
Triad

Part Two of the Future Possible Saga

TRIAD

PHOENIX RISING BOOK TWO

GAIL R. DELANEY

Irish Eyes
Books

To Jenifer: Thank you for accessing that part of my brain I hadn't been able to get to yet and helping me see the path for this book.

To William Scarborough: Thank you for lending me your beautiful imagination to design the new flag of the Protectorate. I had a vague idea, and you made it reality. You are precious to me.

To Michael Tanner: Yes, I know you are a fictional character born of my crazy psyche, but I adore you. Thank you for being the best part of Humanity. It makes me sad you will never be real.

To Vicki Gardner: You owe me lunch.

CONTENT DISCUSSION AND AUTHOR INSIGHT

Throughout the whole of the Phoenix Rising quartet, there is a prominent character dealing with the trauma and emotional recovery from childhood sexual assault.

The events are in the past, and are not detailed anywhere in these novels. Doing so would not add anything but unnecessary shock value, and that isn't the type of author I am. I write enough so the source of the trauma is clear, and the reader can understand the extent of the physical and emotional trauma inflicted on this character.

There will be times when the memories are very raw and near the surface, and I recognize this may be very difficult for some readers when it parallels their own experience. Some books delve deeper than others, but the past events come into play in all four books.

There will also be a point when children are removed from a similar situation. Again, no details. I can't even go there myself.

I don't wish to blindside anyone. I hope perhaps the journey to recovery, very unique for the characters, will be worth the read.

THE FUTURE POSSIBLE SAGA

THE PHOENIX REBELLION QUARTET

BOOK ONE: REVOLUTION

BOOK TWO: OUTCASTS

BOOK THREE: GAINING GROUND

BOOK FOUR: END GAME

PHOENIX RISING QUARTET

BOOK ONE: JANUS

BOOK TWO: TRIAD

BOOK THREE: STASIS

BOOK FOUR: LIBER

THE FUTURE POSSIBLE SAGA STORYTELLING STYLE

The Future Possible Saga is a continuous timeline, in which any give book extends the story of the book prior to it and sets up for the next book while also telling its own story. The books must be read in order to have full understanding of the saga.

This means each book has its own story arc, but also extends the greater saga story arcs.

There will be cliffhangers, but as the author I will always provide you with a payoff within the book you're reading. Each book has its own plot, it's own storyline, and its own resolutions. Each book (with the exclusion of the final book in the saga) will have setup for the next book. These may or may not be considered cliffhangers by some. But, be aware, they exist.

The good news is the saga as told through The Phoenix Rebellion quartet and Phoenix Rising quartet is complete. You don't have to wait for a cliffhanger resolution. Just continue to the next book.

I hope you enjoy, and complete the journey with us.

"Beauty, truth and rarity,
Grace in all simplicity,
Here enclosed in cinders lie."

The Phoenix and the Turtle
~William Shakespeare

PROLOGUE

22 December 2011, Thursday
Earth-Areth Collaboration Building
Washington DC
United States of America

*D*avid Forte's breath curled in front of his face in white puffs and drops of cold rain clung to his dark clothing. His nose and lips were numb with the cold, the night temperature barely into the forties. The light rain had frozen to a slippery sheen on all flat surfaces, making stealth movement precarious at best.

He pressed his back to the wall of the three-story building now designated as the Earth-Areth Collaboration, a building housing laboratories and research facilities, conference areas, and living quarters for the visiting Areth "Dignitaries." A blue beam shot straight into the night sky, blocking out the stars, acting as a beacon for the Areth ship holding orbit over the country's capitol. Somewhere beyond what the Human eye could see, their massive ship hid beyond the clouds.

David sneered, staring upward. The whole idea of aliens strolling into the capitol and making nice made the hair on the back of his neck stand on end; which was probably why General Packard sent him in under the cover of darkness to investigate the Areth claims, without so much as a dog tag to ID him if things went south. Negotiations and "talks" had been proceeding "exceptionally well," if one believed President Woosley, and while David should hold loyalty to his commander in chief, he couldn't swallow the "We come in peace" cock-and-bull story. Who better to send in than someone who would gladly look past the rose-tinted promises of Utopia to the truth underneath?

Kelly believed there had to be someone better.

"When have you given enough, David? When will your kids be more important than 'giving your all' to your country?"

She didn't understand he did what he did for Davey and Anthony, especially with the appearance of these galactic "ancestors from the stars." If the Areth delivered everything they so magnanimously promised, and it really was all done without ulterior motive, then great. Bring on a brighter, better future. But, David had grown up on way too many sci fi movies and television shows to swallow the idea of a far superior race appearing out of the blackness of space to "reconnect with their lost descendants." Part of him hoped to be proven wrong, but it was a small part, the greater and louder part being common sense and gut instinct.

He slipped into the lower level of the parking garage and ran close to the floor, keeping to the shadows as much as possible, until he reached the freight elevator. The building was old, the security system only partially updated, so it only took seconds for his electromagnetic scrambler to decipher the keypad code and open the stairwell door beside the elevator. The elevator would be quicker but would call more attention than he wanted if the wrong people were in the wrong place at the wrong time.

General Packard told him to stick to the labs, and any files he might be able to find there. Some of the types of data the Areth had requested had set off warning bells for some high-ranking geneticists, and the coalition committees wanted assurances their requests were on the up-and-up before handing over the known secrets of the Human double helix.

The fact alone they'd asked for the information put David's teeth on edge, and he wasn't even a scientist. If they were supposedly mankind's ancestors, if Humans were their forgotten children from an expedition thousands of years before, wouldn't the basis of Human DNA structure already be known to them?

He reached the second level and used the EM scrambler to unlock the door, easing it open to check the dimly lit hallway before he exited the stairwell. He had the security guard's schedule for walking the floor, and had the cameras timed to the second, thanks to intel from the general, and maneuvered across the floor to the specific room he wanted. The lock was slightly more sophisticated on this door, but the scrambler did its job and the lock disengaged. Keeping low, David slipped into the lab and headed directly for one of the terminals. If his misspent youth hacking computer systems and building his own GUI from the microchip up would ever pay off, it was now.

The computer terminals were set up on a continuous desk space wrapping three sides of a small room, the wall parallel to the door made of massive glass windows looking on a lab beyond. Everything was still except for the subtle hum of electronics. David slipped into a chair and powered up the computer. It was Windows based, so hacking would be quick and relatively painless.

Thirteen minutes later David was near being sick, and rage pounded in his temples like a snare drum. Every nightmare he had about the Areth was just blown away by reality. The worst of it was they already had Americans working on the genetic cleansing projects they had lined up for at least the next twenty years. Genetic filtering, selective breeding, all under the guise of aiding Humanity. Humans with specific genetic markers would be effectively removed from the gene pool, while Humans with genetic markers the Areth found more appealing would be harvested and used as breeding machines.

It was Nazi Germany on a global, technology-fueled scale.

God help them. God help them all.

President Woosley knew. That damn son of a bitch knew and was fully on board.

He'd sold out his country, possibly the whole damn world.

David pulled a chain from beneath his black turtleneck, unclipped a dongle, and plugged it into the front USB port of the terminal he used. With a few clicks, the data flowed onto the 6-terabyte drive, the hard drive of the computer churning. The biggest question he had no answer for yet was "Who to trust?" If Woosley knew, the entire chain of command could be compromised.

When the download finished, he pulled the drive free, clipped it back to the chain around his neck, and tucked it beneath the shirt. His thin gloves hid any fingerprints, and leaving no other evidence behind, David shut down the terminal. He pushed back from the desk as voices sounded in the hallway; three voices, muffled, but in full conversation. David moved to the door and stood with his back to the wall, straining to hear.

Hearing the voices louder did him no good. They spoke in a guttural, gurgling dialect he supposed was Areth, but if tone was universal, one of them was angry. A woman, he believed. Since their bodies and biological makeup were so close to Human, he could at least discern between male and female. The other two voices were male, and when one barked out a harsh sounding command, the female fell silent.

"You have failed your assignments numerous times," the same harsh male voice chastised. "Your unwillingness to submerse yourself in the Human's culture is likely the cause."

The woman cleared her throat. "Yes, Lord Warrick."

Warrick . . . he was the lead Areth, the commander of the group who made first contact. The one all chummy-chummy with Woosley.

"We have yet to locate an acceptable Human male for your new experiment. I would urge you to work harder on this, Kathleen. Your failure with obtaining the Tanner child has made you look very bad to Barnabas. It would behoove you to rectify your error."

"It has been several years now—"

"Barnabas has a long memory."

"Yes, Lord Warrick."

The other male voice spoke. "I have heard from Barnabas. He predicts a five-decade timeline before we have viable bodies for transfer. It will take that long to filter out the recessive Areth markers. If left unchecked, the recessive markers would become prominent."

"Do not speak the name of our enemy!" Warrick snapped. "We must maintain this guise for now, and to speak of them otherwise is to imply our differentiation."

David squinted. Warrick's demand made no sense. If these aliens weren't Areth, then who was? And who were these sick bastards?

The voices grew faint as they moved away. It was a damn good thing they walked away. David's anger nearly had him pounding the wall and chasing them down to kill them, here and now, and end the ruse.

He waited until the hallway was silent, then eased the doorknob to open the door and slipped into the hall. His watch counted the seconds so he knew when to move and which way to avoid the cameras. With a glance to the left and right, he hugged the wall and headed for the stairwell he'd used to access the second floor.

The sound of boots, heavy and fast, preceded the shout of a single, guttural command he didn't understand but got the gist of. David drew his Beretta and fired at the two guards running straight for him. They dodged his shots and lifted their long-muzzled weapons. They were alien in design, and David had only heard about what the Areth weapons were capable of. They fired, the air reverberating with a powerful pulse he tried to dodge by diving into the stairwell. Hit by the wave, searing pain shot from the back of his legs up his spine to the back of his head and he dropped hard.

Conscious, but unable to move, David was helpless when the two approached and dragged him into the hall. One spoke into a communication device while the other rolled David onto his back. He stared at the ceiling. All he could do was listen and try to think through the pain in his chest as his heart tried to continue beating against the paralyzing effect of the weapon.

On the edge of his peripheral, he saw three figures approach and recognized one as the infamous Warrick, accompanied by a man and a woman.

David tried to move, tried to fight, to escape. If they killed him, the charade would go on unknown by anyone who cared. His eyes burned and watered, unable to blink. Both guards snapped to attention when Warrick and the others reached them, standing rigid with their arms straight at their sides and their fists clenched.

"Who is this?"

One of the guards began to speak, but Warrick silenced them with a backhand across their face. The guard's head snapped to the side, but otherwise, he didn't react.

"Speak in their tongue, idiot," Warrick growled.

"We discovered him trying to escape. We have not determined his identity."

"Search him."

The other guard dropped to a crouch beside David and searched him, finding nothing but the data drive around his neck. The guard yanked it free, stood, and shook his head. "He has no form of identification."

"Kill him and discard of the body," Warrick ordered and turned to leave. "We will not tolerate this behavior."

"Wait," the woman he now knew to be called Kathleen said, crouching beside David. He could only shift his eyes now, able to watch her as she looked him up and down. She moved her hand over his body, blatant to the point of violation. "I would need to scan his DNA structure, but physically, he is just the type of specimen we will need in the future. His body structure and facial features indicate inherent strength and intelligence. If he lacks the Areth abomination in his genomes, he will work well for cloning or breeding stock. If the Areth DNA is present, well, he might serve other purposes."

David tried to shout, tried to fight . . .

"Take him to the *Abaddon* and have him placed in stasis. I will deal with him later."

The guards bent at the waist in a rigid, sharp bow. One then hooked his hands behind David's knees and the other under his arms.

His ex-wife Kelly's voice whispered in his head.

"Someday, David, you're not going to come home. Your righteous crusade to serve your country cost you our marriage, will it cost your sons their father?"

CHAPTER ONE

19 FEBRUARY 2054, FRIDAY
ALEXANDRIA HOSPITAL, SECURE WING – INTENSIVE CARE
UNITED EARTH PROTECTORATE, CAPITOL CITY
ALEXANDRIA, SEAT OF VIRGINIA
NORTH AMERICAN CONTINENT

42 YEARS LATER . . .

"We're losing him!"

Michael ran as quickly as he could, using his cane to help propel himself forward. Victor and Doctor Corbin led the way down the hall to the intensive care rooms set up for the four nameless souls they'd found in stasis aboard the *Abbadon*. The shouts of doctors and wail of alarms mixed in a confusing cacophony. Victor shoved open the door first, and the sound amplified.

The room was in chaos, doctors, nurses, and attendants rushing around the prone body of John Doe, the one of the four they knew had been held in stasis the longest. He had been yanked from the pod when they realized he'd shut down and rushed to the surgical room. He now lay on a table, his arms hanging limp away from the narrow bed. His upper body was laid bare, electrodes stuck to his sallow skin wherever they had found space amongst the variety of mechanical and technological interfaces that had been infused with his flesh. An oxygen mask covered his lower face. His vitals had been the weakest when they were found, but they'd hoped to have more time to find a safe way to wake him from his deep slumber.

Hope had failed them.

"What have you tried?" Victor demanded, slipping the loops of a sterile mask around his ears.

Michael had already put on his mask and worked on gloves.

"Once we had him clear of the pod we put him on forced pressure oxygen and injected adrenaline and atropine and performed chest compression to restart the heartbeat. We've picked up a rhythm twice, and lost it twice, never long enough to defib and get a steady beat," Doctor Lois Maybourne shouted over the alarms. "It's hard, sir, to work around the hookups, but we didn't see any of them until we cracked the pod." She paused. "Many of them are integrated into his system, sir. We can't remove them."

Michael looked to the heart monitor. The line spiked and plummeted in random patterns. The line dropped to red and didn't move.

"He's flat lined, Doctor," a nurse Michael didn't know announced over the din. "His brain functions are decreasing rapidly."

"Damn, we really are losing him," Victor cursed, and leaned over the still man's body. He laid his hand across the man's forehead, a motion so familiar it brought to Michael a flash of memories from his earliest years on to the day he left New Mexico. Memories of Victor, even when he was tormented by the Sorracchi consciousness haunting him, caring for Michael and bringing him back to life. "I'm so sorry," Victor said softly, spoken only for the man slipping away.

Michael pushed through the group surrounding the table, yanking the gloves free from his hands. "I can help."

Victor raised his head and looked at Michael, his forehead pulled in speculation. "We've done everything we can medically. He was in stasis too long. His body is worn out, we—"

"I'm not talking about medicine," Michael said in dismissal.

Very little color tinted the unknown man's face, and the only color to his torso was an angry shade of red where the interfaces had been joined with him with clearly more speed than precision or care. His flesh had grown around them, just as the doctor said. Metal plates with light indicators, now dark with no power source, merged with him over his heart, from each side near the lower lobes of his lungs, and some hanging off the edge of the table from beneath him like tentacles. A cord, reminding Michael of an umbilical, came from the back of his neck at the base of his skull. Michael laid his hand on the man's chest over his still heart, the metal plate sliding into the space between Michael's fingers and thumb, his skin already cool to the touch, slightly clammy. His chest didn't rise and fall with even the slightest of breaths, his body more dead than alive.

"No," Victor shouted, yanking Michael back from the bedside.

"Yes!" Michael shoved away his friend's hands. "I've learned to control this both ways, Victor. I can give as much as I take."

"I know you can," Victor argued, holding Michael away from the bed with a grip on the front of his shirt. "You pulled *me* back from death, remember? It nearly killed you."

"Bringing you back didn't nearly kill me, Vic. Kathleen nearly killed me." Michael took hold of his longest friend's wrists and tugged them away from his shirt. "He's important enough to try."

Victor pressed his lips into a tight line and he released Michael's shirt. "Don't make me regret this."

Michael offered a short nod and turned again to the bed. He drew in a long breath, closed his eyes as he released it, and rested his palm again on the still chest. It had taken weeks of prayer and meditation to harness the power Michael had finally accepted he possessed, and with that control had come the ability to turn the power outward. This would be the first time he'd tried to save a life since he'd yanked Victor back to the world of the living, just over a year before, but he was a different man now. He only hoped it was enough.

He turned his focus inward and blocked out the sounds of alarms and murmured voices around him. Slipped deeper until all he heard was the steady rhythm of his own heartbeat and the rush of blood in his own veins.

Give me the strength to bring him back.

He visualized a sparking, electrified ball of blue/white light spinning in the center of his chest, tendrils of power branching outward like an electromagnetic sphere. Michael drew in another breath and with a mighty mental shove, pushed the energy away and toward the cold, still hole where this man's life should be.

*D*avid was in the same dream.

Somewhere along the way he'd accepted everything happening around him was just a dream, but since he never actually woke up, he couldn't get himself free. He was doomed to live the same day—a day he never actually lived—over and over again like some bad Bill Murray film.

He blinked and brought the room into focus. Seated on the right side of the couch, he faced the Scotch Pine Christmas tree he had bought with the boys and brought home to the townhouse he had once shared with them and their mother—his ex-wife—in the nice-but-not-too-nice part of Manhattan. The lights twinkled through the thousands of strands of silver tinsel the kids had tossed on the tree so thick they hid most of the ornaments. The smell of coffee and pine permeated the air.

David counted to five, and right on time, he heard his sons thundering down the stairs with squeals of excitement. They tore into the living room and headed straight for the tree and David watched, his heart aching. Trapped in this purgatory, he both knew everything was a lie and hoped it never stopped.

"Say good morning to your father before you open those gifts," Kelly said from the doorway leading into the front hall.

David looked to his left. She stood where she always stood, a cup of coffee in her hand, dressed in the pink chenille robe he'd bought her three years before. Her blond lightened hair was piled on top of her head in a white scrunchie, as always, and the smile she sent him was as flat as ever. *For the benefit of the boys.* His psyche couldn't be so kind as to at least give him the wife he'd loved for so long, the one who smiled at him with open love rather than resolved indifference.

The boys scrambled from the floor to race to the couch in a bid to see who could get in his lap first. As always, they tied. Little Anthony, at seven, still wanted to sit on his father's lap. He wore his favorite SpongeBob SquarePants pajamas he'd had so long his toes poked out through the feet, and his light brown hair stuck up in odd directions. He perspired in his sleep and his hair always dried in crazy ways. Davey, his namesake, was too old at ten to sit in his lap so he knelt beside David and hugged him. He wasn't too old for that yet. He opted for fleece pajama pants with a camouflage pattern and a black tee shirt because he said it looked like the clothes David used to wear when he was in the Army.

David hugged them both, and kissed each forehead, inhaling the smell of his boys. Even though he had lived this morning more times than he could count, he lived each one as if it were his last . . . just in case it was.

After hugs and kisses, both boys bolted off the couch to the stockings hung in front of the cold fireplace. Davey dumped out his stocking first, and his "Whoa!" made David smile, just as it always did.

"Mom! Check it out! A signed Papelbon Red Sox card!" Davey looked to his father, his eyes wide and his jaw open. "Thanks, Dad!"

"Daddy didn't give it to you, stupid. Santa did," Anthony argued.

"You're such a baby. There's—"

"Davey . . ." Kelly warned and Davey went silent, his smile never wavering.

David loved that moment. When he saw pure glee on his oldest son's face. In another five minutes Anthony would open the Spider-Man Dual Action Web Blaster David had gone to four toy stores to hunt down.

The air crackled and the lights dimmed, flashing back on as bright as before. David looked around. That hadn't happened before.

"The wind must have kicked up. I heard we might get snow," Kelly said.

"Maybe . . ." he mumbled in response, edging forward to stand. The jeans and sweater he'd worn every other time were replaced by a simple pair of cotton pull on pants like he'd wear in a hospital, and his shirt was gone.

Something wasn't right.

The lights dimmed again and a pounding sounded at the door.

"Who on earth could be here on Christmas morning?"

David suddenly felt sick and lunged for Kelly to stop her, but she was already down the hall. She looked at him over her shoulder and scowled before reaching for the door. On the other side stood two men in dress greens, hats set low over their eyes, misted with the fine snow falling outside.

"Can I help you?" Kelly asked.

"Kells, shut the door," David demanded. She didn't even respond. The boys ran from the living room, right past him. "Kelly, shut the door!"

Kelly was still, silent.

"Mrs. Forté?" the sergeant asked.

"Forte," she mumbled, an automatic habit to correct the pronunciation of the name. "The e is useless." The correction seemed out of place.

David took the three long strides needed to put him between her and the two officers. The bite of the winter air outside tingled against his bare back. She looked right through him, tears in her eyes.

"Mrs. Forte, the necessity to deliver this news today is unfortunate, but we felt it couldn't be delayed. We regret to inform you your ex-husband Lieutenant Colonel David Forte has been killed in the line of duty. "

The mug fell from her hand and shattered on the floor, splattering coffee on her pink chenille.

"Where's my daddy?" Anthony cried. "Where's my daddy?"

Davey stared, eyes brimmed with tears, his mouth pulled into a tight, silent frown.

"No!" David dropped to his knees in front of his sons. He tried to touch them, but his hands had lost their substance. "No, boys. I'm right here."

This was it. No more looping. He'd lived his last day. What waited for him now? Heaven? Or Hell?

The house disappeared in a flash of white light and David turned toward the open door, shielding his eyes with his raised arms.

"*A*re you crying?"

Katrina Bauer swiped at her cheeks with the back of her hand and sniffed, avoiding her brother's taunting smirk. She kept her chin down and blinked to clear the haze, freeing another tear to run down her cheek.

"You are. You're crying."

"Shut up, Karl," she mumbled.

"Why are you crying? Geez, you seriously need to get some sleep. I never knew you to be a weepy female."

Katrina slammed her soldering tool down onto the stainless-steel table tray beside her, the other tools and parts bouncing with the force. She glared at her older brother, silently wishing he would just leave her alone to her work. All he did was tease and poke and distract her.

"You want me to go get Doctor Tanner?" He wagged his eyebrows and winked. "I bet he'd be willing to—"

"Shut. Up. Karl," she said again through clenched teeth. She shook her head and picked up her EM calibrator. How could she explain if he didn't already know?

John Doe lay completely still in his infirmary bed, living more off machines than his own body's need to survive. In the hours after Michael Tanner had—in a way Katrina couldn't even begin to comprehend—pulled him back from death, Katrina and Karl had worked frantically to interface the alien technology that had maintained his body in the stasis pod with their Human technology enough to keep him alive. Running on just a few hours' sleep, Katrina logically understood her emotions and comprehension were compromised, but how could her brother not be affected by the butchering inflicted on the man?

Karl pushed back from the computer console he'd been working at, a mix of Sorracchi and English scrolling in various windows on his screen and stood. She refused to look at him but registered in her peripheral as he came around the foot of John Doe's bed and to her side.

"I get it," he said, the teasing gone from his voice. "I guess I try not to think about it."

"You're not the one working on him," Katrina whispered, wiping again at her cheeks. "He's alive, but what did they leave him with? What if I do fix all this . . ." She motioned with the tip of her calibrator to the tangled mess of life support and electronics surrounding the bed, " . . .and all they left was a shell?"

"You tried, Trina. That's all you can do."

Karl squeezed her shoulder and leaned over to kiss the top of her head. "I need to run a diagnostic on the sub-system, but the access program is set up in the lab. I'll be there for a bit. You going to be okay?"

Katrina nodded but couldn't find a voice enough to say anything. He left her alone again, with only the sound of electronics and the synthetic push and pull of oxygen through John Doe's lungs. In perfect rhythm, his chest rose and fell and the heart monitor never wavered in its constant beep-beep. Everything perfectly timed, perfectly controlled, without falter.

"What kind of sick minds did this to you?" Katrina mumbled, shaking her head. She glanced toward John Doe's still face but looked away just as quickly. He hadn't moved in two days, since the doctors had yanked him from the stasis pod, and for two days Katrina and her brother had worked around the clock to keep him stabilized and find a way to remove the invasive tangle of mechanical interfaces brutally thrust into his body.

Fatigue dragged at her, but with each system interface she bypassed or stabilized, another broke down and threatened to take him with it. The intricacy of the machinery fascinated her, but the way the connections violated his body and organs went beyond butchery to sloppy cruelty. He'd been joined to his stasis pod with meshing of machine to flesh, without consideration of the damage the violations would cause.

Katrina hunched over the thick cable protruding from his left side beneath his arm. She did her best to be careful, to avoid irritating the flesh-to-metal connections, but despite her caution, the skin around the interface had split and wept a thin line of blood. Blinking against a new wave of hot tears, Katrina held the cable in place the best she could and twisted to reach back and grab a few squares of gauze from the table behind her.

White light surrounded him. The townhouse was gone. His children were gone. He spun on the balls of his bare feet, looking for something in the blank whiteness. David flinched and hissed, looking down at his side. Blood wept from a circular wound beneath his left arm, the skin stinging. He touched the blood with the fingertips of his right hand and held the bloody tips in front of his eyes. The blood was warm, slicking his skin.

"I'm sorry," she whispered and sniffed. Her hands trembled, making it hard to tuck the gauze beneath the wound. "I'm trying . . ."

"You're going a great job."

Katrina jumped and looked up, her cheeks flushed hot from embarrassment at not hearing Michael Tanner come into the room. She blinked and focused again on the bleeding wound.

"I'm afraid I'm hurting him more than I'm helping him." She couldn't force her voice to be any louder than a rough rasp.

Michael took three limping steps, leaning heavily on his cane, to retrieve Karl's chair and drag it back to settle beside the stool she sat on, pulled to the side of John Doe's bed. He took away the gauze she'd used to dab at the torn skin and leaned forward to examine the small wound. "I'll treat these to avoid infection. His wounds aren't your fault, Katrina."

She folded her hands in her lap and slid back a few inches, giving Michael room to work. The respiratory system interface was now connected to the reverse-engineered support system computers banking the bed, and his lungs had begun pulling in air again, even if only because they were forced to do it. The alien machines kept his systems going, for now, until Katrina and Karl found a way to disconnect him. Her focus had been in deciphering the system and the commands so his body didn't go into shock from losing the only functionality it had known for decades.

Butchers.

The hum of a stratum basale stimulator joined the low-frequency mechanical buzz of the computer systems and the steady rhythm of John's life support system. The SBS would knit the skin and stop the bleeding . . . until she jostled him again. Katrina closed her eyes, letting Michael do his work as a healing physician, a gift she could only admire.

A strange buzz drowned out the silence, he couldn't identify the source, couldn't recognize the sound. David looked up, looked around, but the sound stopped as abruptly as it began. He focused on his hand again, and the blood was gone. His side was healed, no sign of the bleeding wound.

She lost awareness until her body tipped and she jerked awake just a second before Michael Tanner caught her from falling off the stool. "I'm sorry," she stuttered, shaking off the tendrils of sleep hazing her senses.

Michael gripped her elbows and pulled her to her feet, supporting her while she blinked through sandy eyes. "You are doing a great job, Katrina. You need rest before you do any more."

She nodded, knowing he was right, even though her mind wanted to keep going. She didn't want to leave John—or whatever his name was—like this. It felt cruel, wrong, and she didn't want to be as thoughtless as the masochists who did this to him.

"He shouldn't be alone . . ." she mumbled.

"I'll come back once I know you're resting."

She nodded, her head feeling light and heavy at the same time.

Michael led her out of the room, her resistance shot. Katrina paused at the door, glancing back to the prone stranger on the bed, as much machine as man. "Why would someone—" She couldn't even finish the thought.

"I don't know," Michael answered. "We'll find out."

He led her a few doors down to what had, for lack of imagination, been named the pod room. The other three pods, housing the three men they knew only as The Triadic, were hardwired to power units and spliced to Katrina's computer system that had been temporarily migrated to the room. Michael pushed open the door and leaned on his cane to let her step past him. The room was in darkness except for the eerie blue glow from her monitors and the array of lights and screens on the fronts of the pods.

"I had them bring you a bed."

Her sleep-deprived brain wouldn't let her form an actual question, all she could manage was a long, tired stare at Michael. He smiled and touched her arm, urging her forward.

"I wouldn't want to be far away if it were me."

She managed a nod, moved past him, and made it to the bed on the other side of the room before he eased the door closed and left her alone. Katrina collapsed on the bed, toed off her shoes, and rolled onto her back to stare at the ceiling. A low electronic hum lulled her with white noise, the combined power system of the three pods and the computer systems constantly working on deciphering, cataloguing, and coding the various files she'd downloaded from the *Abbadon*'s database.

Katrina yawned and flopped her arm over her eyes, already halfway to sleep.

She could have been there an hour, she could have been there thirty seconds, when her decipher program twittered with three distinct beeps, yanking her from sleep. Katrina groaned and willed herself to ignore it, but the insistent program twittered again. She rolled out of bed and didn't quite make it upright before she got to the desk, dropped into the chair, and tapped the key interface to open the data file the program had translated.

It was a video-based file, the angle and immobility of the shot indicating it was probably a standard surveillance and observation recording. The room it recorded looked familiar in that it reminded her of the design of the rooms on the *Abaddon*, dark and cold and low ceilings in comparison to a Human or Defense Alliance ship. A man and a woman were in the shot, and despite the slightly grainy quality from the translation program, they struck Katrina as familiar. If she were rested, even more awake than asleep, she might be more cognitive.

She rubbed her aching eyes and contemplated just watching the video in the morning, but her curiosity wouldn't let her, no matter how enticing the siren call of her bed. Slumped over the desk with the lead weight of her head supported against the knuckles of one hand, she tapped in the command to play the recording.

The woman shouted at the man, her hands waving wildly. She was tall, slightly taller than the average Human woman, with dark brown hair twisted into an intricate coil around her head. The familiarity Katrina felt was frustrating, but she couldn't get a clear view of the woman's face. She shouted in Sorracchi, guttural and harsh. Katrina paused the video, backed it up, and played the shouting again. She couldn't get it all, and syntax and exact translation didn't coincide between English and Sorracchi, but what she got was the woman demanded to know how someone, a plural because the word was equivalent to "they," had found some sort of record she never wanted them to see.

By the time Katrina closed the file two hours later, she had watched and looped the video enough to know the Triadic, the three men silent and still in the pods behind her, had discovered some sort of information the Sorracchi wished to keep secret; specifically, the woman who appeared responsible for their training, and possibly their creation.

Kathleen.

That single name incited any member of or person associated with the Tanner family to a deep and righteously justified rage.

Kathleen: the Human name chosen by one of the most advanced, and most sadistic, minds of the Sorracchi race.

Kathleen: the Sorracchi slug who had stolen the body of a Human woman no one knew how many centuries before and used that stolen body to birth Michael Tanner as part of an experiment for a purpose they had yet to fully understand.

Kathleen: Michael Tanner's tormenter, the woman who brought him near death, and *to* death, more than once and left him nearly crippled. The traitor who had tricked Nick Tanner in his youth to father a child with the woman he thought was his Human wife, who had contrived to make Nick believe he had lost his wife and his infant son, and the woman who had held the child for over two decades as her personal lab rat.

Kathleen: killed by the hand—or the mind—of the boy child she had birthed, tortured, and pushed to the breaking point when she threatened not his life, but the life of the woman Michael loved.

Even though she was dead, the destruction she left behind seemed never ending.

Katrina pushed away from the desk and forced herself to stand. Before she stumbled to the waiting bed to steal whatever precious hours of sleep she could, she crossed the small space to the three pods, and stood in the center of the half-circle they formed. Low level lights within the edge of the observation window let her see their faces, still and unchanged, relaxed in a forced sleep. The powers that be planned on cracking open the pods in the next day or two, to see if the Triadic had been butchered during the process of implanting them in the pod, if their flesh-to-tech interfaces were as sloppy and scarring as it had been on John Doe. But, tonight, they stayed still in slumber.

Now that she knew Kathleen had some hand in these three men, a sense of dread settled in Katrina's stomach. Nothing touched by Kathleen survived unscathed.

"I'm sorry," she said to the still room. "Whatever it was, I'm sorry."

CHAPTER TWO

21 FEBRUARY 2054, SATURDAY
PRESIDENTIAL RESIDENCE
UNITED EARTH PROTECTORATE, CAPITOL CITY
ALEXANDRIA, SEAT OF VIRGINIA
NORTH AMERICAN CONTINENT

One of the first senses Michael learned to connect to his father, to family, was smell. The morning after he was rescued from his lifelong prison in New Mexico, Nick Tanner—a man more mystery than reality to Michael—had given Michael a stack of his own clothing for Michael to wear. The flannel and cotton held a mingled scent of soap and shaving cream Michael quickly learned to associate with his father. The smell of leather reminded him of the leather jacket his father gave to him the day he said he had to leave Earth to find help.

That first morning, his father had taken him to breakfast and he had eaten a meal like none he had experienced in twenty-five years: pancakes and bacon, syrup, coffee, and cooked eggs. Caitlin often chided Michael about his appetite, but he couldn't quite explain it wasn't always about the food . . . it was about the company.

Just like tonight.

Michael had been back in Alexandria for barely more than two weeks from his self-imposed exile, and this was the third time his parents had filled the house with people and the smell of food. Tonight, it was in celebration of Nick and Caitlin's first wedding anniversary. Watching them from his place on one of the couches, Michael saw a love so much greater than a single anniversary and it made him ache for what he might have lost.

"Daddy, up," Nicole cried, tugging at the legs of his jeans to pull herself into his lap.

Michael smiled at his daughter and scooped her up under her arms to set her in his lap. She held out a baby doll, a bit tattered and worn and clearly well loved, and launched into a long story told completely in her own language, punctuating her tale with a random kiss to the baby's cheek and a toothy grin to him.

He listened obediently and nodded his head, letting her know he hung on every word. How he had made it through each day during the weeks he was gone without Nicole's stories, he didn't know. He wasn't sure how he made it through now without Jacqueline to wake up to each morning, fall asleep with each night, and share his life with each day.

Nicole pointed across the room and he picked up Lumpy and Gumpa, her personal version of Grammie and Grampa, and kept telling him the story of her day. By her wide eyes and vehement nods, it had been a very exciting day. Then Dog slowly made his way into her line of sight, his old body finally showing signs of his unknown but advanced age, and with a squeal of delight, Nicole scrambled from Michael's lap to chase down her favorite animal.

Michael chuckled at the pitiful glance Dog sent his way when Nicole wrapped her tiny arms around his neck and hugged him.

Hand in hand, Caitlin and his father came into the sitting room. Tonight was another night of both family and friends filling the house. Victor, Michael's oldest friend, sat in one of the deep chairs and scooted to his right so his wife, Vice President Beverly Surimoto, could squeeze into the chair beside him with a giggle. Michael's father celebrated a year of marriage, and Victor and Beverly weren't far behind. Connor Montgomery, Caitlin's brother, usually joined them for

21

these dinners but tonight he had begged off, saying he had work to do for Nick.

Nick helped Caitlin ease herself down onto the couch, despite her look of exasperation. If his father was this protective now of his pregnant wife, with her barely into her second trimester, Michael wondered how bad he would be as the months progressed.

Caitlin batted her husband's hands away, but her smile and the sparkle in her eyes belied her scolding. Nick kissed her cheek before straddling the arm of the couch beside her. With one last wink at his wife, he looked between Michael and Victor.

"What's happening with Buck Rogers?"

Michael chuckled, just as much at Beverly's look of confusion as his father's reference to a hundred-year-old science fiction icon. Victor leaned into his wife and spoke softly, something he couldn't have done a year ago before her hearing had been restored and whispered. Beverly nodded and smiled.

"Katrina and Karl Bauer have been working nearly around the clock on the life-sustaining implements fused with his body." Victor's eyes darkened, and he scowled. "I know the Sorracchi hold no compassion for mankind, but there is a level of sadism to the way he was connected to that pod. With absolute disregard for damage or long-term ramifications. The more we treat him, the more I am amazed he has lived this long even with life support."

"I suspect we will never be able to fully remove some of the hardware," Michael added. "Some of them are so deeply imbedded into his biology to remove them would cause greater damage than leaving them behind. I'm working with Katrina to determine how much can be removed, her knowledge of the mechanics and programming far exceeds mine, and how much will have to remain and be adapted to provide him with some quality of life."

"It's that bad?" his father asked, his face twisted in a wince.

Michael nodded. "Since Thursday she has managed to shift the functionality of his lungs from the alien connection to a respirator, and we are slowly weaning him off forced oxygenation in hopes his lungs will remember how to function on their own. We've removed the connections along his spine, which Katrina determined fed a pharmaceutical cocktail to his muscles to keep them from degrading completely and replaced with muscle stimulators for most of his major muscle groups. When and if he wakes up, he will likely have to teach his body to move again."

Nick stood, moved to the fireplace to rest his elbow on the mantel so he could rub his fingers across his forehead. Michael recognized the look in his father's eyes, even if no one else did; a mix of disgust and anger, rage against the inhumanity of the Sorracchi. "If . . ."

"He has brain activity, but it's very low level. Katrina determined the connections to his cerebellum had a direct effect on his hippocampus, creating an illusionary—"

His father held up his hand, and Michael stopped.

"Sorry. The Sorracchi tapped into his dream center and had him on a perpetual loop. Karl is working on deciphering the code, to see where his mind has been for the last forty years."

Nick cursed under his breath and looked away, rubbing again at his forehead.

"How terrible," Caitlin said softly, tears glistening in her eyes when Michael glanced toward her.

Nicole toddled across the floor and handed Michael a ball, kissed his cheek, and took off again. He watched her for a moment before looking back to Caitlin. She offered him a weak smile and Michael did his best to smile back.

Nick cleared his throat, turned away from the fire, and pushed his hands into his front pockets. "What about the other three. What'd you call them? Triad?"

"Triadic, according to the designations on their stasis pods."

"After we pulled John Doe from his pod, and got a look at the set up, we decided to crack open theirs to see if we're facing the same mess," Victor explained, shifting forward in the chair he shared with his wife. He linked his fingers together and let them hang in front of his knees. "We did that today. They aren't nearly the mess John Doe was in. More care was taken with them, perhaps they were handled by someone else."

Victor slid a glance toward Michael, the implications going unsaid. Kathleen. Katrina had told them, with tears in her eyes, she'd found proof in the files that Kathleen had been the Sorracchi in charge of the three men. Nick had cursed and nearly punched a hole through his office wall when he was given the news.

"Or, she just left the cleanup to someone else," Nick said, considerably calmer than when he had heard the news, probably for the sake of Caitlin. Silence settled for a moment, the only conversation the one Nicole had in the corner with a reluctantly attentive Dog. "What are we doing with them? Can we do a better job if we're starting with a cleaner slate?"

"We have every reason to believe so, yes," Victor answered. "As long as they remain stable, we keep our focus on John Doe and learn what we can from him. Hopefully, we'll garner enough to be effective with them without the trauma."

Firm footsteps approached down the hall from the back of the house where Nick maintained a satellite office and everyone looked to the doorway as Sergeant Annie Nodal stepped into view. "I'm sorry to interrupt, Mr. President, but a secure message has come in on your private connection. Off planet."

"Thanks, Sergeant." Nick laid his hand on Michael's shoulder as he passed and ruffled Nicole's hair before leaving the room.

Nicole crawled on her knees to the chair where Victor and Beverly sat and grabbed hold of Victor's pant leg, just as she had with Michael, to pull herself to her feet. Victor chuckled and offered his hand, but she ignored it. Once on her feet she ran to the couch and climbed up beside "Lumpy," already chattering. Caitlin stroked her hair and smiled. Nicole scooted forward and laid her cheek on Caitlin's stomach, still talking. Then she kissed Caitlin's sweater and scrambled off again. Caitlin looked up at Michael, shaking her head.

"It's like she knows, she already understands."

Michael smiled, warmth spreading through his chest, as Nicole chased Dog from the room with a hearty, pure child's laugh. "I believe she does."

Minutes later, his father's heavy footsteps came back down the hall. Nick clapped his hands together as he came back into the room. "Well, kids, I've got some news."

Michael already faced his father, but everyone else either shifted or turned to look at him. He continued into the room and resumed his spot in front of the fire, his hands pushed into his pockets again. "I just received confirmation John and Jenifer have reached Aretu."

Caitlin gasped and Beverly's mouth fell open. Michael supposed he felt some twinge of surprise, but the announcement made sense. Last Michael knew for sure, John and Jenifer had transported from Florida where he had been staying with Jace and Lilly Quinn to Alexandria over two weeks before. Since then, his father had said nothing about either of them, and Michael let it lie in the light of the many attempts on John's life as ambassador to Earth.

"I know everyone wants to know why I didn't say anything, but until I knew they were safely off planet I kept it between myself and Connor, no one else."

"But, they're safe?" Caitlin asked.

"Yes. They met up with Jackie and Silas . . ." His gaze shifted to Michael for a moment at Jackie's name. "and the four of them continued on to Aretu aboard the *Steppenschraff*, not the *Constellation*. They arrived there a week ago."

"Thank God," Beverly said, her hand pressed to the base of her throat.

"It wasn't without incident. We had intel that led us to believe a Xeno assassin had followed Jackie and Silas with the intent of killing Silas. Another way of getting to John."

Panic, raw and vicious, slammed into Michael, but before he could say anything his father laid his hand on Michael's shoulder and squeezed. "She's fine. They *were* attacked when they landed on Aretu, but the Xeno was subdued and captured. Unfortunately, he also died in custody. We all know this isn't the end of it, but there's one less assassin with John's name on his to do list."

"What are they going to do? Stay there?"

"The message didn't go into much detail on that, except to say John and Jenifer will remain on Aretu until at least the sixth of next month, when the *Steppenschraff* is scheduled to return to Earth. Whether just Jenifer will be coming back then, or John *and* Jenifer, we don't know yet. It seems to be up in the air."

"I hope he returns. John has done so much good," Beverly said.

"Tough to do good when someone wants you dead." Victor squeezed his wife's hand. "I wouldn't blame him if he didn't."

"What about Jacqueline," Michael managed to force through his restricted throat.

His father met his eyes, a small grin turning his lips. "Jackie left Aretu three days ago on the *Axanadu*. She's the one who sent ahead the message. She's on her way back."

Michael's heart went from normal, to paralyzed, to a thundering beat in a matter of seconds and with such ferocity his chest hurt. He'd grown accustomed to the emotion of fear, and fear was exactly what he felt. Fear she wouldn't forgive him for his foolishness.

"The *Axanadu* is a military transport, one of the slower ships," Victor said, his voice registering on the edge of Michael's peripheral awareness.

Nick nodded, still looking at Michael. "It's going to take her two weeks of travel and layover at *Gateway* to get here. She'll be home by the one-year commemoration."

Michael didn't remember turning away, didn't remember making the decision to leave the room, but he blinked and found himself in the dark kitchen leaning over the counter with his head down and his eyes burning. Small, gentle hands touched his back and Michael raised his head to look at Caitlin. When his father had been gone, it had been Caitlin who guided him, took care of him, answered his questions, and rejoiced for him when he finally found the courage to act on the pull he felt to Jacqueline Anderson. Despite their closeness in age, she was the mother he always needed. She smiled now, her eyes glistening with tears from the moonlight streaming through the kitchen window.

"I'm afraid," he admitted.

"That's good," she said. "I know it probably doesn't seem good, but your fear of losing her will make sure you do what you have to so you keep her."

"What if she won't take me—"

She laid her hand on his cheek, touching her thumb to his lips. "She will. She loves you, Michael. So much. It wouldn't have hurt her so much when you left if she didn't."

The acceptance of how much he might have hurt her made his

chest ache and he bowed his head in shame. Caitlin rubbed his back and laid her cheek against his shoulder. "I don't say that to make you feel bad, Michael. I say it because you see the truth most clearly when we don't try to hide."

He nodded and swallowed hard, unable to say anything more.

The medical center had settled into its night rhythm, with dimmed lights and hushed tones. The only constant sounds were those of monitors and machines, and the occasional squeak of safety shoes on polished floors echoing in the empty halls.

Katrina bit into her apple and cringed at the way it echoed in the quiet room. She sat on the floor, cross-legged, with her back against the wall across from the foot of John Doe's bed. The steady suck and whoosh of his ventilator sounded loud and obtrusive in the otherwise quiet room. She'd stopped working on the system interface coding an hour before, when she'd looked up and realized the hospital was silent but hesitated to leave him alone.

She didn't understand her need to stay. She just knew he shouldn't be alone. He could wake up, and if he did, he shouldn't be alone. He'd been alone in that pod for probably more years than he'd lived before his capture, he shouldn't be alone when he realized he was out of it.

Karl teased her about it relentlessly, saying she'd switched one crush for another: from Michael Tanner to John Doe. He didn't get it, no matter how much she told him she didn't have some stupid schoolgirl crush. For either man. He didn't understand her admiration for Michael Tanner, or the intimidation that smothered her in his shadow. The man had come through so much, survived so much, and become someone so amazing she could only stare in awe. How did you speak to someone as big as Michael Tanner and not stutter a bit?

John Doe made her ache deep in her chest. She mourned for his life, the life he lost decades before, even though she had no idea what that life may have been. What would he do when he finally woke up and found out nothing he'd known and loved still existed?

If she tried to tell her big brother all that, he'd tell her she was being a sappy, emotional little girl and to get over it.

Her PAC tablet buzzed and shimmied across the floor near her hip and she picked it up, flicking on the screen with a slide of her thumb.

Where are you?

Katrina sighed and contemplated not answering her brother. But, she knew if she didn't he'd come looking for her and he'd come here first. She set her half-eaten apple on her knee and stared at the screen for several moments. It buzzed in her hand.

I KNOW YOU'RE READING THIS. WHERE ARE YOU?

Katrina groaned and rolled her head against the wall. She started typing before she looked at the screen, her fingers already knowing by rote every movement to type on the touch screen. She looked down before hitting send

YOU KNOW WHERE I AM. DON'T GIVE ME A HARD TIME.

He didn't come back with a response; which either meant he honored her request or all he really wanted to know was where she was. Karl took serious their parents' mandate to watch over her if anything ever happened to them, so after she and Karl came to Alexandria, she sometimes felt like she had a Siamese twin rather than a big brother.

Katrina was tired. Bone tired. A huge yawn threatened to crack her jaw.

ARE YOU COMING HOME TONIGHT?

She hadn't slept in her own bed since the night they pulled John Doe from the pod. Karl had brought her changes of clothes and her "girlie stuff," but she had barely stepped outside in days. The trip the few blocks to the civilian housing where she and Karl had been given an apartment seemed a waste of time when she wanted—needed—to be here. Katrina drew up her knees and cradled the tablet against her legs, pushing her fingers through her curls. Maybe she should go home, just for tonight, to appease him.

The thought of walking down the hall to her lab was exhausting, how could she make it home?

I'M RUNNING A DECIPHER PROGRAM. I WANT TO STAY HERE IN CASE SOMETHING SHOWS UP THAT MIGHT BE USEFUL.

She waited for several minutes with no response from her brother, and just began to relax when the tablet vibrated again.

OKAY. I'LL SEE YOU IN THE MORNING.

Katrina set the PAC tablet aside, picked up the apple again, and stared from the strange angle up at the bed. From here she saw John Doe's hand near the edge of the mattress, an IV taped to the back, and the shape of his body under the blankets, but not his face. She considered talking to him. Michael had told her it had long been believed comatose patients could hear those who visited and cared for them; he told her he'd read to Victor every day while he had been ill well before the War, before the revealing of the truth, before Katrina knew any of them. Victor swore he didn't remember, but also admitted he felt a special sense of calm when reading *The Odyssey*, Michael's reading material of choice.

She groaned as she rolled to her feet, retrieved the PAC tablet, and stood near his feet beside the bed. Katrina tilted her head and studied him. "I wonder what you would like to hear, hmm?" When he offered no answer, she kicked off her shoes and pulled herself up onto the bed to sit alongside his feet, her back to the low footboard. There was just enough room to keep her from falling over the edge. She drew her knees up to her chest and hugged her legs, resting her chin on her raised knee. "I don't see you as much of a classics guy. Something . . .

exciting." Katrina hummed. "I wonder if Michael would lend me one of those science fiction novels he likes to read." She chuckled. "I bet when you wake up you're going to think you woke up in the middle of a science fiction novel."

With another hum of thought, Katrina slid her fingertip across the screen of her tablet to activate it again and exited the communication program. With a few taps, she accessed the digital literature archive. She didn't know much about the genre of science fiction, but she'd heard Michael talk about the books he read, and a particular author stuck in her mind. Moments later, she opened a file and smiled.

"Okay, I've never read this, but I hear it's good. Better than nothing, right?" She glanced up at his face, unchanged, still, deceivingly serene. Katrina cleared her throat and began to read. "Book One—Dawn. Chapter One Arisia and Eddore. Two thousand million or so years ago two galaxies were colliding; or, rather, passing through each other . . ."

David sat in the center of nothing, surrounded by light but no substance. A woman's voice carried to him, somewhere in front of him, or maybe behind. He couldn't be sure. He closed his eyes and listened to a story about far away galaxies and Eddorians and Arisians and worlds he would never know.

CHAPTER THREE

24 *February 2054, Tuesday*
Office of the President
Robert J. Castleton Memorial Building – The Castle
Center for United Protectorate Government
United Earth Protectorate, Capitol City
Alexandria, Seat of Virginia

"*W*hen is everyone due to get here?"

Connor looked up when Mel stepped in front of him, holding a mug of coffee. He let himself enjoy the view over her hips, her waist, her breasts barely disguised by the basic brown, military-issue thermal shirt, to her beautiful face. With a tilt of her head, her short brown hair fanned across her cheek. She pulled her lower lip through her teeth, a sexy twinkle in her dark eyes, and held out the mug. Connor sat back, pausing for a moment in his study of the records and files spread out on the oblong table situated between Nick's two couches. He took the offered cup in his right hand and flipped his left to check the watch on his wrist.

"Probably twenty minutes. Nick had a meeting with Colonel Ebben this morning about the celebrations, and then Michael is coming with

Victor and his team for a briefing on the files Doctor Bauer has translated."

"Twenty minutes . . ." she repeated with a slow, sexy smile.

Connor returned the smile and set the mug on the table before reclining into the couch cushions. "Yep, twenty minutes."

He groaned his appreciation as his second-in-command leaned over him and braced her hands on the back of the couch, holding eye contact as she straddled his lap and settled across his hips with a seductive wiggle. She angled her mouth over his, but held back enough to prevent contact, even when he tipped his chin to catch a kiss. Melanie chuckled and touched the tip of her tongue to his lower lip. "Mmmm, twenty whole minutes."

Connor chuckled and slid his hands up her thighs to her waist. "Damn dangerous in the president's office, don't you think?"

One side of Mel's sexy, succulent, *talented* mouth tipped higher and she tugged at the bottom of his thermal shirt until she got her hands beneath and on his abdomen. His traitorous body responded instantly and intensely, and he curled his fingers into the utilitarian fabric of her field uniform to pull her tighter against him. Connor dropped his head back against the back of the couch and closed his eyes, giving in for just a few forbidden, court-martial worthy moments of sin.

Melanie relaxed against him, her breasts pressed to his chest, and ran her lips along his jaw before she whispered, "I thought you got off on danger, *sir*."

Connor groaned and flipped her onto her back on the length of the couch, sliding his body along hers, letting his mind relive the now-familiar sensation of skin-on-skin with Melanie Briggs in his bed screaming his name. He covered her lips in a deep, open mouth kiss. He thought he did a damn good job ninety-eight percent of the time ignoring the ramifications of his illicit affair with his second-in-command, but the denial only made moments like this as combustible as gasoline on fire. It amazed him now it had taken so many years of being a commanding team to come to this, the spark and desire had been there for a long time.

He rocked against her, holding her head in his hands as he dove into the kiss. Her moan vibrated through him. Connor only allowed himself enough of Melanie to drive him crazy all day long, until he could steal away to his room and wait for her to come to him, just as she had for the last three weeks, three intense, powerful, life-altering weeks.

Connor groaned in frustration when he forced himself away from her kiss and rested his forehead on her shoulder, inhaling the scent of her skin. Melanie chuckled softly and pushed her fingers through his short hair.

"You are a cruel tease, Captain."

Mel kissed his ear, and whispered, "I can't help it if I steal every moment I can."

"One of the many reasons I love you," he said with a chuckle. He lifted his head and looked at her, and the glisten in her eyes made his breath check. Connor leveraged up onto his elbows to bring him over her, her teary gaze tracking him. "*Qu'est-ce—*" He stopped mid-sentence. "What's wrong?"

She shook her head. "You said you love me." Melanie sniffed and looked away. "You were probably just kidding, but—"

"I wasn't kidding."

Her eyes shifted back, tears sliding from their corners.

Connor balanced his weight onto one arm so he could brush the thumb of his other hand along her skin. She opened her mouth, but before she could say anything the sound of voices in the hall had them both scrambling.

 id we remember to back up the translation files before we left the—"

"Yes," Karl said, cutting off Katrina's question.

"Did we initiate the encryption translation—"

"Yes." Karl set his PAC on the low oblong table in front of them.

She gasped. "I forgot the video fi—"

Karl held up a disk. "No, you didn't."

33

She let out a long breath and offered her brother an apologetic smile. He smiled back, shook his head, and crouched at the table to finish loading the program she needed.

Katrina took a moment to look around the president's office. She hadn't ever been in this room, though she had been in the building. There was something regal yet basic about the space. Two couches faced each other and sat perpendicular to a large fireplace with a mantel level with her ears. Above the mantel, rather than a painting or other art, hung a large vidscreen with access to the main computer system. The long table sat between the two chairs and was currently spread with files and various PAC systems. She had her back to the burning fire, and directly in front of her across the room was President Nick Tanner's wide, deep desk of dark wood scattered with papers, computer interfaces, and pictures.

The room was full, with people seated on the couches, in two chairs tucked to the side, and some standing, including President Tanner who leaned against the edge of his desk talking to his son. Colonel Ebben, the Chief Security Advisor, stood near the door with a young, blond haired woman Katrina believed to be either President Tanner's assistant or part of his security detail. Lieutenant Commander Connor Montgomery sat at the far end of one of the couches, a PAC in hand, with Captain Mel Briggs seated beside him. Also seated was Vice President Beverly Surimoto, Victor's wife, with Victor standing at the end of the couch near her. The way Victor's eyes smiled when he spoke to Ms. Surimoto made Katrina's chest ache, but in the best of ways. She'd only heard rumors and stories about their relationship, but everything she heard was beautiful.

Also present were the members of Victor's team, scattered about the room.

Katrina worried her hands together, then forced them apart and clenched them at her side. Her stomach flipped and twisted and her heart felt like it might pound right out of her chest. Victor had insisted she was the best person to present the findings since it had been her decipher programs and conversion software that extracted and translated the data they had already retrieved, which constituted currently about thirty percent of the *Abaddon* database, but the idea of speaking openly to all these people made her want to toss her breakfast.

Victor touched his wife's cheek and stepped away from her toward Katrina, his smile intended to be confidence-infusing, she was sure, but it didn't quite work. "You look ready to bolt," he said, leaning toward her. "You'll do fine, Doctor Bauer."

Katrina swallowed, acknowledging somewhere in the back of her mind he used her title to further encourage her, but again it didn't quite work. She tried to smile back, but instead clenched her teeth against the tremor that shot up her spine. Victor laid his hand on her shoulder and squeezed, then looked to Nick Tanner and nodded once.

President Tanner pushed away from his desk and slapped his hands together, rubbing the palms together. "Okay, kids. We've got a lot to cover."

Immediately everyone fell silent and looked to her.

Katrina felt dizzy.

Victor cleared his throat, and thankfully gave her the few moments she needed. "Since we brought the four pods back from the *Abaddon*, Doctor Katrina Bauer has been working on the files we downloaded from the Sorracchi database. She and Doctor Karl Bauer created a software program designed to translate the Sorracchi logs and she has developed a program to convert their video files to a format we can view. She's going to cover for us the bones of what she discovered."

With that he nodded to her and stepped back to his place beside his wife, sitting on the arm of the couch.

Katrina knew her cheeks had to be scarlet for the way they burned. "Th-thank you," she scratched out, then cleared her throat and tried again. "Thank you." She shifted her hands behind her back and laced her fingers together to keep from fidgeting. "The records we've deciphered so far relate only to the Triadic, the three men still in stasis. No actual mention has been made of John Doe that we know of. It's difficult since we don't know his name . . ."

She trailed off and turned toward the large monitor screen hung on the wall over the fireplace. Luckily the bottom was low enough she could reach it and she tapped the screen to activate the programs she'd already loaded. A new window popped open, scrolling the angular

Sorracchi language. With her back to the group some of her nervousness waned, and when she reached again to tap the screen most of the shake was gone.

"The translation program isn't perfect, but it would take years for a native speaker of Sorracchi, like Victor for instance, to translate it file by file for us. There are inflections and syntax a computer can't quite translate because we would need a more thorough understanding of Sorracchi etymology, but we get the general idea. We've gone through a few years' worth of records and pieced together a rudimentary history for the three men."

When she turned back, her heart slammed against her ribs at everyone watching her. Katrina tried not to look at anyone in particular, so she looked straight ahead and met Michael Tanner's eyes. He paused just a moment before offering a small smile. She drew in a slow breath through her nose, and with solid determination, tamped down her anxiety. She knew what she was talking about, even though some of it broke her heart, and they needed to know. Katrina swallowed and smiled back.

"Translating what we know of the Sorracchi method of marking dates to our Gregorian calendar, we estimate the Triadic were . . . *created* . . . in 2013 after numerous failed attempts. They are biologically engineered and are the result of a combination of genetic manipulation, external gestation, and artificial DNA structuring."

"What does that *mean*?" President Tanner asked.

"They are clones of a sort," Victor provided. "While their DNA structure may be the combination of more than one genetic contributor, it was structured and designed to create a very specific outcome, and then cloned to create three men identical in appearance."

President Tanner nodded. "That means they're over forty years old. And all this was going on before the globalized government."

Katrina nodded. "Yes. We've also determined their aging process has been manipulated. Once they were proven viable—" Her throat tightened at the word she repeated from the files. She had wept when she read of the dozens of embryos created and destroyed when some flaw in their creation deemed them unacceptable to the process. "—the scientist in charge of the experiment accelerated their development through their youth to bring them to what she termed a 'trainable' age, somewhere around pre-adolescence, then we believe they were allowed to age at a normal Human rate until their physical development was deemed optimal."

"Do we know why?" Vice President Surimoto asked.

"Only hypothetically," Katrina answered. "It seems she wanted to manipulate their moral development and curb their maturation to meet the experiment's purpose."

"Which was . . ." President Tanner led.

"Creating a super soldier," his son answered, watching Katrina.

She nodded. "According to the files we've accessed, they have strength, intelligence, and dexterity exceeding any normal Human by at least two hundred percent in some cases. They are a unit in every sense of the word. They were trained to think independently when necessary, but as a single mind as well, which implies some sort of psychic ability."

Connor Montgomery scowled before he spoke. "I thought the Sorracchi were trying to breed out the latent Areth genes for Talents."

"For the potential hosts, yes," Victor answered, and Katrina mentally thanked him for fielding some of the questions. "As we've witnessed with myself and others, those genetic markers either hinder or completely exclude the Sorracchi's ability to overwrite a Human consciousness. But these three were never intended to be hosts, or husks, as the Sorracchi term it. They were created to be pawns, tools. The purpose of controlling their development and curbing their individuality was to create soldiers completely complacent to the will of their masters, without question or hesitation."

"Do we know why they were in stasis, for what, seven years?"

"I've found a few mentions of concerns with them, but not one specifically documenting the reason they were shut down," Katrina explained. "The first file I was able to access was a surveillance video of sorts, and from it I learned the Triadic had inadvertently found out something they weren't supposed to know. Their . . ." She stumbled over the word, always mindful of the emotional impact the cursed name ignited. "The head scientist was furious they had discovered whatever it was. That was some time in 2046, so just months prior to their placement in the pod."

Michael took a step away from his father's desk, the movement drawing her attention. He pushed his hands deep into his front pockets, his expression tight. "It's okay, Katrina. You can say who it was."

Attention shifted first to Michael and then to her. Some in the room knew who she was talking about; she had already told Victor and knew he had told the president and his family. Katrina swallowed and nodded, a small tip of her chin. She had to look away, focusing on Vice President Surimoto, who was at least not a Tanner. "The Sorracchi scientist in charge of their indoctrination and creation was Kathleen."

The shift in the room was tangible. The woman's name was enough to incite all ranges of emotion, but none more clear than the tightening of Nick Tanner's face into a restrained but righteous rage.

"If she was responsible for their training, we have no idea what kind of evil we're going to face when they wake up," Captain Briggs said, the first she'd spoken since Katrina arrived.

Katrina shook her head and turned back to the monitor, calling up some other records, this time roughly translated into English. She figured they would read past her, but she gave the rough translation. "I don't believe that. Chronologically, one of the last entries I deciphered before the timeframe we figure for when they were placed in stasis actually seems to say the opposite. Apparently, the Triadic were off world on a planet I wasn't able to translate because the computer files had no etymology for the word, and there was an incident. Although she doesn't give specifics of the situation, I get the distinct impression she is furious with them."

"What did they do?" Vice President Surimoto asked.

"It's what they didn't do," Katrina answered with more enthusiasm than she actually intended. She couldn't help it. After reading file after file of what had been done to them, and others, the entry had actually given her hope. "They were ordered to kill the remains of a settlement —women, children, and infirmed, those who couldn't fight back—and they didn't. She rages about how they didn't even bother to act hesitant. They just . . . didn't move. As a unit they defied the command and refused to hurt the innocent."

Again the atmosphere in the room shifted and some murmured between themselves. Katrina only caught one comment about their punishment for disobeying. She glanced in the direction of the statement, though she hadn't been able to pinpoint who it was.

"Their punishment was severe," she said, widening her eyes. "Records paralleled these entered by their medical officer who indicated the three of them nearly didn't survive what they called Kathleen's retribution."

In her peripheral vision she caught President Tanner reaching out to set his hand on his son's shoulder. They had all heard of Kathleen's retribution when she deemed herself wronged in some way. Michael's scars and limp were testament, let alone the scars inside no one saw. Katrina had to grit her teeth against the flush of tears she couldn't prevent. She looked down and turned, putting her back to everyone. Keeping her mind occupied, she opened a medical file.

"I haven't been able to work it all out yet, the translation program has issues with some of their native words and the linguistics and etymology of Sorracchi is . . ." She shook her head and made an annoyed sound. " . . .frustrating. All I've determined so far is Kathleen installed—for lack of a better word—some sort of failsafe that was supposed to discipline them when they didn't perform as desired." She turned back and focused again on Michael, just to have someone specific to look at. "I don't know if it inflicted pain, or altered their actions, or what. I'm still working on it."

"You've done an excellent job," Victor said, stepping to her side again. "We're still gathering information, but we at least have more than we did before."

"Good enough," President Tanner said, his voice heavier than when he opened the meeting. He patted his hand on his son's shoulder before stepping into the midst of everyone gathered. "We'll just keep going. Let me know if anything else significant comes out of the files."

Katrina nodded. "Yes, sir."

As she walked out with Victor and the team, she heard President Tanner speak to his son.

39

"She's dead, and we still can't get free of that bitch."

Earth Time: 24 February 2054, Tuesday
Smith Estate—Devon on the Hill, Callondia District
Aretu

*J*ohn came awake with a jerk to the shrill twitter of his alarm, bracing himself on one elbow. He blinked against the bright sunbeam hitting him in the face and moaned his frustration. After a restless night, being yanked from what sleep he'd finally managed left him practically growling.

"Off," he mumbled, but the twitter didn't stop, the voice command program designed to recognize the tone of a fully awake voice versus one still half-asleep. "Off!" he snapped, and the alarm silenced.

He flopped onto his back and laid his arm across his eyes, shielding the intrusion of the sun. John didn't need to look, or to reach out his arm, to know the bed beside him was once again empty, just as it had been for the last several nights. Where Jenifer took herself during the dark hours, where she found her rest, he didn't know. He knew better than to search; whatever reason kept her away was her own, and she wouldn't have any hesitation in telling him he had no right to ask. Jenifer hadn't re-grown her prickles and burrs, and by the light of day nothing was different, but four nights before she had slipped from the space beside him and not come back.

After having shared a bed, even if only for the necessary act of sleeping, the entire trip to Aretu and before; John had more than become accustomed to Jenifer's presence. More than being accustomed to it, he craved it. He hadn't rested so well in years as the nights he held her and hadn't rested so poorly as the nights she'd been gone.

John tossed back the covers and sat up, lowering his feet to the warm wood floor. He scrubbed his face with his palms, the scratch of his one-day beard abrading his skin. Today they headed back to

Callondia Capitol to meet with the captain and security staff of the *Constellation*. They would discuss if investigations had determined whether the murdering Xeno who had snuck aboard the *Steppenschraff* at Gateway had any accomplices aboard the ship, and whether those accomplices were on the *Constellation* after the *Axanadu* led the way to Aretu. The *Constellation* had arrived on Aretu the day before, and if things hadn't changed so drastically, Jacqueline Anderson and his son would just now be arriving on Aretu. Knowing the assassins had been aboard with them from Earth to Gateway made John's gut clench every time he let himself acknowledge how close he might have come to losing his son. He'd sent Silas away from him to be safe, and he had put his son at more risk by separating them.

Unwilling to dwell on it so early in the morning, he left the emptiness of the bed and forced himself into action. Minutes later he entered the large kitchen of his ancestral home, greeted by his son's exuberant cry and the smell of breakfast meats and chichi eggs.

"Miss Jenifer made me breakfast, Papa," Silas told him before biting off a mouthful of pan-fried toast with sweet butter. "Do you want some? She said she left some for you."

John smiled at his son's adoration for Jenifer; Silas might even be more smitten than he. He smoothed his hand over his son's coarse, dark hair and kissed his brow. "Perhaps in a bi'. Where is Jenifer?"

Silas pointed out the large, multi-paned window that bowed out from the kitchen to give a panoramic view of the eastern property and the hills beyond. His great grandfather had put in the window for his great grandmother because she said there was nothing more beautiful than watching the sun come over the hills. When John looked out, he had to disagree. Jenifer was on the hillside, exercising her newfound Talents with a six-foot wooden rod, pivoting and sparring with the rod like a training partner. With a ruffle of his son's hair, he left the kitchen through the side door and headed into the sun.

She moved with grace, the kind of grace only found when accompanied by strength. The rod spun and flipped around her, a dance of woman and wood. Since boarding the *Steppenschraff* and arriving on Aretu, she had worn the softer, free flowing clothing common amongst the Areth. A long tunic, with long sleeves to stave

41

off the morning chill with the approaching end of summer, fit and accentuated her body, flaring around her like a skirt at the hips as she turned. Long panels of cream brocade fabric usually fell to just below the knee, but they flittered in the air around her in ruffling waves. Dark, loose pants stopped at the ankle, showing off bare feet as she flipped and maneuvered to avoid the flying wood.

John raised his hand, and with a hard mental tug the wooden rod stopped its dance and flew into his grip with a solid smack against his palm. Jenifer rotated mid-flip and spun to face him, breathing hard, crouched with one leg extended at a twenty-degree angle and her hand flat on the grass.

"Good morning," she said with a smile.

"Good mornin'."

She straightened from the crouch, as elegant and smooth as a reed in the wind, brushing a bit of dark hair from her brow. John turned the rod vertical to the ground and set its tip on the dirt and enjoyed each sway of her body as she walked toward him. Jenifer confused him, she frustrated him, she made him happy, and she made him crazy, all at the same time.

As soon as she was close enough, John let the exercise rod drop to the ground with a thud and reached for her, drawing her to him with his hands set at her waist. Her lips curved into a seductive curl before she tipped her chin up to meet his kiss. By the time John forced his lips away from hers, her taste had set fire to his soul and he had to consciously focus on releasing the clench of his fingers in the back of her tunic. Jenifer stroked his cheek and rubbed her thumb across his lip.

"You are a puzzle," he said low between them, his forehead rested against hers. With a tip of his head, he slid the side of his nose along hers and inhaled the scent of the morning clinging to her. "I have spent every minute since I met you tryin' to figure you out."

Jenifer moved back to look him in the eyes. "I'm not the one you need to figure out, Ambassador."

"You're no'?"

She shook her head, stepped away, and held her hand out to her side. The rod shot up from the ground with as much precision and accuracy as if John had done it; he had over seventy years of practice, and she had not quite two weeks. Just another testament to the raw power this mystery woman held in her mind, power she had only begun to harness. Stepping back far enough to clear him of the swing, Jenifer spun the rod hand over hand until it was a blur, her self-taught skill in command of the weapon.

"I told you when we got here, John, I'm just waiting for you to make up your mind."

"Abou' goin' back to Earth . . ."

She just smirked, stopped the spinning of the rod with a snap, and headed toward the house. "Better come eat your breakfast before we go, Ambassador."

John followed, embracing the warm spread in his chest when Silas bolted from the house to meet Jenifer halfway, wrapping his short arms around her hips and pressing his cheek to her stomach. Jenifer hugged him back and ruffled his hair. Their voices carried to him, but not with enough clarity for him to understand. It didn't matter, not really, when it was the vision they presented that moved him. By the time he entered the kitchen, Jenifer sat at the table with Silas, who was on his second dish of food John knew of. He retrieved the plate of food left for him and enjoyed the company.

The false sense of security the foolish Areth ambassador and his Human whore had fallen prey to amused her. From three hills away, she watched through ocular enhancers as they played the parts of a family: the soldier, the whore, and the orphan. She waited and watched as they exited the massive, rambling house that looked rather like the result of the imagination of many insane men. The boy followed them to a conveyance and waited beneath a tree until the craft disappeared from sight, then ran off toward the barn.

They would make this far too easy. Blood would be shed before they had a chance to realize the error of their complacence.

CHAPTER FOUR

26 FEBRUARY 2054, TUESDAY
ALEXANDRIA HOSPITAL, SECURE WING – INTENSIVE CARE
UNITED EARTH PROTECTORATE, CAPITOL CITY
ALEXANDRIA, SEAT OF VIRGINIA
NORTH AMERICAN CONTINENT

"Constant air pressure push at ten percent," Doctor Lois Maybourne said from the other side of John Doe's bed. "Lung function maintaining adequate absorption and expulsion rates, external pulmonary system still regulating rhythm."

Katrina tried to focus solely on the extension unit she'd set up to the right of John Doe's bed, but the constant chatter between the doctors crowded into the room kept pulling away her full attention. She didn't understand much of it, most of it being not much more than gibberish. They might as well be speaking the language of the Fourth Sovereign of Raxo for as much as she really picked up.

Didn't matter if she understood or not, what they were about to do, the events of the next few moments were based on her word and her planning. No pressure. No pressure at all.

"Stand ready to engage bypass systems," Michael instructed. He stepped to Katrina's side, and despite the fact she knew he was there, she jumped when he laid his hand on her shoulder. "Are you ready?"

Katrina looked up and tried to smile. Her heart pounded so hard behind her ribs she thought it was going to just spasm and stop, and she couldn't seem to still the tremble in her hands. "I have to be, don't I?"

Michael smiled, and with his hand still on her shoulder, looked to the doctors and nurses standing at the ready to react if this went terribly wrong.

Please don't let it go wrong. Please, please don't let it go wrong.

"Disengage the respiratory junctions in five . . . four . . ." Doctor Anson counted down.

Katrina pushed out a shaky breath and forced herself to set her fingers on the control screen, the commands illuminating beneath her touch.

"Three . . . two . . . one."

She entered the single touch command to disengage the Sorracchi respiratory junctions and held her breath in sympathy. The constant hum of the machine slowly softened with a long hiss. Silence settled in the room like a heavy mist. Katrina looked up and stared at John Doe's exposed chest, wincing still at the scars and wounds left by the brutal machinery. Parts of the machine were still lodged in his body, buried too deep for them to remove until he was stronger, until his body could handle the shock.

If that day ever happened.

David dropped to his knees, clutching his chest. White light blinded him, cold prickling his skin. He tried to suck in air, but an invisible vice squeezed his lungs. He fell forward, bracing his body weight with one arm, clawing at his chest with the other to free his lungs. His ribcage threatened to collapse in on itself like a vacuum.

"Please. Please. Please," Katrina whispered.

"Heart rate dropping, no spontaneous respiratory activity," Doctor Anson snapped out, his voice unnaturally loud in the stillness of the room.

"Begin manual respiratory resuscitation," Michael ordered.

He kept his attention on the heart monitor. There was a rhythm, but it was too slow. Even Katrina knew that. Her pounding heart seemed to want to make up for it.

A nurse retrieved a pale blue bulb with a mouthpiece and placed it over John Doe's nose and mouth. She squeezed the bulb, forcing air into John Doe's lungs, then released the bulb, waited and did it again.

"Twenty seconds, Doctor."

"Recommend intubation, Doctor."

Michael held up his hand, and Doctor Anson immediately halted his move toward the intubation tube laid out at the ready in case everything went wrong. Katrina couldn't even blink. Her eyes burned. She looked from Michael to John Doe, and back to Michael. He moved away from her to the side of John Doe's bed.

"Thirty seconds . . ."

Michael nodded, staring and John Doe's still chest. "I know, Richard. Give him a few more seconds. He can do it." He didn't look to her, but waved Katrina to join him.

She glanced at her monitor. "Do you want me to reengage the—"

"Come to him, Katrina."

Swallowing hard against the desert in her throat, Katrina took a shaky step to the side railing. Michael reached out his hand and laid it on John Doe's chest. "He's still here." His voice was so low she didn't hear him.

Katrina leaned closer, looking at Michael's calm face. How could he be so calm? Why didn't he do something? She knew she was stupid when it came to biology, physiology, but she knew a body had to breathe, a heart had to beat. Tears burned her eyes and panic squeezed her chest. After surviving in solitude for decades, she couldn't bear the thought of this man dying so simply, without ever knowing they'd tried to help. Knowing he was with people who cared.

Doctor Tanner looked up and into her eyes. "Tell him."

She felt her jaw moving in a pathetic attempt to speak, but no sound came out. All she managed was to shake her head.

"You have been with him every day since we brought him from the pod, Katrina. I know you've spoken to him. Talk to him now."

She blinked and looked at John. His skin had gained some color in the last few days, but now he was ashen, his lips edged in a dusky pink. Katrina had grown accustomed to the hum of the machines that kept him alive, the rhythmic rise and fall of his chest with forced oxygen. Now, he was too still. Like he was already gone.

"Forty seconds, Doctor."

Doctor Anson's insistence pushed Katrina. She toed up and leaned over the edge of the railing, throwing her arm across his chest to grip his far arm. She was too short to lean over him, forced to lean on him.

"You're not alone," she cried out, desperate. "You're not in that coffin anymore. Just . . . just take a breath. Just open your eyes."

"Fifty seconds, Doctor."

"Come on!" Katrina cried, her voice cracking. "Please." She closed her eyes and bowed her head. "Please. Take a breath."

"Prepare for intubation," Michael said softly, "and atrial fibrillation."

"No," Katrina hissed through her teeth, and dropped the side of the bed. She cursed being so tiny but managed to hook her knee on the mattress edge and hoist herself up so she looked directly into his still face. A bit of her unfocused awareness acknowledged Michael's hands on her waist, helping her, but she was driven now. She couldn't let him go. She shoved away the nurse and her respiration bulb and laid her shaking hands against his cheeks, shocked by the coolness of his skin. "Don't you dare!" she shouted. "Don't you dare!"

David cried out, the smothering pain in his chest dropping him to his knees. He couldn't take a breath, couldn't stop the dead heat behind his ribs. His heart wanted to beat, but he couldn't make it. He clutched, willing himself to reach into his own body and rip his heart free. He screamed again, arching off the white nothing beneath him.

"Come on!"

Tears ran free down his temples and he flailed for purchase, finding none. He desperately looked for the source of the voice. That same voice that had read to him, had talked to him, had kept him from going crazy in the silence.

"You're not alone. Please, just take a breath. I want to say hello . . ."

"Hold! Hold!"

Katrina looked to the heart monitor beside the bed, trying to focus on the steady, strong rhythm through the haze of tears. She panted each breath, trying to hold back the sob. His chest suddenly expanded beneath her, the natural sound of life replacing the synthetic hiss she'd associated with him for too long.

"We have a steady sinus rhythm, Doctor," Doctor Anson said from beside the bed. "Respiration is spontaneous. Blood oxygen level at seventy-six percent but climbing. Brain activity increasing."

Katrina laughed and cried at the same time and laid her cheek against his chest, tears flowing to slick the contact as she listened to the rhythmic thump of his heart against his ribs.

Michael laid his hand on her back. "You did a wonderful thing, Katrina."

She opened her eyes and looked at him but couldn't say anything.

*A*wareness came to him one sense at a time.

First the comforting weight of blankets covering his body and the warmth trapped beneath, a contrast to the coolness on his neck and face. He'd been cold for so long, only experiencing the illusion of warmth in his dream, the warmth was soothing. The air he breathed was fresh but lacked the aroma of pine and coffee he'd tricked himself into smelling. There was a slight antiseptic scent, laced with some false air freshener.

At first all he heard was the rush of blood in his ears, intense and deafening like when he wore ear protection at the firing range. Beyond the muffle he heard the low hum of voices, but he couldn't make out the words. Until then, he wondered if he had finally died, but with each new sensation he accepted he was indeed alive.

The questions remained. Where was he? Who was with him?

His ears popped, like breaking the surface of water, and sound assaulted him. He'd been either in his looping dream, or trapped in bright white and silence, for so long even the simple sounds were abusive. David winced and tried to turn his head away from the noise. He swallowed and the sounds shifted, popped again. His throat was dry, his mouth pasty.

"He's waking up," said a woman's voice. "Go get Doctor Tanner."

The light coming through his closed eyelids already made his head pound. He dreaded opening his eyes, but he needed to know where he was, and whether he was in the hands of a friend or enemy. David turned his head to the side and blinked his eyes, the sensation of scraping his eyeballs with sandpaper making his eyes water. Everything was blurry, he couldn't focus beyond the fact he was in a bright room and darker shadows moved around his bed. A small shape he faintly determined had blond hair and was dressed in light blue, beyond that he made out no other details, stepped to the side of the bed and a gentle touch brushed his shoulder.

His skin tingled with the contact, both foreign and familiar.

"Take it easy," said a soft female voice. "You're going to be disoriented for a bit, but you don't need to worry. You're with friends."

David tried to raise his hand, but his arm weighed too much. His muscles shook from the meager effort. He knew he opened his mouth, knew he tried to speak, but nothing more than a strangled choke managed to get out of his throat.

"Let me get you a drink. Just a little. Your stomach hasn't had anything in it in a very long time."

How long had he been out? Had he been in a coma? What happened?

He wished he could ask the questions.

David blinked harder and a petite woman with short, curly blond hair took shape wearing a pale blue medical uniform. She smiled and held a cup in front of him, a straw extended in front of his mouth.

"Ready?"

He nodded and she touched the straw to his lips. The effort involved in closing his lips around the straw and drawing in the cool liquid was as exhausting as climbing a mountain. The bed was inclined and he rested on a cushion of pillows. If he had been forced to sit up under his own power, he never would have been able to. The coolness of the water made his breath catch and spread through his chest.

She withdrew the straw and turned at the waist enough to look over her shoulder at the doorway. As the room came into focus, he decided it was some type of medical facility, because it looked like a basic hospital room. Or laboratory? He hadn't forgotten the files he'd found, and since the Areth looked Human, he could just as easily still be in their facility. Until he knew, he was helpless since just raising his hand was near impossible.

A man who looked maybe thirty came through the door, leaning heavily on a cane, and approached the bed, smiling. "It's good to see your eyes open," he said with perfect enunciation, no accent David could determine. Not the schooled speech of someone with too much education for their own good, just lacking in any distinguishable lilt. "I'm Michael."

David rolled his eyes to encompass the room, swallowing again. He didn't think his throat would work quite yet. Michael turned to the nurse holding the straw to his lips again. "Susan, please warm some honey with just a touch of lemon and bring it to him. It will sooth his throat and give him some calories."

She let David take another sip and stepped away with a nod.

David watched the man who called himself Michael and wondered if he was the Doctor Tanner the nurse had sent someone to retrieve. He didn't look like a doctor. His hair was a mix of light brown with dark blond and looked like he needed a good haircut about two months ago. Not intentionally grown out long, just never bothered to get it cut. He wore a blue and maroon plaid flannel shirt open over a dark blue tee shirt and faded jeans and leaned on a knobby wood cane.

Michael slipped a pair of wire rim glasses from his front pocket and put them on before he took a small tablet from the table beside the bed and turned it on with a touch, scanning the information. Watching the screen upside down, it looked like a medical chart with actively changing readouts. Michael smiled before setting the tablet back down and looking at David. The glasses came off again.

Unable to do much, David focused on every minute detail, hoping something would give him the answers he needed. Thus far, he felt no threat, but he wasn't sure his judgment was the best.

"You're growing stronger, even just since this morning," Michael said, limping forward a step so David could see him a bit clearer. With each blink the world came more into focus. "We worried about you for a while. I know you have a lot of questions, and I promise we'll answer them."

The nurse returned with a small bowl. Michael leaned his cane against the side of the bed and stirred the contents, the aroma wafting to David. His mouth watered at the simple scent of warm honey. As soon as Michael let him take some of the warm honey from the spoon, and he managed to swallow, his throat immediately felt better.

"We'll see how that works in your stomach before we move on to anything with more substance. Does that feel better?"

David nodded, swallowing repeatedly. He cleared his throat, ready to risk speech. Michael curled both hands around the railing along the side of the bed and watched David.

"The electrodes attached to your limbs are for muscle stimulation. You might not feel it yet, but they're causing the muscles to restrict and relax. You haven't moved in a long time, and this should help get you moving faster. I know you probably can't move much at all right now, but that will change. It will take time, but it will change."

"Permanent damage?" David managed to force from a throat unwilling to cooperate.

Michael smiled, apparently pleased at David's ability to ask a simple question. "I don't anticipate anything permanent. Regardless of the intent, the stasis pod you were held in was advanced technology. Your body needs to learn to function on its own again."

David squinted. *Stasis pod?*

"Take him to the Abaddon and have him placed in stasis. I will deal with him later."

"Don't let this question alarm you," Michael said, interrupting David's memories. "Can you tell me your name?"

David cleared his throat again before croaking. "You don't know?"

Michael shook his head, never looking away from David. He met David's eye with the confidence of honesty. David had had the displeasure only once of meeting an Areth in person, and the alien had made his skin crawl. They looked him in the face, but never quite full in the eyes, and always hovered on the edge of smirking at their own inside joke.

The other male voice spoke. "I have heard from Barnabas. He predicts a five-decade timeline before we have viable bodies for transfer. It will take that long to filter out the dormant Areth markers."

51

"Do not speak the name of our enemy!" Warrick snapped. *"We must maintain this guise for now, and to speak of them otherwise is to imply our differentiation."*

The Areth weren't the Areth. Pieces slipped back to him, one at a time.

"We found you thirteen days ago aboard an alien ship floating derelict in space. You had been there a very long time, and because of that I don't want to overwhelm you with excessive details. You were listed only as Human male, and because our historical records are incomplete at best, we haven't found anything to help us know your name. We took your fingerprints once we removed you from the pod, but it will take time. You nearly died." His tone was level, David was sure to keep him calm.

A ball of lead dropped into his gut and his heart jerked. A sick panic hit him.

Michael glanced to the tablet he'd put back on the table and set his hand on David's shoulder before looking at him again. "You need to trust me. I know what I ask is immense, but . . ." Then Michael paused and pressed his lips together, his eyebrows tugging down. He nodded, just a tiny jerk. "You are with Humans again," he finally said. "The aliens you knew as the Areth are effectively gone. A great many things have happened, but if you wonder who we are, we are Human."

David blinked and tamped down the rush of adrenaline making his heart pound. He flexed his hands and cleared his throat again. If he was going to get answers, he had to start somewhere.

"David," he managed to force from his throat. "Lieutenant Colonel David Forte. Homeland Security."

Michael nodded and smiled. "It's good to meet you, David." He gripped David's hand lying dormant on the blanket and gave it a small pump, despite David's inability to shake hands in greeting.

A soft sound, like someone yawning, came from the corner of the room. Michael turned his head to look, and David tried to follow his track of sight. He hadn't seen the small couch against the wall, at least it hadn't been clear enough for him to make it out until now and hadn't noticed the small girl curled up in a ball. Her cheek rested against her folded hands, and fat ringlet-like curls framed her face. Even though it was a small couch, she looked tiny. Like a child.

Michael looked back to David with a smile that made David think Michael held a great deal of pride for the girl. "She . . ." he said, "is your guardian angel, and the reason you're here with us. She wouldn't let you go."

David swallowed again, a name slipping into his mind without hesitation. "Katrina," he choked.

Michael nodded. "Doctor Katrina Bauer. She'll want to know you're awake. She's been waiting."

Michael limped around the foot of the bed, his steps nearly completely dependent on the cane he used and made his way to the couch. He stood so David could still see her face and touched her shoulder.

"Katrina . . ."

She inhaled and stretched a little before opening her eyes, humming on the exhale. Dark brown eyes blinked open and she looked up at Michael. He tilted his head toward David's bed and she looked his way. Her eyes widened to match the instant smile that lit up her face and she sat up, scrambling to stand. He was right, she wasn't any bigger than a sneeze and didn't look much older than her teens. But, Michael had said doctor, so unless she was Doogie Howser's sister, she had to be older than she looked. Even though she rushed to her feet, she stopped still when she finally stood, watching him. He wouldn't be convinced the voice he remembered was hers until she spoke, but she seemed stuck like a deer in the headlights.

David attempted a smile, but at this point he didn't know whether it was a convincing reassurance or a frightening grimace. It had to be convincing because she rushed forward to the side of his bed and curled her hands around the side railing. Michael joined her, setting his hand on her shoulder.

"Katrina, this is Lieutenant Colonel David Forte."

Her eyes rimmed with shiny tears and she swallowed before she spoke. "Hello, David." Her voice matched her, soft and small and delicate.

"You're not alone. Please, just take a breath. I want to say hello . . ."

Even though he remembered the white light with no substance or escape, and the voice speaking to him from the nothing, part of him assumed it was another trick of his mind, a way to cope with the nothingness. All doubt fled when she spoke. It had been her, talking, reading to him, telling him it was okay to come back.

David swallowed, the benefit of the honey nearly lost now. He'd only been awake a few minutes, but exhaustion pulled at him already. "Hello, Katrina."

She looked to Michael. "Is he okay?"

Michael nodded. "Better than any of us anticipated. I've already told David his recovery will take time, but he's awake and with us, and that was the biggest obstacle."

She bounced on the balls of her feet, her curls bouncing with her. The smile she turned on him gave him hope.

"One question," David forced through a throat already irritated again.

Michael nodded.

"What year is it?"

Michael's smile faltered for a moment. "That may be the most startling question you could have asked, David. Today is the 26th of February 2054. Based on the records we found, you have been in artificial stasis just over forty-two years."

CHAPTER FIVE

27 FEBRUARY 2054, SATURDAY
OFFICE OF THE PRESIDENT
ROBERT J. CASTLETON MEMORIAL BUILDING – THE CASTLE
CENTER FOR UNITED PROTECTORATE GOVERNMENT
ALEXANDRIA, SEAT OF VIRGINIA
NORTH AMERICAN CONTINENT

"*L*ieutenant Colonel David Forte was reported missing during an undisclosed mission in December of 2011. He was an agent for Homeland Security at the time."

Nick looked up from the information he scanned on his PAC tablet, focusing on Colonel Ebben across the table. "Undisclosed . . . no record at all?" Around the table were various other key personnel involved since the pods came back to Earth: Michael, Victor, Beverly, and Connor.

Ebben shook his head. "None, sir."

Nick looked at Connor, and Connor confirmed what he thought. "Black Op?"

"Sounds it. What was going on in 2011?"

"We were three years post first contact," Connor said. "Woosley was president."

"Ah, yes . . ." Nick said with a grimace. "A shining light in the history of American presidents. He practically handed over the keys to the capitol."

"Mr. President, it's my recommendation we keep the prisoner isolated—"

"Whoa. Whoa. Whoa." Nick held up his hand to stop Ebben. "Prisoner? Lieutenant Colonel Forte is not and *will* not be treated as a prisoner. Don't you think this guy has been through enough?"

"We don't know where his loyalties lie, sir."

"Neither does he, most likely. You want to be the one to explain to him what the hell has happened in the last forty or so years?"

"Even if he wanted to pull something, I doubt he could," Connor said.

"So, we move him to a rehab wing until he's on his feet and brought up to speed. Then we'll see where we stand." Nick leaned back in his chair and tapped the table with his fingertips. "Did we find any personal records?"

Ebben cleared his throat. "He was thirty-six at the time of his disappearance, divorced from his wife Kelly about eight months prior. He had two sons with her, David Junior and Anthony, ages ten and seven at the time of his capture. He was a police officer in New York City until early 2002 when he joined the United States Army."

"Probably in response to the terrorist attacks in 2001," Connor interjected and Nick nodded, then motioned for Ebben to continue.

"He was recruited after First Contact to join Homeland Security. He took part in numerous covert missions, none of which have solid records, prior to his disappearance."

"When was Homeland Security disbanded?" Nick asked Connor.

"Mid-2012."

"Just before his VP was elected."

Connor nodded. "The last United States President before the global union of governments in 2017."

The beginning of the end.

"Have we tracked down any of his family?"

"Good luck with that. We were lucky to find his service record," Connor said with a chuckle. "Census information is spotty at best."

"I hadn't bothered, sir," Ebben answered. "I didn't think it would be relevant."

"The guy just woke up after forty years in a deep freeze. I think it'd be nice if he had some family to connect with," Nick tossed out with enough edge Ebben knew he was ticked. Yeah, he'd selected Ebben to serve as security advisor, but sometimes the guy just seemed plain heartless.

"Yes, sir."

"How is he doing otherwise? Considering," Nick asked.

"He's progressing," Michael explained, shifting forward to rest his arms on the table. "He's been very quiet since waking. I'm worried more about his mental wellbeing than his physical."

"He must be very confused," Beverly said in her soft, rounded voice. She had been given back her hearing ten months before, and with each day her speech became clearer. "To wake in a strange place and have so much be so different."

"He doesn't believe us yet," Michael explained. "Not fully. I sense a deep hesitation in him and wonder how much he knew before he was captured. With time he'll accept what we say as truth, but until he understands all that has happened since 2011, he has to take us at our word."

"Considering what was going on when he was captured, I can see why he wouldn't," Victor said. "If he was on a mission to infiltrate a Sorracchi facility, even if it was under the guise of the Areth name, then someone was already questioning the lies. Maybe even himself. He may see what we tell him as trading one lie for another. What makes what we say any more true than what the Sorracchi said in the beginning?"

"So, how do we convince him?" Nick asked. "How do you dump that much information on someone and have him get it all?"

Michael shook his head. "I took it on myself to study history once I was free to do so, but I came from a different place than David. My life laid the groundwork. I wasn't seeking truth as much as information."

"Do you think Katrina Bauer can assist us? She seems very

GAIL R. DELANEY

concerned for his wellbeing," Beverly said. "Victor has told me how much time she spent with him before he woke up."

"She will, I have no doubt," Michael said with a nod. "She might be a better person to answer some of his questions, or at least set him at ease. I've never seen anyone remember with such clarity the experiences while in a coma." He pointed toward Victor. "You told me you have no clear memory of your time comatose. He remembered her name and her voice without provocation."

"What about physically?" Nick asked. "He was in stasis for four and a half decades."

Victor tapped the screen of his PAC, opening some schematics of the pods "The technology of the stasis pod is highly advanced, to the point some of our Areth and Umani peers don't recognize its origin. David is weak, and his muscles were in an advanced stage of atrophy when we took him from the pod. I believe we can bring him to some level of mobility, but with our technology, I don't know if we have the capability of bringing him near where he might have been prior to this."

"With *our* technology," Nick said, catching Victor's play on words. "Do you have a thought?"

"I've been communicating with some doctors within the Coalition. There may be options, but I'm not ready to commit to anything quite yet."

"Keep me informed."

Victor nodded.

"What do we do first?" Beverly asked. "Heal him or teach him?"

"We have to do both," Michael answered. "I read his service record. David Forte is highly intelligent. He won't settle for not knowing."

Nick shifted and rubbed his fingers across his chin, his gaze toward the floor.

"What are you thinking, Dad?" Michael asked.

Nick jerked his head up and sat straighter. "Jace Quinn."

"What about Jace?" Beverly asked.

"I wasn't here when Jace was brought back from the Sorracchi prison, but I read the reports. I heard how bad he was. Physically and mentally."

58

Michael nodded. "I understand."

"Do you think it would help?"

"Their history is different, but the result is the same."

"I'm going to get a hold of Jace," Nick said to everyone rather than just Michael. "See if he can come to Alexandria for a while. Just a few days. Maybe it would do David some good to talk with someone with a similar experience."

"Jace wasn't held in stasis . . ." Victor said.

"No." Michael turned to face Victor and Beverly. "But he was tortured and abused by the Sorracchi, like David. He was left barely alive and wasted physically. David doesn't have memory loss, but he doesn't understand the last four decades, which in a way is a loss of the past."

"I suppose it wouldn't hurt," Victor agreed with a nod.

"I'll call him in the morning—"

"Afternoon," Michael corrected. "Tomorrow is Sunday. He'll have service in the morning."

"Right." Nick tapped the table. "Set up a time for me to get in to him," Nick added, and probably shouldn't have felt the urge to smile at Ebben's surprised expression. "I want to meet Buck Rogers."

Alexandria Hospital, Secure Wing – Intensive Care
United Earth Protectorate, Capitol City
Alexandria, Seat of Virginia
North American Continent

*D*avid joined the police force in New York straight out of college and served for four years until the terrorist attack on the Twin Towers. His son was just a baby, and when David witnessed the atrocities of that day, he felt driven to do more to protect his son. Kelly hadn't been happy about his decision to join the military, but she had let him go. He served in Afghanistan for six years before he was approached by General Packard to join a new subdivision of Homeland Security, an agency with a new definition after First Contact.

In his years of service, he spent more nights in a hospital than he cared to count. More than Kelly even knew about, because he didn't want to feed her fear while he was thousands of miles away. Sometimes it was for him, sometimes he sat at the bedside of a comrade in arms. He supposed he found some comfort in the familiarity.

The hospital was still, nearly silent, and cast in a soft glow from the moon outside reflecting off the snow covering the city. Alexandria, Virginia looked more like Rutland, Vermont. David lay awake listening, what he hoped to hear he didn't know. His own immobility scraped at his nerves like steel wool on an open wound.

He couldn't take the mutilation of his own body, and mutilation was the only thing he could call it. He'd only seen some of the bits of technology and interfaces when Michael Tanner had done an examination. Michael had explained David had been found in a stasis chamber, attached directly to the device through alien probes and tentacles forcibly attached to his body, running his life systems for him for over forty years. He also explained they couldn't remove some of the internal mechanisms until David was stronger, if ever. They had fused to his biology, like a malignant, invasive tumor . . . inoperable. At least Michael seemed honest, if not hesitant to commit too much.

David rolled his head on the stack of pillows keeping him slightly raised, though the staff had laid the bed nearly flat for sleep. He didn't like being down like this, it left him feeling vulnerable. Though, sitting upright, he wasn't much of a threat either.

The nurse, Susan, had been thoughtful enough to set all the controls he needed either immediately beside or beneath his fingers so he could gain some independence. He fumbled in the dim light to find the bed control near his left hand and engaged the control. He raised the head of the bed until he sat at a slightly obtuse angle, up enough he could easily see the flat monitor mounted on the wall. The monitor control was beneath his right hand, and he maneuvered shaking fingers enough to turn on the monitor and mute it before he drew too much attention. The control worked like an iPad or iPod, slide and tap, but that was a workout.

The right corner of the screen read 23:47, and across the bottom were the words *Aired Previously*. A blond woman, attractive but not stunning, a far cry from made up and dolled up anchorwomen he was used to seeing, spoke to the camera with a video of a burning building in the background. A story box to the left of her head read *Xeno Attack Kills Seven in Toronto*.

His hand shook when he turned up the sound, bringing it up just enough he could hear her speak. He glanced toward the door. No one had come looking yet.

"An attack on a sizeable settlement in Toronto today left seven civilians dead and several injured. Reports indicate the death toll was exacerbated by the severe cold in the region, and the inability for Firebird rescue teams to access the area for over an hour and a half. A local Xeno cell has claimed responsibility, stating they will continue their attacks until the Earth is free of outside alien influence. A shipment of all-weather supplies and shelf safe food stocks were recently delivered to the settlement as ordered by Areth Ambassador John Smith. The attack is believed to be in retaliation for the rescue supplies.

"Ambassador Smith's whereabouts have been unknown for nearly three weeks after an attempt on his life within the Aretu-Raxo embassy in Alexandria on the third of last month. Ambassador Smith is seen here engaging in negotiations with President Tanner just a few days prior to the embassy attack."

The image behind her changed to a video of an office with several people either seated or standing. A tall man with hair more silver than brown leaned against the edge of the desk, his arms crossed over his chest. David had seen enough random clips to know this was the infamous Nick Tanner, president of the whole damn planet. He looked far less pretentious than his title implied.

Another man, not quite as tall but more lanky with light brown hair, stood near a hearth and spoke animatedly with one hand moving through the air, the other shoved in his pocket. It wasn't an angry discussion, just passionate, by what David interpreted. The camera focused on him and *Ambassador John Smith of Aretu* overlaid his image.

"What kind of name is John Smith? He couldn't do better than that?"

A woman stood at the edge of the image, behind the ambassador. She wasn't part of the conversation, appearing more the observer than a participant. She was a steel beauty, stunning but with a dangerous glint to her eyes. She wore a weapon, and her attention never left the ambassador.

Bodyguard?

"Although President Tanner's office has been reluctant to provide any details regarding the Areth ambassador, sources have indicated Ambassador Smith is being held in a secure location until the numerous assassination attempts can be quelled and the originating Xeno cell can be shut down."

"Xeno," David said to the empty room. "Xenophobe?"

He squinted and scowled. Had he really been reduced to speaking to empty rooms? Heck, he'd feel better just having Ruger to talk to. His pal and buddy had proven to be a great companion in the months following his divorce, and Ruger never gave him a hard time about not rinsing out his cereal bowl or not stopping for milk on the way home. David figured since he was a German Shepherd he was a born cop, and always listened attentively to David's ramblings.

"In happier news, a small colony in the Texas region has welcomed their first post-war birth," the anchorwoman said with a wide grin, and once again the image changed, this time to a dark-haired woman holding a wailing baby. The woman smiled at the camera, her hair still slick to her forehead from the exertion of birth, but her eyes shined bright with joy. A man stood beside her, his hand protectively on the head of the screaming baby. "Parents Eric Geurrero and Denise McKenna welcomed baby Nicholas into the world today, the first baby to be born in the colony since it formed last summer. They said they named the baby after President Tanner, and they aren't the first." She smiled and winked. "In a few years, we're going to have more Nicholases than we know what to do with. Congratulations to Eric, Denise, and Nicholas."

David shook his head. Getting details from anyone was like pulling teeth from an angry polar bear, but it didn't take a genius to know the world had to be in bad shape for the birth of a single baby to make the news. In 2011, he thought things were bad, and knew it would get worse after he hacked into those files. But, this . . . this he never imagined. It was like a bad SyFy Channel movie.

A soft tap preceded the door opening, and a diminutive shadow partially blocked the light from the hall. "David?"

"Yeah," he said, trying to project his voice but it came out as little more than a crackle. He cleared his throat and tried again. "Yeah, come on in."

She slipped into the room and eased the door shut behind her. "I didn't wake you, did I?"

"I've done enough sleeping to last me 'til I'm dead."

She came further into the room, the light from the monitor taking her out of the shadow. She still didn't look any older than eighteen, twenty if he were generous, but she had made it clear she was twenty-four and not a year younger. He still smiled remembering her adamancy.

"I've gotten so used to coming here before I go back to my lab I guess I feel out of sorts if I don't." She paused and tilted her head toward her left ear. "Michael told me you remembered me reading to you. I didn't think you would, but he told me it might help."

David nodded and smiled at the way she rambled. She reminded him of his little sister Stacy, and that realization pinched something in the center of his chest. He purposefully refused to think about what being in a stasis pod for over four decades meant for the people he loved.

"Don't you go home?" he asked.

She climbed onto the foot of his bed and pulled her bent knees to her chest as if she did it every night. "Not since—well, not since you were taken out of the pod. I just sleep here and my brother Karl brings me stuff from home."

"Because of me?"

"You . . . and them. They're called the Triadic. They were found with you. Do you remember anything about them?" She shook her head. "Never mind, of course you wouldn't. They weren't even born, or whatever you'd call it, until a few years after you were put in there. They might know you, but I don't think you'd know them."

The more she talked, the more he smiled, and the more he remembered her voice. When she hadn't been reading to him, she'd talked. About things he didn't understand, about things that didn't make sense, just talked.

"What do you read to them?" he asked, teasing her because he got a kick out of the blush in her cheeks. Just like he used to with his little sister Stacy.

She smiled and blushed. "Nothing, but maybe I should."

"So, tell me about it."

"You sure you don't want to sleep?"

"I told you, I've slept enough to last me a lifetime."

*I*t was nearly three in the morning before Katrina left David's room. Despite his claims to never want to sleep again, he'd nodded off eventually, and she slipped off the bed to let him rest. She always felt the need to walk on light feet through the hospital this late at night, and her walk was longer now that they had moved David to a private room away from the intensive care space he'd been held in since being pulled from the pod.

David.

Lieutenant Colonel David Forte to be exact. He'd explained how his name was spelled with an 'é', but didn't sound it, the point seemed important. It was nice just to know his name rather than just "John Doe." He was alive, awake, and real.

The realization made her vision haze and she swiped at her cheeks before anyone happened to see her. Karl accused her enough of being a weepy female, but she couldn't imagine not being moved by David's story. Michael had told her about what they had discovered that afternoon once they knew his name. He'd had a family, a wife, and two young sons. He was the middle child of three siblings, with an older brother Mark and a younger sister Stacy. They had no idea if any of them were still alive, but President Tanner had insisted they find out. For David's sake.

She reached the pod room and walked past her desk to the half circle space in front of the three coffin-like machines. They had opened the containers a few times, determining how intricate the interface was, but for the most part they stayed closed for effective functioning of the equipment. Katrina crossed her arms and gripped her elbows, stepping closer to Omega's pod.

"Would it help if I read to you?" she asked.

She wasn't surprised by the lack of response. Just before she turned away from the pod, a red warning light flashed along the readout screen. Katrina leaned closer and squinted, trying to read the scrolling Sorracchi language. She had a rudimentary understanding, but it took her time especially when the symbols were moving. It was much easier to build a program to translate for her than read on her own. She got enough from the readout to indicate a connection had lost communication.

The pod door was heavy, but she disengaged the seal and pried open the lid. Once she began the process of opening the pod, the hydraulics kicked in and the lid folded back with a slow hiss. The pod was slightly inclined with security straps holding Omega in place across his thighs, hips, and chest. The first time they'd opened the pod they'd discovered the three were naked but had since been clothed in infirmary pants as much for their modesty and Katrina's flaming cheeks. She was too short to reach all the way to the top of the pod, even with it tilted, but she could reach most of the connections.

"Hmmmm," she said as she examined each of the umbilical connections. "I don't see anything off or unhooked. How would it happen anyway . . ."

She nudged his right arm away from his side to get a better look at the connection into his lungs. At least whomever Kathleen had ordered to put them in here had taken more care than with David. The interfaces were still fused with their skin, but it wasn't as sloppy and brutal as with David. It would still be a challenge to disengage and remove them without leaving damage behind.

The connection looked off center. She slid into the space in front of the pod and laid her hand on his stomach to leverage herself into a better position. The abdominal muscles beneath her palm tightened reflexively, and Katrina gasped, stumbling back. She looked up at Omega's face, truly expecting to see his eyes open, but his face was as placid and unchanged as always. Katrina swallowed and again tried to examine the connection, this time without touching his bare skin.

The cord had partially disengaged, and she slid it back into place with an audible click. Once it was seated again correctly, she stepped back and reached for the edge of the lid, pausing again to look at him. Even though the logs put them at about forty years old, their faces were deceivingly young. They had been cleaned up after the pods were opened, their faces shaved, their bodies cleansed. They looked young, very young, too young to have gone through all Kathleen's logs said they had.

Guilt niggled at her when she closed the pod again. She had to find the right way to disengage them, to save them the trauma David had survived, to bring them out of stasis with as few problems as possible. They didn't deserve to be in there. No more than David did.

The hydraulics eased the pod lid closed, and she pressed the command to seal it again. This time, she avoided looking at his face through the viewing window. She only had a few hours to catch some sleep, but she couldn't just go to bed without checking on some of the programs she'd left running while she was visiting David.

She sank into her chair and tapped her control board, the screens lighting up in response. The front panel of her center monitor had a scrolling image of their brain patterns, three rows, with Alpha on top, Omega in the middle, and Beta at the bottom. The readings were consistent, which was expected with comatose patients. As she scrolled back through the last hour or two, she noticed something minor but distinct. To be sure, she tapped in a time twenty-four hours earlier.

"Activity is increased," she said to the room. "Not enough to read as a jump, but . . ." She swiveled in her chair to look back at the pods. "I hope to God you don't wake up in there."

CHAPTER SIX

EARTH TIME: 2 MARCH 2054, MONDAY
SMITH ESTATE—DEVON ON THE HILL, CALLONDIA DISTRICT
ARETU

*T*he same gnawing unease Jenifer had felt when they landed on Aretu two weeks earlier had been chewing at her for days; a constant ball of acid in her gut, a tingling at the base of her skull, and a tension across her back keeping her ready to lash out at any second. She had been blissfully free of any "fight or flight" needs the first couple of days they'd been on Aretu, and at John's family estate, but then a snap of anxiety had yanked her from her sleep—and from John's bed—and she hadn't been able to shake it since.

With each day, and most specifically each night, the dread had gotten worse.

In the long hours of the night, when sleep eluded her and she kept herself away from the bedroom upstairs where John slept, she had learned the many sounds of the home his family had built over the generations. When the wind blew over the east hills, a window in the salon clattered in its housing, and when it rained water gathered in the old eaves of the kitchen and dripped hypnotically on the rock garden along the foundation beneath the large bow window looking out on the property. A north wind chilled the dining room, but when the sun was warmest the room was nearly stifling. In hundreds of years of advanced technology, she wondered how the Areth had gone without developing better climate control. Or, perhaps, it was just the nature of the home to let it ramble and settle and whistle.

In truth, she loved learning the nuances of the house.

She'd also discovered a few things in her nighttime wandering; a library tucked in the south corner of the house with massive windows and even larger bookshelves reaching all the way to the twelve-foot ceiling and covering all four walls. The more she saw and learned of the Areth, the less alien and foreign they were. Thousands of light years and thousands of *years* of development, and they were more Human than some Humans she knew.

The moon was massive, a white and silver orb dwarfing the stars. It was so bright it lit the library nearly as well as any of the lamps stationed around the large room. Jenifer found her way here every night since discovering the library, and four nights before had found the section of shelves reserved for the Smith family history. Journals and albums, some so old the images of his ancestors were drawings or paintings on brittle pages. She knew he was the thirty-fourth John Smith in his family and had managed to track back the archives to the twentieth John Smith, a farmer and common man. He had not lived on this farm, the Smiths didn't come to Devon on the Hill until John Smith the twenty-seventh, but John's people had always been workers of the land. Some had gone on to other things, some had died in the war with the Sorracchi generations before, some were even men of the clergy and men of science and medicine, but the majority were men of strong backs and worn hands.

Guilt niggled at her—a sensation she wasn't accustomed to—for digging into his family history without telling him so much as her real name, but it was clear John held no qualms about who he was or where he came from. She had yet to read anything to make her think he had anything to hide. Tonight, she sat curled into the eight-foot-long window seat ensconced amongst the piles of pillows, thumbing through a book so old the pages crackled when she turned them.

Fatigue pulled at her, but she knew if she were to go to John's room
and lie down her mind would snap awake and keep her from sleeping.
If she dozed here eventually, she dozed here. At least John wouldn't be
disturbed.

A tale of travels across what the Areth called the Northumbra Sea
let her mind drift briefly from the ever-present knot, enough she
settled back into the pillows and closed her eyes. Even an hour of rest
would do her good.

She was on her feet, the book hitting the wood floor with a loud
thump, before her sleep-deprived brain had enough fire power to
connect with what her body already knew. Something was wrong. A
noise didn't belong.

Someone was in the house.

She left the book on the floor and moved silently across the library
to the door, easing it open. The old hinges creaked, and she winced,
glancing left and right along the narrow, slightly curved hall. Jenifer
loved the many and large windows of the mishmash home, varying
styles and ages, and right now she loved it for the moonlight glow
lighting each passage. The hall was empty, no sound carried from any
nearby room.

Staying close to the wall, Jenifer moved on light feet to the kitchen
and through the salon, past the main staircase leading to the second
floor. An intruder would take those stairs unless they knew the layout
of the house and knew about the narrow staircase in the back leading
from one of the various sitting rooms. She entertained a quick glance
up the central stairway as she passed, confirming the winding stairs to
be empty. A slight creak of the floor above made her skin tingle and
bitter adrenaline burned the back of her throat. The upstairs hallway.
Outside the bedrooms.

Jenifer ran silently through the house to the back stairs and skipped
every other step, her feet near the wall to keep the old boards from
announcing her arrival. Her heart pounded viciously against her ribs
by the time she reached the top, not from exertion, but fear.
Unmitigated, unquestionable fear. John and Silas. The mantra repeated
again and again in her head. *John and Silas. John and Silas.*

She passed several empty rooms, pausing at each curve or corner to glance ahead. Silas' room was the first occupied room she reached, and she paused outside the door, her ear pressed to the wood. Jenifer risked closing her eyes for a few moments and concentrated, reaching out in a way she didn't fully grasp but had finally accepted. The room was still, peaceful, the only sound Silas' soft snores.

Right now, she wished for little more than Damocles in her hand, but her weapon was in the bedroom. Her senses practically sparked the closer she moved toward the end of the house with John's bedroom. With each step, the rush of adrenaline pushed harder, and she forced herself to keep from rushing forward. The hallway curved, blocking her clear view of the bedroom door, but she knew before she leaned against the wall someone who didn't belong was just feet away. The malice and hatred tainted the air like a foul smell, sticking in her throat and burning her nostrils.

"Show yourself," slithered a voice from the darkness. "Unless you prefer to hide in the shadows like a coward."

Jenifer tensed and pressed her back to the wall. The voice was female, and now that she had a sound point of reference, she knew whomever it was stood not far from the bedroom door. Wishing again for Damocles, she took the step needed to come into view. A woman stood several feet away, a weapon of unknown origin in her hand trained on Jenifer. The moonlight lit her from the back, casting her face in shadows, but Jenifer new instantly it was the woman from the video that had convinced Jenifer to take on the task of being bodyguard to John Smith, Ambassador to Aretu. The woman who had stood in the crowd and thrown the flash-bang grenade that nearly blinded Connor Montgomery and nearly killed John and his son. A Xeno.

But this woman was more.

More evil. More deadly. More dangerous.

"You've been lazy," the Xeno said, stepping toward Jenifer. But at least it was away from John's door. "Complacent." She stepped away from the window, the shadows flittering away from her face. Cold, dark eyes and a self-satisfied smirk. "I've watched you for days. I could have killed the boy a dozen times."

Jenifer's heart jerked as she thought of all the times they'd left Silas alone.

"I'm not playing this game," Jenifer said through clenched teeth.

She brought up her hand and reached out to snatch the weapon from the woman's hand the same instant she pulled the trigger. The shot went wild, ripping across Jenifer's shoulder before tearing a rift across the plaster wall. Jenifer stumbled back, the weapon bouncing off her hand before it clattered across the floor. With a primal scream, the woman launched forward at Jenifer. They both fell and Jenifer landed on her back. Pain seared through her arm and shoulder, the smell of blood, scorched skin, and singed plaster burning her nostrils. They grappled together, fighting for dominance. The back of Jenifer's head slammed hard into the wood floor, all concentration she'd drawn to fight the woman with her mind broken by the blinding pain. She kicked out and got a leg between them. With a grunt of exertion, Jenifer kicked out and broke the woman's hold on her throat, sending her stumbling back toward the far end of the hall. A sound behind her caught her attention and she rolled to her knees, her heart slamming into her gut at Silas' wide eyes staring at her from the darkness.

"Run, Silas! Get Anson!" she shouted and twisted to face her attacker.

She was on her feet, her hand braced against the wall. A sharp snap of her eyes made Jenifer look, too, at the weapon discarded on the floor. Her attacker, huffing for breath, growled deep in her throat. A primal, enraged sound. Jenifer extended her hand and pushed through the pain. The action ripped through her skull, commanding the weapon to come to her. As it slapped into her hand, the bedroom door opened and one single blast sent the woman hard into the wall in a boneless slump. She slid to the floor, motionless.

Jenifer lowered her arm and looked to John, Damocles in his hand. Never before had she been so glad she had programmed his DNA signature into the weapon so he could try her toy. He looked to her and took one step. It was all the invitation Jenifer needed and she was in his arms, holding on tighter than she had ever held on to anything. Or anyone.

*J*ohn sat in the front salon, facing a fire someone had built in the hearth, holding his sleeping son in his lap. The boy's cheeks still glistened from the tears he'd wept when he came back to the house, Anson Barclay behind him with a pulse rifle in his hand. The house bustled with activity. Just a few feet away, Jenifer sat on a long lounge with a physician from Devon Township treating the weapon burn on her left shoulder. John knew Evan Gralwayne, they had been classmates the years John had attended school to be a physician; before he realized his calling was as a soldier, not a healer. The shot had torn through the fabric of her tunic, leaving the edges burnt and stuck to her raw skin, and John had winced with her each time the doctor had to pull the material away from the flesh to treat it. The Sorrs used weapons designed not only to kill, but to maim and cause as much pain as possible in the process, and somehow this Xeno had gotten her hands on one.

Two surety guards came into the room, wearing the yellow sash of the civilian delegation, and two others moved down the hall past the doorway, the woman held securely between them. She thrashed and fought, a silencer band over her mouth muffling her cries of profanity and threats. Silas stirred and drew a shuttered breath but didn't open his eyes.

Both guards stopped in front of him and bowed deep. One took another step toward John. "We will take the prisoner to Devon Township tonight, Ambassador, and arrange transportation to Callondia Capitol in the morning."

"Thank you, Captain," John said in a lower voice to keep from waking his son.

Anger flashed through him, hot and fierce. Silas had believed he would be safe here, no harm would come to him on his Papa's farm, and yet his life had been put at risk even here. Would there be no safe place for his son to have a childhood?

The physician stood and snapped shut his medical bag. "The

wound will need treatment with a skin grafter to fully heal," he said to Jenifer, then turned to John. "Do you have one, John?"

He nodded. "I can see to it."

Evan offered a small smile and looked at Silas asleep in his lap. "He's a fine boy. I heard how he ran for your caretaker."

John nodded, his response stuck in his throat.

"Are *you* fine, John?"

"Yeah," he managed to choke, glancing past Evan to meet Jenifer's watchful stare.

She pulled the cut, burned edge of her tunic over the gauze bandaging her shoulder and stood, never looking away from him. John drew in a long breath, releasing it in small degrees as she crossed to him. He tipped back his head when she reached the chair and closed his eyes when she slid her fingers through his hair and rested her palm against his cheek. John turned into the touch and kissed her palm.

"Right, then. If you need anything, miss, you let me know."

"Thank you," Jenifer said softly. "I'll see you out."

Her hand left his cheek, his skin immediately feeling bereft. John blinked open his eyes and watched her leave with Evan. A lump choked him and his eyes burned. Once again, he came close to losing everything because of Sorrs hatred. Where could he go, where could he take his child, that the people he loved would be safe? Was there a place?

Or would he have to make it?

John shifted his son against his bare chest and stood, the sound of Jenifer speaking with Evan drifting through the house as he climbed the main staircase. Plaster rubble littered the hallway floor and crunched as he walked over it in bare feet. Silas' bed was a rumbled mess, but it didn't matter. John laid him down and pulled the blankets up to his chin. Silas sighed in his sleep and curled onto his side, settling into the warmth of the bed. He took a moment to lay a hand on his son's dark hair and kiss his equally dark cheek before leaving the room.

He avoided acknowledging the damage to the wall outside the bedroom but couldn't help the clench in his gut when he saw the dark stain on the wood floor left by Jenifer's wound. The bedroom was empty, just as he'd left it.

"John . . ."

Her voice was rough, soft, uncharacteristic. Comforting arms wrapped around his body, warm hands on his chest. He inhaled, drawing in the feel of her body against his back, her lips touching his skin. John turned in her embrace, took her head in his hands and covered her mouth in a kiss ripped from his soul. Words were useless, he'd had enough of nearly losing her, enough of swallowing his heart as she bandaged a wound, enough of holding back the desperation, not the desire, but the need for her. More than an attraction, she was a compulsion, a fulfillment.

John never took his lips from hers but released his hold on her to work at the buttons of her tunic. Any other woman he might have asked if this was what she wanted, he might have asked permission to be bold, but if he had learned anything about Jenifer it was nothing happened she didn't want. Her kiss, her touch, the fervency of her hands told him all he needed to know. He wrapped her in his embrace, her arms around his shoulders, and lifted her feet off the floor. With gentle care to protect her shoulder, John lowered her to the bed and found her mouth again.

*J*enifer woke with the sun, rather than watching it rise, blissfully free of the knot of dread that had kept her from resting nearly since they'd arrived. She inhaled and stretched, smiling at the languid lack of tension. The bed beside her was empty, but she didn't have to look to know John was in the room. His presence was a constant, steady warmth. She rolled toward the center of the bed and saw him standing at the window, his bare back drawn tight with his arms crossed over his chest.

"Good morning."

John turned, a slow smile curling his lips. "Good mornin'." He came back to the bed and dropped beside her, lying on his side supported on his elbow. John pressed a quick, firm kiss to her lips before settling back again. "How do you feel this morning?"

Jenifer smiled and touched his cheek. "I never thought you to be the type of man who needs your ego stroked."

The look he gave her sent a flush from head to toe.

"That's no' what I meant, but I think it answered my question."

Jenifer winked. "Tell me what you were thinking about."

"I'm done thinkin'. I decided something this mornin'." He shrugged one shoulder. "Or maybe it was last night."

"Decided . . . or figured out . . ."

He released a huff. "A'right, fine, I figured it out, just as you said."

"When?"

"The *Constellation* leaves today for its return trip to Earth, but if we leave on the *Steppenschraff* in another three days we'll be back to Earth before the *Constellation* arrives."

"And we're taking the Xeno back with us," she stated, not really asking a question.

"She may have attacked an ambassador on foreign soil, but she is wanted for multiple acts of terrorism and murder on your planet she'll answer to first."

"So . . ." Jenifer smiled and sat up, bracing herself on both her elbows. "You're still an ambassador."

"Don't act so surprised," he said with a chuckle, swinging out of the bed again. "Come on, up with you. Silas will be up soon."

CHAPTER SEVEN

Earth Time: 3 March 2054, Tuesday
Defense Alliance Transport Vessel Axanadu
On approach to Earth's solar system
Estimated Time to Earth: 17 hours

"*Y*ou are doing great, Ms. Anderson." The onboard Areth physician set aside the touch tablet he used for making notes and moved to a computer interface unit hanging on the wall. He woke the system with a touch and entered some commands as he continued talking. "I am, however, pleased you will be off this ship in a few hours. While there has been no evidence interstellar travel is detrimental in the early stages of pregnancy, we do advise expectant mothers to remain in a natural gravity atmosphere for the last two-thirds of their term."

Jackie pulled her tunic over her head and frowned a bit at the way it stretched across her lower abdomen. Another week on the *Axanadu* and she would have had to resort to buying larger clothing. She may be just beginning her second trimester, but the physician said her thin frame wouldn't let her disguise her physical state for long. Not that she minded. She smiled and ran a hand over the slight extension of her waist.

"So, there's nothing I need to worry about?"

"None whatsoever. You are a young, healthy woman with a healthy child. I see no cause for concern." He turned to face her, a slight dig between his pale green eyes. "Is there something you're concerned with you didn't share with me?'

Jackie shook her head and finished buttoning her tunic. "No, it's just . . . we doubted we'd conceive. This was a surprise, I guess I'm waiting for the bad news."

"Were your doubts because of your missing ovum?"

Jackie nodded, her fingertips automatically brushing over her clothing where she knew the small scar marred her skin. The Sorracchi had held her prisoner for a handful of days, and in those days they'd taken from her something infinitely precious. She didn't even remember it happening, hadn't been aware enough to realize she'd undergone surgery, and didn't know the ovum was gone until weeks later after she'd recovered and Michael told her. The greater question wasn't when did they do it, but why?

The answer terrified her.

"Granted, losing an entire ovum drastically reduced your likelihood of conception, but didn't preclude it completely. You've been given a miracle, you and the father."

She nodded again, her throat thick with tears. Jackie wanted to be able to blame the hormone swings she'd heard about during pregnancy, but she knew hormones were only part of her emotional imbalance. She missed Michael so much it hurt, and it had only gotten worse since John and Jenifer told her Michael had returned to Alexandria. He was there, waiting for her.

And she would be able to tell him he was going to be a father.

First, he would have to explain to her why he left without a word. Jenifer had been more than willing to tell Jackie why she thought he'd left. In Jenifer's eyes, Michael was a coward for leaving. John had given a different view: Michael had left because he thought he had to in order to protect her and Nicole.

She wanted to hear Michael's words of explanation.

The doctor laid his hand on her shoulder and squeezed gently.

"Don't let things of the past taint this for you, Ms. Anderson. Every child is a gift."

Jackie swallowed hard and blinked until the tears subsided. She raised her head and looked him in the eyes. "Thank you, Doctor. I appreciate everything."

She left the medical bay for the last time and returned to the small single quarters she'd occupied for the last two weeks for the return flight to Earth. She longed to breathe fresh air, even if it was cold enough to freeze her nose hairs and be in her own home. After two weeks onboard the Alliance transport, the next few hours would take an eternity.

3 MARCH 2054, TUESDAY
ALEXANDRIA HOSPITAL, SECURE WING – INTENSIVE CARE
UNITED EARTH PROTECTORATE, CAPITOL CITY
ALEXANDRIA, SEAT OF VIRGINIA
NORTH AMERICAN CONTINENT

"*H*ey." Karl slapped his hand against the doorjamb, and Katrina bounced in her chair with a squeak. Her brother smirked. "I'm going for some dinner in the cafeteria then heading back to the apartment. You coming?"

Katrina scooted closer to her desk, willing her heart rate to slow down. She scowled, keeping her focus on the data files open on her tri-panel monitors. "No," she snapped out. "I've got work to do."

Karl came into the storage-cum-stasis-pod room and crouched beside her desk. Everything she needed had been brought to her so she could access the records they'd downloaded from the *Abaddon*, and with every hour she spent on the decipher programs she had more information to work with. She just knew she was close to finding something significant.

"Sis, you need to get some real rest. You have been going non-stop since those damn pods came back from space."

She shot him a look, then shook her head. "Not until I'm done."

Karl laid his hand on hers, halting her typing. "Trina, promise me you won't stay here all night again. Come back to the apartment and we'll watch one of those old classic movies you like. How about that one you like so much, *Enchanted*, right?"

Katrina smiled. "You must mean it if you're willing to watch a love story to get me home."

"I worry about you."

"Okay, fine. Get me something to eat, and I'll meet you at home."

He tapped the desk and stood again. "Okay."

Alone again, Katrina sighed and looked at her monitor. She had left a diagnostic running on some of the life support umbilical units they had removed from David both before and after he woke. She would check on the results and then leave for the night. Katrina locked the computer access and stood. She tapped the light switch when she reached the door, the light from the monitors casting a pale blue glow that didn't quite reach the half circle formed by the three stasis pods.

A thunk stopped her short of stepping out the door. Katrina paused, her hand on the door handle, and looked back into the room. The only sound she heard was the low electronic hum of the computer system. Maybe it was just the chair popping a hinge. It was old and had threatened to either drop her to the floor, or send her catapulting across the room, more than once. She stared through the dim light to the three pods, the viewing windows dark and shadowed. She had to squint and stare to see the barely lit planes of the men's faces within the pods.

Katrina twisted her lips and hummed. She left the door partially open and headed down the hall to the R&D bay where the implements had been left for study. The bay required a passcode to enter, and she typed it in with barely a thought. It was early evening and most of the staff had headed to wherever they called home for the night. This end of the building housed no patients, even David had been moved to the patient care wing of the hospital. Njogu was still working, seated at one of the workstations. He looked up, his large, black eyes focusing on her. It had taken Katrina several weeks not to be creeped out by the Umani's different eyes. Like large pools of black ink, with no color, no iris, and no whites, they startled her nearly every time he looked at her. She had learned everyone from his particular sovereign, or with a lineage leading back to his sovereign on Raxo, had similar eyes.

"Good eve, Katrina." His voice was so deep, she swore it had to come from the tips of his toes.

"Hi, Njogu. I'm checking on my analysis program."

"I do not believe it is finished," he said, his English only slightly broken. "I have not heard de program indicate completion."

"Hmmm." Katrina went to the array of machinery stretched over a table along the outside wall and bent forward to check on the progress. "Dang, not even sixty percent done. I guess I'll have to finish in the morning."

"It would seem wise."

She nodded. "Okay, then. Good night, Njogu."

He waved an unnaturally long hand with fingers much longer than any Human she'd ever seen. "Good night."

The halls were empty going back to the pod room. She wanted to begin a new data encryption translation program before she left, knowing it would run most effectively if she wasn't doing anything else at the same time. Not bothering with the light when she opened the door, she pushed her malfunctioning desk chair out of the way and bent over the desk to begin the program. The chair rolled away and clanked against the far wall. Katrina glanced at the chair, a tingle going up the back of her neck. She looked back at the chair, then slid a glance at the pods. They looked the same as always, dark except for the small square of blinking lights and data scrolling in Sorracchi.

She shook her head and turned back to the computer. A few taps had the program open and running. Katrina shut down the monitors to preserve power and took a step back.

Into something solid.

She sucked in a breath to scream, but all sound was silenced by the hand clamped over her mouth and the steel strong arm wrapped around her body, nearly lifting her off the floor. Katrina forced a scream against the cold palm of her captor, but nothing more than a mumbled huff got past the hand. She thrashed and kicked, clawed at the arm around her waist.

"*Yesheti Tchotchu,*" a male voice whispered against her ears.

Katrina pressed her eyes closed, hot tears running down her cheeks. Fear burned her throat and her heart wanted to pound out of her chest. She whimpered and tried to shake her head in the iron grip. The words were Sorracchi, but she couldn't focus enough to translate. She blinked her eyes opened again to see two shadowed figures moved into her line of sight, one each side, and Katrina realized with a dizzying rush she was held by one of the three Triadic.

"Human?" her holder whispered again.

She nodded within his hold or tried to.

"English?"

She nodded and hated the whimper his hand muffled.

"We will leave this place. You will take us."

Even when she had huddled against her brother and watched the Sorracchi bomb the world she hadn't been this afraid. She felt sick and lightheaded, and doubted her knees would hold her if he let her go.

"Do. You. Understand," he hissed against her ear.

Katrina nodded, unable to do anything else.

CHAPTER EIGHT

Squatter District
Falls Church, Seat of Virginia
North American Continent

The cold air bit into Omega's exposed skin, stinging and burning like thousands of syringes of hot oil. He had lost the feeling in his toes, relieving the throbbing pain, but he knew hypothermia threatened his frozen limbs. He and his brothers had no protection against the raw weather. The thin infirmary pants they had woken in did nothing to stave away the cold. The open wounds left on his sides and spine stung in the cold, but the bleeding had stopped shortly after they had left the facility.

The sound of loud voices echoed off the dark buildings, some windows barely lit from within by a meager, flickering light like candles or some other non-power light source. The voices were a mix of raucous and pitiful, someone wept loudly, perhaps at a window so her wails carried through the streets. A stomach-knotting stench sat heavy in the cold air, a mix of body discards, mud, and possibly even death.

Many buildings were nothing but shells, the upper floors gone, the lower floors hollow and dark with windows blown out and walls partially gone. Garbage and filth littered the snow and ice crowding the sidewalks and stairwells.

Somewhere someone screamed.

They had been indoctrinated with the knowledge the Humans were lawless, filthy, just short of barbarians. This place of destitution supported those concepts, but the facility they had left behind had been in sharp contrast to all this. Perhaps they had run from safety into danger, rather than the reverse.

They moved as quickly as possible through the dark, wet streets of the foreign city. They had deduced the planet to be Earth, based on the architecture, the languages they heard while escaping the facility in which they woke, the celestial patterns in the night sky, and the physiology of the young woman who both clung to him and held herself stiff and apart from him as best she could.

She trembled violently, her frail body nearly in spasms, and her teeth chattered together so hard he wondered if it hurt. Dark brown hair twisted into wet, spiral curls around her fair face, and bright red blotches marred her pale, wet skin. She at least had shoes on her feet and a sweater, though now wet with the snow; he feared if she had less she would have already been beyond hope.

We need shelter, Beta's mind snapped out to both him and Alpha.

This woman isn't conditioned for this climate. She will become ill soon, Omega told his brothers.

She should have been left behind. She's nothing but an encumbrance. Alpha looked over his shoulder at them, scowling when his gaze flicked to her.

She was oblivious to their conversation, never raising her head from where she pressed it against his chest. His bare skin was no warmer than hers, but he could at least shield her from the wind.

Until we know where we are—

Don't tell me the situation, Omega. I am fully aware.

They reached the end of a narrow alley that opened onto a wider roadway, perhaps twenty feet from the wall of the building where they stood to the wall of the building on the other side. The road was manmade of a slick, black surface iced over by the night weather and precipitation. Wind whipped down the natural tunnel made by the tall buildings, hitting them. The woman whimpered and pressed harder to him even though he himself was stone cold, and he tightened his arm across her shoulders. He feared doing more, already aware of her frailty and weakness in comparison. She was clearly not any kind of soldier; though she'd confirmed she was Human. She raised her head and looked at him, her body jerking from the cold. The shining fear in her dark eyes twisted in his chest. His immediate mental reaction was to shove aside the snap of compassion. Such things had brought them to this place.

If she is to be here like a weight around our ankles, put her to use.

Omega looked to Alpha, meeting his hard stare. He knew the glint of anger was a show, felt it as sure as he felt his own emotions. They stared, until Alpha clenched his jaw and waved dismissively. Omega took a step back into the alley, reducing the wind by a small degree. She resisted and he tightened his hold, just enough to keep her close.

"We require shelter."

She stared at him, wide eyed.

"You require warmth," he continued.

"L-l-let m-me go b-b-ack," she stuttered through chattering teeth.

"We require your assistance. For now," he added, hoping it might help.

She blinked, a new trail of moisture sliding from the corner of her eye and shook her head, sending droplets of moisture free from her twisted curls. When she looked away she took in their surroundings, peeking around the corner of the building to look up and down the street. "I d-don't know this area, b-but I th-think there's a sh-shelter t-two streets d-d-down there." She only drew her hand far enough away from her wet sweater to point with one finger in the direction they had been heading.

"We cannot stay where we will be seen."

She closed her eyes, her lips pressed tight together, trembling with such violence he thought she would shatter. She shook her head again before looking at him. "I-It's a p-part of the city with h-hotels and apartment buildings. Y-you could f-find an empty one."

Alpha nodded. Omega looked to Beta, who watched the woman he held with intense concern, it rolled off him like the wet wind. Beta raised his chin and met Omega's look. Then he turned away and went to Alpha's side. Omega took a step, the woman against his side, but she stumbled and nearly fell.

She is in distress.

So shall we all be if she has led us astray.

They reached another corner, a multi-story building in front of them. Dim light flickered in nearly every window, this building seemingly whole in comparison to the buildings around the area. A large white sign had been attached to the front, white with the single word "SHELTER" painted in black. Alpha shook his head and pointed to the right to a hill leading up and away from the designated shelter.

She whimpered and stumbled along with them, not fighting but her fatigue and discomfort clearly made it difficult for her to keep up with them. If they weren't hindered by the cold and their reluctant bodies, stiff and resistant after an unknown period of time in the stasis pods, she might have been left behind already. This portion of the city seemed in better repair by a margin in comparison to the area they had come through. The buildings were more whole than crumbled, but still draped the streets in depressing shadows of destitution. Something catastrophic had happened to this world.

In recent history . . . Beta project to them, responding to Omega's observations.

They reached a large brick structure, seven stories tall and taking up a quarter block. Broken ladders and platforms clung to the sides of the building, hidden in an alley leading to an open space behind the structure. The doors were barricaded with steel bars, the windows enclosed, and large signs posted "Condemned" and "Structurally Unsound—Do Not Enter" warned them away. No forms of illumination flickered in any of the upper windows. The building appeared completely empty.

No communication was required. Alpha's wish was as clear as Omega's own thoughts. He moved into the alley, Alpha continuing down the street. Beta stayed with Omega until they came to the second group of twisted ladders. With the slightest clack of metal against metal, his brother leaped to the lowest rung and scaled the structure.

She stumbled trying to look back, and Omega followed her glance. By the time they turned, Beta had disappeared into the darkness. Omega's feet slipped on the slick surface, but he maintained perfect balance, surprising since he no longer felt the soles of his feet.

"Wh-where are we g-going?" she mumbled through chattering teeth.

"Shelter," he answered.

Images flittered through his mind. Alpha had made it to the other side of the structure, and confirmed he had no sign of inhabitance in the building, though there was a structure further along with indications of light and inhabitance. There were three buildings along the street with signs of habitation. Beta found an accessible window into the building into a hallway littered with refuse, but the air inside the building was less raw although the stench of enclosure and death hung in the air. Omega and the woman reached the back of the large building to a flat area littered with burned out vehicles of varying sizes, encrusted with ice and camouflaged with snow. The ice and snow were thicker here, undisturbed by regular traffic. Here he saw the building they reconnoitered was a four-section structure surrounding the center space. One entire side of the building was gone, a massive hole blown through the center of one side, gaping like a projectile wound.

A screeching squeak several dozen feet away indicated Alpha's arrival from the other side through a metal gate. They moved toward each other as one of the ground floor doors opened outward with a crack of frozen hinges.

I find no sign of occupancy. There are signs of structural failure, worse in some portions over others. I recommend the juncture to our left, center levels. They have the least immediately visible damage, and the architecture indicates those habitation units provide the means for primitive combustion as a heating source.

Alpha nodded at Beta's assessment and they moved toward the door. The interior of the building was in near complete darkness, the air stale and musty. They entered into an open space, with a few pieces of furniture, and a wide staircase leading to the next floor. Beta motioned them forward toward the steps. She held back when they moved, shuffling her feet. The way she tilted her head made it clear to him she could not see the way they could in the lack of light.

"I will not let you fall," he said, and she startled at his voice, turning blindly toward him. Her dark eyes shifted, trying to see him in the lack of light. "Come on. We will rest soon."

Omega led her to the stairs, instructing her when they took the first step and allowing her to hold the railing and she pulled herself along.

Seek an appropriate habitat. I will come with the woman.

Alpha and Beta nodded from the mid-flight landing and turned together, running up the stairs. She raised her head at the sound of their departure but didn't release her grip on the railing. Omega guided her, holding one elbow with his hand against her back. She made it to the first landing, at a painfully slow pace, before she fell against the wall, the soft sound of her cries echoing off the chipped plaster. She flinched away from him, hugging the wall, when he knelt beside her.

Heavy eyelids half-hid her dark brown eyes and she swayed. Then she lowered to her knees and gripped her hands on her lap, her head bowed while she wept. The sound filled the hollow, silent space despite her muffled attempt to suppress it. Omega shifted to sit on the step slightly above her so he faced her. His body protested the movement, but pain was irrelevant. Sensation worked its way back to his hands and feet, the pain telling him blood flowed warm again. His metabolism had staved off hypothermia much longer than any Human on this planet could have withstood, but concern for this diminutive woman made him cold from the inside, curling in his gut like smoke. It was a foreign sensation, and although he understood and acknowledged what it was, the expected reaction was unknown to him.

"I am sorry we have brought you to this place."

She lifted her head, her face glistening damp in the darkness. "You don't have to run," she whispered, her voice rough and cracking. "We want to help you. We wouldn't do you any harm. I swear."

Omega wanted to assuage her concerns but knew anything he said would be little more than a platitude. He reached for her, tempted to touch her cold cheek and smooth back her damp hair, but he held his hand still just an inch from her skin. She stared at him, wide-eyed, unaware of his near contact.

"Come," he said, gaining his feet again. "We must locate my brothers."

He cupped her elbows to draw her up, her cold hands curling around his arms when she tried to stand. She stood, but her body swayed and her head tipped back before they could take a step, and Omega lifted her into his arms. His body objected with spastic fatigue, but he pushed it aside to climb the stairs. His brothers had found a suitable habitat. By the time he reached the habitat marked 312, she was still and limp, her shaking stopped. The door opened without him reaching for the knob, and Beta let him into the room. The habitat was spacious, though sparsely furnished. A lounge sat crooked to a cold hearth, a table with two chairs to the right near a doorway leading to an adjacent room. Dust and crumbled construction debris coated everything. Boxes and discarded personal items, books, and papers scattered the floor.

A hallway led away from the open space to Omega's left, and as Beta closed the door behind him Alpha came from the hallway.

There are three sleeping quarters, the largest sharing the chimney with a fireplace in the room. I have inspected the structure as much as possible, and it appears at least temporarily safe to build a fire for warmth.

Omega moved past his leader to the first door he reached. A large bed frame sat against the wall opposite the dark hearth, the mattress pulled half off and stripped bare. Alpha had laid some blankets on the floor near the hearth, and as Beta lowered to his knees Alpha went to work on sparking a fire in the fireplace with a flint left in a bin to the side of the tile flooring.

Does she still live?

Omega looked over his shoulder to Alpha and nodded.

The cold was too much for her. It was nearly too much for us.

We will not stay here long. Long enough to regain our bearings.

Omega nodded, acknowledging Alpha's command, but focused on removing the worst of the young woman's wet clothing. Her socks peeled off with a sucking pop, revealing bright red toes and swollen feet. Her skin was waxy and damp and frigid, the flesh without give.

The crackle of the first embers of a fire stirred in the hearth. Soon the room would be warmer and her exposed skin would soak in the heat. He left her uncovered until he knew she would warm better under the blankets. There was no resistance in her limbs while he worked to remove the saturated sweater, the yarn heavy with melted snow. It left a damp circle on the blanket beneath her, but once she was bundled, it wouldn't matter. She wore a long-sleeved shirt and lighter undershirt beneath the sweater, layered most likely to keep her warm. He took off the long-sleeved shirt, still too damp to leave on, but the undershirt was only barely damp and sufficient to provide some level of warmth and modesty. Her trousers were heavy and utilitarian. They shucked off after several tugs to peel the wet fabric from her damp skin. The worst of the cold seemed localized in her upper body and her feet.

Curled on the blankets, she looked like little more than a child. Omega had never seen a woman so petite and frail. Someone so small would have been useless to his masters. Guilt curled in his chest for the pain she would likely experience when she awoke, and for the fear he had seen in her dark eyes.

The temperature in the room had already risen several degrees with the fire now burning in the hearth. The flicker of flame danced across her still features. Once the flame had caught, Alpha stood and crossed to a chair with another rumpled blanket draped over it. He retrieved it and came back to Omega, holding out the blanket.

Cover her.

Omega looked up at his brother, Alpha's recrimination heavy on his shoulders. He reached out and Alpha dropped the blanket into his hand. As Omega draped the blanket over the woman child, Alpha went to the bed, yanked the mattress free of the frame and set it against the wall, completely blocking the window.

This window faces the courtyard, but the fire may create enough light to be seen.

Omega nodded, satisfied he had done all he could do for the woman until she warmed. It would be preferable to give her something warm to eat or drink, but until they could reconnoiter further and find supplies, the warmth of the fire would need to suffice. He stood and took several steps back, bringing him closer to the fire.

The heat spread across his exposed back and worked to dry the fabric of his thin pants. The blood flowing to his extremities had already warmed, his flesh returning to a natural color and temperature. She would take longer, her genetics alone prevented anything more expeditious, but until she was fully warmed and conscious again, he wouldn't be able to be free of the cold curling in his chest.

CHAPTER NINE

4 March 2054, Wednesday
Alexandria Hospital, Secure Wing – Intensive Care
United Earth Protectorate, Capitol City
Alexandria, Seat of Virginia
North American Continent

"*I*'ve sent a message via Gateway on to Aretu to request a consultation with Doctor Olivia Cole. She is one of the Defense Alliance's leading cybernetic prosthesis developers," Victor said, handing a tablet to Michael as they walked the halls toward David Forte's room. "With the deep, excessive degeneration in his muscular system I think her prosthetic systems would be a huge benefit for David."

Michael wedged his cane beneath his arm so he could hold the tablet and scroll through the images on the screen, their progression slowing as his limp became more pronounced without the aid of the cane. Victor slowed to match his hitched pace. The images showed a variety of patients with internal and external prosthetic devices attached to both arms and legs. Some appeared to be external only, and just as many had both external and biologically fused internal connections. He winced, his mind immediately paralleling the devices to the brutal machines they had worked for days to remove.

"Aren't we trading one aberration for another?"

"I thought of that, but . . ." Victor took back the tablet and their pace increased as Michael leaned again on the cane. Victor sighed. "If we don't take some radical steps in his treatment, it could be years before he has any kind of mobility, if he ever regains the ability to walk on his own. Even with intense therapy. Doctor Cole's equipment is not designed to be permanent but can be programmed to work internally to help a patient regain lost motion and strength."

"His atrophy is that bad . . ."

Victor nodded. "Even with the muscular stimulators we've had going twenty-four-seven since he came out of the pod, he's only able to lift his arms a few inches and has been unable to move his legs, although he has full sensation. He was in there for decades, Michael. I don't think it's just about weakness, I think his muscles have forgotten how to move."

"Instead of muscle memory, muscle amnesia. How is he doing otherwise?"

"Do you mean mentally? Emotionally? Without knowing the man he was, I can't speak to his change in mental state, but speaking as an observer, I would say he's not in a good place. Considering his record, he was a man of the military. A man unaccustomed, I'm sure, to being powerless."

"Jace Quinn is coming." Michael pushed his hand into his pocket, rotating his shoulders to ease the tension that had been sitting between his shoulder blades for a week. "He'll be here next week."

Victor nodded, tucking the tablet under his arm as they neared David's room. "He'll be a good one for David to speak to, man of faith or not." Victor looked at him sideways as they walked. "How long until the *Axanadu* lands?"

Michael smiled, despite the nervous twist in his gut. It was an odd combination of emotions he'd been taunted by since returning to Alexandria, and since learning Jacqueline was on her way home. He teetered between joy and anticipation to paralyzing, sickening fear. "Two hours."

Victor clamped his hand down on Michael's shoulder, drawing him to a stop, and Michael turned to face him. Victor's expression, which hardly was anything other than a smile since being freed of his Sorracchi entity, never lost its smile but his eyes pinched just slightly and the smile wasn't quite as pure. Victor drew a slow breath.

"I understand the feeling of dread, knowing you made a mistake and knowing you have no right to ask for forgiveness. I also understand the smothering feeling when you realize you may have lost the woman you love."

"Beverly forgave you. She understood you didn't consciously hide anything from her. Victor, you were nothing less than compromised." Michael clenched his jaw. "I have no such excuse."

"You *were* compromised, my friend. Compromised by your overwhelming need to protect your daughter and the woman you love. Perhaps you weren't compromised in the same way as I, but you were." He squeezed Michael's shoulder. "Jacqueline will understand."

Michael couldn't find anything sufficient to say, so he turned away and moved down the hallway again, focusing on the act of leading each step with the top of his cane.

"$\mathcal{T}$he stasis chamber you were in was advanced technology, but poorly executed. Your atrophy is severe, but it could have been exceedingly worse," Michael explained, seated in a chair beside David's bed at an angle so they looked directly at each other. "The technology adapted to the lower power levels and kept you alive much longer than I'm sure your captors expected. For a man who hasn't moved in four and a half decades until a few days ago, you're in very good health, David."

David chuckled completely without humor and relaxed his head back on the pillows behind him. "Yeah, I'm the image of vigor and vitality."

"I suspect you were in good health before you were put in there."

93

He shrugged, the action pulling across his chest and back, but the muscle strain felt good. Like the burn after an intense workout. A sign of progress. He wasn't much better than a newborn when he woke up, barely able to hold up his own head. "I guess. I had to be in my line of work."

"We have a woman coming from Aretu. She specializes in advanced technologies that can help you get on your feet again."

"Will I get back to where I was before . . ." He swirled his fingers, not lifting his hand, having not yet figured out yet how to word what had happened.

"I have confidence you will, yes."

David nodded, flexing his fists in his lap. It wasn't much, but it was motion. "So, when do I get to hear the full story?"

Michael tipped his head slightly. "Story of what?"

He looked up and focused on Michael, motioning toward the window of his room with a jut of his chin. The view beyond was a city in mid-destruction. Some parts of the skyline looked normal, save the snow coating everything far more than he'd ever known in Virginia. Unless they were lying and he was further north. Other parts of the city were jagged, razed, and depressing. The view itself stood as a symbol for his question.

Michael followed the direction of his indication, squinting at first. Then he nodded. "No one knows the best way to do that, David. You're a unique situation. I can answer questions, but some of it is purely a history lesson for me as well until three years ago."

"Three years ago . . . is that when they thawed *you* out?" David said with a laugh.

Michael's grin was impossible to interpret. "In a way. It's a story I'll tell you some time when you understand more clearly."

"Does it have something to do with that nasty limp?"

Michael's eyes shifted to the shillelagh he had left leaning against David's bed. "Intricately connected, yes." He drew in a sharp breath and focused on David again. "You are going to have visitors shortly."

"Great." He rolled his head on the pillows.

Since waking, a parade of doctors, specialists and gawkers had moved through his room. He'd been poked, prodded, studied and felt a bit like the Roswell aliens . . . ironically. He didn't mind Michael, not even Victor, and had come to look forward to the odd hour visits each evening from little Katrina Bauer. She provided a level of calm in all the chaos and confusion.

"Don't worry, he isn't here to dissect you. He wants to meet you." Michael turned in the chair to look toward the room door. "I think he's here now."

"Who?"

"My father," Michael said, leveraging himself from the chair with a small stagger before retrieving his cane. "Nick Tanner."

Realization came swift, like a bucket of ice water in the face. David's jaw dropped when he realized he'd never made any connection between "President Tanner" and "Doctor Tanner".

"The president of the *planet*?"

Michael grinned. "Yes."

Moments later there was a sharp rap at the door. Victor pulled it open for a female soldier dressed in familiar battle dress green with the emblem of a mythical phoenix on the arm, stepped inside, holding the door. President Tanner stepped in with a nod and smile toward Michael. David recognized him immediately from the news footage he'd often watch at midnight, but it wasn't until he stood beside Doctor Tanner that David saw the similarity between them. He wore the same drab green cargos as the soldier, with a brown sweater and heavy boots, looking more like a soldier than a president. A woman walked hand in hand with him, looking not much older than Michael with blond hair pulled back from her forehead, but flowing down her back, and a bright smile.

The woman, whom David had to assume was First Lady Caitlin Tanner he'd heard snippets about, also a doctor if he remembered right, went immediately to Michael and gave him a hug and kiss on the cheek. David's first thought, being there were two doctors in the family, was that Michael followed in his mother's footsteps. But First Lady Tanner most certainly was *not* Michael's mother. Not when she couldn't be more than half a dozen years older than him, if that.

Michael motioned his father forward. "David, this is my father.

Nick." The fact Michael didn't use his father's title again didn't go unnoticed.

President Tanner crossed the room, extending his right hand to David. "Good to meet you, son."

David tried to raise his arm, getting it a few inches off the blanket before the tremors set in. President Tanner gripped his hand, not acknowledging at least externally the weakness David despised. "Same here, sir."

President Tanner grabbed the chair Michael had used previously and sat, leaning forward with his elbows on his knees. He didn't look like any president in the history of the institution, lacking the navy-blue suit and solid color red or blue tie and polished shoes, clean cut hair and photo ready smile. His posture was one of a trained soldier, ready to move, and he looked the part of a soldier, perhaps even slightly uncomfortable. His wife came to the bed and squeezed David's hand.

"Hello, David. I'm Caitlin."

"Ma'am." He nodded.

"Michael has been keeping me up on your progress," President Tanner said, motioning over his shoulder to where Michael sat on the other, empty bed, his shillelagh beside him. Victor had moved to stand near the window. "You're doing great, he says."

"Doesn't quite feel it, sir."

"I'm sure it doesn't." He looked down at his hands for a moment before looking at David again. "The last few days must have been confusing."

David squinted and he grimaced. "That's a mild word, sir. I remember having this dream, over and over again, but other than that I feel like—" He had to stop and swallow hard, the memory of kissing and hugging his sons goodbye sharp, vivid and painful. "I feel like it just happened."

Nick nodded and worked the palms of his hands together, the slight scraping sound speaking to calluses and years of hard work, not politics. "We found some basic records for you, said you had two sons. Two siblings. Didn't find much else, but I want you to know we're working on locating some of your family."

David snorted. "My sons would be in their fifties by now. They won't remember me."

"They will," Michael said, his voice catching David by surprise. The weight of his tone made David wonder if Michael had first-hand experience.

He looked to Michael, and as he'd learned was Michael's way, the younger man looked back without wavering. David gave a nod and looked back to Michael's father. He caught the expression on his wife's face, and it made him pause. Her eyes glistened with unshed tears and she offered him a compassionate smile, patting his leg through the blankets.

Nick sat back and cleared his throat, rubbing his hands down his legs to his knees a couple times. "Do you remember what happened?"

David hadn't yet found any reason to doubt the truthfulness of anyone he'd seen, but a part of him still warned to keep back information until he had the whole story. He wasn't about to lay out all his cards until he saw a few other people lay down first.

"Not much, sir. I was hit with some type of weapon, not a gun, and it paralyzed me. I couldn't talk, could barely hear, and it's all kinda fuzzy."

"We've pieced together enough from the Sorracchi files to know you were captured breaking into one of their facilities . . ." President Tanner led.

David nodded. "Reconnaissance, sir," he said, giving the simplest answer he could.

President Tanner seemed satisfied, then suddenly jumped to his feet and took his wife's hand, leading her to sit down where he'd been. They shared a smile and she sat. Tanner moved to the foot of David's bed and stood with his feet apart and his hands pushed into his front pockets.

"I also read enough of your file to know just sitting here is probably driving you nuts."

"David and I were just discussing his recovery time," Michael offered.

"You pretty much nailed it, though, sir."

"Don't let it get you down. I've seen men come back from worse . . .

physically. I've asked someone to come talk to you. His name is Jace Quinn. He's been through something similar, and I think his perspective might be good for you. You've had a lot thrown at you in the last couple of days," President Tanner said, his eyes squinting at the corners as he studied David. "How are you dealing with it?"

"My mother used to say there was only one way to eat an elephant, sir. One bite at a time."

President Tanner chuckled and rocked on his feet. "That's how we take on most things these days." He stared for a moment before taking in a quick, sharp breath. "I know you've only been given the basics, son, but the world is a very different place than when you last walked around."

David swallowed, wishing he could reach for the cup of water on the table beside him. "Could I ask a few simple questions, sir?"

"Sure."

"How long did it take for us to figure out the truth?"

President Tanner's smile flattened, his expression darkened. "Too damn long."

The door burst open and everyone reacted, the soldier who had led the way drawing her weapon. David shifted enough to see past the president and recognize Karl Bauer, Katrina's older brother. He looked flustered, breathing hard.

"Stand down," President Tanner said, holding up his hand to his guard. "It's okay."

"I'm sorry, sir," Karl stuttered. "I-I had hoped to find Katrina here."

Victor moved to the young man. If David had it figured out right, both Katrina and Karl worked on a team Victor headed. "What's wrong, Karl."

The man shook his head. "She didn't come home last night. I know she's stayed here all night before." He looked to David, a sharp jerk of his head, then back to Victor. "But I talked to her last night before I left and she was going to come home, I got dinner. She never did. She didn't answer any of my messages. And I can't find her. Anywhere . . ."

"Where would she go?"

Everyone turned in surprise to look at David, almost like they'd forgotten he was there. He tried to sit forward, tried to move, tried to do *something*, and his frustration had never tasted so bitter.

"She's usually here, with you . . . or with the pods. I looked in real quick, and she wasn't at her desk in there."

Victor went to what looked kind of like a cross between a phone and the wall unit communicators David remembered from the *Star Trek* movies and pressed a button. "Njogu, this is Victor. Have you seen Katrina in the R&D room today?"

"No, sir," came a deep, slightly accented voice through the speaker. "I have not seen her since yesterday evening."

"What time?"

"Around seven, sir. She came to check on a diagnostic program."

"That's right after I left her," Karl said, rubbing his hand across his forehead. "Geez, where the hell is she?"

Victor extended his hand and laid it on Karl's shoulder, offering a small nod. David felt useless, a lump in the corner. He clenched his fists, trying to quell the rage.

"Njogu, could you please go to the pod room and see if she might have gone back there? We're looking for her."

"Yes, sir."

Victor closed the line as Michael pulled a small communication device—just looked like a fancy cell phone to David—and pressed the screen before bringing it to his ear. After several moments he shook his head. "She isn't responding."

"Geez," Karl mumbled and paced the floor between the door and the window. He pulled up short and looked at President Tanner, wide eyed. "I'm sorry, sir. I-I didn't meant to—I just—"

President Tanner raised his hand in a small wave. "Don't worry about it. This is important."

The wall speaker beeped, and Victor went to it, tapping the screen. "Victor."

"Sir, we have a problem."

"She's not there, Njogu?"

"Far worse, sir. De pods are empty."

Every man in the room, and woman, looked at Victor. Katrina had spent her visits telling David about the three men they'd found with him on a derelict alien ship floating nearly dead in space. She said they were some type of genetically manipulated super soldiers, the stuff of science fiction, designed to be some sort of fighting machines for the Sorracchi. They'd been put in stasis like him because of some glitch in their programming, and she'd been working on a way to remove them without the damage inflicted on David.

"Empty?" President Tanner demanded.

The voice on the other end had to have heard him. "Yes, sir. Empty. Dey have been opened and dere is no sign of the occupants. Or Katrina. De implements are bloody and dere is blood on de floor."

They all moved as a unit, save for President Tanner and his guard, heading for the door. David slammed his head back, as much as it was possible, against the raised head of his bed and cursed. Michael paused at the foot of his bed and waited until David looked at him.

"I understand," he said simply. "I'll come back when we know more. I promise you."

David nodded, his jaw clenched. He swallowed and nodded again, unable to say anything. Michael moved to follow the others, but his father gripped his arm. He stopped short.

"I'll make sure Jacqueline gets home," his father said.

Michael frowned and drew in a slow breath. "Thank you. Tell her . . ." He paused and shrugged. "I don't know what to tell her."

His father took his hand from Michael's arm to pat his shoulder. "I got it. Go."

Then everyone was gone but President Tanner, his guard, and his wife.

"Nicky, what can we do?" she asked, her voice trembling. Then she looked to David and he saw tears in her eyes. "I'm sorry you're in the middle of all this, David. She's just such a sweet girl."

"I know. She's been . . ." He was surprised by the choke in his throat. David swallowed and sniffed. "She's . . ." He was done.

100

CHAPTER TEN

"*L et me go . . .*"

Katrina bolted from sleep, every muscle and joint screaming in pain. Her heart pounded so hard it hurt; she couldn't suck in enough air to fill her burning lungs.

"No harm will come to you."

Katrina screamed and scrambled to get free of the bundle of blankets and sheets wrapping her. She was on the floor in a room of which she had no recollection at all. The room was grey, like it might be daylight but the windows were covered. Between her rough pallet and a fireplace stood one of the Triadic, still dressed only in cotton infirmary pants. He took a step toward her and dropped into a crouch, but before he could touch her Katrina tossed away the blankets binding her legs and scurried across the floor toward the empty bed frame on the other side of the room. She used the frame to gain her feet and bolted for the door, running straight into the hard chest of another of the three. He gripped her arms, preventing her from escaping, the pressure of his fingers shooting pain up her already hurting limbs.

"Let me go!" she screamed, trying to pull away.

The one holding her tightened his grip. He stared down at her with cold hazel eyes, not saying a word, his head tilted slightly to the right. Tears burned her eyes, blurring her vision, and she couldn't take a breath.

"Please," she begged. "Please . . ."

His head snapped up and he looked past her. Then he released her and she stumbled back, falling against the bare frame, her back hitting the metal and wood slats intended to support a mattress. The pain was excruciating, every vertebra of her spine burning with the impact. Black spots danced in her vision, and she felt hands lift her from the frame. She couldn't suck in enough air to speak, unable to protest when the first carried her to an upholstered chair a few feet away. The chair puffed dust when he set her down, making her nose tingle. She huffed through the pain, squeezing her eyes shut to quell the nausea.

In the easing of the pain and the passing of the twisting in her stomach, Katrina realized she was missing half her clothing, and her blood ran cold. A new wave of fear and panic hit her, her insides shaking. What had happened after she lost consciousness? Oh, God! What had they done?

"No harm will come to you," said the same voice.

Katrina flinched and tried to swallow her sob. She blinked open her eyes and looked into the face of the half-dressed of the three, with the other two now standing behind him, at least wearing clothes, though clearly castoffs, torn and mismatched. He crouched in front of her, his hands on either side of her on the arms of the chair. With the fireplace to her left, the light of the flame revealed the features of his face and she knew it was Omega, the small scar on his upper lip distinguishing him from the other two.

He stared at her, studying her. Katrina fought the urge to scurry back and over the chair but saw nowhere to go. The other two stood between her and the door. She tried to breathe, but her lungs didn't want to cooperate and she couldn't stop shaking. Omega shifted his gaze down to her body, then back to her face.

"You are still cold."

Before he finished, one of the two behind him turned back to the open bedroom door and picked up a pile of clothes from the floor. He crossed the room, holding them out to her. Katrina shoved back into the chair and drew up her legs so hard it scraped across the floor. He stopped and looked to Omega. Omega nodded and took the clothing himself.

"Your clothing has not yet dried. We have found these. They should do until your own are suitable."

He set the clothing on the edge of the chair by her hip, then stepped back and gave her space. Doing her best to watch all three, Katrina unfolded from the chair and looked through the clothing they had given her. A pair of children's yellow pajama pants with white cartoon cat faces, a pair of brown sweatpants at least two to three sizes too big for her, a pair of boy's jeans, a hooded sweatshirt, and a sweater with the elbows worn through. Although they would be too big, she opted for the brown sweatpants because they looked the warmest and stood to pull them over her hips. There was a string tie and she pulled it as tight as it would allow. The hooded sweatshirt was also big, but the extra fabric and layers gave her a sense of camouflage, as false a sense as it might be. There were no socks, but when she sat again she tugged the long legs over her bare feet.

"Thank you," she said automatically, having the passing thought she wasn't sure what she was actually thanking him for. "I'm Katrina."

Omega looked up at them, and the two looked at each other. The one behind Omega nodded toward the one who had brought her clothing, and he nodded, turning away. Without a word, he went to the door and left the room.

"We are searching now for sustenance and water," Omega said, apparently the spokesperson for the three.

"Where are we?" she asked, hating the quiver in her voice.

The two looked at each other, and the one—either Beta or Alpha, she didn't know which—nodded to Omega.

"It was our hope you might tell us," Omega said.

Katrina pushed her fingers into her tightly twisted curls, her hair reverting to its natural inclination to tight curls after being drenched in the rain. She only vaguely remembered stumbling through the night, so cold she swore her insides shook. The memory made her shiver and she wrapped her arms around her body, curling as close as she could into the chair. She closed her eyes, inhaled, and tried to grab hold of the wisps of smoke to form images. She tilted her head, focusing on smells and tactile sensations.

Her body jerked involuntarily when everything snapped into place like a program download. Katrina gasped and opened her eyes, finding the two of them watching her. She blinked and swallowed, wishing for a drink.

"Falls Church," she said softly, her voice scraping in her dry throat. "Virginia. Um . . . North American continent. We're near Alexandria, the capitol of the United Earth Protectorate."

"Is this the ruling government?"

Katrina nodded, looking at him. "Yes. Formed after the war with the Sorracchi."

They exchanged looks.

Katrina's head hurt so she looked away from their stoic faces, her attention shifting to Omega, still dressed in pajamas. Pink, puckered wounds ran down his sides and one on each forearm, in all the places she remembered the mechanical appendages of the pod attaching to his body. Had they ripped themselves free of the connections? How long had they been free? They were nearly healed. She still felt chilled to her bones from the walk here, and she had worn three layers, thick socks, and winter boots. They had been barefoot, unclothed from the waist up, and what they had worn accounted to little more than nothing. They should have been hypothermic, but beyond the healing wounds, they appeared perfectly fine. Katrina looked to Omega's bare feet, healthy toes and no swelling. He stood, his harms hanging at his side, long fingers free of any sign of exposure. She had to blink and force herself to look away.

"How long have we been here?" she asked.

Omega looked to her again. "We have been in this structure eighteen hours and thirty-seven minutes."

"Eighteen hours. How—" A whole new wave of cold panic hit her, she unfolded from the chair, and jumped to her feet. "Oh, god. Karl must be going crazy."

"Time is irrelevant," the one *not* Omega stated. "We require information."

The fact he spoke made her start. She had begun to wonder if any of them knew how to speak except for Omega. She blinked, staring at him. She remembered now. They had talked about how she would give them answers. They needed her to figure out where they were, when they were. They had no idea where they had woken, where they had been taken, or how long they had been in the pods. She didn't know if they had been placed in the pods while on the *Abaddon*, or somewhere else.

The door to the room opened, and the third returned. Moisture glistened on his hair and dark spots sprinkled the shoulders of the heavy jacket he wore. It had to have been a scavenge. The hem was frayed, a tear leaving one pocket gaping open, a hole in his sleeve. But it was better than nothing. He had more clothing in his hands, but nothing else. The two looked at him, the only indication of communication, psychic she assumed, was the shift of their eyes. The first non-Omega nodded and motioned with a tilt of his head for the new arrival to hand Omega the clothing.

Katrina sank to the chair again, and hunched forward, holding her head in her hands. Her stomach rolled with hunger, her head hurting. If she'd been here eighteen hours, it had been close to twenty-four hours since she ate anything and she barely remembered what it had been. She had a vague recollection of some kind of sandwich, but she'd spent the day at her terminals. If she understood what verbal communication there had been, the newcomer had been sent again in search of food and apparently clothing. He'd come back with clothing from somewhere, could have been from any of the abandoned, condemned apartments in the building, left in the rush to find something safer or left because the ones who lived here were dead.

She raised her head in time to see Omega pull a blue sweater over his head. He had shucked the soiled infirmary pants, apparently quite quickly since he already wore faded jeans. The one who had been with them since she woke turned his head and stared down at her, his hazel eyes hard. She couldn't determine if they were cold in anger, or because he was focused, or concerned, or . . .

"Which one are you?"

He tipped his head, staring at her.

Katrina swallowed and pointed at the only one she recognized. "I know you're Omega." Then she motioned between the other two. "But I don't know which of you is Alpha and which of you is Beta. I-I can't keep thinking of you as 'Not Omega One' and 'Not Omega Two'."

"I am designation Alpha," the one she had addressed stated.

She looked to him, forcing herself to look into his eyes that, although they were the same color of Omega's, held a hardness Omega's didn't. Not a frightening hardness, but something different. Omega and the one she now knew as Beta looked to Alpha. She would be fine as long as Alpha and Beta didn't move, but unless she figured out a way to tell them apart, she'd be lost once they did. Neither of them said anything, the only indication they weren't statues being the shift of their eyes between them.

Alpha's head snapped around to look at her again. "What year is it on your calendar?"

"2054. March. Um, if you took me . . ." She stuttered the end of the sentence, then cleared her throat. "I think today is the fourth. Wednesday."

They looked at each other again.

"Could you please . . ." She waited until they looked at her. "Could you please *talk*. I mean, I think you're talking to each other, but it's disconcerting to have you . . ." She stopped and let out a breath, relieved her heart had finally stopped pounding. Katrina closed her eyes and rested her forehead on her raised knees.

She still hurt, every part of her. After sleeping for nearly eighteen hours, how could she be so tired?

"Who commands this world?"

She had no idea who spoke but forced herself to raise her head. Lucky for her, none of them had moved so she still knew who was who. "Is there a particular answer that will get me killed?" she asked.

Omega's head ticked just slightly and his eyes shifted to look to Alpha. It was becoming clearer. Alpha was just as the name indicated.

He was the leader, the one who said "yes" or "no" to anything. Omega turned back to her.

"You continue to fear us. No harm will come to you."

"I'd love to believe that," she mumbled, unfolding again. "But considering the fact you dragged me out of my lab into the cold, and now have me holed up in some . . ." Katrina looked around, processing the room. She remembered again, snippets at a time, coming to the Squatter District and the condemned apartment building. Katrina shook off the rest of the explanation and focused again on Alpha and Omega.

I am the Alpha and the Omega.

The Bible quote was completely out of place, but it seemed to fit all the same.

"There are no Sorracchi here anymore," she finally said. "Not to speak of. There was a war. Almost a year ago. Them versus us. Humans. We won." She added a shrug. "At least, those of us left won."

They all exchanged looks.

"You're doing it again."

Omega shifted his focus to her. "We are unaccustomed to the necessity of using spoken language."

"Clearly." Her stomach rumbled again. "We have a president, named leader in the days following the end of war. His name is Nicholas Tanner."

"*H*ow is it three men and a woman were removed from this facility without a single person taking notice?" Connor Montgomery demanded. "I want surveillance footage and a list of every man and woman who worked here last night, civilian, military, or otherwise."

Everyone scattered except for Connor and his 2IC Melanie Brooks, and the two of them headed for Michael and Victor where they stood with the majority of Victor's team, with the exception of young Katrina

Bauer. Connor rubbed his forehead as he approached, and Mel said something to him low enough only he heard, and a small, almost undetectable smile curved his lips. Michael also noticed the subtle brush of their fingertips as they walked, and the conscious way Connor's fingers curled to make contact. Then he looked up and the smile was gone again, and the serious commander of the Firebirds was back.

"What do we know?" Victor asked when Connor reached them.

Connor sighed and set his hands at his hips. "Precious little. We know when Karl spoke to her, when she spoke to Njogu, and we have a time stamp from her computer when she last accessed it. Based on the last known physical status of the Triadic, I want to assume someone removed them from the pods and took her with them. I won't begin to attempt to understand the rationale of the Xenos, so they are my first thought, but what interest would they have in three men stuck in stasis?"

"Could they have woken?" Michael asked.

Victor looked to him and shrugged. "We have been carefully monitoring their brain activity and physical state, and even last night there are no changes in the readings to indicate a spike in consciousness or a change in their status. The appendages in the pods are bloody, possibly torn free of their connections. Whoever took them removed them with extreme prejudice. Even if they did it themselves."

"Self-removal seems unlikely," Doctor Averill Jones said from behind them, stepping forward. The Areth doctor's features were pinched and his hands worked like a nervous tick in his pockets. "The amount of pain inflicted at that kind of violent removal would be near insurmountable. They will be injured and in need of medical care, no matter who took them or how."

"And what about Katrina?" Karl Bauer snapped. "Everyone is talking about the Triadic, not her."

"It isn't that, Karl," Connor said, shaking his head. "If we can understand who would be interested in the Triadic, and who would be capable of removing them, we can narrow down the search for Katrina."

"So we agree someone had to remove all four of them?" Doctor Anson asked.

"A young woman in no outer gear and three men dressed in pajamas don't just wander into the streets. Katrina's coat and hat were still in the lab," Connor said, shaking his head. "Logically, I say someone removed them. There has to be some footage somewhere in the records, and we'll search them until we find an answer."

A Firebird stepped into the R&D bay where they had gathered and called to Connor by rank. He and Mel turned and walked away, leaving Michael again with the team. He looked at his watch. Nearly seven. Nine hours had passed since they discovered Katrina's disappearance, and they had nothing to go on. Over six hours since Jacqueline had landed.

Victor set his hand on Michael's shoulder. "Go home, my friend. There is nothing more you can do here. You're standing around waiting just like the rest of us. Go home and see her."

Michael nodded, knowing his friend was right. It was time to find out his future.

CHAPTER ELEVEN

*M*ichael paused outside the room that had served as his bedroom for the weeks since he'd returned from Florida, a room he'd learned to hate coming back to each night because it was his and his alone. He and Jacqueline had slept together in this room enough times visiting he felt the absence of her presence with keen clarity. He had hated lying in the bed made for two without Jacqueline beside him.

His father said Nicole had refused to leave Jacqueline's side from the time they picked her up at the landing bay, the child desperate to hang on to the mother she had missed for weeks. What sadness and fear had they implanted on their daughter in their absence?

Michael leaned forward, resting his forehead on the painted wood. Jace Quinn had taught Michael the power prayer held to give peace and wisdom, and in those moments before he opened the door, he prayed for both. He took a breath, turned the knob, and opened the door.

The room was only softly lit by a small light beside the bed, casting a soft glow over the two most important people in his life. Michael's heart swelled, and warmth spread out from the center of his chest at the sight of Jacqueline asleep with Nicole nestled against her.

Jacqueline lay on her side, facing the door with Nicole against her bosom, both covered by a blanket. At that moment he wondered if he had ever seen anything quite so beautiful. Jacqueline's dark hair fanned the pillow, Nicole's blond curls a beautiful contrast to Jacqueline's light olive skin. Michael crossed the room on careful feet, limping slowly to avoid use of the cane, and stopped beside the bed, studying them both in the pale light.

He had no right to destroy their peace. Michael smoothed his hand over Nicole's curls and she released a shuddered breath, sucking hard on her thumb a few times before settling again into deep sleep. He wanted to brush his fingers along Jacqueline's cheek, to touch her skin and confirm she was there, but he knew she'd wake. She was a trained soldier, and he was surprised she hadn't woken already. He leaned on his shillelagh and watched them for a few more moments, drinking in the fullness filling his chest. Then he turned and left.

His father waited in the hallway, leaning against the wall with his ankles crossed and his arms over his chest. Michael spared a short glance before he eased the door closed and held his breath until the latch clicked into place.

"They're asleep," he said in a low voice.

"I know," his father said. "I'm the one who told you."

Michael took several steps down the hall, away from the door and past his father.

"Go back in there, Michael."

He stopped and turned, using the cane as a pivot. "She's resting."

Nick moved away from the wall, shoving his hands into his pockets, his feet set wide. "She's not angry you weren't there. When we told her, she—"

"Understood," Michael snapped, banging the tip of his cane on the hardwood floor. "Jacqueline understood. Jacqueline will understand. It's all I have heard since I came back. Jacqueline will understand. Perhaps I should be able to offer her more than acceptance of my shortcomings." By the time he reached the end, his voice bounced off the walls. Michael sucked in a deep breath and leaned again on his cane, his head down.

His father stood silent for several moments, watching him. Then he slowly drew in air through his nostrils and released it. "That's been brewing for a while."

Michael rubbed his forehead with his free hand, willing back the low headache that had been building since the realization of Katrina's disappearance. Bad things tended to happen when he couldn't tamp down the pain. He longed for a quiet place to focus, to find his balance.

To hold Jacqueline.

"You could have told us to shut the hell up," his father offered.

"Would you have *understood*," Michael hissed through clenched teeth.

"Somehow I don't think my honest answer is going to help."

Michael raised his head and looked at his father through a haze. "I want to be more than someone you must excuse, Dad. Someone you must forever be justifying."

His father walked toward him, and with each step closer, Michael's spine tightened like the string of a violin. Since accepting his reliance on a cane, Michael no longer looked his father straight in the eye, but when Nick Tanner reached him he forced himself to stand upright despite the discomfort in his hip.

"How many times are you going to attempt to reinvent yourself before you realize the only person asking you to change is you?"

Michael ground his teeth together, looking away. "I want to be deserving of her."

"Every man who can claim the love of a good woman should want the same thing," his father said with a small chuckle. "How many times do you think I've looked at Caitlin and thought 'what the hell is she doing here?'"

Michael glanced past his father to the closed bedroom door. "I have been trying to find what I can say to her to assure she will forgive me, and all the while I keep thinking I have no right to ask."

"None of us have the right."

He looked to his father. A lump stuck in his throat that hurt to swallow past. Nick looked away and sniffed, then cleared his throat. "All you can do is try not to screw up, but when you do, mean it when you tell her you're sorry." Then Nick looked at him again. "Go back in, Michael. She'd rather you wake her up, I swear. Give me

Nicole, and then make it right. There's more at stake than you know."

Michael nodded and moved past his father. Just as before, he eased open the door and stepped into the shadowed room. Neither Jacqueline nor Nicole had moved. His father followed him into the room and met Michael when he slowly edged Nicole from the safe haven of Jacqueline's body and handed her off to her grandfather. She never blinked, barely sighed, safe in the child's knowledge no one would hurt her. His father said nothing else, but turned and left the room, crouching to reach the knob and pull the door closed behind him.

Michael tossed the shillelagh upward, catching it mid-shaft, automatically shifting his weight to his left leg to take the strain off his right hip. He stared at the cane for a moment, and considered just sitting on the bed, but leaned it against the wall beside the bedside table.

It hurt, and Michael cursed his damaged body, but he slowly eased himself down to kneel beside the bed like a man supplicating in prayer. She hadn't moved, her breathing hadn't changed, she still slept. He knew intimately the sound of her rest, and the sound of her waking, even though he'd missed it so badly the emptiness of their bed nearly smothered him every night. Michael sat back on his feet, folded his arms on the bed, and rested his forehead on his arms. His fingertips brushed her arm laid across the pillows and he touched her skin, reveling in the first contact in so long.

Jackie drew in a breath, long and slow, her skin tingling at Michael's familiar touch. She blinked open her eyes, and her breath caught when she saw him kneeling at the side of the bed, his head down. Jackie shifted further onto her side so she could reach for him with her other hand and combed her fingers into his hair. Perpetually in need of a haircut, his hair was soft and the act soothed her as much as she knew it soothed him. She had thought for weeks what it would feel like to see him again. Would she be angry? Would she be smothered by the hurt? Had she had enough distance to let her think and act without anger? None of that came over her, only a warmth like warm honey spreading out through her when she saw him, and a flutter of joy when she touched him after so long. It still hurt, but the hurt seemed too far away to matter.

He slid his arm across the coverlet and caught her hand, drawing it to him to press it between his cheek and the bed, the touch gentle and almost hesitant. He kissed her palm, drew her other hand from his hair and brought it to his lips before raising his head to look at her.

The dim lamp on the table cast his features in angular shadows, but she clearly saw the pinch around his eyes, and the glisten of emotion Michael always wore for all to see. He kissed her palm again, holding it there when he spoke against her skin. "I have missed you. So much."

A flutter danced through her lower stomach. Was it his voice? Jacqueline smiled, the sound of his voice as much a panacea as his touch, to both her and maybe even their child. Instinct. She ran her hand along his cheek and brushed her thumb over his lips. "I've missed you, too, handsome." She smirked. "What do I have to do to get a kiss?"

Michael leveraged himself to half-stand, using the mattress and the bedside table for support. She caught the pained pinch around his eyes when he stood on his right leg, but let it go until he could tell her himself what had happened since the surgery. If anything, he looked more encumbered than before, not less. He sat on the bed beside her and she rolled onto her back just enough to reach for him and pull him down for the kiss she had thought about for weeks. Michael's kiss never failed to ignite her every sense, but this one more than most after so long without him. She was dying of thirst, and he was the only way to quench it. He held her face in his hands and kissed her deep, holding back nothing. That was what she had always loved about him. He never played games, never withheld anything, and when he touched her she knew he gave her everything. It was amazing to know when she looked in his eyes, she saw nothing but truth.

And maybe that was why his departure had hurt so much. She never had the chance to see his reason in his eyes.

Michael kissed her jaw and throat until he could press his face into the curve of her neck and slid his hands behind her shoulders, holding her. A shuddered breath moved through him and she felt the slick warmth of tears against her skin. Her own eyes burned and she pressed them closed. Then he pulled back and braced himself over her, looking down at her.

"Jacqueline . . ."

"Are you sorry?" she asked, touching his cheeks.

Michael swallowed and bowed his head. He nodded against her hand, holding it to his cheek. She had no Talents, as the Areth called them, to her everyone was just as much a blank slate as any anyone else. But she swore she felt the anguish and repentance rolling off him. Finally, he sucked in a breath and looked her in the eyes. "Yes." He took her hand from his cheek and held it between his. "Yes, Jacqueline. I am so . . ." He pressed his lips to her palm, his eyes closed. "I am so sorry."

She smoothed her thumb across his cheek. "I've heard everyone else's opinions about why. You tell me."

Michael shook his head. "I won't give excuses. You deserve better than that."

"I don't want an excuse. An excuse is justification without a reason. I want to know your reason. Michael, I know you never do anything without reason."

He kissed her fingers and sniffed, releasing a shaky breath. Tears ran from Jackie's eyes along her temples, wetting her hair, but she didn't want to pull away from his hold even long enough to wipe them away. She had expected and contemplated many scenarios when they saw each other, but this fully contrite Michael exceeded anything she'd imagined.

"I woke from the fever, and they told me you had collapsed. I knew it had happened again, the way I'd pulled from you and Connor and Dad last year."

"When you died, twice, and that strength saved you."

Michael shook his head, focusing on their hands and not her face. "I had no control over it. I had no way to stop it. I could have hurt you. I could have hurt our daughter." She squeezed his hand. "I left before I could hurt you more. I didn't dare go to you." Michael looked to her. "I left to find control."

Jacqueline nodded against the pillow and raised her free hand to wipe at her cheeks, sniffing softly. "Did you find it?"

"Yes. And more."

She smiled. "You'll have to tell me about that some time."

Michael nodded, then stilled, some of the resolution returning to his features. It was when he looked like this, when his eyes were this calm, she knew whatever he said was the full truth. Nothing less. "I know I was wrong. I won't justify it."

"You *were* wrong," Jackie said, her stomach suddenly fluttering. She'd anticipated many courses of the conversation, many ways it could go, but not in any of them had she figured out how to tell him about their baby. The baby they'd thought wouldn't be because of the Sorracchi. She'd fumbled through the words even in her own head, none of it ever coming out right. Maybe she didn't need words, ultimately. " . . .but not about what you thought." Michael raised his head and looked at her.

"I don't understand—"

"You were wrong about why I collapsed," she rushed over him. "I had been sitting with you, watching over you, and hadn't slept much, but . . . there was more."

The baby had been moving since the first words he spoke, and she hoped the baby was big enough maybe he could feel it, too. Jackie pushed aside the blanket she'd kept draped over her body, knowing he would see the difference in her if she hadn't, and sucked in a fortifying breath. Holding his gaze, she guided his hand beneath her sweater to rest on her stomach. Her pulse raced and she struggled to keep her breathing steady in anticipation of his reaction.

Her prayer was answered when as soon as his large hand spanned her waist, the baby beneath his touch shifted again, pushing out toward him. Tears hazed her vision and she blinked quickly so she wouldn't miss his face. His eyes widened and his mouth fell open, then he looked at her. A slow, wide smile bowed his lips and Jackie matched it, laughing softly. She scooted her arms to her side and pushed herself up on her elbows so she could better look down on his hand resting on her bellybutton.

"That's your baby," she said softly, then cleared her throat. "I just finished my fourth month. I was pregnant when you went into the hospital, I just didn't know." As she talked, Michael shifted and slid down her body to rest his cheek against her stomach, looking up at her along the length of her body. He still smiled, and she knew she smiled just as wide. "They told me when I woke up."

Michael sat up. "Jacqueline, I—"

"No." She shook her head. "You said you were sorry, that's all I need. And I'm sorry, too. I told your father going to Aretu with Silas had nothing to do with what happened, but that wasn't the whole truth. I shouldn't have—"

"There's nothing to forgive, Jacqueline," he cut her off, his voice rough.

She nodded and smiled. "Are you happy?"

His answer was a laugh. Full, unadulterated laughter was something Jackie had only heard from him perhaps two or three times since she had known him. The sound filled the room and wrapped around her, and he finished with a long, deep kiss that stole her breath. He eased her back onto the pillows, following her, kissing her so thoroughly and completely he left her feeling limp and liquid. He pulled away only enough to look her in the eyes, their rapid breath mingling between them. His smile was so beautiful, it made her heart swell.

"There was a time in my life I didn't dare imagine what happy might feel like. Had I tried, nothing would have compared to what I feel today." His gaze slid down to her lips, and she welcomed the warm curl of anticipation. "I want to make love to you, Jacqueline, but I think my parents are waiting to make sure we are okay."

She inhaled a deep breath and tried to ignore the ache. "That's okay. We can come back to this. Soon."

He smiled again and kissed her one more time before sitting up. "Caitlin is expecting, too."

"I know," she said, sitting up next to Michael as he moved to the edge of the bed. "She's a little further along."

Michael chuckled. "Something my father said makes sense now."

"What's that?"

He turned at the waist to look at her. "He told me there was more at stake than I knew. They knew about the baby." His eyes shifted down to focus on her body. Another smile and her heart warmed. "Two children. Nicole will be a sister."

"What do you want? A boy or a girl?"

Michael looked at her. "It doesn't matter. I take whatever God wants us to have."

Without looking away from her, he held out his hand and the cane he'd left leaning against the wall snapped into his waiting grip. She's seen him do such things before, but it still amazed her. Michael used the cane to stand, leaning heavy on it to find his balance, then offered her his other hand. As soon as she stood, he drew her against him and kissed her again, deep and slow and thorough. Jackie groaned against his mouth.

"That's not fair," she whined.

Michael smiled, and she realized just how much she loved to see it. He moved toward the bedroom door, drawing her with him. The difficulty she noted in his steps, worse than before the surgery, made her chest tighten, especially when she saw the pinch around his eyes. He stopped at the door and looked down at her.

"I'm fine," he assured. "I'll be better when it warms up again."

"Can they do anything more?"

"Don't worry about it right now." He held the head of the cane in the curl of his thumb and pinky and used the other three fingers of his right hand to turn the doorknob and open the door. Before she stepped into the hall, he held her back. Jackie turned to look up at him, her chest to his. "I love you, Jacqueline."

She smiled. "I love you too, handsome."

CHAPTER TWELVE

5 March 2054, Thursday
Squatter District
Falls Church, Seat of Virginia
North American Continent

*Y*our primary objective is information, Omega. All else is secondary.

Omega clenched his jaw, silencing the argument against the order Alpha projected from the building where they had found shelter. *Understood.* His answer was simple, but adequately non-committal but to avoid further argument he consciously blocked his internal emotional reaction to his brother's limited view. His opinion of priorities varied from Alpha's.

He had walked four street divisions and approached the building Katrina had previously indicated as the military-managed safe haven. She explained such sites had been established by the ruling government to provide necessities to the citizens remaining in the rubble of the city of Falls Church and the surrounding area. They provided food, water, in some cases clothing and blankets, and a place to sleep if those who came had no other place to go.

Military personnel oversaw the running of the shelters, commissioned by President Tanner to provide for the displaced citizens left in the city. By what Katrina had told him, shelters like this existed anywhere the populous had gathered, all over the planet. The question still remained for Omega and his brothers whether the man named president and known as Nicholas Tanner could be the same man so engrained in their own history. The possibility of another man carrying the same name wasn't without likelihood; if he were the Nicholas Tanner they knew of, Alpha would have to reconsider their final objectives. Their lives had been affected far too much simply by the existence of Nicholas Tanner, and in tandem, the existence of Michael Tanner, to allow the investigation of their situation to go unexplored.

Alpha wanted information, but Omega intended to gather anything he could; intelligence, yes, but also food, water, and clothing. He and his brothers had yet to take in nutrition since waking from their pods, and while they hadn't required it as of yet, clearly having been provided with supplementation while in stasis, they eventually would. Katrina was Human and weaker in constitution. He knew she already felt the need for food, though she had yet to say so.

He reached another corner, a multi-story building in front of him. Dim light flickered in nearly every window, this building seemingly whole in comparison to the buildings around the area. A large sign had been attached to the front, white with the single word SHELTER painted in black. One soldier stood under the protection of a torn awning. There was no precipitation tonight, but the wind was wet and cutting. The temperature had dropped once the sun went down, prickling at his exposed skin.

The soldier nodded to him as he passed but made no move for his weapon. Omega appeared no different than any other man crossing the threshold. The door glass was shattered, held together by mesh netting embedded in the pane, and reinforced with a panel of wood. The words Heritage Hotel arched in a half circle on each door in black letters with gold trim. Omega pushed the door open and went inside.

The lobby of sorts smelled of body odor, dank fabric, some kind of hot food he couldn't distinguish, and burning wood. A large fireplace, which appeared to perhaps have once been more a decorative element than a means to heat, burned with a large fire barely contained within the boundaries of the mantel. People lingered in the room, some eating food from bowls, some huddled near the fire. Single light source lamps scattered the room, casting circles of light just touching each other, but providing sufficient light to navigate the room.

A man crossed between Omega and a long counter, dressed in drab olive-green utility pants and a long-sleeved black shirt covered with a matching green jacket. A hand weapon was strapped to his thigh, but he made no move for it. Omega's immediate instinct drew power from around him, but he held it repressed, unwilling to play his hand until when and if action required it. An embroidered patch on the man's jacket read Torres. The military emblem on his sleeve was unfamiliar, likely a result of the regime, but the rank markings were reminiscent of the markings taught to them in their studies of Human culture and establishment. If they remained the same, the man was a lieutenant.

"Welcome," Lieutenant Torres said, rounding the end of the counter to move behind it. He set his hands on the worn wood, spread wide, relaxed and non-threatening. Omega wondered if the stance was practiced or learned. "What can we do for you tonight, my friend?"

Omega tilted his head and listened momentarily to the conversations in the room, keying in on voices and discussions. He focused again on the soldier. "I need to get out of the cold, just for a while."

Torres nodded and smiled. "Sure thing. Do you have some place to go tonight? It's going to be almost as cold as last night."

Omega nodded.

"Okay, good. Come by here on your way out, and I'll make sure you take some food with you. You don't need to stay in the shelter to be fed. Are you with anyone?" Omega tilted his head, attempting to discern the meaning of the man's question. "You takin' care of anyone?" Torres explained.

"My wife," he lied, the words falling from lips trained in deceit as much as combat. "Two sons."

Torres winced. "Sorry to hear that, but hey, at least you've got each other. Right?" he finished with a smile.

Omega nodded and moved into the lobby. He crossed the room to the fireplace and crouched down in front of the fire, not directly engaging any particular person. The heat felt good, the small fire they had built in their temporary habitat never quite enough to remove all of the chill. There were several worn couches and chairs scattered around the room, some clustered into groups, some turned toward the source of heat. To one side of the lobby were several tables and chairs, nearly every one occupied by people of all ages eating the warm food provided by the shelter: old men, women with children, a varied blend of the inhabitants of this world. A group of men sat around one table eating hot food from bowls. The smell of coffee and chicken battled with burning wood.

In front of the fire to Omega's left sat a woman on the floor with a young child in her lap and an older boy on the floor playing with some pieces of wood. He stacked and restacked, apparently satisfied with the game. She smiled at the boy as he played and bounced the child to amuse him or her, Omega couldn't be sure the sex of the infant. She looked up and saw Omega watching and offered a smile. Omega hoped his smile back was convincing. He looked away and focused, attempting to single out the bits of conversations around the room.

"I'm not saying he's doing a lousy job, I just think Tanner could do more than he is," carried from one of the tables off to Omega's right.

"Like what? Geesh, look around, Ed. Look what he's dealing with? The planet was half-dead even *before* the war. He was put in charge of a smoldering rock. If he can find you, he makes damn sure you're not hungry or cold. Sometimes it may not be more than a nutrition bar and a blanket, but it's more than you started with for damn sure."

"We wouldn't be in this situation if it weren't for the damn aliens—"

"Which ones? Seems to me there are a hell of a lot more out there than we ever thought."

The first guy grunted and a loud thump echoed through the room, perhaps from a mug or cup being set down hard. "I say it's the Areth and the Umani that brought this hell down on us. I heard the whole damn reason the Sorracchi slugs came here to begin with was to get some kind of twisted revenge on the Areth. They wouldn't have given a damn about Earth otherwise. I say we kicked the Sorracchi's asses, let's get the Areth and the Umani off Earth, too. Get our damn planet back."

Chair legs scraped across the floor. "You're an idiot. Once you open Pandora's Box, you can't close it again."

Heavy footsteps walked away and in his peripheral Omega saw a man cross the lobby and head up the stairs. The man left at the table mumbled under his breath, followed by the sound of an eating utensil scraping in a bowl. Omega shifted his focus to all conversations within hearing, from the far side of the lobby to the people tucked into the corners of the room. Two people played some sort of game with cards in the far corner, two lovers talked of their plans for later in the evening, a few discussed President Tanner—in their case, praising him for his work to revive the planet after the war—and one man sat alone mumbling to himself.

The boy playing with the blocks pushed himself up and came toward Omega, holding out one of the blocks.

"Ethan—" his mother said sternly.

Omega raised his hand and tried another smile. Then he held out his hand so the boy could place the block in his palm. He had no memory of this age. Their aging process had been accelerated from infancy to pre-adolescence to better prepare them for their training, but they had been well educated in the stages of physical and mental development in every race they encountered. Weaknesses. Average intelligence. Possible strengths. A child this size and age was completely vulnerable, no way to defend himself, no way to understand the risks surrounding him even though he lived in it daily.

Omega rolled the block in his fingers, each side carved with an Anglo-Saxon letter and painted in primary colors, long since chipped and faded. He rolled it, watching the boy's eyes shift with each movement. Omega held up the block, a red painted A on top.

"Do you know what letter this is?"

The boy shook his head, long blond hair falling across his face.

"It's an A." He turned it again until a green E showed. "This one?" This time the boy nodded vigorously. "What is it?"

"E!" the boy shouted. "Like Effan."

Omega smiled and held the block back to the boy. "Very good."

Ethan returned to his mother, and she smiled at Omega, mouthing, "Thank you."

Omega nodded, watching the boy play. Despite the squalor around him, Ethan seemed completely content to sit near his mother and build towers from pieces of wood. He probably had never known any other life, either born just before or immediately after the beginning of the war Katrina described. Chair legs scraped again behind him at the table.

"I heard what you had to say, my friend," said a new voice. "I'm with you. We need to purge the planet of anything not Human."

Ed chuckled. "Hell, the Earth has practically been purged of Humans anyway, what the hell is left?"

"Either way, we deserve our own planet. Don't you think?"

"Hell, yeah."

There was a long pause before the newcomer asked, "How far would you be willing to go to see that happen?"

When Ed spoke again, his voice was lower and no longer carried as before, but Omega still heard him without issue. "As far as it takes." He cleared his throat. "You a Xeno?"

"That's a name given to us by those who don't want us to speak the truth, those who wish us to appear as villains. We are Separatists willing to take the steps no one else will. We are no more villains than the glorified Phoenix group was before the Sorracchi destroyed us."

"Well, whatever the hell you want to call yourselves, I'm in. I'm sick and tired of eating lousy food in cold shelters. I was important before all this. I was a man of wealth."

"Do you want it back?"

"Of course I do."

"We are on our way back to the world we once knew. We have friends in powerful, influential places." The chair scraped again. "We have plans for his big speech on—What pretentious name did he give it? Victory Day? —when he tries to convince the bleating sheep of this planet everything is great and we're so much better off than we were a few years ago. Stands there with his wife and that freak of a kid of his." The nameless voice made a disgusted sound and huffed. "We had hoped for the assassination of Ambassador John Smith, but since he's scurried off like the Areth cockroach he is, we'll have to settle for another example. The biggest."

"You sure are brave telling me all this," Ed pointed out.

"I've been watching you for quite some time, my friend." There was a pause and Omega resisted the urge to turn his head and look. "Join us and help us regain what is ours."

"Tell me what to do."

"Be back here tomorrow. The kickoff for this farce of a celebration is early Friday morning. We only have days until we put our plan into action, and every man counts. I'll return at mealtime to give you more information."

Scraping noises indicated one or both men rose from the table. Omega angled his head a slight degree and watched in his peripheral vision. A tall man with hair mostly grey dressed in blue utility pants styled much like what Katrina had worn and a dirty brown jacket crossed the lobby to the counter. He said something to Lieutenant Torres, who nodded and smiled, and went through a door behind the counter. The man Omega suspected to be the Xeno, as the one named Ed had designated him, scowled as soon as the soldier was gone and cast a stern glare around the lobby. When Torres returned, he had a sack filled with something—supplies perhaps—and handed it to the man. With barely a nod of acknowledgment the man exited the lobby.

He plotted the death of his president, and willingly accepted the provisions freely given by the same man. He was more than a traitor, he was a coward and a hypocrite. Omega held no loyalty to the leaders of this world, but such deceit scraped against his nerves.

Two men entered the lobby, dressed in full military clothing, both carrying large pulse weapons across their chests, pistols strapped to their thighs. They barely spared a glance in the direction of the lobby and walked directly to the counter. Where he sat, Omega could easily watch the exchange, and with little effort, he honed his senses to hear each word.

"Hey, Rick," said one of the new men to the lieutenant. "Exciting night?"

Torres shook his head. "Nah, just typical. Something going on?"

"Yeah," one of the new men said on a long sigh. "A woman was abducted from Alexandria hospital Tuesday night. Guess she works with the head honcho doctor in there. The one emancipated just before the war."

Omega tensed and clenched his fists. They spoke of Katrina.

"Abducted? Geez . . . by who?"

"Hell if we know. Did you hear about the four meat popsicles they found on an abandoned slug ship a few weeks back?" Torres nodded. "Whoever did it took her and three of the four. The other woke up a while back, but he's a cripple. Montgomery's guess is probably a Xeno cell, but no one knows what they'd want with these guys since not even the eggheads know who or what they are. Other than the fact they were frozen by the Sorracchi."

"Poor bastards," Torres said with a shake of his head. "Do they think the Xenos brought her out here?"

"There are no leads yet, but we're passing on the word." The officer took from his vest a small computer device and held it out for Torres to see. Omega assumed it was an image of some sort, but from this angle he couldn't see what was displayed. "This is the girl. Name's Doctor Katrina Bauer."

"Damn, she looks about twelve."

The soldier chuckled and put the device back in his pocket. "I met her once. She's no bigger than a kid." The man's smile faded, replaced with a serious pinch around his eyes. "Too small to defend herself."

Torres nodded, his expression grim.

"We doubt whoever took her would let her be seen, if she's still alive, but keep an eye open. The other three were removed forcibly from their stasis, so we don't know if they're awake or even alive. Hard to miss, though. They're apparently identical. We haven't gotten any images of them yet."

"Got it," Torres said. "I see anything, I'll call in to base."

The two soldiers tossed off a passive salute and exited the lobby. Omega focused on the flickering flame, analyzing the conversation. It was assumed he and his brothers had been taken by force, along with Katrina, not that she left with them. How long that theory stood, he couldn't know, but it was clear she could not be seen. Not yet. Where this course of events would end, Omega couldn't see, couldn't even hypothesize. They may have escaped from enemy hands, or they may have run from their final hope.

It was only a matter of time before they knew if Mother's poison still laced their bodies.

Frustration pushed Omega to his feet, and he wove his way through the clusters of people back to the counter. He would find out little more tonight, and the promise of food to bring back to Katrina and his brothers had him anxious to leave again. Lieutenant Torres looked up as he neared the counter.

"Feeling warmer?"

"Yes, thank you," Omega answered. "I need to get back, though."

"Hang on, okay?" Torres went through a door into the back room and came back moments later carrying a fabric sack. "I didn't know if you had a way of heating up anything, or keep anything cold, so I gave you a meal of sandwiches to eat tonight so they won't spoil. There's some fruit and nutrition bars, MREs, that sort of thing. Stuff to hold you over. And I put in some water sanitizing tablets. They're pretty effective, just give them about fifteen minutes once you put them in untreated water to make sure."

Omega reached for the bag when Torres slid it across the counter toward him, an unfamiliar conflict in his chest. He wondered if this man would be so willing to help if he knew Omega and his brothers were the ones who had taken Katrina, and kept her hidden in a cold, abandoned building just blocks away. Was this the care offered to all men under Nicholas Tanner's leadership?

"Thank you," he finally said, fisting his hands in the loose fabric at the top of the sack.

Torres leaned closer and dropped his voice. "You didn't say how old your boys were but looking at you I figure they've got to be little guys. Don't tell anyone because I'll have everyone lined up here for some, but I threw in some packaged cookies I smuggled in a couple days ago. Let the kids have a treat, right?" He winked.

Omega stared for a moment, unsure how to process the man's facial gesture. Seeming not to notice Omega's bafflement, Torres leaned back and looked under his counter.

"Do you need anything else? Our clothing and blanket supplies are low, but I still have some. Won't get more probably until this weekend."

Omega started to shake his head, then stopped, the image of Katrina tugging the cuffs of her baggy pants over her bare feet. "Socks."

Torres arched his eyebrows. "Yeah, I think I can do that. For you or the kids?"

"My wife."

"Well, I've got adult and I've got child. Here." He pulled a bundle from under the counter and opened the top of the sack, tossing in a pile of white socks tied together with a string. "Need any for the kids?"

"No, just for my wife."

Torres nodded. "Good enough. Come back when you need anything. If it gets too cold where you are, we can find you room here. The rooms are warmer than outside."

"Thank you," Omega said again and took the sack, turning toward the door.

Mother Kathleen had indoctrinated them with the idea the Human race were barbarians barely capable of flight, criminals and filthy savages to be repressed. Worthy only in the fact their bodies could be manipulated to garner strength, and their minds were weak enough to be controlled—wiped out—as the Sorracchi saw fit. Those precepts had been the justifying reason why he and his brothers had fled the facility they woke in once they garnered enough knowledge to know it was inhabited by Humans.

Now, all he thought he knew was cast in shadow.

He and his brothers had long ago accepted their teachings were tainted by Kathleen's rage and bias. It was their rebellion to her instructions that had led to their punishment, their poisoning, and ultimately their imprisonment within the pods. They understood enough to cast doubt on all. But, could there be *any* truth in her words?

Omega pulled open the doors and cold wind pushed into him. He tucked his chin, held the sack to his chest, and headed back up the hill to his brothers. And Katrina.

CHAPTER THIRTEEN

*T*he room hadn't been touched in years.

Stuffed animals coated in dust sat against the white painted headboard of the small bed, staring with hazed eyes toward the door. All the furniture had been white once, now gray with dust and debris, and pink was the prevailing color; pink walls, pink curtains, pink blankets on the bed, pink lampshades on little ballerina lamps.

In carved wood letters the name JESSICA LYNN arched on the wall above the bed.

Katrina stood just inside the door of the bedroom, transfixed. She had thought to explore the apartment, maybe find a pair of socks, or more wood to burn in the fireplaces. The other bedrooms had been rummaged through and cleaned out just like the rest of the apartment. The inhabitants had taken with them anything they could carry, whether it had been before or after the war Katrina would never know. The room was frigid in comparison to the rest of the apartment. Her logical mind knew it was because they had a fire burning in the dual hearth so the bedroom and the main living space both had some source of heat, but her soul told her the room was cold because life had been stolen from it before the apartment was ever empty.

She took a step into the room, the soles of her bare feet poked and pricked by the debris on the floor. The cuff of the sweatpants helped protect her toes, but not her soles, and her shoes weren't dry yet. The long, low bureau to her left had been decorated with carousel horses, snow globes that had long since cracked and shattered in the cold, and plastic rhinestone tiaras. The sight made Katrina's eyes prickle and her throat tighten. She touched the carousel horse, her fingertips coming back gray with dust. Three tinny notes played before the music box fell silent.

Taped to the mirror with no less than half a dozen oversized strips of yellow cellophane tape was a child's drawing in crayon and marker. Four stick figure people standing side by side, hand in hand, with names written beneath in mostly block letters. DADY MOMY PETUR and the last, JESSICA.

A dozen scenarios played through her mind like the worst scenes of a horror movie. None of them had any kind of happy ending.

The sound of the apartment door opening and closing carried through the empty shell of a home, magnified by the hollowness. Katrina swiped the back of her hand across her cheeks and sniffed. Both Omega and Beta had left what she figured to be about two hours before, leaving her alone with the stoic, brittle Alpha. His silence had spurred her into exploring as far as he would allow, and even then, she knew he didn't like her being outside his direct line of sight. Where did he think she would go? Without shoes, she wouldn't get far. Maybe they could run around Alexandria barefoot, but she couldn't.

Katrina turned and shuffled toward the door, needing to escape the depressing air in the room. She reached the open doorway just as Omega stepped into the space, and she pulled up short with a gasp, taking a step back.

He followed her. "Are you hurt?" he asked, reaching out his hand to her, but he stopped short of touching her arm.

Katrina shook her head and crossed her arms over the bulk of the sweatshirt. "No, you startled me."

"You're crying."

"I'm fine," she said too quickly, she realized, and sighed. She had to swallow hard before she could speak. "I'm just . . . this room breaks my heart."

He looked past her, his eyes shifting as he scanned the room. Katrina blinked again, clearing the haze from her vision so she could watch him. A slight tilt of his head and dig between his eyes was the only indicator of his reaction.

A voice in the back of her head—a voice that sounded too much like Karl—told her she should be terrified, and a bit part of her was more afraid than she'd ever been even when the world had shattered, but a greater part of her remembered the files she'd found while digging through the *Abaddon*'s records. The clinical descriptions of the Triadic's creation, their indoctrinations, the detailed description by their educator of their punishments and the experimentation performed on them to create what the Sorracchi deemed to be the perfect team. Killing machines trained and brainwashed to take every order without question, no matter how gruesome or heartless. All that should have been enough to make her believe she might never leave this condemned building alive, but it was the final records she remembered the most.

They had refused an order.

And it had infuriated her.

It was that act of rebellion, their refusal as a single unit to slaughter the remains of an alien village filled only with women and children and infirmed that kept Katrina from being afraid. Well, mostly. That act of rebellion had landed them in the stasis pods. They had been deemed a failure, a dangerous commodity with too much time and energy put into them to simply kill them, a project to be set aside until the cause of their flaw was discovered and removed. That day never came.

Their show of compassion didn't completely wipe out the fact they'd taken her from her lab by force, and now had her holed up in a deathtrap abandoned building somewhere in the Squatter District of old Alexandria.

He stepped past her into the room, his arm brushing her as he passed. When he reached the middle, near the foot of the small bed, he stopped and scanned the room, turning a circle to face her again.

"Why?"

"Why what?" she asked.

"Why does this room upset you?" He looked toward the bureau and the array of little girl treasures. "It is abandoned, as is everything."

Katrina shrugged and tugged the rolled sleeves of her oversized sweatshirt over her hands. The chill seeped into her bones. "I don't know what happened to this family, but I can guess, and every guess I come up with says this little girl died before they ever left here. I've heard of people doing this when they lose someone. It's like a shrine, or something. But they left it when this part of the city was attacked."

"This was a child's room." She wasn't sure if he meant it as a question or a statement, but she nodded. "It makes you sad to know a child died."

"Of course it does. Doesn't it you?"

He canted his head a slight degree, his hazel eyes shifted to a non-distinguishable point. Katrina waited, holding her breath. His answer was important, though she couldn't define why. She just knew it was.

Omega took the two steps needed to close the space between them, his gaze still somewhere else. He brought his hand up and pressed his palm against his chest, then snapped his attention to her, his eyes pinched. "An empty feeling . . ." His voice strained. "Something should be here but isn't." He straightened and swallowed. "Is this sadness?"

She couldn't have answered him, even if she knew what to say. The words stuck in her throat and she could only nod vigorously. He looked down at her, jaw clenched, the only movement the slight shift of his eyes when he studied her. Katrina stared back, wondering what she saw in the change of his eyes, and wondering what he saw when he looked at her.

Then his head snapped up and he looked toward the open door leading back to the hall and the rest of the apartment. "Come with me," he said, curling his fingers around her elbow. "I've brought food." Omega looked down at her feet, hidden in the sweatpants like the feet of a child's footed pajamas. "And socks."

She was proud of herself for not breaking away and running for the end of the hall. It didn't really matter what he found to eat, she was so hungry it hurt. The main room was considerably warmer than the hall, but it was still far from comfortable. It was also empty. There was no sign of Alpha and she hadn't heard Beta return.

A green fabric sack sat in the middle of the table. One of them had cleared away the dust, and a bottle of water sat waiting in front of a chair. Katrina did give in to the impulse to jog forward and pick up the bottle, twisting it open to take a long drink. It was the first she'd had to drink since waking up, and she sighed as it rinsed away the coating in her throat. She didn't know how long they would be able to stay here with no heat, no fresh water, no facilities. The bathrooms were only functional in that they were gravity-driven waste units designed to work without electricity. They weren't exactly sanitary, and Katrina had fought the curling in her gut the times she'd been forced to finally give in to the need, but she knew it could have been worse.

Anything could be worse.

"Where did your brother go?" she asked, curling into one of the wooden chairs with her feet tucked on the edge.

"Reconnaissance." He pulled the sack toward him and reached inside, first handing her a plastic rectangle package of sanitation towels.

It was ridiculous how happy Katrina was to see something so simple, a basic personal item given to the refugees, but she didn't care. She tore open the package and took out one of the moist bits of disposable towel, going to work on her soiled hands. Before she finished, Omega set a wrapped sandwich in front of her.

She looked up and smiled, her stomach growling loudly at the possibility of food. "Thank you. Did you go to the shelter for this?"

"Yes."

"I thought Alpha preferred you didn't go there."

He paused in reaching into the sack again and looked down at her. "We have to balance the risk with what can be gained."

Katrina nodded and unwrapped the sandwich, not caring at all it was ham and cheese and she didn't like ham and cheese and took a bite. "Are you going to eat?" she said, very unladylike, around a mouthful in her cheek.

Rather than answering, he turned away from the table and crossed the room to the fireplace. With his back to her, he crouched in front of the hearth. Katrina tried to see what he was doing, but when she couldn't, she went back to the sandwich. Nothing had ever tasted so good, ham or not.

He stood and came back to the table, grabbing one of the chairs to drag it in front of her. Katrina nearly choked when he gripped her right ankle and pulled her foot toward him. She tried to swallow, but the chunk of sandwich wouldn't yield. He freed her foot of the elastic cuff of the sweatpants, pushing the pants up past her ankle, and slipped a warm, clean sock over her exposed toes.

Katrina sighed at the heavenly warmth. He had to have had them by the fire, warming them. He glanced at her before setting her socked foot back on the edge of the chair where it had been, and took her other foot, doing the same.

"Oh . . . thank you," she said on a pleased groan.

He nodded, his common response she was learning, and started to stand. Katrina lunged forward and grabbed his arm before he was gone again. "Wait." He lowered himself back into the chair, watching her. Katrina drew in a deep breath. "Have you eaten since you . . ." she winced, not sure how to even describe what happened, " . . .woke up?"

He moved to stand, and this time she didn't stop him. "It is more important you eat," he said over his shoulder, walking back to the fireplace.

She reached for the sack and crossed her legs, keeping the nice clean socks off the dirty floor, and set the sack in her lap. There were two more sandwiches in the bag and based on the empty wrapper on the table she assumed Alpha had eaten one before he left, dried fruit, nutrition bars, water sanitizer, all general supplies provided by the Protectorate. Omega came back and set her boots on the floor in front of the chair.

"Thank you," she said, took out one of the sandwiches and held it out to him. He looked from the offered food to her, then sat back and took the sandwich from her hand. "You might want to eat slowly, though. It's been a long time since you digested real food."

"I will have no issues."

She couldn't help but watch, or maybe she was more curious than concerned, while he unwrapped the sandwich with exacting movements. No tearing it open. No turning the package to find the best way in. Each motion was the exact action needed to open the package, as if he'd studied every possible way in and this was the most efficient. He set the package with half the sandwich on the table and met her gaze when he bit into the half he held. Katrina smiled and took another bite of her own.

She relaxed against the slatted wood back of the chair and let out a long breath. They ate in silence. The three of them were still a mystery, but she had figured out a few things, one of which they had no problem with silence. Mostly, she believed, because the three of them had their own little conversations in their heads she couldn't be a part of.

Katrina finished the sandwich and took a drink of the remaining water, clearing her throat. "Do you have a name?"

He finished chewing his bite and brushed his fingers over his mouth. "I am designated Omega. You know this."

"That's your designation. Don't you have a name?" He shook his head. Katrina sighed and leaned forward, bouncing her hands off her knees. "I'm a doctor of computer technologies, that's my *designation*. It's more what I do than who I am. My *name* is Katrina."

"We have no necessity for a name."

"Of course you do. You're a person." When he didn't offer any argument for nor against, nor an acceptance, Katrina sighed and held out her hand, waving it toward him. "Well, what if I don't *want* to call you Omega?"

She wasn't positive, would never be sure, but she thought *maybe* one corner of his straight, never wavering lips ticked up in just the slightest, barely there smile.

The apartment door opened and both Alpha and Beta came in, leaving wet footprints in the dust. Omega looked up, stood, and strode across the room to them until they stood in a triangle formatting facing each other.

She watched them in fascination as a conversation clearly took place. They shifted their attention between each other, one perhaps tilting his head, another nodding. Then all three turned their heads simultaneously and looked at her. She stared, wide eyed, until they turned back to their conversation.

"You know, some people would consider that exceptionally rude."

By the strained expressions, she surmised the topic wasn't pleasant. Popping the last bit of bread in her mouth, she lowered her legs and pulled the boots on over her new socks and laced them, then thunked her feet down on the floor, the sound loud enough to echo in the space, and stood. "Use your words, boys."

Omega glanced her way for a brief moment, then back to his brothers. "Until we determine friend from foe—"

Katrina stumbled forward to stand in the middle of all of them, facing Omega with her back to Alpha. "What do you mean, friend or foe? We're friends. I told you that. The Sorracchi are gone."

"Because you were enemies of the Sorracchi does not imply you are an ally," Alpha said behind her.

She twisted only enough to look up at him and his condescending glance.

"The enemy of my enemy is my friend. Right? Haven't you ever heard that?"

"The Vashadi are a race of massive creatures who feast on the brains of their fallen enemy and ferment their blood into wine. They are the enemy of the Sorracchi, but I would not wish to find myself their ally," Beta said, his arms crossed, looking at the floor.

Katrina turned her head and looked at him, wide eyed. "Did you . . . did you just make a *joke*?"

Beta raised his chin enough to look at her. "My intent was not to amuse."

She nodded, giving him the same stare she shot at her brother whenever he was a pain in her backside, then turned her head slowly to look at the other two. "Well, *we* don't eat brains. We don't write over brains, either. When we found you on that ship, *abandoned* by the Sorracchi, I might add, we brought you back here to save your lives."

"To what purpose?" Alpha asked.

"To save your lives," Katrina repeated, stressing each word. She shook her head. "We had no idea who you were, why you were there, anything about you. All we knew was you had been left there to die and, darn it, we aren't the kind of people who leave other people to die. Whether we know who you are, or not."

Katrina put her hands on Omega's chest and pushed him aside, marching past him to the fireplace. She picked up a wrought iron poker and jabbed at the red embers at the bottom of the woodpile. Sparks flared and drifted up the chimney, crackling and popping. Warmth flared, heating her cheeks. It had to be the fire making her face flush.

She tossed the poker back into the bin and shoved the loose sleeves of her scavenged sweatshirt up past her elbows, swiveling to face them again. She lectured them as she walked back. "And frankly, since then, with the information we found from the *Abaddon* records, we've grown more and more convinced you were worth helping." She held up one finger, wagging it at them. "And no, it's *not* because you're this . . . superhuman super soldier." Katrina finished with a wave of her hand. "I know that's what you're thinking."

They exchanged looks.

"Yeah, see. I knew it."

Omega took a step toward her, close enough she had to tip back her chin to look him in the eyes. "If not for what we are, then why?"

She faltered and had to look away to tamp down the visceral reaction to the thought of the woman who caused all this. She drew in a calming breath and raised her chin again. He hadn't moved, still watched her. "Because of who did it to you."

"We were under the instruction of many. Whom do you mean?"

"Her," Katrina said, her throat itching with each word. "The woman who created you. The woman who was responsible for your training. Do you know who she was?"

Omega looked over his shoulder at his brothers, and Alpha nodded. Then Omega looked to her again. "She was known by two names. In Sorracchi, she was Tosk Rak'blon, but in your language she was known as—"

"Kathleen."

Omega nodded. "Yes."

"We know who Kathleen is, too. Some people on our team more intimately than others, and not in a good way. One of the men who found you, Michael Tanner—" Omega tensed, and she caught in her peripheral the visual exchange between Alpha and Beta. "Sh-she was his mother. Biologically, I mean. The Human body she—the Sorracchi consciousness, or whatever—had taken was the body that birthed him. Or some early clone of that body. I'm still wrapping my head around a lot of it.

"We are aware of Michael Tanner," Omega said, his voice sharper than she'd ever heard. "Is he the son of your president?"

She nodded. "He was rescued, too, just a couple years ago from a Sorracchi facility in New Mexico. He'd been there his whole life."

"Who was responsible for his liberation?"

Whenever Beta spoke it startled her, he said so little. Katrina looked to Beta, then back to Omega. Something she said had affected them, and the one thing she could pinpoint was the mention of Michael Tanner.

"Ultimately, I guess you'd say it was his father. Nicholas Tanner. He went in with several others to free Michael and several other Humans they'd discovered to be held there." She tilted her head and took a step back so she could see all three of them. "How do you know Michael Tanner?"

"We don't know him," Alpha corrected. "We know of him."

Omega's head snapped sharp to his brother, a deep scowl digging at his brow. The glare his brother returned was just as dark.

The first round of pulse fire yanked Katrina from sleep, her heart pounding hard and erratic against the back of her ribs. She sat up with a jolt and tried to focus in the dark room, the walls dancing with shadows cast by the flicker of the dying fire. The bedroom door flew open and she jumped again. Omega held his finger to his lip and crossed the room, crouched low until he was beside her.

"What's going on?" she whispered when he reached her.

He shook his head. "Alpha is investigating."

Another round of weapons fire, louder, closer, and more intense than the last, ripped a scream from her. She was halfway to her feet before she realized she'd jumped up, but on her back again just as quickly when Omega yanked her down onto the pallet. He covered her mouth with his warm hand to smother another scream, his body held her down

A scream echoed from somewhere outside—someone else's—a woman's scream—and another shot. Katrina bit her lip and fisted her fingers in Omega's sweater, burying her face against his chest now to hold him down as much as to hide from the firefight. His heart beat steady against her fingers. She tried not to tremble, bit her lip to hold in her own screams. Another blast.

"Stay still," he whispered near her ear. "Stay low. The fighting is not immediately outside this structure. It is three grids over, but the fire might carry without obstruction."

The blasts accelerated, filling the night so rapidly she couldn't distinguish them anymore. Voices overlapped each other, demands to stand down, to stop firing, to go to hell. The building shuddered and shook when a random blast hit it somewhere, not close enough to hurt them but close enough to make the walls shake and debris crumble from the ceiling. Omega wrapped his arm behind her head and drew her closer.

Several minutes passed in silence before Katrina could finally let herself relax. She drew in a shaky breath, eased her fingers free from his sweater, and tipped her head back to see his face. He held her, but his attention was on the window across the room.

"Did it stop?" she asked, her throat so tight she could barely force out the words.

"It appears so."

A pop and bang made her jump again.

"It's okay," he assured her, relaxing his hold so his hand settled near her waist. "Don't stand but look."

Katrina tried to tip her head back to see the window but couldn't. She flipped to her stomach, still within the shelter of Omega's body, his hand heavy against the small of her back. Several pops and bangs, in rapid fire, accompanied an explosion of light and color that lit up the room through the ragged curtains. The fireworks show continued for at least five minutes.

"This is not an attack. What is the purpose?" Omega asked when the sky fell dark again.

"It's Revolution Day," she answered, turning onto her back again beneath his angled body. He squinted, the expression she'd learned to interpret as the only show of confusion he would allow. "One year ago today, President Tanner and the Earth's new allies—the Umani and the Areth—led a global attack force to rise up against the Sorracchi as a single, unified rebellion. The fighting continued for three days until the Sorracchi surrendered."

"The purpose of the lights—"

"Are to commemorate. To celebrate."

He canted his head a slight degree. "Your world is in ruin."

Katrina nodded. "Yes. But it's our world. If we hadn't risen up we would be slaves, even more of us dead, with no hope. At least now . . . there's hope."

His scowl deepened and he looked to the window again. A sound in the hall made her jump, and Omega's flat hand settled on her stomach to keep her from moving away from him. She wished her heart would stop pounding so hard; the danger was over, but she couldn't steady her breathing or make herself let go of Omega. He turned his head toward the door he'd left open.

"It's Alpha returning. The fighting was between a group of Humans several blocks away but has ended with the intervention of several soldiers."

She stared at him, trying to process the extent of their abilities. How amazing to communicate with others so easily, so freely. He shifted his weight onto his bent arm and looked down at her again, the light of the flame reflecting off his eyes. They shifted in the dim light, then his features pinched and he rolled away from her and to his feet in a single, effortless motion.

"Go back to sleep, Katrina," he said. "You will be safe."

Before he reached the door she called out to him and he stopped. "Thank you," she said, settling into the blankets again.

He shut the door as he left.

CHAPTER FOURTEEN

6 March 2054, Friday, 11:07 hours
Revolution Day
Office of the President
Robert J. Castleton Memorial Building – The Castle
Center for United Protectorate Government
Alexandria, Seat of Virginia
North American Continent

hree sharp raps on the door preceded Connor's entrance into the office, his second-in-command right behind him. Michael set his cup of coffee on the long narrow table between the two couches facing each other and stood.

"Did you discover something?"

Connor looked around. "Hell, yeah. Where is Nick?"

"He had a meeting with Colonel Ebben. He should return soon." Michael nodded toward Melanie Briggs. "Good morning, Melanie."

She smiled. "No one calls me Melanie, sir. Mel will do."

"Michael has a thing for full names," Connor said as an aside and walked around the other side of the long table to the monitor mounted over the fireplace mantel. He popped a chip from the PAC he carried and turned on the massive screen. "We were way off," he said, working the touch commands in the bottom right corner of the screen. "Way, way off."

Michael scowled, but before he could ask for clarification the office door opened again and his father came in with Beverly Surimoto and Colonel Ebben. His father was mid-stream discussing something with the colonel but stopped short when he saw Connor.

"Did you find something?"

"Yes, sir," Connor said, his voice heavy with something Michael wasn't quite sure he could properly identify. Anger, maybe. But he wasn't sure. "They were damn good to skirt just about every security camera we've got, and I'd just about decided they'd been beamed up by the Areth or something, but then I found this . . ." He tapped the screen. "An old-style security system in the back corridor behind the old kitchen area we had to shut down after the fire a few months ago. No one goes down there, no reason to. But, the camera is motion activated and it kicked on night before last."

"So, whoever took Katrina and the Triad knew the building."

"Not likely, sir. Unless it was Katrina telling them the way." Connor slid his fingertips across the screen and a video window opened, the stilled screen grainy and unfocused. "Watch this."

A tap on the screen set the video to play. Michael took his glasses from his shirt pocket and slipped them on before he stepped closer to the screen. His father stepped beside him to stand shoulder-to-shoulder with Michael. The image flickered and played, with no sound. The image showed a bad angle of what had once been the facility kitchen in the lower levels, now with charred walls and tarnished counters and appliances from a fire caused by ancient wiring damaged further by fallout from the war. They had shut down that wing of the hospital seven months earlier when it made more sense to open the auxiliary kitchen rather than try to repair what was there when resources were practically non-existent. For several seconds the image didn't waver except for the flicker and shift of the static created by the poor-quality recording system.

Then four figures came into view. Michael blinked and took a step forward, squinting to make sure he actually saw what he thought he saw. Three men, wearing only the blue cotton infirmary pants Michael remembered dressing them in when they first opened the pods, and Katrina Bauer led along by one of the three, his arm securely around her shoulders. She didn't fight hard, but she clearly wasn't with them out of choice. Michael stepped to Connor's side and tapped the screen to pause the image.

It was grainy, the finer points lost, but by what Michael could make out all three men had open wounds wherever pod connections had been integrated directly into their biological systems. Study of the pods had presented as a forcible, abusive extraction. Could they have removed themselves from the pods? How could that be possible?

"Is she okay?" his father asked.

"She appears to be," Melanie answered, and shook her head. "She's not leaving by choice, though. Watch." She engaged the image again.

The four of them reached the back door leading to an alley behind the facility once used for delivery and storage. One moved ahead and disappeared into the night. The second approached the door but paused and looked back to the third who led Katrina. She shook her head and tried to pull free of her captor's hold, but he held her firm. There appeared no excessive brutality in his handling over her, but it was clear he intended for her to leave with them. The two still within the room exchanged looks, but neither spoke. Katrina said something, but the image was so unclear Michael only knew she spoke and couldn't even begin to make out what she said. He doubted even Beverly Surimoto could read lips in this situation.

The one at the door looked into the alley then disappeared. Katrina shook her head more adamantly and tried to step back. The one remaining of the Triad moved his arm from her shoulder and gripped her arms. He pulled her to him and spoke and she suddenly stilled. Whatever he said convinced her to stop fighting and she let him lead her out the door.

"They have no winter gear. Hell, the three of them are barely dressed," Nick mumbled. "They could have frozen to death for all we know."

"At least we know who we're looking for, sir," Connor said, turning off the video. He turned to face them, his hands set at his waist. "Three identical men dressed in pajamas dragging an unwilling woman through the streets of Alexandria would be memorable."

"They had to have found shelter, or they wouldn't have survived the night. There is no way . . ." Michael said.

"My people are gathering now. We'll be sending them out in teams, half working out from the hospital in an expanding concentric search pattern, half beginning at one mile past what we believe to be a possible travel distance and working inward. We're also sending reports to all shelters, stations, and ration facilities with details ordering all personnel to report any persons of interest."

"I want reports every hour," Nick ordered, the tension in his voice drawing Michael's attention. His father's lips were pressed together in a thin, tight line, his features hard. "I want her found."

"Yes, sir." Connor nodded to Melanie, and they both headed for the door.

*Y*ou feel the poison.

Omega swallowed against the nausea twisting his stomach and looked to his brother. Alpha stood near the window of the main room, looking down into the street. The day had turned warm and the sun was so bright it made the snow glow. Omega couldn't look outside, the reflection off the white surface painful to his eyes. It pierced his head like an acid needle. Even the light through the window was painful. He closed his eyes and turned his head away from the glow, nodding in answer.

Yes. It began last night. It is not insurmountable.

Alpha left the window and sat with Omega in one of the other chairs at the table. *Beta is also affected. The nausea and pain.* He tapped his temple with one finger. *He tells me he has noticed a faltering in his precision and focus.*

I've felt it in both of you. Omega squinted his eyes to try to block some of the burning sunlight. *I sense you are trying to block us from knowing the pain you are in, Alpha. Hiding it does no good.*

Neither does it do good to add to what you're already fighting.

Beta had been fighting the pain for several hours, and Alpha had been ignoring his own pain for nearly as long. It was useless to deny it to each other; a burn at the base of their skulls like hot acid pulsing in their veins, a tension in the gut like their insides were slowly turning to stone, and a crawl under the skin akin to a thousand tiny sand gnats crawling to be free. It was tolerable, still, but they knew from experience it would grow increasingly worse until they would seek either death or insanity. Kathleen had brought them close to that point, as punishment for their rebellion or failure to learn.

She wasn't here to stop it this time.

Which led to the inevitable question . . .

What are we going to do? He raised his head and looked at Omega. *We've come from an existence like death only to face death. There has to be another way.*

The room door opened and Beta came in, glancing around the room for Katrina.

She hadn't slept the remainder of the night after the initial gunfight in the city and the light show she called fireworks. There had been more fighting, more pulse fire, throughout the city well until sunrise. Even when she began to drift to sleep, the echoes of blasts would wake her again. Omega had gone to the room with the second round of pulse weapons and had watched over her for the rest of the night. Now, with the light of day, she had been able to rest and slept now in the bedroom.

She sleeps.

Beta nodded and sat in the third chair at the table. His eyes pinched at the corners, the same nausea and pain inflicting Omega ebbing off Beta to touch both his brothers. He took one of the sanitized water bottles and drank a portion of it before leaning back in his chair.

The lights last night were a form of commemoration for the Human's uprising against the Sorracchi, and the Humans' alliance with the Umani and the Areth. It would seem she has told us the truth. The Sorracchi have been exorcised from this planet's existence and Earth is close to joining the Coalition.

Alpha shook his head and rubbed his hand over his short hair. *When we were put in those pods our captors ruled this world. We have woken in an alternative reality with no loyalty and no masters.*

How bizarre a twist of fate for this world to be governed by the one man who inspired such hatred and rage? It was an irony Omega still found too bizarre to accept.

Nothing of their creation or purpose had ever been held from them, and in equal parts, they knew they were the tools of the Sorracchi to wield power over weaker species the Sorracchi intended to overtake. Their mother creator reminded them constantly, and in many ways, how the Humans were the enemy of the Sorracchi—and her—on many levels. The two years she had been absent from their training in their youth had been a pleasant reprieve, and they knew only that she had committed a crime Warrick had deemed punishable by humiliation of the worst level for a mind such as hers. She had been forced into the guise of a Human and required to conceive and birth a Human child to continue the Sorracchi's experimentation into genetic filtering. Physical gestation was not necessary—the three of them were proof, having never grown within the womb—but Warrick had wanted to denigrate Kathleen and defile the body she had so long coveted.

The name Nicholas Tanner was like a curse to Kathleen, and the mention of it always enraged her. The only other name that could incite her in equal measure was the name of the child she was forced to birth. Michael Tanner.

They had been surprised when Katrina revealed a man named Michael Tanner had been amongst the ones who found them. Their last knowledge of Michael Tanner had been of a young man held in one of the many facilities where Kathleen oversaw research and experimentation, and her cruelty was well known.

It had been unintentional when during some of his additional training, Beta had inadvertently opened Kathleen's personal records, files not categorizing the details of an experiment, but her personal motivations and insights into the rage and psychosis behind her actions. In those files, she had raged against the boy Michael who refused to bend to her abuse, who had the audacity not to die, and who had the strength of character to remain somehow kind and compassionate despite her machinations otherwise. His refusal to be cruel seemed to anger her more than his existence. In those records, she boasted of discovering a young woman who seemed to have turned the then young man's attention. Entry after entry spoke of her plan to allow Michael to care for the girl, named only as Renae, only to plan ultimately to rip the girl away to break down Michael's resolve.

Future dated entries indicated her plan had failed. No matter what she did to the boy born from her, she couldn't destroy the character born to him despite her manipulations.

They had assumed he hadn't survived adolescence.

Someone having the same name would have been coincidental.

But to now learn the man responsible for the planet was Nicholas Tanner, the coincidence had to be discarded for ironic truth.

If what Katrina said was to be believed, he was a man to be trusted.

Simply because he was Kathleen's enemy does not make him our friend. We told her as much already.

Omega looked to Alpha, accepting his brother had come to all the same conclusions he had. He nodded and shrugged.

Nor should it exclude him as a possible ally.

CHAPTER FIFTEEN

Earth Date: 6 March 2054, Friday
Revolution Day
Smith Estate — Devon on the Hill, Callondia District
Aretu

"*P*apa!" Silas ran into the kitchen, holding a book out in front of him so John could see the cover. "Can I take this?"

John drank half his jubai juice, looking at the book over the rim of the glass. He swallowed and set the glass on the counter. "Yes. Silas, you don't need to ask me about each thing you want to take. If you can pack it, you can take it."

Silas grinned wide, ran forward, and hugged John around the waist. "Thank you, Papa." Just as quickly, he bolted from the kitchen past Jenifer, back up the stairs to his room, his feet pounding on the steps.

"We're leavin' in thirty minutes!" John called after him.

A distant "Okay" answered him.

"Are you sure we have enough room in the transport to take everything he wants?" Jenifer asked with a chuckle.

"I'm beginnin' to wonder." He smiled, then saw the single bag she

148

had set on the floor in the receiving hall behind her. She hadn't arrived on the *Steppenschraff* with anything more than Damocles and the clothing she wore, but even then, the small bag represented very little going back. "What about you?" he asked with a jut of his chin toward the bag.

She didn't look back but crossed the room to him, reached around him to pick up his half-empty glass of jubai juice and brought it to her lips, watching him over the top. John smiled and laid his hands on her hips, drawing her closer to him. She settled in the space between his spread feet, finished the juice, and set the glass where he had left it.

"I'm going to miss fresh orange juice." She licked her lips.

"Jubai juice," he corrected.

Jenifer shook her head. "That," she said, pointing at the glass, "is orange juice."

John chuckled. "Just because your people couldn't come up with a fruit name more creative than a color doesn't mean we've go' the wrong name." He took his hands from her waist to take her face in his palms, taking the moment of pleasure to rub his thumbs over her lips. Jenifer smiled and he leaned in for a kiss. She tasted sweet and tangy, and he lingered on her mouth, taking his time. He hummed and felt her smile. "You taste like jubai—"

"Orange," she whispered and nudged his chin with hers, welcoming another deep kiss.

"Greetings!" came a voice outside just before the house door opened.

"In the kitchen, Anson," John called back, and gave Jenifer one more kiss before he went to greet his estate manager. He met the older gentleman with a grip in his forearm just below his elbow, and Anson matched the hold. John slapped his other hand on Anson's shoulder. "We're just about ready to go."

"Don't you worry, John," Anson assured him, his weathered voice rough as rustling leaves. Anson Barclay had watched over the Smith estate in John's absence for nearly forty years. He looked up the front staircase leading to the upstairs hallway with crumbled plaster and pulse charge burns on the walls. "Don't you worry," he reiterated. "It'll be like nothin' at all happened here when you come home."

"Thank you, my friend."

Anson looked past John to the kitchen doorway, and a wide, honest smile spread across his weathered face. He yanked his wool plaid cap from his mostly bald head, leaving the remaining white hairs to stand on end. "It's been good to have you here, Miss Jenifer. Been nice to have a woman within these walls again. Been too long."

"Thank you, Anson."

He nodded and smiled. "The boy, too. Done my old bones good to have a young one like him to keep me on my toes."

Anson's grandsons Colwyn and Ianto came up the walkway toward the open house door, raising their hands as they approached. John returned the gesture and Anson turned to look.

"The boys come to help load the transport," Anson told John.

"No' sure we need tha' much help," John said with a chuckle.

On cue, a thumping noise at the top of the stairs had them all look. Silas was near the top of the stairs, trying to keep his balance and make it down the stairs carrying a bag as big as him, with another sack on his back. Colwyn called out for Silas to wait and bounded up the stairs to take the bag.

"I take that back," John corrected.

Colwyn came down the stairs with Silas, and he and Ianto gathered the few bags in the hallway. Anson went with them, Silas beside him, leaving Jenifer and John in the house again. He turned to ask her if she was ready and found the hall empty. John stepped into the kitchen again; empty. He crossed the hall to the front parlor where they had sat after the Xeno attack, and also found it empty. He went to the hall again and headed toward the back of the house and the various rooms branching off from the main hallway. Dens, a downstairs bedroom, a music room, a room full of things no one knew where else to put, and the library.

The library door was partially open. John pressed his hand to the heavy wood and pushed. Sunlight warmed the room from the wide, bowed window taking up much of the outside wall, a deep window seat filling the length of the space with piles of various pillows. Dust motes danced in the sunbeams and the room smelled of leather and ancient parchment.

Jenifer stood by the window, her hands tucked behind her, staring out the window into the morning sunlight. Light crystals hung in front of the glass panes, catching streams of light to cast dancing rainbows across the shelves of books.

"Those crystals come from deep in the mountains. Mountain streams carried small crystals down the rivers to settle in shallow beds," John said, crossing the room to her. His voice echoed in the large space, the ceiling two stories above them. Jenifer glanced at him but turned back to the dancing light. "It took us an entire summer, but my brother Conrad and I collected enough crystals to make our mother a light catcher."

"You made these?" she asked.

John stepped behind her and wrapped his arm around her waist to draw her back against his chest. She moved readily into his hold, her hands sliding over his arms. He took one hand away long enough to point at the most rough of the light catchers, crystals of different colors and sizes hanging from varying lengths of string.

"Just that one. The others were here before I was born. Do you like them?"

"They're beautiful."

"Jenifer," he said, leaning into her to set his lips near her ear. He kissed her lobe and tightened his hold on her. "You are welcome to take from this house anything you want. Anything."

"This is *your* home, John," she said in a voice uncharacteristically soft for Jenifer, then drew in a slow breath. "And everything in it."

"And I offer it all to you." He tightened his hold.

She only allowed him the embrace a moment before she slid his hands away and moved out of his arms. John caught her hand before she was out of reach, and she halted. He held his breath until she turned her head and looked him in the eyes. One corner of her mouth ticked up only the slightest degree.

She squeezed his hand and pulled free without saying a word.

Alone in the library, John pushed his empty hands into his pockets and sighed. She had opened herself to him more than John was sure she had ever opened to anyone, he had no doubt of that. But she still held herself apart, still guarded herself. He wondered if she would ever be fully his.

He looked up at the light catchers, remembering the distant, daydreaming way Jenifer had looked at them. She told him the nights she'd stayed apart from him she'd been here, reading, sleeping as she could. John smiled and raised his hand. The string holding the light catcher eased from the hook on which it hung, and the strands of crystals came into John's palm. He looked at the stones, remembering the summer, then folded the crystals as carefully as he could and slipped them into his pocket.

"*J*'m going to check on Ms. Jenifer," John told his son, ruffling the boy's tightly curled hair as he stood. Silas only nodded, too intent on the game he played with Aubrianna.

John crossed the audience room, decorated to appear like a casual sitting room except for the gold brocade fabrics, cream walls, and its presence on the sixth level of one of the many turrets in The People's Palace. He'd been in nearly every room of the palace at one time or another, and despite the opulence, he knew there were rooms with much more elegant grandeur. This room was sufficiently informal to allow the children to play without concern. A balcony door stood open on the other side of the room overlooking the garden on the east side of the palace.

Jenifer stood on the balcony, her hands wrapped around the glimmering railing, her head down and her eyes closed. John paused in the doorway, taking in the beauty of her against the backdrop of the royal gardens. Flowers and distant mountains held no comparison to her beauty.

The heady smell of thousands of flowers drifted in on a light, cool breeze, lifting her hair off her shoulders. She tipped her head to the sun and smiled, and the now-familiar swirl of warmth stirred in John's chest. He recognized it for what it was; more than attraction, more than a pull, it was something with too much substance and importance to be labeled with such a simple word as love.

He stepped across the balcony and wrapped his arms around her just as he had a few hours before at the house in Devon on the Hill. Jenifer leaned into him, resting her head against his chest over his heart. John rubbed his cheek against her hair and inhaled. "You're unsettled," John said and kissed her cheek. "I've felt it since we began packin'. Before that, since last night." She ran her hands over his arms and encouraged him to hold her tighter. He willingly obliged. He'd hold on forever if it meant she stayed close. "Will you tell me?"

She didn't answer right away, drawing in several long, slow breaths first. "You asked me to do something when we arrived here. Do you remember? Standing on a balcony." Jenifer turned in his arms but leaned back against the railing.

John settled his hands at her waist. "I remember. I asked you to stay, not because you were my bodyguard, or because you had to. I asked you to stay because you wanted to."

She nodded and turned her head to look over her shoulder toward the garden. Another breeze swept up and fluttered her hair around her face. "And I said I knew when we went back, you'd be going back as the Ambassador to Earth for Aretu."

"Yes, you did. Do you no' want to go back, Jenifer?"

"It's not about me." She looked back to him, squinting against the bright sunlight. "When we return to Earth, I return as your bodyguard, John."

Her expression was neutral, but despite her once foolproof ability to erect walls so thick no one got through, she couldn't keep him out. Not completely. She could buffer her emotions, but he knew her too well now to be convinced by her show of singularity. He would be willing to bet the case of casha cream he'd had packed for her if he could reach inside her right then, he would feel the tremble of her insides trying to keep her calm. John leaned closer and pulled her against him.

"Do you really think that can happen?"

A sound in the room behind him prevented her from trying to argue her point. John linked his fingers through hers, and without a word, drew her into the room where Queen Bryony and his brother Conrad waited. They had already shared a meal upon arriving at the palace, but Bryony and Conrad had excused themselves and left Aubrianna to play with Silas while they went to greet some other travelers that would be accompanying John and Jenifer back to Earth.

A man and a woman had returned with Bryony and Conrad. The man was mostly bald with skin the color of rich caramel and his hair, what he had of it wreathing his scalp, was stark white. He was a bit paunchy, and smile lines fanned out from the corners of his dark green eyes. John had seen him months before working with Victor's team, and hoped he remembered the man's name before Bryony had to introduce them.

Corbin Lordahl.

John smiled and looked to his brother, who smiled back and tipped his head. Apparently John needed to work on putting up his own walls again. Living on a world where he'd yet to meet anyone who had a Talent for mental communication, he had lost the sense of necessity to shield his thoughts and his emotions. And with Jenifer, he had intentionally allowed his buffers to fade to give her the outlet she needed.

The woman was older, her hair nearly all steel-grey and pulled into a knot at her crown, the hair thick and wavy as it rose from her brow. She had the slight thickness of age, but easily recognized sincerity and pleasantness transformed her aged face.

John stepped forward, extending his free hand while he kept hold of Jenifer's hand in the other. "Doctor Lordahl, it's good to see you again."

"You as well, Ambassador."

"And this is Doctor Olivia Cole. She is a premier specialist in—"

"Cybernetic Prosthetics and Augmentation," John finished and smiled. "I have heard about the breakthroughs you've made in the last thirty years, Doctor Cole. You were a teacher at the university when I was still studying medicine."

Doctor Cole tilted her head with a wide smile. "It's good to meet you, Ambassador. I have heard some wonderful things about your accomplishments as well. It seems we all feel we are in good company."

Stay behind, John, when the others leave. We need to speak with you.

John acknowledged his brother's request with a tilt of his chin. He caught Jenifer staring at him, and she raised an eyebrow. She hadn't shown any indication before now of being able to pick up on anyone's thoughts other than his, and only when he specifically intended to communicate with her. Her Talents had inclined toward the kinetic, though some of the most powerful kinetic abilities he'd ever seen outside of Aretu.

Did you hear that?

She looked away and crossed her arms over her chest, a self-satisfied smirk tipping her lips. *Maybe.*

He managed not to laugh, but not by much.

The conversation for the next half hour was inconsequential, small talk between a queen and her guests. John learned the purpose of Doctor Cole returning to Earth. Victor had a patient suffering from severe and almost total atrophy, as well as damage to his musculoskeletal systems resulting from abuse, possible torture, and cryostasis. Victor had contacted Doctor Cole to return to Earth and possibly help the man. Her details were limited, and she said she would be studying what Victor had provided on the trip back to Earth to at least offer thoughts for therapy. What she did speak of intrigued John and made him wonder where the man had come from. If he was found in cryostasis, the likelihood was he was some forgotten Sorracchi victim.

"Did Victor tell you how long he's been in stasis?" John asked, leaning forward with his elbows braced on his knees. Despite the morbidity of the man's situation, John couldn't deny his fascination.

"Nearly fifty of their years," she said with a touch of sad resignation. "He nearly died but was revived by a man Victor called by the name Michael Tanner."

Bryony's eyes lit up and she smiled. "Nicholas' son?"

John nodded. "There can be no other. I would be willin' to bet whatever Michael did wasn't your standard medical practice."

"What do you mean?" Doctor Cole asked.

"Michael is exceptional," John said, with a smile and a shake of his head. "I've never met anyone like him, on Aretu or anywhere else. He has Talents far exceedin' anythin' I ever thought possible in a Human." He cut his hand through the air in emphasis. "And I believe he has yet to realize his potential."

"He's Human . . . My understanding was their capacity for Talents had dwindled to little more than . . ." Doctor Cole's gray eyebrows arched high, and then she looked to Jenifer with a deep blush darkening her weathered cheeks. "I'm sorry, my dear. That probably sounded much more condescending than I intended."

Jenifer just raised her hand and dismissed Doctor Cole's apology. Before anyone said anything further, she rose from her chair and crossed the room to crouch by the children. The conversation continued, but Johns' focus was now on her. It wasn't long before she sat on the tapestry carpet with them and Aubrianna quickly scrambled to sit in her lap, as if Jenifer had been in the palace all of Aubrianna's life. Silas scooted closer too, and the three of them were soon engrossed in what might have been the most important conversation in the universe. Jenifer smiled, then laughed, and John chuckled himself, immediately clearing his throat to cover the sound.

You are lost, my brother.

John snapped his gaze to Conrad, who wore a satisfied grin. He looked back to Jenifer, who had raised her head and watched him across the room. John stared back, then offered a small smile. She smiled back and went back to focusing on the children.

Conrad was right; he truly was a lost man.

Eventually, Doctor Cole and Doctor Lordahl made their excuses and said they would see John again on the *Steppenschraff*. Although Doctor Cole called a farewell to Jenifer, she didn't rise from the floor. She probably couldn't have if she wanted, both Aubrianna and Silas either sat on or leaned against her. She drew children to her like steel to a magnet.

With the two doctors gone, Bryony closed the door and waved a hand near a camouflaged panel near the door. John looked toward Jenifer when he caught her movement in his peripheral. She kissed Aubrianna on the cheek and lifted the girl from her lap so she could stand, then walked across the room to join John and the ruling couple. A low hum began at the panel and spread out, encompassing the room; a dampener field, powerful enough to prevent any type of external eavesdropping and smother Talents used to surveil private meetings. Espionage wasn't unheard of despite the extreme, unseen security in the palace. As much as crafts like the *Steppenschraff* were designed to enhance Talents, the field did the opposite.

"Whoa . . ."

Jenifer reached him just as the field hit, and she swayed, fisting her fingers in his sleeve to keep her feet.

"It's a dampening field," he explained, wrapping his arm around her waist so he could lean close. "Give it a minute, you'll adapt."

Bryony turned from the door, her rehearsed smile she wore for visiting dignitaries and special guests now gone, replaced by a strained smile attempting to assure. "As much as I hate to see you leave, my dear John, I regret I must send you away with troubling information."

"What's wrong?" John asked.

"Coalition intelligence has intercepted several communications on the outer rim. The Urdo Khantan have formed a new alliance."

Cold dread slid through John's gut. The Urdo Khantan were warmongers, assassins, pirates, and soldiers for hire. They were a vicious race, raised from birth to be heartless killers, and had come up against the Defense Alliance several times; each time under the orders and on the payroll of a Coalition enemy.

Jenifer's hold on his arm strengthened. She had to feel his trepidation.

"It is the worst you can imagine, John," Conrad confirmed. "The Sorrs have found the most horrendous allies in the universe, next to themselves, to plan retribution against the Coalition and the Human race."

CHAPTER SIXTEEN

$\mathcal{K}$atrina ran her hand over the tight plaits she'd woven into her hair and dragged her tired body down the hall to the apartment main room. Only Beta was there to babysit her, as far as she could tell. He sat at the table, the guts and parts of what looked like an early generation PAC spread out in front of him. He looked up from his work when she stepped into the room, offered a small nod and even smaller smile, and went back to the open case.

"So, you're my elected babysitter for this afternoon?" she said, dropping into the chair beside him and hunched over in a tired, achy slump.

Three nights and one restless afternoon of sleeping on a hard, dirty floor bundled in old blankets had left her sore and stiff, and she'd give about anything for a hot shower. She was hungry, tired, and frustrated.

"I don't understand babysitter," Beta said, setting down a fine point screwdriver.

"It means you are the one the other two left in charge to make sure I don't skitter off home when you're not looking."

He tilted his head. They were so much alike, so near to identical it was a bit freaky, right down to shared body movements and facial expressions; but after three days she no longer had any problem telling them apart. They definitely were different. It was something in their eyes.

"I am here to assure your safety."

"Yeah, that's what I said." She picked up a quantum board and turned it in her fingers. "Wow, I haven't seen one of these since I was fourteen, and even then it was approaching obsolete."

"It is archaic and fundamentally flawed; however, it is possible we may be able to obtain additional information using it."

"When those were made access to the global net required accounts and passwords, but with some adaptation I can probably set it up for open access." She set her elbow on the table and rested her chin on her hand. He raised a single eyebrow. Katrina smiled and took her hand from her chin, holding it out palm up. "Let me see that processing core."

He stared at her for a few moments, then slid the processor across the table. Katrina gathered some of the old, practically inadequate tools and leaned close over the part. In the hands of anyone else, they probably *would* be inadequate, but as much as Victor had faith in his skills as a surgeon, Katrina knew exactly what she was capable of.

They settled into silence, each working on a different part of the PAC. As old as this one was, she thought it probably dated back to maybe 2020 or so when everything still processed off two distinct and very different operating systems. The OS for this device was, just as Beta said, fundamentally flawed. It couldn't even run a qubit detangling algorithm, and that particular format had been outdated at least fifteen years earlier. She might as well be working with Softech at this point.

It had been a long time since she'd worked on the innards and parts of a machine, and it felt good to dig into something so basic. She'd built a quantum quad-core system from parts she harvested from her dad's discarded units—and a few from his brand-new set up—when she was seven. It had been then her parents had recognized what they said was both her potential and her death warrant. Perhaps death had been an exaggeration, but they believed if the Sorracchi—still known as the Areth fifteen years earlier— learned of her inherent knowledge and skill she would be taken away in a heartbeat and used to the will of the aliens who had infiltrated their world.

"Don't let them know. Don't let them see. Don't look them in the eyes. Don't draw attention."

Her parents had drilled her from the age of seven until they died in the initial attacks to be invisible, to blend in and never stand out from anyone else. Don't ever seem smarter, more talented, more knowledgeable, or more attractive. The more attractive part was easy enough, no competition with anyone there, but sometimes she wanted to grab stuff right out of people's hands and show them how ignorant they were. Two years and she still had a hard time looking Victor or Michael in the eye when they asked her for her opinion.

She kept her head down but looked at Beta through her lashes. His jaw was clenched, deep lines digging into his brow. Katrina thought maybe he looked a little pale, though the light was so bad in this little cubbyhole of a hideout it was hard to tell. The circuit panel beeped, and Beta looked up, his eyebrows arched. Katrina smirked and pointed toward the power transfer cell, motioning for him to give it to her.

He did and handed her the relay cycler he'd been working on, which was good since she planned on asking for it next. Rather than continuing, Beta instead watched her with interest and handed her the parts as she needed them.

"Are you feeling okay?" she asked, angling a look at him before she tried to reroute the data store through a backup relay. He gave her the same look as he had when she called him her babysitter. "You look like you may feel ill."

"I am of sufficient health."

She didn't think it was possible for their voices to give away any *less* emotion or hint at what they thought, but apparently it was. Which made her suspect he wasn't being completely truthful. Maybe not *lying*, maybe he considered himself sufficient, but she saw easily he wasn't. She let it go and let them fall back into silence for a few minutes before she tried again.

"Omega told me you don't have names," she said as nonchalantly as she could.

He handed her a fusion coupler. "We have designations."

"Yes, he made that clear," she mumbled and sighed. "You know, having a conversation with the three of you is like . . . like trying to decipher code on one of those ancient CISC language-based computer systems they had fifty years ago. I always feel like I'm not asking the right questions. Using the wrong code."

"My brother does not answer your questions."

She wasn't sure if he asked a question or made a statement, the fluctuation of his voice was so minimal.

"He gives me that same look you do. Like the fact I ask the question I ask is so absurd you can't imagine even answering it." The board sparked and she jerked back, waved the spiral of smoke out of the way, and leaned over again.

"We don't find you absurd."

She held the coupler at an angle over the board, giving the circuits a few moments to cool before she tried again. A few moments to stare at Beta and wait for him to proceed. He looked away toward the window. The sun was very bright even for the late afternoon, and despite the fact the fire had reduced to glowing embers the apartment was comfortable.

"It is strange to us someone would ask questions such as if we have a name or if we are well. We are of no importance other than to serve at the will of the Sorracchi."

Katrina shook her head and set the coupler on the table, leaning back in her chair. "You're wrong, Beta. Maybe that was all you were to them, to the Sorracchi, to Kathleen, but you're more important than that. Not because of what you are—because, frankly, we only have a basic idea of what you may *be* or what they intended to use you for— but because you just . . . *are*."

"We are what?"

"You are alive." Katrina tried to smile, but the weight of their reality made her chest tight and her eyes burn. "Beta, we have lost so much. So many people have died at the hands of the Sorracchi, every life is precious, every person worth fighting for." She leaned across the table to lay her hand on his arm, his bicep tensing at the contact. "I swear to you, *no one* in Nicholas Tanner's administration wants to hurt you in any way. You and Omega and Alpha, you have to believe me."

He clenched his jaw and swallowed, then stood abruptly and crossed the room to the window. Katrina watched his retreating back and swallowed the thick emotion in her throat. She had hurt for them even before they woke up, but now, knowing them, she wished she knew how to make them understand they were so much more than machines in flesh and bone to be used at the will of others. To redirect her thoughts she pulled the tablet casing across the table and worked on putting the entire mechanism together. If the circuitry was salvageable, she would be able to connect to the global web.

If she could do that, she could slip in the backdoor of her own system and . . .

Her skin prickled in gooseflesh and a cold sweat skimmed across the back of her neck. She could reach Karl or Victor and tell them where she was. She could call for rescue.

Katrina looked across the room to Beta. Just as quickly as the idea came, she shoved it aside. She would go back to Alexandria, but only when they came with her. Of their own free will. She wasn't giving up.

She blinked to clear her eyes and focused again on reviving the ancient tablet. The screen fluttered and blinked like a massive Degauss, and the tablet emitted a low hum. A launch screen flickered into focus. The background image was a picture of a blond girl, maybe three, smiling wide beside a golden yellow puppy. She lay on her belly on a green grass lawn, the puppy on its back with its tongue hanging out. Katrina smiled instinctively. The icons on the screen indicated various personal-use programs—they had been called apps—from games to photo programs.

"Beta, where did you find this?"

"During exploration of this building. The unit was found on the second floor—"

"So, not in *this* apartment?" she asked, raising her head.

"No. Is there a reason you wish to know?"

"No, I—" It was hard to explain. The idea this smiling girl might be the Jessica Lynn of the forgotten room would have been too much. "I have it working. Come see."

"*Y*ou're here. Should I assume you're serious about joining us?"

Omega's attention snapped to the familiar voice from the evening before, but he kept his head down and feigned sleeping in the chair nearest the table seating area of the shelter's lobby. There were fewer people here today, likely because of the drastic change in weather. The sun was bright, the sky cloudless, and the temperature had jumped thirty degrees in twenty-four hours. Only embers burned in the fireplace, and four people ate at the tables. He predicted others would arrive later when the sun went down and the temperature dropped again.

"I almost didn't," answered Ed, his tone lacking the fluster and anger of the day before. "Going in with you might bring me more grief than I want."

A chair scraped across the floor and creaked when the Xeno recruiter sat. Omega released a long breath, focusing his senses on the two men. He couldn't look, but the men's tone and meter told him just as much.

"Regardless of what you hear from anti-Separatist propaganda, we don't force anyone to join our ranks or fight for what they believe. If you don't care enough to take up the cause, then you don't care enough, my friend."

The chair creaked again.

"Wait," Ed snapped. "I didn't say that. Sit down."

Another creak. The Xeno knew how to play the game. "What *are* you saying, Ed?"

Ed cleared his throat. "Like I said, joining up with you could bring me a lot of grief. I'm living on the streets now, but that's a hell of a lot better than in a detainment center for acts of terrorism. This administration holds little mercy for anyone they consider anti-Tanner."

"You'll keep living on the street while Nicholas Tanner holds power." The Xeno's voice dropped until it was low and harsh, his prejudice tainting his words. "He hands out just enough to say he's 'doing what he can,' but don't believe it. We have proof he has enough food, clothing, and materials stockpiled to rebuild at least a dozen cities. But he doesn't. Because holding back gives him power. Control. The Areth and the Umani are as bad as the Sorracchi ever were, and Tanner is in their back pocket."

"I get it. I'm in."

"And we will take care of you, Ed. You won't have to scrounge around for Areth and Umani scraps Tanner decides to toss your way. Hot food and a warm place to sleep every day."

"I want more than that. I want my life back."

"And you'll get it."

Chairs scraped again and Omega raised his head to watch the men cross the lobby away from him. The man he had initially identified as the Xeno shook Ed's hand before he exited into the street. Ed stood at the door for several minutes, then pushed his hands into his pockets and looked around before heading out himself. Omega rolled forward and pushed up out of the chair, clenching his teeth at the pull along his side. His wounds had flared red during the day, throwing off heat where the edges had pulled away from the metal appendages still lodged in his skin. The torn flesh when they escaped had closed and healed within hours, but with the inevitable onset of Mother's poisoning, infection had begun to set in, making the skin raw and weepy.

He had hoped to learn more from the two men, though he hadn't yet determined what he would do with whatever information he garnered. The conflicting opinions regarding Nicholas Tanner intrigued him, though he recognized the fanatical hatred he heard in both the Xeno's words and tone. The man's views were far from unbiased, but Omega recognized the positive views of the current administration weren't without their own bias.

Katrina's opinion was biased as well, but in her expression he sensed honest conviction. She believed without doubt or hesitation Nicholas Tanner was a good man who would do and had done all he could to help the devastated people of his world. He and his brothers still held judgment, but it was difficult to deny her fervor.

"Hey, friend," called Lieutenant Torres as he came down the staircase emptying into the lobby. Omega stopped and the soldier walked to him, smiling, with his hands at his waist. "Did the kids like the cookies?"

"Yes," he answered easily. It was simple to recall Katrina's smile when he'd given her the confection he'd told his brothers would be for her and her alone. "Thank you."

Torres winked and made a clicking sound in his cheek. "Kids deserve something once in a while. Why don't I put some stuff together for you?"

"I don't wish to take from those who need—"

Torres waved him off as he rounded the counter to the back. "Everyone needs. You've got to take care of your family."

To argue more might draw undue attention, and if the man believed Omega was a father caring for his family, he wouldn't suspect otherwise. Instead, Omega followed him to the counter and willingly accepted the cloth sack the man offered. "May I ask a favor?"

"Sure. What do you need?"

"Basic first aid."

Torres scowled. "Everyone okay?"

"Yes, simple abrasions."

Just as quickly the man smiled. "Little boys, right? Always falling down or roughhousing."

He wasn't sure what roughhousing was, or whether it was an activity only young boys were prone to but nodded in agreement. Torres reached beneath the counter and withdrew a small canvas zipped pouch, dropping it into the sack. His unhindered willingness to provide assistance caused a pang in Omega's chest, the same type of pang he had felt when he took Katrina into the cold night. He struggled to categorize and recognize the physical reactions to his thoughts and intended to ask Katrina when he returned what this feeling might be.

A sudden wave of gut-twisting pain clenched his insides and he bent forward, gripping the counter. A low, strangled grunt curled in his throat before he was able to silence it. He braced himself for the instant punishment his logical mind knew wouldn't come. She wasn't here to dole out her lessons against showing weakness.

"Hey, you okay?" Torres asked, already at Omega's side, his hand on Omega's shoulder.

Omega clenched his jaw and swallowed, managing only to nod. He forced himself to stand upright, ignoring the wave of pain lancing up his spine. Torres scowled, studying him, seeming to wait until Omega could prove he was able to stand and leave on his own. Focusing all his attention on each simple movement, Omega retrieved the bag and held it in a tight fist grip at his side.

"I am fine," he answered, the act of speaking a strain on his restricted throat. He squared his shoulders and exhaled. "I appreciate your concern."

Torres still scowled and nodded, a single jerk of his head. "We've got a doc coming by here tomorrow. If you're still sick, or in pain or whatever, come back. They'll check you out. Okay?"

Unable to trust his voice again, he acknowledged the offer with a nod and walked with stiff steps to the door. The air outside had turned slightly while he was in the shelter, a bit cooler, and the sun had begun to set. The bracing air revived him a little and let him stand straighter.

He headed up the hill toward the condemned building where he had left Beta and Katrina. The effort to stretch his legs to stride up the incline made his thighs burn. The poison, once released, worked with powerful efficiency. He paused at the corner past the shelter, a street branching off to his left, and braced himself against the building with a flat palm. As he gathered his strength, he caught the muffled echo of voices a few feet away around the corner. He drew in a deep breath and focused his senses.

"We got 'im?"

"Like a lamb to slaughter," said the familiar Xeno voice. "He's ready to throw all in. He'll do whatever we tell him if we give him a soft bed and warm food."

The new voice chuckled. "So, when Tanner goes down his assassination is pegged on a zealot with no known connection to us."

The voices faded as they walked away from him. Omega clenched his jaw, anger rolling in his chest. Since his first day of self-awareness at a few months old, when he and his brothers were brought to consciousness and inducted into their training, Omega had been trained to be the very same deceivers as these men, manipulating and bending those unaware of the truth to accomplish whatever goal the Triadic had to accomplish. They had been trained loyalty by punishment, and knowledge by download. Every element of their existence had been twisted and formed to become machines void of free will, void of conscience, void of opinion.

Triadic.

The designation felt foreign, but the intent felt too real in the words and actions of these Xenos. Perhaps it was the comparison that angered him most.

He pushed away from the wall and steeled himself to make the climb up the hill. After soaking in the darkness of these Humans, he looked forward to the lightness Katrina drew from his chest when he saw her smile.

Omega stopped and tilted his head.

And realized he also smiled.

CHAPTER SEVENTEEN

7 MARCH 2054, SATURDAY
SQUATTER DISTRICT
FALLS CHURCH, SEAT OF VIRGINIA
NORTH AMERICAN CONTINENT

17 June 2022

In spite of the extensive cleaning and genetic handling genoma to propagate desirable characteristics, Triadic began to expose the emotional tendencies. During the exercises of formation, second of three down. Instead of continuing the formation both first and all break to help. All of they were punished for second of three down and his drawback what break imposed without permission. This will be be an opportunity to examine the function of cure [no translation—morphology indicates plural noun]. Working correctly, all the broken bones will be going to increase them inside two days. Triadic progress will be carefully monitored in the future to guarantee what about emotional weakness it is not allowed. The creation of Triadic by six years, they should have been taught well at the moment against emotional Human basic answers.

3 October 2022

Mental perceptiveness began to manifest exceptionally well between Triadic. They are carrying out, agile, and that an only one unification collective. Next we strictly control process begins them to me to expand in the power that they will be going to practice. We begin the second phase of the quick growth; more weak Human organs it took three years to be recovered of the first phase. When manipulating the Triadic accomplish functional level, physical development accelerate caused what we suppose to be painful faults in skeletal system; however, they quickly learnt the pain it is not an option and it must be ignored or face the reality of bigger pain.

17 January 2023

We have been introducing Triadic neural connection with [no translation— morphology indicates plural noun, possible mechanical or technical origin] control. Initial tests show positives transmission [no translation—morphology indicates possible plural noun, possible mechanical or technical origin] incorporated in systems. [no translation—morphology indicates plural noun, possible mechanical or technical origin] helped continuously in the aging, development, cure and the process of formation, and be going to act as an indicative controls emotional deficiency it keeps on being a problem. Also it was necessary to contain joined curiosity. First presented questions of his instructor in his creation. [No translation—morphology and syntax indicate proper name] granted information of mortal mistake describing Triadic formed of biological resources for creation was gathered in the husk I am joined. He was killed by his stupidity, with no transfer of conscience. It is a pity as he educated with a hand heavy and when strong physical discipline was maintained, his mouth was the problem.

28 January 2023

[No translation – morphology and syntax indicate proper name] is without satisfaction by the progresses by the Triadic, specifically with those insistence continued to question origin and intent. We begin the handling of the wave of sleep to manipulate standards of thought when in way of hibernation. While

[without translation-morphology and syntax to indicate his name] and I to have convinced [No translation – morphology and syntax indicate proper name] to maintain the program, he warned, he is going to see an improvement accented in the general performance Triadic, or he is going to begin a new study. This is hypothetical, though with facts without determinable date, synthetic gestation and quick growth can have compromised the program. Second phase will wrap a study in the long term, raising a soldier by way through Human gestation and the natural development, in spite of genetic handling it will be wrapped so much they highlight and repress the wanted results. One is not known to mean [No translation – morphology and syntax indicate proper name] intends to begin this new phase.

Trying to further decipher the choppy, sideways translated journal entries made Katrina's head hurt, and every time she heard a sound somewhere in the apartment she tensed, afraid one of them would find her and discover she'd accessed her files through the back alley system. It had taken her most of the day working on the archaic system, but she'd finally gotten a look at the decryption files she'd left running.

Sorracchi was a difficult language to translate via program, and it had taken a staff of six linguists three months to create the program she used to translate the data files. If there hadn't been so much she might have tried doing it herself, but time and mass quantity had prevented it. Now, she was stuck with these less-than-eloquent renditions of Kathleen's journals.

Even broken and faulty, the entries gave her chills and a tight knot in her stomach.

Each one documented a progression of development, and Kathleen's growing dissatisfaction with the Triadic, purely because they exhibited concern for one another. If Katrina read it correctly, which was a challenge, the first entry told of the three of them in training and one of them—Beta, she believed—stumbled and fell. Alpha and Omega stopped to help him, and for that act of Human emotion, they were all punished.

Punished for helping a fallen brother.

If she didn't want them to hold regard for each other, why use brothers?

The second translation seemed to indicate the entrance into a new phase of their development. The data implied they appeared much older than they were, excluding the fact they had been in stasis for several years. Their first phase of development had accelerated their aging until they were probably old enough to learn, to function physically, but young enough and small enough to be controlled. The image of young light haired, hazel eyed children being beaten and abused into submission played in her head like a horror film, she wanted to look away but couldn't. Part of her hoped she misunderstood the entries because of the rough translation, but her gut told her she wasn't wrong. Whatever Kathleen had done to first accelerate, then halt, then accelerate their growth was painful for them. Of course it would be, she didn't need to be a doctor to know as much. Children who grew too quickly, even naturally, experienced pain throughout their musculoskeletal system.

The cold detachment of the entries may have been a result of the translation program, but she doubted it. A Sorracchi was executed for apparently telling Alpha of their biological parentage. She knew now that a Sorracchi female contributor had been their mother, biologically at least. Her stolen body had provided the maternal DNA to create them, but who had been the paternal contributor? Another husk stolen to host a Sorracchi? Where else could they find a willing participant? Katrina, and anyone close at all to the Tanner family, knew Nicholas Tanner had been deceived by Kathleen and had thought his "wife" and child dead. Perhaps Nicholas Tanner wasn't the first to be fooled? Or maybe all contributing factors had been gathered from Sorracchi husks for use by Kathleen.

She jumped at a sound in the hall and quickly tapped in the command to close down the translation file and shut the door of the program to hide her access. The screen flipped to a news channel, the image placeholder an archive photo of President Tanner shortly after accepting the emergency presidency several months earlier. She engaged the video, knowing it would take several minutes to load on the archaic machine.

The door opened and Omega stepped into the room, looking side to side.

"I'm over here," she said loud enough he could hear and spot her tucked against the wall.

The deep dig centered on his brow eased when he saw her, and he strode across the wood floor, his shoes creating a hollow thud in the bare room. When he reached her, he dropped to a crouch in front of her knees, his feet on either side of hers, a wrapped sandwich in his hand. Despite herself, her stomach growled. Omega smiled, just a tip of one corner of his lips, and held out the sandwich.

Katrina set the tablet aside, Omega's gaze following it, and took the sandwich. It was a simple cheese sandwich, but the cheese was sliced thick and butter moistened the bread. She hadn't had a simple cheese sandwich since she was little. Taking a bite of one half, she held out the other half to Omega. He hesitated.

"It's okay," she said around the sandwich in her cheek. "I don't mind sharing."

Omega took the sandwich but shifted to be beside her and sat with his back to the wall. "Thank you."

She noted the twinge and pinch at the corners of his eyes, and just as quickly the wince passed. He settled beside her with his legs bent, his forearms resting across his raised knees. With one bite, he took out nearly a third of the sandwich portion. Katrina smiled and chuckled.

"Something amuses you." As usual, his tone lacked the inflection of a question.

Katrina shrugged. "Sort of. You remind me of my brother Karl when he eats. He's like a bottomless pit."

He looked away, studying the half-sandwich between his fingers. "You speak of your brother with affection, although often the things you speak of seem points of frustration to you."

Katrina shrugged and pulled her next bite off the sandwich. "I don't think there has ever been anyone in my life who frustrates me more than Karl." *More than you.* She stomped down the response. "Sometimes I think he does things *just* to frustrate me." She chuckled and looked toward Omega, who now watched her. The studying scrutiny made her pause. She took a slow breath before going on. "But, other than my parents I know no one has ever loved me as much as Karl." The words caught in her throat and she had to look away.

She took the last bite of the sandwich and chewed slowly, hoping the act of eating would push down the lump of emotion. Each finished their sandwiches in silence. Once she choked it down she lowered her knees to sit cross-legged, her leg bumping his.

His head was bowed, his gaze cast down. Then he raised his chin and looked to her. "I have no concept of family." His tone was unsure, more so than she was accustomed to hearing from him.

Katrina smiled, hoping the bloom of sadness in her chest didn't show in her eyes. "Of course you do. You have two brothers, Omega." The scowl between his eyes deepened. Impulse made her reach for his hand and lace her fingers through his, leaning toward him until their shoulders touched. Omega stared at their hands, his fingers stiff between hers; then he turned their joined hands so her hand was on top, parallel to the floor. Slowly, he curled his fingers to hold her hand, her puny one lost in his hold.

Her pulse jumped and heat infused her neck and cheeks.

"Is that a family?" he asked, focused on their hands.

She had to blink fast to clear her thoughts but squeezed back against his gentle hold. "It's more than some people ever have."

He slid his other palm across the back of her hand, sandwiching it between both of his. His skin was warm, but rough, calloused, strong. Katrina scooted closer until she could rest her cheek against his shoulder.

"My grandfather was in the British Armed Forces," she said, watching his apparent fascination with their handhold. "He and my great uncle served together in Afghanistan in twenty-ten. Do you know about Earth history?"

"No," he answered simply.

"It's way too much to explain, let's just leave it we were in a war on a continent on the other side of the ocean from here. They were holed up, taking gunfire, with half a dozen other soldiers. An American extraction team was on its way to get them out—" He looked up, his brief look of confusion making her pause. "This continent was once called the United States of America. They were allies with the British

Armed Forces." He nodded and she continued. "They heard the choppers coming in and moved to get out. My Great Uncle Casper was hit on the way out. A bullet in the back." Katrina swallowed, the familiar emotion of the family story catching her, mostly because her heart ached at the reality she'd never hear her grandfather tell the story again. "My grandfather went back for him, picked his brother up, and ran for the extraction team. But he took a bullet in the thigh twenty feet from the chopper. He fell to his knees, but never dropped his brother. Two other soldiers had to jump from the chopper and get them, helping them both. The Allied hospital was twenty minutes away, and Grandpa held his brother's hand the whole flight. He wouldn't leave Uncle Casper's side until he passed out from hemorrhagic shock. The two of them woke up two days later in adjacent beds."

Katrina rubbed her cheek against his sweater to clear a tear before it dripped off her face and sniffed. Omega didn't say anything, just watched her the way he always did. She cleared her throat and turned away enough to look toward the fire and the fireplace.

"When I was little I asked my grandpa why he wouldn't leave Uncle Casper when they made it to the hospital. They were safe, after all. He said . . ." She tried to deepen her voice to mimic her grandfather, but her throat had roughed with the story and she couldn't quite pull it off. "'He was my brother, poppet.' It was years before I understood."

"What made you understand?"

His question startled her and she looked back to him. He already understood, she saw it in the tension around his mouth and the dig between his eyebrows.

"My brother Karl," she said, shrugging one shoulder. "Our parents died during the first Sorracchi attacks; not the first day, but later when we thought we were safe. Since that day Karl has taken care of me. He brought us to Alexandria, he found a way to join the rebellion, and we have been part of the rebuilding efforts since then. He watches out for me, even though he gives me a hard time." She chuckled with a smile. "I would do anything for Karl, and I know he would do anything for me."

He nodded and looked to their hands again. Katrina watched him for a few moments. He didn't seem to mind she watched him.

"My grandfather's name was Phineas, but he went by Phin." Katrina settled against his shoulder again, her hair brushing his ear. She tipped her head back. Her breath caught when he dipped his head toward her, bringing his nose within inches of hers. She had to work her tongue to try to swallow, her throat suddenly too dry to speak clearly. "Would you let me call you Phin?"

She thought maybe, just maybe, his lips ticked up in a small smile. "You find names to be very important."

"You deserve a name." She smiled back at him. This close, she could differentiate the small flecks of gold in his eyes. "And I think you and my grandfather are very much alike."

She held her breath, hoping he would understand. Hoping he would accept. It was an odd request, she knew, but despite the way she had come to be with them, she couldn't deny she saw the desire in them to be more than they had been created to be. For that, they deserved more than just designations.

He nodded and smiled, the expression still small, hesitant. Like he didn't quite know he was doing it. "I accept the name you have chosen."

Katrina smiled wide, the acceptance of the name pleasing her much more than she expected. "Thank you."

"Shouldn't I thank you?"

She shrugged. "You might not want to thank me when someone finds out your name is Phineas. It's not exactly a common name, but I think it's regal and ancient and important." She shifted her gaze toward the door, but didn't change her position, didn't move away from him. "All three of you deserve names."

"You should choose them."

She looked to Omega—Phin—again. His expression was softer, the v-dig between his eyes gone. "Do you think your brothers will allow—"

"The Phoenix is an immortal creature, unique, the only one of its kind. Legend says—"

Katrina startled and let go of his hands to twist and snatch the tablet off the floor, tapping the pause button on the video she had left to load.

"What is that?" Phin asked, reaching for the tablet.

Katrina turned back, holding the tablet out to him. "I was able to access some news files and records. I thought maybe if you and the others see some of our history it might help." She held it between them so she could identify the people on the screen. "This is a speech President Tanner gave shortly after taking the presidency. That's him at the podium, and his wife behind him there." She pointed but didn't touch, not wanting to initiate the video again. "Seated there is Michael, his son. Standing beside him is Jackie Anderson, she's Michael's . . . well, I don't know what they call each other, but the baby she's holding is Nicole. She and Michael adopted her." She pointed to the area to President Tanner's right. "That woman there is Beverly Surimoto. She's the vice president. And the man beside her is Victor. He's her husband, but he doesn't use a last name. He used to be a host to a Sorracchi consciousness but was emancipated just before the war." Phin's gaze cut to her when she mentioned Victor's emancipation. "He is a doctor and heads the team I work on. He's one of the men who worked on helping you before— Would you like to watch it?"

Phin took the tablet and held it in his palms, scowling deeply as he studied the still image of Nicholas Tanner standing behind a wooden podium. He looked tired, worn. This had only been a couple of weeks since Michael had woken from his coma. The world had only begun to realize the extent of the damage the Sorracchi had rained down on mankind, how many had died, how much destruction left behind.

"Why is Michael Tanner seated when all others stand?"

"He was hurt," she explained, waiting until Phin looked at her again. "He was recaptured by Kathleen before the final war, and his father had rescued him. She tortured him; he died twice but the Areth doctors brought him back." Phin looked back to the tablet, the dig between his eyes deeper than ever.

"You've been trained to read body language, right?" she asked.

Phin looked to her. "Body language?"

"Watch how people act, how they speak, their voice inflections, to determine their intent. I would imagine that would be important if . . ." She trailed off before she said more than she wanted. He nodded. "Watch President Tanner and decide what you think." He nodded

176

again and looked back to the screen. She reached across to restart the video.

"—that at the end of its life, the Phoenix builds a funeral pyre, dying in the flames. From the ashes of the fire, the Phoenix rises and begins its life again. Reborn." President Tanner turned his head slightly to look behind him to where Michael sat.

"My son..." He stopped, visibly struggling to swallow after his voice cracked, diverting his eyes again for a moment. Then he canted his head and seemed to find an inner strength. "My *son* told me this story after my return from Raxo and Aretu. I wonder if, fifty-odd years ago, the founders of Phoenix had any idea how appropriate the name would eventually be."

President Tanner braced his hands on either side of the podium and looked out over the small gathering of citizens. "We've been through hell, and we've thrown ourselves into the flames, and now it's time to dig ourselves out and get on with the job of rebuilding our world. There's no point in pointing fingers and playing the blame game. What's done is done, and what is—is."

He straightened, taking his hands from their perch on the lectern, tapping long fingers in front of him. "The Earth is in bad shape. That's probably not the way my official speechwriter would want me to lay things out, but there it is. Our population is twenty percent of what it was two years ago, but we're still here. Our environment has been damaged, but not irreparably. We're battered and bruised, but we're not defeated. Not by a long shot. I'd rather have the crap beaten out of me and live to fight another day, than be a slave or lab rat."

The crowd broke into applause and President Tanner looked down until they quieted again. When he raised his head, his features had tightened, strained and tense. He stood straight and tall, shoulders squared, and his voice held no waver. "This government is new, and we're still working out the kinks, but we've got a plan. No one wants to see this planet return to the fractured and divided way it was before the Sorracchi came. Maybe that's the one good thing that has come from this. We are unified. We are one. Together we stand. Together we kick ass."

He smirked; an expression Katrina recognized. The crowd

applauded again, with whoops and hollers. He did smile, slightly, and leaned forward. "My speechwriter just had another heart attack."

He waited again until the crowd quieted, the smile still present but without mirth. He looked out over the crowd, then to the sky, and back. "I know the biggest question on everyone's mind is, what are we going to do with the Sorracchi. They have been confined, and as I write this, we are working with Areth scientists to divide the Sorracchi identities from their Human hosts only when we believe there's a chance of separation. The success rate sucks, but even if we only free a handful of Human minds, that's better than what we had." Only because Katrina knew Victor, and knew his friendship with Victor, did she notice his quick glance toward Victor and Beverly. His emancipation was not public knowledge, but those within and affiliated with the administration knew. "These newly liberated Humans have to adjust to a world they don't know, and deal with thousands of years of memories that aren't theirs. Let's remember that these new citizens had nothing to do with their capture, their possession, or the acts committed by their hands. They are not the bad guys."

A solemn silence replaced the cheers and shouts of the crowd.

"As I said before, our government is new. We are working on a model that will give each major population a voice. Each continent will have two representatives who will sit in counsel for the people they serve. From each continent, a panel of judicial representatives will be selected to help maintain and create law to keep our new world civil. We have formed an Executive Council similar to the previous government; with a president, vice president and a pyramid of leaders who will provide guidance and a balanced power. This time around, all the representatives and council members, including myself, have been selected through emergency elections. This is just to get us off the ground. Next time, the choice will be yours. Every Human will have a vote."

Cheers again. This time, the crowd began chanting "Zeus! Zeus! Zeus!"

Phin looked to Katrina. "Zeus?"

"It was his call sign when he was in Earth Force." He still looked confused. "He was a pilot. He flew gliders, and he was one of the best. Pilots have nicknames, call signs, and his was Zeus."

Phin nodded, but she wasn't convinced he understood. President Tanner's voice broke through the crowd noise. "Queen Bryony the Fourteenth of Aretu, and the Council of Seven of Raxo have promised aid and support until we are on our feet again. Before anyone worries that we'll have a repeat performance, just know we're going into this with our eyes wide open. We are making it clear that while their help is appreciated, Earth belongs to us." Cheers. "No shared government. No shared powers."

The screen scrambled and the video paused, freezing in still frame.

"I was afraid I wouldn't be able to access the whole video," Katrina grumbled, taking back the tablet. She shifted to press her back firmly to the wall before attempting to reload the video.

Phin leaned closer, watching her. "Beta told me you fixed the device. He—"

"Daniel," she blurted, her head coming up on its own. Phin stared, and she smiled. "His name is Daniel."

He nodded, a slow dip of his chin. "Daniel was pleased with your skill."

She grinned. "Thanks." Then went back to work.

After a few moments, Phin asked, "What will Alpha's name be?"

Katrina looked up and pulled a face. "Hmmmm . . . I don't know yet. But, when I *know*, I'll tell you."

CHAPTER EIGHTEEN

8 March 2054, Sunday
Squatter District
Falls Church, Seat of Virginia
North American Continent

You cannot go to the shelter, Phineas. You are too weak, and if you continue your wounds will open again. At the least, your condition will draw unwanted attention when your intent is to remain inconspicuous.

Phin winced against the pull and burn along his sides, using the mantel of the main room fireplace to keep himself upright. He glared at Beta—Daniel, now, since he had also accepted Katrina's name—and swallowed against the nausea rolling in his gut. Perspiration made his neck itch and his sweater stick tacky to his back.

I am no worse than you or Alpha.

Daniel tilted his head and raised a single eyebrow, a new expression he had developed in the last day. *Brother, you are by far the worst of us.* His smile held a distinct and uncharacteristic glint of humor. *I am unsure whether I should pity you or envy you.*

Alpha strode across the room to the table, taking up one of the bottles they had refilled with water purified with the tablets provided by the shelter, his irritation and annoyance a tangible buffer around him. His commands rolled over their thoughts powerful enough to silence them in the space their thoughts shared.

Beta will go to the shelter in your stead and listen for further information —

She has named me Daniel. He smiled, despite Alpha's deep scowl.

It is unlikely the Humans will notice it isn't you.

"You use Human as if it is something foreign, so different from who we are," Phin forced through clenched teeth, a chill ratcheting up his spine.

Alpha slammed the open bottle down on the table, some of it spilling out the top and over his hand. He stomped across the room in three long strides, stopping short beside Phin. "You are as much an alien to them as they are to us."

"Only because you demand we keep ourselves separate."

I will not revisit this discussion. Once we determine a way to be rid of —

"I caution you to choose your words wisely, brother."

"And I caution you to choose your allegiance wisely, brother."

"My *allegiance* is not in question."

Alpha, Phineas weakens with this confrontation. Please allow him to rest.

Daniel's voice of reason went completely ignored. "Remove the blinders you have allowed Katrina Bauer to strap to you, *Omega,* and realize she has compromised your mind. Your perception is twisted. She poisons you. She poisons all of us."

Phin stood straight despite the pain and faced his brother. "I accept Katrina has *changed* me, and I willingly accept that change; however, brother, you are as much a fool as you accuse me of being if you cannot see we *all* have been compromised by Katrina."

"She has compromised *us,* Omega." Alpha clenched his jaw, sucking in sharp, deep breaths and despite his efforts at buffering his pain, Phin felt it twist at his brother. "Since the day of our creation we have functioned as a unit."

"Is your issue with our differing opinions, or with the fact I am not blindly following behind you into our deaths because you will not consider another alternative?"

"The weight of decision is mine!"

"No! The decision has been and always will be *ours*."

"*Enough*," Daniel hissed out, looking toward the hallway. "Arguing will not resolve this."

"Nor will ignoring reality—" Alpha snapped.

"I agree," Phin cut him off. He looked to Daniel, purposefully away from Alpha. "It would seem the argument is our definition of reality. Alpha would have us hide in this prison of our own making and die slow, painful deaths rather than—"

"Rather than lead us into the shackles of a new slave master!"

"You know as well as I there is no prison on this planet capable of holding us once our strength is regained," Phin said, dropping his voice. "The only surety we face is death if we remain hidden like spiders in a hole."

"Enough!"

"I will not stay silent on this!"

Their voices echoed in the empty apartment, bouncing back to them off the old, crumbling walls. There was no doubt by now Katrina had heard the arguing, but she hadn't appeared from the bedroom down the hall.

Alpha clamped shut his jaw with a crack of teeth, and sucked in several deep, harsh breaths before he turned sharply and went to the door, exiting the apartment with a loud thunk. With him left the palpable tension, and Phin swayed at the lack of it. Daniel came to his side and helped him to the ratty couch facing the fireplace. One cushion was missing, the other a home for previous four-legged residents, but Phin needed to sit before his legs forced the issue.

"Alpha is right on one thing," Daniel said once Phin sat. "We have never fought amongst ourselves. Though we have not always agreed completely, we have never had this level of dissent."

"Do you believe Katrina is the cause?" Phin hunched forward and pressed his hand to his side, heat emanating through his sweater.

"Perhaps not the cause, but her presence is not without effect."

"The intent was never to keep her here indefinitely."

"No, but our intentions were based on little more than the need to escape with neither knowledge nor understanding of our situation."

Phin raised his head and looked at his brother. It was appropriate Katrina had given him a new name because his brother had changed. Just as Phin told Alpha, they had all changed—they had all been changed—by the presence of Katrina Bauer.

"This is a different place," Phin said through deep breaths to push aside the pain. "We are different than we have ever been. We are doing the one thing she didn't want; we are evolving. Even in our arguments we are more. We have our own minds, our own thoughts—"

"Our own varying emotions."

Phin shifted his eyes to look to his brother. Daniel tilted his head and shrugged one shoulder before standing from his crouch. "I will return within two hours." He picked up one of the cloth sacks Phin had brought back previously from the shelter and went to the door leading into the hallway. He paused with his hand on the knob to look back at Phin before closing the door.

As soon as the mechanism clicked, a tight groan forced its way from his throat despite his weak attempt at silencing it. He slid his hand beneath his sweater to the burning circle of flesh along his ribs. The skin was hot and slick, and clear liquid tinged with blood coated his fingertips when he withdrew his hand.

The very technology intended to empower them and elevate them physically above their enemies was now the instigator of their destruction.

Summoning his reserve of strength, he pushed up to his feet and staggered toward the table and the basic first aid kit he'd brought from the shelter. His skin pulled painfully as he dragged his sweater over his head and he swayed to keep his balance, dropping the garment on the closest chair. He raised his right arm, put his hand behind his head, and tried to twist enough to see the source of the radiating heat.

They had been fused to their pods with appendages and cables used to regulate and maintain their systems while in stasis, but when they woke and removed themselves from the pod they had been forced to yank the connections free leaving behind the metal interfaces. His skin had healed over the edges of the metal within a couple hours of their departure, the process accelerated by the microscopic yet powerful technology infused into their physiology.

Now, the same technology served its second purpose: punishment. Their creator made sure they understood what she had done when she modified their cybernetic functions, and the extent of their punishment should they continue to defy her. What gave them strength, would steal it. What healed their bodies, would turn against them. What maintained their life would now end it.

Only she could stop it.

And she was not here.

His skin was swollen around the plates and bright red. Clear fluid, his body's natural defense against the infection, mixed with the slow weep of blood. With each shift, the skin pulled and puckered, stinging pain radiating from the bond of skin to metal.

"What happened?"

He instinctively twisted toward Katrina's startled voice, the movement searing pain along his side with such vicious efficiency he swayed and reached for the table to stay upright. Katrina's small hands supported him and she slid her body between him and the table, holding him up. It only took a moment for him to push past the wave of pain and nausea and he straightened.

"Phin, answer me." Her delicate fingers skimmed his skin, soothing despite the sparking of his nerves like ignited hydrogen sulfate. She pressed her palm flat to his stomach. His abdominal muscles tightened beneath the touch. "You were healed. I saw . . ."

Warmth infused him, a different heat than the infectious fever, and far more appealing. It was nearly enough to negate the stab of pain at the base of his skull. Phin managed to swallow his groan before answering.

"The infection was inevitable. It was no more than a matter of time."

She raised her chin to look at him, a deep line of concern furrowing her pale forehead, and laid her hand against his forehead, then cheek. "You're burning up." Katrina turned away and rummaged through the pile of first aid supplies, tossing everything back in a pile. "There is *nothing* here for fever or even an antibiotic. What kind of first aid kit doesn't have an analgesic at least?"

He wasn't sure she intended the question for him, nor if she expected an answer from him and since he had no adequate answer, he remained silent. She huffed and went back to picking up supplies, holding them to her chest. With her free hand, she took his and slid her fingers between his just as she had the day before, and the same sensation danced up his arm as it had then. Their education had included an understanding of the basest of Human biology, sexuality, and the Human drive; a vulgar and primitive need Humans had no control over, pushing them to violence even to the point of murder and destruction.

How could this warm sensation, this desire to bring Katrina close and seek contact with her, no matter how simple, be the sordid and obscene and malicious evil embedded in the core of Human existence she wanted to suppress and punish?

"This kit is pathetic, but I'll do what I can." She walked away, tugging him along with her. Phin fell in step behind her, following her down the hall to the room she used as her bedroom.

None of them had slept since freeing themselves from the pods, their enhanced physiology capable of going several days without sleep, but at the sight of blankets gathered to form her pallet a wave of fatigue hit him, nearly making him stagger.

"I can clean and dress the wounds, but I think it'll be easier if you're lying down."

"I am capable of treating the wounds—"

"You probably think so," she said, reaching up to put her hands on his shoulder, pushing gently to urge him toward the bed. "Doesn't mean I'm going to let you."

He lowered himself to the blankets, his skin pulling painfully. A warm trail of blood ran from the plate closest to his heart. Before the fluid could drip to the blankets Katrina scrambled to press a gauze square to his skin. Lying down seemed to magnify his fatigue, his limbs suddenly heavy. Nearly as heavy as his eyelids. He tried to fight the weight of sleep, but the cushion of the blankets, the warmth of the fire, and Katrina's presence beside him was too soothing. He gave in to the slow slide toward rest.

"I don't think I've ever met anyone as stubborn as you. Except maybe Alpha," she mumbled, more to herself than to Phin, as she tore open more gauze packages.

The strain in her voice, and the soft sound of a sniff forced him to open his eyes. Katrina focused on the packaging in her trembling fingers. Heaviness filled his chest, and a tightness in his throat, another in a daily stream of sensations and emotions he could only experience but not name. He only knew he didn't like this feeling, not only because the burning in his veins amped up at its presence, but because he understood this reaction was born by the distress he sensed in her. He wanted it to stop, not his discomfort but hers. Phin lifted his hand from the blankets to lay it on her leg. Her head jerked up, a tear sliding down her cheek from glistening eyes.

"Why do you weep?" he asked.

She looked away again and swiped the back of her hand across her wet cheek. "Because I'm scared."

"You have nothing to fear from us, Katrina—"

"Not from you, you dolt," she cut him off, wiping at her cheeks again. "*For* you." She scooted back and scrambled to her feet, stepping over him to head for the door. "I have an idea about how to cleanse those wounds. I'll be right back."

He intended to remain awake until she returned to ask her to explain, but the need for sleep overpowered his need to understand.

atrina used the water purifying tablets in some of the already purified water to create what she hoped would be a sanitizing wash for his wounds. In the short time it took for her to go to the main room and collect the tablets and water and return to the bedroom Phin had slipped into sleep. It might have been better that way. She wasn't sure she would have been able to take seeing him in more pain when she washed the wounds. The red, weeping edges bubbled when the water made contact, at least confirming for her the water did what she hoped, but no doubt would have hurt had he been awake.

As it was, he barely flinched in his sleep.

Katrina cleansed the wounds along his side and above his heart near his clavicle, then treated the wounds with the miniscule supply of antibiotic creams and bandaged them as best she could. Phin never stirred. Once she'd done as much as she could, she stoked the fire to keep away the chill, especially since he still wore no shirt, and settled beside him to wait for him either to awake or for one of his brothers to come back.

Darkness had begun to settle outside before she heard the outer door and heavy footsteps carrying down the hall. A moment of panic hit her at the thought it might not be Daniel or Alpha, but the steps were too sure, too confident in their destination to be anyone other than a brother. She sat at Phin's side, between him and the fire, her back to his feet so she could watch him sleep. When the bedroom door eased open, she drew up her knees and looked to whoever had come in. He was halfway across the room before he reached the light from the fire and she saw it was Alpha. His brow pulled low over his eyes and he looked from her to Phin.

"He was bleeding," she said, barely able to force the sound from her throat. "He's running a fever. There was nothing in the medical kit for infection or fever." Her voice faltered and she paused long enough to swallow. "I did what I could, but I don't think it will be enough."

"How long has he slept?" Gideon asked.

As simple as that, she knew his name.

Katrina shook her head and looked at Phin. "I don't know how long it's been. Since just a little bit after you and Daniel left." She looked up again. "I went out after the shouting stopped, and he was trying to bandage the wounds."

Gideon came to Phin's side and crouched, the light from the fire casting distinct shadows across his concerned face. He touched Phin's forehead, his scowl deepening, then touched the edges of the bandages she'd applied. Katrina watched him, the clear and undeniable distress in his eyes, as he tended to his brother.

"Why is he so sick, Gideon?"

His gaze shifted to her. "So, you have decided to gift me with a name as well?"

"No," she said, softer. "I just realized the name. I didn't want to give you a name that wasn't right." He didn't say anything, so she asked again, "Why is he so sick?"

"He leads the way for all three of us. Given time."

Katrina clenched her jaw, fighting back a sharp retort. An answer that had nothing to do with the question wasn't an answer. She tried a different approach, wondering if he would answer more truthfully if he knew she would understand. "Okay, let's try this. What did she do to you to make you this sick? I know she did it, I read some of her journals."

"Did she not say?"

Katrina shrugged and shook her head. "Our translator programs are rough, and I haven't read the original in Sorracchi. I will . . ." She made sure to wait until he looked her in the eyes. " . . .when we go back. Or, you can just tell me."

Gideon sat, matching her position on the other side of his sleeping brother. She waited for him to speak, watching until she saw the shift in resolve. For a moment, she let the bloom of hope ease her.

"I do not know the word in your language for the technology she used, only what it is and what it does."

"Can you write it? In Sorracchi?" He scowled and she huffed. "I have no ear for Sorracchi. I can't talk it. I can barely understand when someone speaks it. But if I see it, I can understand. It's like code, and I understand code."

When he didn't argue, she reached for the tablet she'd left on the floor. It took a few moments for it to power on, the ancient workings barely able to keep up with the simplest of commands. She hadn't managed to get back into her system since the day before, the demand just too high. She opened a simple tablet program and held it out for him. Gideon stared at her for a few moments before settling the tablet in his right palm. He was left-handed, something she hadn't noticed with any of them. Then again, none of them had written anything for her. With his finger, he wrote on the screen a series of swirls, slashes, and dots common in the Sorracchi language. Then he handed it back.

Katrina stared at the symbols, waiting for them to engage into something that made sense. "This part means tiny or invisible, impossible to see," she said, touching her fingertip to a section of the script. "And this part refers to biology, system functions, organic maybe . . ." Katrina tilted her head. "And technology. Integration. Nanotechnology?"

"I do not know this word."

"Tiny technology. Little bits of computer with specific programs, usually designed to complete certain tasks. Fix a machine . . ." Realization hit her when part of the journal entries became clear. She looked at Gideon, her eyes so wide they burned to blink. "Bionanetics. She infused bionanetics into your physiology to age you, make you stronger, help you learn, help you heal."

"My brother told me your intelligence was exceptional," was his first reply. He looked away from her to Phin. "You are correct. This occurred at the time of our creation, and this technology did as you said. Aged us. Enhanced us. And in the end, used to control us."

Cold dread settled into her chest and slid into her stomach like a block of ice.

CHAPTER NINETEEN

9 MARCH 2054, MONDAY
OFFICE OF THE PRESIDENT
ROBERT J. CASTLETON MEMORIAL BUILDING – THE CASTLE
CENTER FOR UNITED PROTECTORATE GOVERNMENT
ALEXANDRIA, SEAT OF VIRGINIA
NORTH AMERICAN CONTINENT

"*H*as there been any word, Nicholas?"

Nick raised his head, tired muscles straining across his shoulders, to look toward the door of his office. Beverly waited, her hand resting on the jamb. There was so much going on in the midst of the week-long celebrations her question could have pertained to just about anything. Regardless, he knew exactly what she wanted to know. He motioned her into the office and toward one of the chairs opposite his desk. He shook his head as she sat, folding his hands over the tablet he'd been reviewing.

"None," he answered on a huff. "Connor transmitted descriptions and images to all Firebird and all Terra teams in Alexandria, Falls Church, and surrounding settlements. Thus far, all commanders have reported no sightings."

She drew in a deep breath and released it, a delicate hand pressed to her chest. Her emotions played clearly across her face, sad eyes looking to the window. "I didn't know Katrina very well, I'd only met her a few times, but Victor feels so much anxiety over her disappearance I can't help but feel it too. He has slept very little since last week."

Nick leaned back in his chair, the old hinges and joints creaking at the strain. "Michael too. I hear him pacing at night after Nicole and Jackie are asleep. I don't know if it's his hip keeping him awake, or worrying about her, or both."

Beverly smiled, though the sadness didn't quite leave her eyes. "I'm so glad Jackie is home again. I look forward to seeing her."

"This weekend," Nick said, tapping the desk with his fingertips, then pointed to her. "Come to the house for dinner."

Beverly's smile brightened, genuinely. "His birthday is this weekend."

Nick nodded. "Yeah, and we'll actually be able to celebrate *together* for the first time. Two years ago, his first birthday after we got him out, I was—" He circled one hand in the empty air above his head, a general reference to his trip across the galaxy to find the Umani and Areth. "And last year, he was . . ." He let the explanation trail off, the memory of Michael's long and terrifying recovery.

His vice president leaned forward across the desk to squeeze his hand. "I'm so happy for you, Nicholas. Look how much has changed, how far you've come, in the last couple of years. When we met, you were—"

"A grumpy old man living in the woods and angry at the world, with no one but my dog to give a damn about?"

Beverly laughed, a soft but lovely sound she'd only grown accustomed to letting free in the year since her hearing had been restored. "Well, you could put it that way. I was going to simply state alone. And now . . . you have your son. You have Caitlin." She tilted her head and smiled again. "You have a beautiful granddaughter, and you have a new baby on the way. Some would say you are a very lucky man, Nick Tanner."

"We're all damn lucky, Bev."

A sharp knock at the door turned his attention, and he motioned for Connor and Mel to come in, the tense lines digging into Connor's forehead making Nick's hackles jump. He stood before Connor reached the desk. "What?"

"We have a communication from Lieutenant Rick Torres in the squatter district of Falls Church. He heads the shelter and distribution center."

"And?"

"He's on the network, waiting to speak with us." Connor rounded the end of one of the two couches and went to the fireplace, and the large vidscreen mounted on the wall. With a few taps and slides of his fingers on the screen, he activated the monitor and tapped into the secure communication system. Nick offered Beverly his hand and drew her from the chair, walking to the other side of the room. Melanie Brooks stood to the side and just behind Connor as he engaged the link. The screen flickered half a second before a young man in an olive uniform with a black stocking cap appeared. He straightened visibly when he saw Nick and saluted with a sharp snap of his hand.

"Good morning, Mr. President. Madam Vice President."

"Lieutenant," Nick said in response, returning the salute. "What can you tell us?"

"It's regarding Doctor Bauer, sir."

"Have you seen her?"

"No, sir," Torres answered with a sharp jerk of his head. "But I believe I have seen one of the men Commander Montgomery indicated abducted her."

"Just one?" Connor asked.

"Yes, sir. He's been into the shelter nearly every day for the last several."

"Has he ever given a name or said anything about where he is?" Connor led again.

"No, sir. We don't push for names, per orders. If they tell us, they tell us, otherwise we just help any way we can. The first time he came, I asked him if he had anyone to support. He said a wife and two sons. And he asked for socks for his wife."

Connor and Nick exchanged glances. "How did he look, son?" Nick asked.

"There was nothing about him that stood out, sir. Not for the first few days at least. But a couple days ago when he came in he asked for a basic medical kit. Said it was for some minor abrasions, implied maybe one of the boys had fallen. But . . ." Torres squinted and shook his head. "He didn't look good. And he doubled up like he was in pain. I told him the doctor would be coming in and told him to come back if he got worse."

"You never saw Doctor Bauer?" Connor asked, shifting his stance to cross his arms over his chest, his feet set apart.

"No, sir. Just him. I never saw her, and I've only ever seen one, but he's definitely one of the three. Looks just like the picture. He came just yesterday, alone, and I haven't seen him today. He seemed different though."

"Different how?"

"This is going to sound weird, but he smiled more. He talked with a few of the people staying here. I've seen him talk, but mostly with kids. Yesterday it was with some of the men and women too."

Beverly touched his arm. "A different one of them?"

Connor shrugged, supplying an answer. "Could be. If the first one is ill, the second might be going out instead." Connor focused on the screen and Lieutenant Torres. "You said you had a concern, Lieutenant."

"Yes, sir," Torres said with a nod. "We have a few . . . citizens . . . who come to the shelter on a fairly regular basis. They talk a big talk, grumblings mostly, but we keep a close eye on them because they can get pretty hepped up. They came in today, and one of them had learned of the report. He's stirred up some momentum and gathered a group. They're out looking for the fugitives, sir. I'm concerned for the safety of Doctor Bauer should they be found."

Cold dread landed in Nick's stomach. "All the transmissions have stated proceed with caution, and do not engage."

Torres nodded. "Yes, sir; but, they've got other ideas. One of my men heard a Separatist state they knew the Triadic were alien, possibly Sorracchi—"

"They aren't," Nick cut off, shaking his head. "At least, not that we know. Until we have them in custody again, and *know* the status of Katrina Bauer, they are not to be engaged."

"I understand that, sir. But these people don't care about our orders. They're getting their information from somewhere else."

"Understood, Lieutenant." Nick pinched the bridge of his nose. "Connor—"

"On it, sir."

Connor and Mel were out of the office before Nick raised his head.

"Where are they going?" Beverly asked, looking from Nick to the door where they had departed.

"To find Katrina before anyone else."

"You're going to let him die?"

"It is not as simple as that!" Gideon snapped.

Katrina took an involuntary step backward but firmed her expression and set her arms at her hips. "Yes, it is. Go back and he at least has a *chance* at life. There is nothing I can do here! There is nothing any of us can do here!"

Tears burned her eyes, born more of anger than anything else. She had sat vigil with Phin all night, with either Gideon or Daniel with her, and nothing had changed despite everything she tried with her limited resources. His body burned with fever and his wounds swelled with infection. He'd developed a rattling, wet cough in the wee hours of the morning. Gideon turned away from her and marched across the room to the fireplace, Katrina glaring at him with each step. His shoulders hunched and he gripped the edge of the mantel, dropping his head forward with a long, heavy huff.

"I understand what is happening," she tried to reason. "I understand the science of the bionanetics, but I can't *do* anything here. In Alexandria are some of the most brilliant, most amazing minds alive —Human or not. We can work together to—"

"I will not submit my brothers to slavery again." Gideon turned on her, the darkness in his eyes so fierce her breath caught. "We would rather die than be her puppets."

"Her?" Katrina squinted and stared at him. "Kathleen? You think . . ." She shook her head. "You think we would give you back to her? Gideon, I told you the Sorracchi are gone. They were beaten. We won."

"She is the only one with the knowledge—"

"She's *dead*, Gideon."

He stopped short, and visibly pulled back, his eyes wide. Daniel stepped into her peripheral vision, having stayed out of the argument until now because he had made his opinion well known already. He sided with her.

"Dead?" Daniel asked.

Katrina nodded and looked between the two brothers. Their expressions were nearly mirrors of each other. "I didn't even think to say it. Kathleen is dead. Michael Tanner killed her a year ago to save Jackie." They exchanged looks. "She is gone. But . . ." Katrina stepped closer to both of them. "Even if she had survived the war, there is *no* way she would have any power over you. If she had lived, she would be prosecuted for her crimes and punished. I'm sorry. I should have said."

Gideon looked to Daniel. "Then we are truly without hope."

Katrina threw her hands in the air and spun a full circle, grinding out a frustrated moan. She came just short of stomping her feet. "*Listen* to me! We can help, I swear to you. No one will be your master, you will be no one's slave."

Gideon groaned and scrubbed his hands over his face, the first action she'd ever seen from him not born of discipline and stoicism. He set his hands on his waist and dropped his head again, his eyes closed. Katrina held her breath and covered her mouth with trembling fingers. *Please . . . say yes. Say yes.*

"Gideon . . ."

Gideon snapped his head toward Daniel, but there was no anger in his eyes. Their silent communication drove her nuts. Finally, Daniel nodded and Gideon dropped his hands from his waist. He moved between her and Daniel and retrieved his coat from the back of one of the kitchen chairs. Without a look back, he pulled on the coat and went out the door. With the click of the lock Katrina sucked in a sharp breath and sniffed, wiping at her rebellious tears. She jumped when Daniel laid his hand on her shoulder.

"He's heard you, Katrina," Daniel said, his voice low. "He needs some time to consider all options. He is right. Neither Phineas nor myself would choose slavery. We would rather die free."

She swallowed hard and sniffed again. "I know. I wish I could make you understand, make you see President Tanner would *never* do that. To him, that would make us as bad as the Sorracchi and that's *not* going to happen."

"Your sincerity is not what Gideon questions, but theirs."

Katrina wanted to scream, wanted to jump up and down in frustration. She twisted away from Daniel and marched to the window. With her back to the wall beside the window, Katrina stared at Daniel from across the room. "You know it's funny, Daniel. I'm the one who you took from the hospital in the middle of a storm, I'm the one who hasn't been allowed to leave these rooms for nearly a week, but I'm the one trying to justify my actions."

Daniel smiled, but it held no humor. "I'm going to check on Phineas."

Katrina just nodded and turned to the window again. She slid the curtain aside just enough to look down into the street. The sun was bright, glistening off the moisture on the streets. Icicles had begun to melt on the eaves of the buildings, dripping into puddles on the sidewalks. The last couple of days had been warm, a sign spring might come soon. After the destruction of the WeatherNet, climates and weather conditions had been extreme and unpredictable. They could have a blizzard tomorrow, or they might not see snow again for months. No one knew.

Katrina sighed and crossed the room to the kitchen area and rummaged through the variety of nonperishable and extended shelf-life foods Phin had brought back from the shelter. She smiled and picked up the remaining cookie package. He had made it adamantly clear to both Daniel and Gideon no one was to have the cookies but her. Just as quickly the warmth brought by the memory fizzled and cooled into a lump of dread. She looked toward the entrance to the hall.

Phin had barely moved during the night, and she had to press her hand to his chest to feel his heartbeat just to make sure he was still alive before she left him alone. He still burned hot with fever, and the skin around his wounds was so red it was nearly purple, swollen. Only once had he stirred when he mumbled her name and his hand slid across the blankets until he touched her, then he calmed.

Katrina set the cookie back down on the counter and sighed.

The door kicked in with a splintering crack and Katrina scrambled back with a scream. At least a dozen men burst through the door in waves, armed with everything from bats to handheld pulse weapons, screaming. Dressed in rags and mismatched clothes, they had to be the homeless and displaced, not soldiers or Firebirds. The ones closest to her turned and caught sight of her. Katrina shoved away from the counter and behind the table, tipping it and its contents over to block their path. One tried to come around and cut her off, but Katrina grabbed the back of a chair and flung it at him, tripping him when the legs slammed into his shins. He cursed and flung the chair out of his way, coming at her again.

A roar of a sound came from the hallway, and her pursuer paused long enough to look. Katrina looked, too, and gasped to see Daniel and Phin burst from the hallway, Daniel leading the charge. One of the men closest to them extended his arm and fired a weapon, a stunner, hitting Daniel full in the chest. The crackling sound carried above the shouts and commands of the men.

"No!" Katrina screamed, drawing the attention again of the man intent on her. Before he could grab her arm she ran away again, dodging behind the couch to keep an obstacle between them.

Daniel slammed back against the wall, his body spasming with the jolt. Phin ran past him, his bandaged and reddened torso still exposed. Katrina's heart pounded so hard in her chest she thought she'd choke on it, desperately trying to both keep her eyes on Phin and Daniel and staying out of the man's reach.

Without even slowing down, Phin attacked the nearest man to him, both deflecting their attack and taking the offensive in two swings of his arms. He grabbed the bat the man held, and with a twist, snapped it around to knock it against the side of his attacker's head, using the man's weight as leverage to pivot through the air and take out two other men with kicks from his bare feet.

Daniel yanked the stun bolts from his chest and shoved away from the wall in time to defend himself against two of them. Katrina's pursuer shot her one hard, cold glare then turned away and entered the fight. With men blocking the door, she had no escape. But she refused to just stand by and watch. She shot past the end of the couch to the fireplace and picked up the wrought iron poker used to stoke the embers. One of the men saw her and cut away from the fighting to grab at her. Katrina swung wide, screaming out all the power she could put behind the blow, and clocked him across the jaw. He stumbled back, wide eyed, then dropped hard to the floor.

Standing with her back to the corner, waiting for another opportunity to take one down, Katrina spotted one of them removed from the fight, crouched near the tipped table, a video recording device held to his eye. He shifted his angle to keep the fight on his screen but stayed clear of the fighting.

The two blocking the door suddenly flew forward into the fight, landing on their faces, and Gideon grabbed the next nearest him. With no visible effort, he tossed the man away, taking down another two like bowling pins.

And then there were three.

Katrina could only stare—in dumbfounded shock—at what she could only describe as a perfectly choreographed dance. Though there were three, they moved in perfect harmony, perfect unity, perfect precision, taking down permanently every man who dared approach. They moved around each other as surely and as accurately as a single man in battle. Weapons were turned on attackers and exchanged between brothers like runners in a relay race, and they arched, flipped, and leveraged both each other and the attackers to their advantage. Katrina held her breath, and in what seemed seconds unconscious bodies littered the floor around them and they stood, back-to-back and shoulder-to-shoulder.

The man crouched at the table with the camera lunged to his feet and bolted for the door. Gideon raised his hand and a pole shot from where it had fallen on the floor into his hand, hitting his palm with a solid slap. With the momentum of the wood, Gideon spun around and released it, hitting the fleeing man solidly in the back of the head and he dropped on his face. The camera slid across the floor.

Finally, Katrina took a breath, her vision hazed. She wasn't sure how many men had run, wasn't even sure how many had finally come in, but at least a dozen lay scattered and still around the room, including the one she had knocked out. She dropped the bar with a loud clatter and stepped over the body nearest her.

"Everybody okay?" she asked.

Phin stood closest to her, having effectively become a Human shield between her and anyone else who came her way. He turned and looked at her, his chest heaving more than the other two with the massive exertion, his cheeks frighteningly pale. A flash of relief brightened his eyes when he saw her.

Then he dropped hard to the floor.

"Phin!"

Her knees hit the floor before she reached him, and she crawled the last two feet to his side, barely beating Gideon and Daniel. She was almost afraid to touch him, the gauze bandages now scarlet. Tears ran down her cheeks, dripping from her chin, when she finally laid her hands on him. He'd gone from burning with fever to deathly cold, his skin clammy and chilled from perspiration.

"Phin!" she cried and touched his face, turning him toward her. There was no reaction, nothing. "Phin!"

"He's near death," Daniel said from somewhere.

She laid her cheek on Phin's chest and closed her eyes, feeling only the slightest bit of relief to hear his heartbeat, though shallow and weak. Katrina sat back on her heels and stared up at Gideon, not even attempting to hold back her tears.

"Please," she begged, whispering through her cries. "Please, Gideon. Don't let him die. Please."

He crouched on the other side of Phin, laying his hand on his brother's chest. Gideon closed his eyes and swallowed hard before he raised his head and looked at her again. "It may be too late. He can't travel. We have no way—"

"Yes," Katrina cut him off.

She scrambled to her feet and leaped over bodies to the scattered items on the floor by the table. She shoved aside bottles of water and packages of food until she found the tablet, a wave of panic choking her at the thought the fall may have broken the fragile, ancient device. She went back to him, trying to turn on the tablet as she navigated the bodies, and dropped to her knees beside Phin as the tablet twittered signaling it powered up. When the screen lit up, she held it out with shaking hands.

"I don't understand," Gideon said, shaking his head as he looked between her and the tablet.

Katrina swallowed and blew out a steadying breath. "I hacked in the backdoor of my own computer system in Alexandria." Gideon's eyes widened, and for a brief moment anger flashed in his eyes, but just as quickly slid away. Katrina nodded and looked between Gideon and Daniel who stood a few feet behind his brother. "I've been reading my files, trying to find a way to help you, trying to find a way to understand what she did. But, that's not what matters. I can call for help. I can bring them here to us."

Gideon looked to Daniel, who immediately came forward. Together Gideon and Daniel lifted Phin off the floor, cradled between them. Katrina stood with them, staring. Gideon looked at her before he and Daniel headed toward the door.

"Do it."

CHAPTER TWENTY

*M*ichael couldn't sleep.

He was exhausted and should have been asleep the minute he slid into bed beside Jacqueline. He thought the reason he couldn't find rest for the last couple of weeks had been the absence of Jacqueline beside him, but she was here now, had been home for five days, and sleep still eluded him. As soon as he lay down, the niggling feeling of anticipation bubbled at the base of his skull. Now he reclined with his back against the headboard, his hands laced over his stomach, staring out the open curtains to the sliver of a silver moon. Jacqueline was warm and wonderful beside him, her back pressed to his hip, but even that wasn't enough to allow him sleep.

He needed to go somewhere, do something, but where and what he didn't know. The sensation was familiar, he had experienced it twice before, but the same outcome was unlikely since each time before the sensation had preceded his father's arrival; once when Michael was taken from his prison in New Mexico, and once when his father returned from his trip across the galaxy. Since Nick Tanner was down the stairs and in his office, most likely, and had been all evening and Michael had been taunted with the growing sensation of necessity for weeks, he knew it had to be something else.

Jacqueline drew in a long, deep breath and stretched, shifting to lie on her back. Her eyes shined bright in the dim moonlight. "What's wrong?"

Michael shook his head, sliding deeper into the bed to rest on his side, his weight balanced on his bent arm so he could look down at her. "I don't know."

She chuckled softly. "It must be serious. You never say you don't know."

He studied her features, the smooth angles just visible in the low light. She was so beautiful she took his breath, and he doubted there would ever be a day she wouldn't. Michael smiled at her teasing and slid his hand beneath the blanket to rest it on her lower stomach. He had to be very still, and sometimes waited several minutes, but eventually he would be rewarded with the small nudge against his palm.

"I've never told you about the night my father came for me."

She tilted her head on the pillow, staring up at him. "Is that what's wrong?"

"No. But it helps explain."

"Okay, so tell me."

"You never met Alexander. He was a man who was with me in New Mexico, but the Sorracchi had brutalized him. He was malformed, his mind like a child, and in pain all the time. That whole day he had been in pain, crying for me. I felt a clawing need, and I thought it had been to go to him and help him. Something I couldn't do."

"It wasn't?"

Michael shook his head. "Perhaps in part. But I realized later it was more. Do you remember when my father came back to Tennessee?"

Jacqueline smiled. "Remember? Kind of hard to forget." She reached up to touch his cheek and he turned into her palm, kissing it. "I know you have this weird way of knowing when your father is about to show up. Is it like that?"

"Now, yes," he said against her skin, his voice slightly muffled. "It's similar to seeing him before he is there. But, this is different. Each time I had no idea he was even near, and before he came I felt . . ." He shook his head, not knowing the right words to tell her. He looked up at the door and tossed away the blankets. "Dad is coming. Something happened."

Jacqueline sat up and swung her legs off the side of the bed. "I should probably be freaked out when you do that."

Michael pulled on his jeans and buttoned them as the soft knock came at the bedroom door. "Michael?"

He grabbed his cane and crossed the room to open the door. "What happened?"

"We found Katrina." His father squinted and tipped his head back and forth. "Okay, not so much. She contacted Victor through a basic text only sub-program through the hospital computer system, of all things."

"Is she okay?"

"We don't know. The message was limited, but she gave an address in Falls Church and asked Victor to come. And bring medics." He motioned with a tilt of his head toward the stairs leading down to his office. "Connor and Victor are on the line, and Connor is already en route. She didn't say much, just to hurry and they needed medics."

"I'm confused."

Nick chuckled and started down the stairs. Michael was slower, using both the railing and his cane as balance to navigate the steps. "It gets better. The Triadic has made a request." He stopped and looked up at Michael. "They want you there."

Michael stopped.

"Why would they want Michael? How can they even know Michael?" Jacqueline asked behind him.

"We find out within the hour. As soon as Victor and his medical team gets here, you head for Falls Church."

*C*onnor slammed his back against the cold brick wall of the condemned apartment complex, his pulse rifle tight to his chest, and motioned for his men to flank out and approach the courtyard entry of the building from multiple angles. They'd scouted the building using magnification goggles, and confirmed four people—three men, one on the floor, and one woman—waited in the lobby. The other Firebirds branched out, following his orders.

Two streets over they had identified a group of men armed with crude weapons. They were clearly agitated, possibly gathering, and Connor suspected they were some of the citizens Torres had said were on the move, seeking Katrina and the Triadic. What they had to do with Katrina's sudden outreach to Victor, Connor didn't know absolutely, but he wouldn't be surprised if they were connected. Especially given the visible condition of the men.

What he didn't like was going in blind.

"The perimeter is clear," Mel said, sliding into the space beside him.

Conner nodded, and motioned for everyone to move in. He rounded the corner and hugged the wall until he and Mel reached the glass double doors leading into the lobby area of the building. Despite their stealth approach, two of the three men stood shoulder-to-shoulder between the door and Doctor Katrina Bauer, who knelt on the floor with the third, his head in her lap, apparently unconscious. Connor held eye contact with the standing men, and pulled open the door, his weapon trained on one and Mel's on the other.

"Stand aside," Connor ordered. "Stand aside!"

Neither moved. Barely blinked.

"Gideon," Katrina said softly from behind them, her voice strained and nearly lost in the cold of the lobby. "It's okay, Connor is just worried. Please . . ."

One of the two turned his head at the sound of her voice, then looked back to Connor. With no change in their expressions, both men turned sideways and stepped back, clearing Connor's view of Katrina.

At immediate glance she appeared unharmed. She wore the clothing she'd been taken in, her hair uncharacteristically braided flat to her head, but had no visible injuries or signs of abuse.

The man cradled in her lap hadn't fared as well. He was dressed in worn, frayed denims, no shirt and no shoes. Bandages on his sides and left shoulder above his heart were saturated with blood. He was still. Too still.

Firebirds filed into the lobby from different entrances, weapons at the ready, and Connor raised his hand for them to stand down. He nodded to Mel, and she nodded back, understanding his silent command. Watch the other two. Connor walked between them toward Katrina and the fallen of the three. She raised her face to look up at him, tears streaking her smudged cheeks, her chin trembling.

"Is Victor coming?" she asked, then sniffed.

Connor nodded. "He went for Michael. So, you *did* send the message."

She nodded and took a hand from the man's chest to snuff her nose. "How long?"

"Minutes."

She sucked in a sobbing breath and shuddered, looking down again at the man she held. "Please," she begged, Connor didn't think of him, "let him be on time."

*M*ichael bit back the need to tell the Firebird navigating the hover to hurry, the niggling push growing worse the deeper they traveled into the Squatter District. The hover was one of three, this one the medivac conveyance. Connor had called en route to advise only one of the four required immediate medical attention, though in his estimation the other two men who had taken Katrina were not well, though they at least kept their feet. The third was unconscious, and severely wounded.

Connor reported Katrina had no outward appearance of harm.

Michael understood harm sometimes hid below the surface and chose to hold his judgment until he saw her with his own eyes.

He stared out the window as they moved through the streets, the depression cold and darkness weighing on him like a wet cloak. There were parts of the city completely destroyed, and then areas like this where Humanity had gathered to be near others as much as to find shelter and food. His father stretched his resources as far as possible, creating shelters throughout the city where anyone could go at any time and find a warm place to sleep and a hearty meal as much as they could offer.

"How much farther?" he asked.

The driver looked over his shoulder to where Michael sat. "We're less than a minute out."

Michael nodded and tapped his fingertips on the armrest to his right. He still didn't know why the Triadic had asked for his presence. He had accepted, once he climbed into the hover, the insistent nudge was to push him toward this meeting. But why? Why had his subconscious acknowledged the need to go before he had any knowledge of their whereabouts?

His father had been initially reluctant first to let Michael go, and second not to accompany him, especially after Michael explained the necessity he'd felt for the last few days. His father's last words as he left the house stayed with him.

"It's time to use some of that new mojo of yours, Michael. Go with your gut. If you feel anything from these three you don't like, tell Connor to take 'em down. I'm willing to give them the benefit of the doubt, and I was ready to do that from the get-go, until they dragged Katrina out of the hospital. She says they're scared, you be the judge. If you trust them, I'll trust them."

The hover turned down an alley along a dark, brick faced building that appeared to have once been an apartment complex, but now condemned, the words written in massive print to keep away squatters. The alley opened to a courtyard, lit in moonlight and covered in snow. The hover doors opened with a pop and hiss and wet, cold air swept into the relative heat he'd enjoyed on the way. Michael gripped the edge of the door to ease his way from the craft, planting the tip of his cane firmly on the slick pavement before testing his step. Victor exited behind him, setting his hand on Michael's shoulder.

"You got it?" Victor asked.

Michael answered only with a nod. It didn't take long for the cold to settle into his joints and make his hip ache.

Anger pulled at his friend's features. Victor had taken Katrina and her brother into his group with unveiled excitement for their skill and knowledge, but Michael knew Victor also looked at his people with more affection than simply a superior and his team. Especially Katrina. She was the youngest of all of them, and Victor admitted, next to Michael probably the smartest.

The need to go inside was almost a tangible shove against Michael's shoulders, and he had to force himself not to hurry. Two Firebirds stood guard at the double doors and pulled them open so Victor, Michael, and the team could enter.

The last Michael had seen of these three men, they were in a comatose state and no one had any idea how to wake them. Now two stood as guards on either side of Katrina and their brother, who was unconscious. Someone had provided a blanket for him, but the lobby was too cold. Katrina supported him in her lap, cradling him with affection, trembling hands stroking his cheek.

A small bit of relief edged away the tension. She looked tired, perhaps slightly pale, but not hurt or manhandled in any way. In fact, an overwhelming sense of protectiveness buffered off the two men guarding her. It was tangible, warm.

Katrina looked up, and the overwhelming sadness in her eyes nearly broke Michael's heart. She looked from him, to Victor, and back. "You have to help him. I promised you would help."

Victor moved around Michael and knelt beside the fallen man. Katrina took away her hands for him to examine but didn't relinquish her position of supporting him. She looked up to the man to Michael's left, then to Michael. The man turned to Michael in a sharp snap.

"I am Alpha—"

Katrina cleared her throat, a small sound and barely audible, but the first of the Triadic paused, his gaze angling down to glance at her and she smiled. More tension ebbed from Michael. She definitely held no fear for these men. Alpha turned his focus again on Michael. "I am now known as Gideon, designation Alpha." He tilted his head toward the other standing behind Michael. "That is Daniel. Designation Beta." Then he looked down at the one on the floor. "Phineas is designation Omega."

Familiarity brushed over Michael's senses, which confused him. It was the same knowledge of presence he felt when his father was nearby. Michael squinted and tilted his head a slight degree. "I'm Michael Tanner."

Gideon nodded, a slow raising and lowering of his chin, his golden hazel eyes unwavering. "We are also familiar with you, Michael Tanner."

"Is that why you asked to see me? Because you know who I am?"

Again Gideon nodded, the same metered movement. "You represented everything she hated, every rage, every evil, every inspiration. Nearly from the day of your birth, we knew of your existence."

"Michael . . ." Connor said behind him, his voice tainted with warning.

He raised his hand without turning, hoping Connor understood there was no reason for concern. He felt nothing malicious or deceitful from them. He shifted, closing the distance between them by a small degree. "If you ever felt her wrath because of her anger toward me, I am sorry."

Victor stood and motioned for his people to come forward. "We need to move him and move him now. He's near death."

"You can help him."

Victor turned to Gideon, his strained expression telling Michael more than anything he said. "We'll try. Katrina told you we'd help, we will."

Gideon's head snapped to the left.

Be cautious. I sense contempt, and the intent to attack.

The words weren't so much a voice in Michael's mind, but a sense of almost thinking the words himself. He looked around, the hairs on the back of his neck bristling. He felt it, too; anger, resentment, and irrational fear. Michael took a step back and spoke to Connor over his shoulder. "Something is wrong."

"With them?"

"No."

Connor spared him a sharp glance, his eyes enough to ask the question.

"I don't know," Michael answered truthfully. "But it's not them, it's directed at them. Someone here."

Melanie raised her hand and set it on the holster at her hip, releasing the safety strap. Connor mumbled a curse.

They draw weapons.

"No!" Michael said, holding up his hand. "No, we're not drawing on you." Michael was suddenly smothered in a wave of malice, focused and with murderous intent. "The stairwell!"

Pulse blasts echoed down the stairwell on the far side of the lobby, and two more Firebirds joined the one at the bottom of the stairs. The Firebirds from outside burst through the courtyard lobby door as the street side door was kicked in from the other side. Pulse weapon fire crisscrossed the lobby.

Protect her!

Katrina screamed, draping her body over Phineas. Victor grabbed Michael's arm and Michael dropped to the floor, pain ricocheting up his leg to his hip. He landed on his hands and knees, his cane skittering across the floor away from him. The Firebirds, with their charges, were corralled in the center of the lobby surrounded on all sides by approaching enemy fire. Connor lunged across the floor, crouching beside Michael as he returned fire.

"Stay down, stay low!"

Michael looked up toward one of the men firing on them, crouched behind the backside of the wide stairwell. With an outward snap, Michael yanked the gun from the man's hands and sent it flying across the room. The enemy stared at his empty grip, his eyes wide. Michael focused on another, the gun getting off several blasts mid-air as he mentally sent it soaring toward the farthest corner of the room. If he could see them, he could stop them.

Then the air grew thick, all the energy sucked away like a great behemoth inhaling a breath. Michael's head was caught in a psychic vice. He collapsed flat on the floor, pressing his hands to his temples. No one around him seemed to feel or acknowledge the high-pitched whine rippling through his mind. Like speaking underwater, Connor's voice carried to him, and he shook Michael with a grip on his shirt.

"Michael!"

Sound popped and came rushing back to him and the pressure released. All weapon fire stopped and Firebirds scrambled toward the men who had attacked them. Connor tugged on his arm until Michael rolled onto his back, trying to find his equilibrium again.

"What's wrong? Did you get hit?"

Michael shook his head, not sure if he wanted to hear the possible volume of his own voice in his head if he spoke. He fought back the nausea and swallowed hard, letting his head rest on the threadbare rug beneath him.

"Get them secure. Now!" Connor shouted, waving his men into action.

"Michael!" Katrina's desperate shout forced Michael to turn his head and his gut clenched to see Gideon and Daniel on their knees.

"Get medics in here!" Connor shouted and stood, stepping over Michael.

Victor came to him and held out his hand, gripping Michael just above the elbow. Michael mimicked the grip and his oldest friend pulled him to his feet. The constant, scraping pain in his hip was intensified by the fall he'd taken, the right side of his body pulsating from waist to knee. He bit down hard to restrain the deep groan of pain when he put weight on his right leg. He stumbled and gripped his friend's arm to keep his feet and looked around for his cane.

"Let me get it—" Victor began.

Before he could step away, Michael reached out and the cane slapped against his palm. "They're being poisoned by something Kathleen did. I can feel it draining them, making them sicker. Especially Phineas."

Victor slid him a look but stepped away to Gideon. Two other medics already worked to lay Daniel out on a gurney they'd brought in from the hovers, so Michael limped to Phineas and Katrina. She looked up at him with tears streaking her cheeks.

"I promised them you'd help," she choked.

"I will." He couldn't kneel beside Phineas, couldn't even if his hip didn't throb with the constant, amplified reminder of his mother's tender mercies.

The two medics came forward to lift Phineas from the floor as several Firebirds dragged the attackers—whom Michael assumed to be Xenos—from the building in restraints. One yelled blatant threats toward Nick Tanner and Michael, threats to teach the Tanner family who held the power on Earth.

"That man . . ." Gideon said as two Firebirds helped him to his feet. "That man knows of plans to attack President Tanner."

"How do you know that?" Michael asked, looking between Gideon and the Xeno.

"We have been monitoring their actions at the shelter nearby. They have recruited several citizens with the intent to let them die."

"Take him to interrogation," Connor ordered, apparently hearing the conversation. "We'll question him there."

Michael stumbled forward, gripping the dusty handrail of the open staircase to shift his weight, sweat pasting his tee shirt to his skin from the pain. The fall had caused damage to his already weak, deteriorating body and he wasn't sure he would be able to walk across the lobby to the hovers outside to get back to the hospital.

As soon as Phineas was strapped to a gurney, Michael opened his arm to Katrina and she came against him, weeping. He embraced her, letting the joy of seeing the tiny woman safe and secure shove aside the smothering panic of moments before. Gideon had gained his feet, and refused to lie on the offered gurney, claiming he could walk and would remain with his brothers. Before he walked away, flanked on each side by medical-trained Firebirds, Michael called out his name and he turned.

"You didn't have a chance to tell me how you knew me."

We are brothers. The words were clear, but silent to everyone else. Gideon smiled despite the pain pinching his features. *Before you were conceived we were created. From the same woman.*

Michael stared in shock as he left the lobby and tightened his hold on Katrina as she wept. Connor and Victor returned from outside, and Connor gave orders to the remaining Firebirds. Victor crossed to Michael, his features tense, and laid his hand on Michael's shoulder when he reached him. "The pain is worse."

Michael clenched his jaw and nodded, using both the chair and Katrina for support. His left leg shook under the strain of bearing all his weight.

"Come. We'll—"

Michael released the chair and stepped away, an intense and smothering wave of pain overwhelming him. He dropped, only vaguely aware of the hands trying to hold him up before he hit the floor.

CHAPTER TWENTY-ONE

"*H*e's burning up with infection. Give me a massive dose of super antibiotics."

"We're losing a rhythm, doctor."

"BP dropping fast."

Katrina pressed her back against the inner hull of the hover, barely able to breathe as Victor and his team worked on Phin. Alarms blared and beeped, orders flew back and forth between them. She could only stare, wide-eyed. Victor snapped out a command and laid out his hand, but it wasn't one of his techs who placed the requested device . . . it was Daniel.

Victor looked up and at Daniel, but only paused for half a heartbeat.

Katrina blinked and looked past Daniel to Gideon, who assisted one of the other medtechs, no words spoken between them.

"The infection is bad, but I don't see signs of any other injuries," Victor mumbled. "What is making him so sick?"

"Nanotech—" Katrina snapped and Victor looked to her. She nodded. "Nanotechnology. Bio-based. Kathleen used it to control them. Make them sick when they disobeyed."

Victor nodded.

An alarm blared loud.

"He's flatlined!"

"*I* tell you, I am *fine*." Katrina batted the diagnostic scanner out of her face and glared at the emergency care physician. Doctor Zavala had been waiting for her as soon as she came through the immediate care doors.

She'd wanted to go with Victor. With Daniel and Gideon.

With Phin.

Even if there was nothing she could do.

"Ms. Bauer, you have been through a frightening ordeal," she said in a voice far too cloying for Katrina, her expression feigned sympathy, a trick Katrina decided must have been in medical school before things went to hell. "Being abducted and held against your will is terrifying, and we need to make sure whatever harm—"

"*No* harm," Katrina snapped, dodging to the side to hop down from the exam table. "They didn't hurt me. They didn't do anything to me. They . . ." She cursed the tears welling in her eyes, an overflow of the pain bubbling in her chest. Katrina clenched her fists and pressed them against her eyes, but the sorrow was at a boil, she couldn't hold it back anymore. It would drown her. Choke her. "They took care of me," she sobbed.

Another sympathetic look as the doctor tilted her head. "It's not uncommon for prisoners to develop an irrational empathy for their captors, though I've never heard of it developing in such a short time span."

*K*atrina stood beneath the flow of hot water, the heat taking away the chill from her bones. But it couldn't touch the cold in her heart or fill the hole in the center of her chest. She stayed there, unmoving, until her skin pruned.

Katrina slumped against the slick shower tiles and slid down to the floor, the water pounding her head. She drew her knees to her chest, buried her face, and wept until her sobs echoed back to her.

She wasn't consciously aware of toweling off or pulling on the clothing brought to her or pulling a brush through her washed hair until she caught sight of herself in the hospital room mirror.

Ringlets framed her pale face. The blooms of color in her cheeks and lips a sharp contrast, but equal to the red rimming her eyes. The tears hadn't stopped since the hover arrived at the hospital, slowing in moments like this only to drown her without warning.

She hadn't ever before felt this cold.

Phin was dead.

"*I* was so terrified," Karl whispered against her hair, his arms tightening.

She wanted to say she was sorry, but her throat wouldn't cooperate. She buried her face against her brother's chest and held on. He held her, but not long enough, before he pushed her away and gripped her shoulders to look into her eyes.

"Did they hurt you? What did they do to you?"

"No!" Katrina yanked free of his arms, finding them suddenly as smothering now as they had been comforting a moment before. "Why won't anyone *listen to me*?"

He reached for her again, his hold not as demanding. "Katrina, you've been held captive for nearly a week. We've been worried sick about you, what could be happening to you—" He clenched his jaw and swallowed hard, and when he spoke his words thrummed through him with such intensity she felt the shake in his touch. "Trina, did they . . ." He swallowed hard. "Did they do *anything* to you?"

"No," she answered immediately, trying to put the weight of truth into the one word. "Karl, they took me with them because—because they woke up in this world they didn't know, a place they didn't know . . . they were afraid. They *didn't* hurt me. They *didn't* do *anything* to me."

Karl drew in three hard, deep breaths through his nose, huffing out his mouth, his grip on her desperate. Finally he set her down and took her face in his hands, the tremble not going unnoticed by her. Karl bent at the knees enough to look her straight in the eyes, his mouth a tight, restrained line, his lips curled in to disguise the tremble in his chin.

"They didn't hurt you?"

"No, Karl." She could barely speak around the lump in her throat and shook her head. "I promise you."

He pulled her back into his arms, rocking her back and forth. "I was so damn scared." Karl kissed her hair. "I wasn't that scared . . . ever."

"I'm fine. I'm back. And I'm fine."

"Yeah, well, doesn't mean I don't still want to kick their collective asses. I don't give a damn if one almost died—"

Katrina shoved him away and stumbled back a step. "Almost died?"

Karl's brow pulled low over his eyes and he nodded, a sharp single jerk of his chin. "Yeah, I heard he died en route—"

"Yes, he *died*," Katrina stressed.

He set his hands at his hips. "He did, yes. But, once they got him here Victor got him back. Got his heart restarted. He was technically dead for nearly four minutes, I heard."

With each word, her brother's ears became more muffled behind the loud thrumming of her heart. She must have swayed because Karl suddenly lunged forward and gripped her arm, keeping her on her feet. Her heart pounded so hard it made it hard to breathe, and she had to hang on to her brother to stay standing.

"Hey, stay with me," Karl said, steadying her again. "You okay?"

Katrina nodded, trying to clear her head and hear past the thundering. "Phin is alive?"

"Who is Phin?"

"Phin. Phin." Her logical mind reminded her Karl probably didn't know their names, but most of her logic was being overridden by the fact he was alive. She was halfway to the door before he grabbed her arm and stopped her short. "I have to go!"

"Why? Katrina, what are these men to you?"

"They are my friends, Karl." His incredulous look made her sigh. "I know you can't understand, I know it seems hard to believe, but Karl . . . honestly . . . they are good men. Despite everything, and you have no idea what I mean by *everything*, they are good men."

"Good men don't kidnap women."

Katrina closed her mouth and turned away, the argument to prove her point not nearly as important as seeing the boys. She *needed* to see them. Now. "Karl, come with me. Come see. They are good men."

He pressed his lips together in a hard line but dropped his hand from her arm. She offered a small smile and went out the door. They had brought her to one of the rooms off the immediate care wing so she could shower and change, but if she had to bet, she'd bet Victor moved the three of them to some of the rooms near the research wing to have them closer to her research. A pinch of guilt hit her as she climbed the stairs. While she was wallowing in her grief, she should have been gathering her research and giving Victor all the data she had and the hypothesis she'd formed.

Don't let it be too late for them.

"I need to tell you a few things on the way . . ."

"*Y*ou keep this up and you could do permanent, irreversible damage, Michael," Victor argued, raising his voice to be heard over the din of alarms and sensors and the excited, rapid-fire communication between medical staff.

Michael gripped the arms of the wheelchair Victor had forced him into, the pain ricocheting through him, radiating from the deteriorating, crumbling joint, biting. The agony was so intense it nauseated him, made his vision flash, the world tilt. The pain hadn't been this intense even before the surgery months before, not before or after.

"We both know the damage is already both permanent and irreversible, my friend," Michael forced through clenched teeth

Victor scowled. "There is no need so great as to rush along the progress."

"The lives of three men—"

"I can see to it, Michael," Victor snapped. "Just . . . sit here if you need to be here, but *do not* get out of that chair." When Michael opened his mouth to argue, Victor cut him off again. "I have effectively been your doctor since you were barely old enough to walk, and I will continue to be your doctor until I am unable. I know better than anyone here what you are capable of withstanding, but because you *can* withstand the pain enough to stand doesn't mean I'll allow it."

Michael drew a slow breath and stared at his longest friend. Then he nodded and settled into the chair as best he could, attempting to shift as much weight as he could to his left hip. Victor's response was a sharp jerk of his chin and he turned away, heading toward the chaos surrounding the three newly arrived patients. He stopped an attendant and said something to her. She nodded and headed out of the room.

As she opened the door to leave, Katrina and Karl Bauer rushed past her. "Victor!" Katrina called out, then saw Michael and crossed to him instead, crouching beside the chair. "Michael! Is it true?"

Michael smiled and nodded, knowing exactly what she asked. "Yes, he's alive. He's stable, and Victor is watching him carefully. Gideon and Daniel are both being sedated until we can find a way to treat them."

She looked past Michael to the beds, and the crowds gathered around them. "Can I see them? Can I see Phin?"

Michael laid his hand on hers where it rested on the arm of the chair. "Not yet, Katrina. Phineas isn't out of danger yet, and we don't know what we're dealing with."

"Did Victor tell you?" she asked, her focus snapping back to him.

"Nanotech. How did you come to this?"

"My first thought about it was the day after we left here." He noted the fact she made no reference to the departure as an abduction. "They ripped out their own appendages and the wounds closed within a couple hours."

"Right," Karl continued. "She said they had a higher resistance to the cold and seemed to recover from it faster than her. Though she's a wimp."

"Hey!"

Michael smiled, unable to deny his amusement at the banter between the siblings. At the thought of their relationship, he made an involuntary glance toward the three men being overseen by Victor's medical staff.

We are brothers. Before you were conceived we were created. From the same woman.

"You said Kathleen had found a way to punish them," Michael confirmed, focusing again on the Bauer siblings, specifically Katrina. "Whatever it is monitors chemical reactions in their hypothalamus."

"Gideon told me they've always known about the bionanetics—that's what they were called based on the Sorracchi translation—since their creation. And a few years ago Kathleen implanted a device at the base of their skulls to use the bionanetics as punishment. Certain chemical reactions in their brains triggered a reaction. It was supposed to be a deterrent."

"What chemical reactions? Do you remember anything specific?"

Katrina shook her head. "Um . . . in the hypothalamus. Oxy—Oxytocin."

"Compassion . . ."

"What?"

"She punished them for feeling compassion," Michael forced through clenched teeth. "Probably any type of chemical reaction indication of an undesirable emotion; anything indicating affection or attention to another, or probably even anger or the desire to rebel against her. Each emotion creates a different chemical and electrical reaction in the brain."

Katrina nodded, color draining from her face. She seemed to shake it off. "Karl thought we should test their blood."

Michael shook his head. "That might prove inconclusive. It would depend on the blood saturation level, and whether the devices are programmed to avoid extraction."

"Then how can we find out?"

"Begin with a full vial of blood and run the entire content through a scan. If we find something, we'll know, but if there is nothing there we can proceed with a full system electronic scan. I'm reluctant to try that first should the technology have security measures to prevent detection that could bring harm to them."

Her eyes shifted and her gaze lingered on the beds. "I'll have someone draw the blood," she said in a quiet voice. "Can we do anything else?"

"Begin there. The results will determine our next step."

Katrina nodded, her attention still held by the three men she had spent the last six days with. Michael disregarded the idea they had held her hostage, as many thought, her concern for them—and in turn, their concern for her—too genuine for something so malicious. What they had done was ill-advised, compulsive, but he had no doubt their intent never included bringing harm to her. Katrina stood and shifted through the crowd of medical staff to Victor, explaining with adamant hand gestures and nods of her head what she needed. Michael didn't need to hear her words to know her conviction.

He looked up at Karl Bauer, who watched his sister with a set determination in his jaw, his eyes pinched.

"I believe no harm came to her," Michael told him.

Karl looked down, but the hard set didn't release his features. "She told me the same thing. Doesn't mean I don't want to—" He dropped the statement without finishing the threat.

Katrina returned to them, stating the blood would be taken and she would oversee the testing immediately. Both she and Karl left the room together, the young girl casting one last glance to the beds before disappearing through the doorway.

The chaos in the room had dimmed, the conversation now low and calm, analytical in the treatment of the Triadic. They had been temporarily sedated in hopes of slowing the progress of whatever poison attacked their systems, and so their poorly mended wounds could be treated with care and without the risk of causing more discomfort than necessary. Michael watched, frustration digging at him with as much substance as the pain radiating along his right side. He'd managed to push the reality of it aside, a task he'd mastered in his youth to give him the strength and focus to survive his mother's "lessons," but he was out of practice and the pain was still too great to be ignored.

Victor came toward him, three vials of dark red blood in his hand. Michael assumed one for each of the Triadic. "Katrina's theory is interesting," he said, crouching in front of the chair, the vials in his open palm. "You think it's valid?"

"It's logical, and it fits her thought process."

Victor nodded. "That it does. Only a woman like Kathleen would devise a way to punish a man for giving a damn." He stood again. "I'm taking it to her in the biology lab, and Lois is going to help her with the analysis."

"Victor . . ." Michael called after him. His friend pulled up short and came back. "I need to ask a favor of you."

"Of course. Anything."

Michael looked at the vials in Victor's hand. "Do you have my DNA on file?"

Victor tilted his head, his brow pulling down in undeniable curiosity. "Not specifically, no. We've never had cause to analyze your DNA, Michael."

"I want you to." Michael cleared his throat and tried to shift, a spike of pain shooting straight up his spine. "Compare my DNA to the Triadic."

"I assume I'm looking for familial comparison." Michael could only nod, the pain ramping up to levels beyond his ability to speak. Victor waved one of the nurses to them. "Please get me an infusion syringe of hydroconophen and an empty sample syringe."

"No, Victor—"

"Yes." He waved off the nurse, then turned his attention back to Michael. "Don't argue with me, Michael. We need to get your pain under control before we can do another treatment. You knew the first wouldn't last more than a couple months, and the fall you took tonight aggravated the problem."

Unable to both hold an argument and focus on suppressing his reaction to the pain, Michael leaned into the arm of the wheelchair and braced his head in his hand. He had mastered the necessary act of pushing away reality, slipping past the pain, by the time he was about ten years old. He was aware of Victor straightening his right arm, tying on the tourniquet, and drawing the required blood. Then the hiss of the infusion syringe.

Gentle fingers combs through his hair and Michael inhaled. The hydroconophen slid through his system like heavy silk threads. He tipped back his head and opened his eyes, the effort exhausting, to look into Jacqueline's strained smile.

"Hey, handsome," she said, her voice sounding too far away for being so close. "I hear from Victor you're being stubborn."

Michael moved through thick air, his body unwilling to respond to his mind's demands. Words rolled around in his thoughts but couldn't make it to his mouth. He managed to grasp her hand and pulled it to him. Jacqueline moved around behind the chair, her hand pressed to his chest and he leaned his temple against her arm, trying to decide whether he should fight the lethargy or give in to the weight.

"It's good to see you again, Jacqueline," Victor said somewhere nearby, yet far away.

Their voices floated around him, only slightly more dominant than the sounds of the machines and doctors and nurses shuffling around the room. Michael closed his eyes and rubbed his cheek against the soft knit of her sweater, wishing he could feel her skin. She smoothed his hair, lulling him. He lost focus on their words, drug-induced sleep edging against his conscience. This is why he hated narcotics. Control was necessary at all times, and the drug took his control away.

"Tell me, Victor, because he hasn't. What happened in the surgery? Why is he worse now? What's wrong?"

"We didn't know what we were dealing with until we were in surgery, and we realized there wasn't much we could do but try to ease his pain as much as possible and keep him mobile as long as possible."

Michael pressed his eyes tighter and turned into her arm. He tried to tighten his grip, not wanting to hear again the reality of his physical fate. The final blow his mother had delivered before he took her life to save Jacqueline's.

"I have seen the evil of the Sorracchi, I know the lengths Kathleen went to torture Michael, and I know he hasn't told you most of it."

Jacqueline's fist curled over Michael's heart.

"When she took him last year, she assaulted his body so severely it is fading away, from the marrow of his bones. The bones of his leg and hip are crumbling."

Her gasp sounded like a siren in his muddled head. He tried to tell her he was sorry, but his brain and his mouth wouldn't connect.

"Sssshhh," Jacqueline said near his ear and kissed his cheek. "It's okay, Michael." She cleared her throat, and even in his muddled state, he heard the tears in her voice. And hated he was once again the reason. "What else?"

"He has no cartilage. I padded his hip joint with a compound as close to cartilage as we have available to us. I am going to do it again come morning, once we have the three men here stabilized, and I'll keep doing it as long as it does any good."

He didn't want to give in, but finally the hydroconophen overpowered him.

CHAPTER TWENTY-TWO

10 March 2054, Tuesday, 00:49 hours
Detainment and Interrogation Facility
United Earth Protectorate, Capitol City
Alexandria, Seat of Virginia
North American Continent

"*J* am one of hundreds, *Firebird*," the nameless Xeno spat out, lunging against his restraints. "Killing me will stop nothing. Tanner will die. We will regain our world. We will be free—"

Connor punched him and he stumbled back, landing hard in his chair.

"You're a little confused, Skippy," Connor said, leaning onto the table in the small, dark interrogation room. "We already regained our world. You seem to be a bit behind the times."

Skippy spit blood on the floor and laughed, giving Connor a crimson grin. "By Victory Day, Nick Tanner will be dead. Victory will be *ours*."

Connor straightened, not looking away from the Xeno. "I wouldn't bet my life on it." Then he turned his back and went to the door, leaving the prisoner in the dark when he hit the illumination control on his way out.

Mel waited for him in the hall, leaning against the wall opposite the door, her arms crossed over her body. Connor held her gaze and pressed his lips together, swallowing against the lump of rage working its way up from his chest. He pivoted left and she fell in step beside him. Firebird Sergeant Hastings snapped to attention as they approached.

"He gets nothing," Connor snapped as he passed. "No food, no water, no toilet. No damn light. Not until he gives up the information."

"Yes, sir."

He and Mel walked together to the end of the hall to the bullpen, dark at nearly one in the morning. Firebirds guarded the facility along the perimeter and outside the cells of the Xenos taken from the Falls Church shelter, and civilian peace officers held various positions throughout the building, calmer for the night shift, but the bullpen was empty. The dim light played with his vision and he squinted at the shadows. It had been weeks since the flash-bang bomb outside the embassy that had taken his vision for several days and left him sensitive to light for days more once his vision returned. He coped fine with the light now, but darkness still proved to be a challenge.

"I'll get a light," Mel said, moving away from his side for one of the desk lights.

"No," he snapped, immediately regretting his temper with her. He closed his eyes and dropped his head forward, clenching his fists against his waist. Connor drew a steadying breath through his nose and released it before he looked at her again. "I'm sorry. You didn't deserve that."

"You're angry, I get it."

"I'm not angry, I'm pissed, Mel. I'm sick and tired of being two steps behind these damn Xenos and their twisted—" He shoved at a chair and it slammed into another desk, the sound uncharacteristically loud in the hollow space. *Merde.*

"Hey." She stepped to him and laid her hand on his arm. "Look, I understand, Connor, but you're not going to be able to think straight if you let them get to you."

"I've been chasing traitors for weeks, and I'm no closer to figuring out who the hell is sabotaging the Tanner Administration from the inside than I was when John Smith was chased out of Alexandria," he said through clenched teeth. "Nick put this on *me* to figure out, and all I've been able to tell him is, 'I don't know.'"

Mel stepped closer and slid her hand up his arm to his shoulder. "And I promised you weeks ago *we* would figure this out together."

Connor looked away, past her to the bank of windows facing the city. They were on the fourth floor of the building, just high enough to see over the tops of some of the lower buildings. Mel touched his jaw and drew his attention back to her.

"President Tanner knows you're trying." She tilted her head, keeping her gaze connected with his.

"That's not it," he cut her off. She arched her eyebrows, the next question in the spark of her eyes. Despite his deep-set frustration, Mel had a way of calming him. She always had. In the hours following the destruction of Paris, she had been the grounding force that kept him from losing his mind. Connor took another calming breath and circled his hand behind her waist to draw her closer, against him.

Beyond her the night sky lit up with a boom of red, yellow, blue, and white. Mel jerked in his arms and looked over her shoulder. "Evacuation Day."

Connor took her face in his hands, and she welcomed his kiss with parted lips. He didn't dare let the kiss go for too long. The world was different, but many rules hadn't changed. He knew he walked a fine line—hell, he'd stepped over the line—but he didn't care for Melanie Briggs any more or any differently now than he did a few months before; the only difference was now he showed her.

And told her.

"I love you, Mel," he said against her mouth and kissed her again. She made a low sound in her throat and wrapped her arms around him, her hands sliding over his backside. Connor chuckled. "We'll talk more about this later."

Mel nodded. "Yes, we will."

Connor took a step back and looked toward the fireworks again. "I have to go to the hospital and brief Nick. He's there waiting for Michael to go into surgery."

"Okay. I'll be here in case the Xeno decides to talk."

Touching her only with his lips, Connor kissed her again. "Keep me posted." He was halfway to the door when she called his name, and he turned back. "Yeah?"

"I have a thought to run by you. Just a . . . possibility for someone to consider."

"Oh, you can't just toss something like that at me and leave me hanging."

The fireworks still lit up the sky, casting the bullpen in color and light so he could see the smirk on her face. "Okay. Sergeant Annie Nodal."

Connor tilted his head, staring at her as he ran the idea. "She serves as one of Nick's personal guards."

"Exactly. She would be privy to a great deal of information, the kind of information Xenos and other enemies of the administration would love to get their hands on, she receives communiqués, she is present in meetings. Just like that Jenifer woman assigned to John Smith. For all we know, she and Nodal—"

"No," Connor said, shaking his head. "Annie and Jenifer didn't work together, but we'll find out who she *is* working with. We'll dig into this further once things are calmer."

Mel laughed. Connor laughed with her when the absurdity of his own statement hit him. He raised his hand and waved her off before heading toward the door again.

"Connor . . ."

He chuckled when he turned. "What?

"I love you, too."

He smiled and winked and left her alone.

"*A*ren't we facing the same risk as with the last surgery?" Nick asked, seated beside his son's bed. His chest ached and he worked his palms together. "You're doing the same thing you did last time, right?"

Victor stood on the other side of Michael's bed, writing orders on a tablet. Michael was asleep, knocked out by the painkiller Victor had given him before Nick arrived, curled on his left side with his head resting in Jackie's lap. Jackie was wide-awake and listening, smoothing her fingers through Michael's hair.

"It's different this time in that we know what we're dealing with, and we know what we need to do. Last time, we thought we were going in to repair damage, and we found deterioration beyond anything we ever expected." He handed off the tablet to a nurse, who left the room. With her gone, Victor set his hands on the raised railing on the bedside. "We had to find a solution with him open, kept under anesthesia much longer than we would have wanted, and left exposed to infection. This time, I don't plan on this procedure taking more than thirty minutes."

"What can we expect?" Jackie asked. "Will he be as bad as he was? Worse?"

Victor shook his head. "I wish I knew, Jacqueline. This will, at the least, alleviate the pain to a manageable level."

"Is that really the best we can hope for?" The weight of her voice was as heavy as the weight in Nick's chest. "Bringing his pain to a manageable level? That means he'll always be in pain. Always."

Nick bowed his head and closed his eyes, swallowing hard.

"For now, yes," Victor admitted, his voice hoarse. "Three years ago, before everything went to hell, there was technology available right in this hospital to help him, but not now. Not anymore. Maybe . . ." He cleared his throat. "Maybe when we've recovered more as a society we can . . ."

Mercifully, he let it go.

Nick sat back and slapped his hands on his knees. "When are you taking him in?"

"We can't for another three hours at least because of the hydroconophen. The drug needs to break down in his system more before I put him under anesthesia. I'll take him into surgery first thing in the morning."

Nick looked to his son, still asleep nestled against Jackie. Silent tears streaked her cheeks and she raised watery eyes to look at Nick. He stood and went to the bedside, holding out a hand to the woman who he considered as much a daughter-in-law as if she bore the Tanner name. She took it, and he squeezed.

A soft knock at the door preceded young Doctor Katrina Bauer sticking her head inside. "I'm so sorry to disturb you," she whispered, and looked at Nick. "I'm really sorry, Mr. President, but I found out what we needed to know about Phin and the others."

Nick looked to Victor. "Phin?"

"It would seem our three new patients have names. Phineas, Gideon, and . . ."

"Daniel," Katrina finished, stepping into the room. She looked to Michael with wide eyes. "I'm so sorry about Michael, I—" She shook her head. "I'm just really sorry."

"We're glad to see you home safe." Nick offered what he was pretty sure was a damn pathetic smile. He'd been filled in on the apparent situation, specifically that Katrina Bauer showed no signs of abuse and insisted they had done nothing to hurt her. Other than drag her out into the cold against her will.

"Thank you, sir."

"What did you find, Katrina?" Victor asked.

She walked toward Victor, holding out a tablet. "It's what I thought, and what Karl suspected. And Michael, too." She looked briefly at

Michael again, and Nick thought he saw tears shine in her eyes. She was a soft soul, strong but compassionate to a fault, as far as he had seen. "According to the journals and files, all three of them have a neural interface inserted near their hypothalamus and their bodies are just full of bionanetic bots. Nothing says exactly where or what it looks like."

"We can determine that with an image scan," Victor interjected, reading the information on the tablet.

Katrina nodded. "The neural interface detects chemical and hormone changes triggered in the hypothalamus by certain emotional responses. It was an attempt by Kathleen—" She looked at Nick, and just as quickly looked away again, color blooming in her cheeks. "—to control their emotions, to keep them from caring, or showing compassion, or sympathy. She wanted them to be emotionless robots. But, it didn't work. No matter what she did. No matter how sick she made them, as soon as they recovered, they would . . . they would do it again."

She talked so fast Nick had a hard time keeping up with her, but he got the point. His ex struck again.

"Daniel slipped into a coma within an hour of arrival, and Gideon is failing. We'll need to decide then what to do within the next twenty-four to forty-eight hours, after I have a chance to go over your findings. I'll go over it while I wait to take Michael into surgery." Victor looked at Michael. "I would love Michael's input on this."

"Me, too," Katrina said in such a small voice Nick almost didn't hear her. "Me, too."

04:13 HOURS

"*P*lease, Gideon. Don't let him die. Please."
"*He's flatlining!*"
"No!"

The voices danced on the edge of a white, blank, existence. The sound of weeping made his chest ache; he wanted it to stop. Wanted to reach out to Katrina and ask what was wrong to make her so sad. She called his name, again and again.

Then silence.

The pain was gone. Perhaps for the first time in his life he was without discomfort, even in his joints and ligaments where a lingering ache always resided, a side effect of accelerated growth. He could breathe without the ragged scrape of steel wool in his lungs. His blood didn't burn like fevered acid.

Not yet, Phineas . . .

Phin jerked, torn from the white dream, the piercing shrill of alarms assaulting his ears. A plastic cup covered his nose and mouth and he stared up at a white ceiling. Phin thrashed, monitor cords and electrodes flailing in his attempt to be free.

"Whoa, whoa," came a man's voice from somewhere on his right just before he came into Phin's line of sight, leaning across the narrow bed to put his hands on each of Phin's arms, holding him still. Phin blinked for a moment, focusing past the mask obscuring his view. His features were familiar: angular and lean, dark olive tone skin, dark eyes, black hair. "You're okay, Phineas. You're with friends."

Phin snapped out with his mind, searching for Gideon or Daniel. Although he felt Daniel, the sensation was heavy and silent.

I'm here, brother.

Where are we? Where is Katrina?

We have returned to her people to save your life.

Daniel?

He is comatose, much like you were, and falters. As do I.

"Can you hear me, Phineas?"

Phin blinked and shifted his focus to the man standing over him. Victor. Somewhere on the edge of his memories, the name and his face came together. He had been on the video Katrina had shown Phin of the president's speech. He was a doctor. The doctor Katrina worked for directly.

"Yes," Phin finally answered. "Where is Katrina?"

Victor smiled, leaning over the bed so Phin could easily see his face.

He felt weighed down, although he recognized there was nothing fastened to the bed to hold him in place, only the man's hands. It was the weight of weakness, fatigue. The absence of pain had been replaced again by a dull ache in his joints, the ache he'd always known, but no searing, bone-scraping pain like he'd felt before the men had attacked. He was tired, drained, but stronger.

"Sleeping, I hope. But I doubt it."

A flash of a memory blinded him for a second, a too-vivid image of Katrina cornered by a man with a wrought iron bar in her hand. She swung, shouting, and the man dropped to the floor. Chaos and noise accompanied the image, and the ever-present awareness of his brothers as they fought as a unit. He gasped again and choked, battling to bring the room into focus.

"Easy, easy," Victor said again and glanced at the wall above Phin's head. "Your brainwaves are spastic and your heart rate is spiking. You need to calm down, Phineas."

Phin inhaled, tamping down the chaos fighting for dominance in his thoughts.

Be still, brother.

Even in his mind, his brother sounded strained. Weak. Faltering.

Are we in danger?

Only if they cannot duplicate your cure.

"I wish to see my brothers and Katrina Bauer," Phin demanded with as much authority as he could muster, which while he was stronger than he had been, he was not yet anyone to be reckoned with. He knew it, and he assumed so did they.

Victor stood straighter, releasing his hold on Phin. "Your brothers are here, in the same room, though none of you are in any condition to get out of bed." He stepped back and Phin rolled his head on his pillow, relief edging away the sharp panic when he saw Daniel; though his brother was still. Silent. "Katrina has been ordered to get some rest, but as I said, I doubt she is listening to me. She's safe, she's fine. We'll do what we can when we can to assure of you that."

She thinks you dead, brother. You died, and these people brought you back.

Phin blinked, processing his brother's revelation. "I died," he said aloud.

Victor nodded. "Yes, en route here. You were gone over three minutes, but we managed to get your heart restarted." The man huffed and shook his head, then ran his fingers over his short hair. "Damned if we know why, but you've been steadily improving since then."

"She knows I live."

Victor nodded. "Yes, and to say she was relieved would be an understatement." He smiled. "I'm sure she'll be here to see you soon."

Despite the fact he had only been awake a few minutes, fatigue dragged at Phin again and he fought to keep his eyes open. He blinked slowly, trying to stay focused. "You are Victor."

He nodded. "Yes."

"She told me you are to be trusted."

Victor smiled. "I will live up to her word."

Phin let himself drift back into sleep.

09:00 HOURS

"You look exhausted."

Katrina smiled, knowing it lacked any conviction, and lifted her head. She sat at the foot of David's bed, her familiar spot with her back to the footboard and her knees hugged to her chest, trying to stay awake just a little bit longer. With a tilt of her head, she rested her cheek on her knee and looked at David.

Even with her muddled head, she recognized the change in him in just a few days. He had more color, a healthier line to his features, his natural strong jaw giving him a look of strength both time and recovery would revive. His eyes were brighter, sharper, and had taken on what she assumed to be his natural golden-hazel color. His dark hair no longer contrasted against his skin to make him look sallow, but seeing him now, she believed she saw the man he had once been. She saw the man he would be again, she had no doubt.

"I'm trying not to sleep," she said, blinking slowly. "Keep my internal clock set right, you know? I figure by the time I go to bed tonight I'll sleep for at least twelve hours."

"Yeah but wearing yourself out doesn't do any good." David smiled, studying her. "As much as I'm relieved you came to see me, you should be taking it easy. You've been through hell; half this facility has been through hell worrying about you." With slow effort, his arms shaking with the strain, he slid his hand across the bed and touched the socks covering her feet. "I went through hell worrying about you, Katrina, and got just as torqued I couldn't help."

She reached for his hand and squeezed, tears burning her overtired eyes as pride swelled in her chest. "You're doing better," she managed to whisper. Her emotions ran on overdrive, magnified by fatigue. "I'm fine, David. I swear."

"Yeah, well, I'm holding judgment until I see these guys. I might not be able to kick their asses now, but don't think I won't."

Katrina chuckled and slowly blinked. As much as she needed to see David, and knew she had to assure him—like she'd had to assure everyone else—she had come home unharmed, physically, mentally, and every other way. "You sound like Karl," she said on a tired chuckle. "I told Phin he'd have Karl to worry about. I didn't think to warn him about my . . ." She chuckled again.

"Your overly concerned adopted uncle," David provided. "I'd say about three generations removed."

She smiled. "I never had an uncle." Katrina unfolded and slipped off the edge of the bed, leaning up to kiss David's cheek. "I'm going to go check on the boys."

David grinned. "The boys?"

She shrugged. "Yeah. I'll come see you later."

Katrina left David's room and made a brief detour to one of the small kitchenettes on the floor manned with coffee pots. She wasn't usually one for coffee, but with enough sugar she could stomach it and she really needed the kick to get her through the day. The beverage was bitter, even with sugar, she drank it anyway. News had come to her throughout the night about their progress, but she needed to see for herself. It was hard to comprehend Phin could be doing as well as the reports said. He had fully stabilized, his fever had broken, the infection in his wounds nearly completely gone and the wounds themselves were nearly sealed again. Minor topical surgery had been performed during the mid-morning hours to remove the metal plates still embedded into his body in an effort to decrease the possibility of further infection. They couldn't operate on Gideon or Daniel yet, a mixture of their deteriorating health and the necessity to remove the interface not being as urgent as with Phin.

The three of them had been moved to an observation room with a long window in the hallway along the length of the room so doctors and nurses could easily observe from outside and act more quickly if need be. She couldn't go in, the room restricted to only medical personnel until their illnesses and infections were under control, but she knew she would feel better if she could see they were okay.

She stepped into the hall leading to their room and smiled when she saw Victor in the hall, speaking with one of the nurses on staff. He glanced up, caught sight of her, and smiled.

"Katrina, come here," he called, motioning her toward him. He walked toward her, meeting her halfway, setting his hand on her shoulder. "I think you will be very happy when you see your friends."

"I can see them?"

"Only in the literal definition of the word, I'm afraid. But, if Phineas continues to improve you will be able to visit with him within the day. Now . . . if we could only figure out why Phin is improving and his brothers aren't."

He led her to the window and she looked inside. Gideon and Daniel were in beds side-by-side, both still and apparently asleep. Monitors above their heads kept a running visual of all their vital life signs. Doctor Jones stood beside Gideon's bed, and Doctor Corbin sat at one of the computer terminals. But it was the third bed that made Katrina gasp.

Phin sat in his bed, the head raised behind him for support, but he was awake and speaking with Doctor Lois Maybourne. The blankets gathered at his hips, and his sides were again bandaged, but the gauze was white and pure. Katrina smiled, tears of relief gathering in her eyes. She touched her fingers to her lips to smother the hitch in her throat. Victor squeezed her shoulder.

"I know a great many questions have risen around the circumstances of you leaving this facility last week—"

"Victor—"

He shushed her and shook his head. "While I don't think we can ever completely forget they took you from this hospital against your will, I believe you—and them—when you say they never harmed you or intended you harm. Whatever happened, those men hold a deep and abiding affection and concern for you, Katrina."

She turned away from the window to look up at him. "Daniel and Phin, maybe, but I'm fairly convinced Gideon has no use for me at all."

Victor laughed and arched an eyebrow. "Well, for a man who has no use for you, he was very quick to ask about your wellbeing as soon as he woke. But, he wasn't nearly as concerned as young Mister Phineas."

"Phin . . ." Katrina corrected and smiled. "I call him Phin."

"Either way," Victor said with a wide smile, "all three will be pleased to see you."

Victor rapped on the glass, drawing the attention of the doctors, and more importantly, Phin. He looked across the room, and Katrina saw in his eyes the moment he saw her. He smiled, and despite Doctor Maybourne's clear objections, Phin tossed back the blanket and slid off the bed. He wore infirmary pants almost identical the ones he'd worn the night they left, and although his steps were slow, he crossed the room to the window. Katrina stepped closer and laid her hands against the glass. When he reached the window he raised his hands and matched her position, aligning his fingers with hers.

Doctor Maybourne followed him and stood just behind him with a scowl on her face. Phin turned his head and spoke to her, the words too low to carry through the thick, mesh enforced glass. She shook her head and looked to Victor, seeking confirmation. He shook his head but chuckled. "As I suspected, Phin is very anxious to see you. *Beyond* the literal sense."

"Soon," Katrina said loud enough to draw his attention again. He stepped closer to the glass, looking down at her. "They said I can come in to you soon." She smiled and nodded. "I'm so glad you're better."

"My brothers are still ill."

His voice was muffled; she got as much from listening as watching his lips. Katrina nodded and hoped her smile showed encouragement.

"We're working on it. All of us. I promised you we would help."

"You have kept that promise."

She smiled and nodded, hoping he couldn't see the tears prickling at the back of her eyes. Doctor Maybourne touched Phin's arm and spoke. He turned away only for a moment to acknowledge her words, then back to Katrina.

"I'll come back later. I promise."

He nodded and allowed the doctor to guide him back to the bed. Katrina waited until he was reclined once again before she turned away. She was determined more than ever to figure out not only how the device fused to their brains worked, how it made them ill, but also why Phin was suddenly better and they weren't.

CHAPTER TWENTY-THREE

10 March 2054, Monday 17:23 hours
Alexandria Hospital, Secure Wing – Surgical Care
United Earth Protectorate, Capitol City
Alexandria, Seat of Virginia
North American Continent

"*A*re you supposed to be out of bed?"

Michael raised his head and smiled. "Is that a reprimand or an invitation?"

Jacqueline stopped short halfway across his recovery room, her elegant eyebrows arched high, then a slow, seductive smile bowed her lips. "Hmm, seems someone is definitely feeling better."

He took a moment to appreciate her beauty. She wore her hair loose, something she hadn't often done when actively training new Firebird recruits, and the dark blue sweater she wore looked suspiciously like one he *thought* was his. It appealed to him much more when she wore it, and because he had knowledge of what the sweater hid, he smiled at the almost imperceptible difference in her body. The baby she carried. Their baby.

Michael shifted his weight just enough to lean onto his shillelagh and beckoned to her with his other hand. "Come kiss me. I've missed you."

She stepped into his embrace and wrapped her arms around him, meeting his lips for a kiss a day and a half in coming. Michael cursed his inability to hold her with both arms, take her face in his hands and deepen the kiss, but he held her tight with the one arm he could and soaked in the rush she inspired. He had thanked God a hundred times over for her love, and her forgiveness.

"That is not resting."

Michael smiled against her mouth and kissed her one last time before drawing her to his side to look at Victor. "But far more therapeutic."

Victor chuckled and looked to Jacqueline, who shrugged. "Don't look at me. I was about to ask you what you've been putting in his IV."

"I doubt Michael's smile has anything to do with anything I've given him." Victor laid his hand on Jacqueline's shoulder and leaned down to kiss her cheek. "It's good to see you, Jackie. We've missed you, but none more than Michael."

Michael hooked his arm around Jacqueline's shoulders and brought her to him, pressing a long kiss to her hair. When she tipped back her head and looked at him, a sparkle in her dark eyes and a smile on her lips, Michael wanted to laugh. Not in amusement, but in acceptance of the gift—the *gifts*—he had been given. Not once, but too many times for him to number. She arched a single brow.

"What?" she said softly.

The answer for her too extensive to word, Michael smiled, a simple expression he'd found difficult for most of his life but one he found easier with each gift given him. He knew now, with absolute clarity, each truly was a gift. Looking into her eyes, an exceptional lightness of being filled his chest.

"We're having a baby," he said simply, sharing the news with his longest friend even though he couldn't look away from Jacqueline.

Victor whooped and Michael found his arms again empty when Victor pulled her free for a hug, then embraced Michael as well. "That's wonderful! Beverly will be thrilled. How far along are you?"

"Sixteen weeks," Jacqueline answered, coming right back to

Michael's side when Victor set them both free. "I'm due in August. I'm not going to be able to hide it much longer."

"Now that I know, I see it. I blame my lack of perception on my lack of sleep." Victor sighed and smiled, perhaps a touch of melancholy in his eyes. With a sudden jerk of movement, Victor embraced Michael again, loudly patting his back. Before releasing Michael, he said with a rusty voice, "I'm so happy for you, my friend. You deserve every happiness."

Then he stepped back and clapped his hands together. "Are you up for a conversation about our newest patients before I let you go home? I am anxious to hear your thoughts." Victor motioned toward the cushioned chair in the corner of the room adjacent to the bed. "We've worked out a few more details since early Friday morning."

Rather than move to the chair, Michael reversed the few steps he'd managed and returned to the side of his bed, easing onto the mattress to sit on the edge. The pain in his hip was little more than a dull throb, whether the final results of the surgery or the pain medications still lingering in his system. He eased himself down and reached for Jacqueline's hand to draw her to the space beside him. Victor didn't question and took the chair he'd initially offered, sitting on the front edge with his elbows on his knees and his fingers linked.

"What have you confirmed?" Michael asked.

"It's definitely nanotechnology, except it's not any kind of nanotech I've ever encountered." Victor shook his head and made a low, hissing sound through his teeth. "If mankind could redevelop technology like this, medicine as we know it would be changed forever. To say the way Kathleen used it is a shame and a monumental understatement."

"Their symptoms are caused by nanotechnology," Michael stated in confirmation, and Victor nodded. "How infiltrated are their systems?"

"That's just it, Michael," Victor said, holding out his hands palms up. "It's not just nanotechnology, it's biomechanical. Their *blood* is the nanotechnology. Their systems are infused with it. I have no way to prove it, but my theory is they were *created* with this technology incorporated into their genetic makeup." He began ticking off each point on his fingers. "It sped up and regulated growth, it increases their speed, boosts their immunity and their strength, heightens their senses, increases their learning capacity exponentially, and during whatever gestation period they underwent it magnified the latent genetic markers that predetermined they would have Talents of some kind whether genetically manipulated or not."

The magnitude of the revelation pushed Michael back and he sat up straighter, releasing Jacqueline's hand to rub his forehead, processing the information. "Did this programming to recognize and punish emotional responses exist from infancy?"

Victor sat back and raised one leg to rest his ankle on his other knee. "No, not if I am correctly interpreting the records Katrina deciphered. Based on those files, Kathleen recognized their emotional reactions as a diversion from their indoctrination, and she had a failsafe implanted into each of them to manipulate the bionanetics. The bionanetics were programmed from creation to be used as tools to progress their development, the poisoning was an added application. Katrina told me Gideon confirmed as much when he told her they knew when the neural interface was implanted. They always knew why. They also knew from the moment they woke up they could eventually die."

"How was that done?"

"A neurological device was implanted near their hypothalamus to monitor brain activity and hormonal/chemical changes. The device is linked to the entire bionanetic system and uses the pre-existing technology to affect every major system as punishment for adverse emotional responses."

"If she didn't want them to feel emotion, why didn't she just use this technology to change their biochemical reactions? Just . . . suppress them," Jacqueline asked, looking from Michael to Victor. "Keep them from happening at all."

Michael stared at Victor, seeing the truth he knew in his friend's grim expression. He found her hand again and laced his fingers through hers, drawing in a slow breath. "Because turning off their ability to feel emotions would be too simple. If she turned off one emotion, she would have to turn off all emotion." He looked away from Victor and to her. "Take away their emotions and they would feel no fear, and no hope."

He saw the slow realization flitter through her dark eyes, and her hold tightened a small degree. Michael lifted their joined hands and kissed her knuckles, never looking away from her. "Hope is a powerful motivator, but fear is just as powerful."

"If they didn't fear her," Victor said just outside Michael's peripheral, "she lost control."

Jacqueline closed her eyes and swallowed hard, a single tear squeezing free to run down her cheek. She leaned into Michael and rested her forehead on his shoulder. "The more I know about this woman, the more I hate her."

He circled his arm behind her shoulder and held her against him, looking back to Victor. "Has Njogu been able to offer any thoughts on reengineering the chip, or do you believe it is something we can remove?"

"We are still working on solutions. I've ordered every kind of non-evasive scan we have the capability to perform, and we are completing the exams on all three of them should there be some kind of variation, but I find that possibility doubtful."

Michael nodded. "How are they doing?"

Victor shook his head and pinched the bridge of his nose. He looked exhausted, and Michael knew he hadn't been home for more than a few hours since they had discovered Katrina's disappearance, and he had slept very little in the last forty-eight hours. His friend scrubbed his face with the palm of his hand and focused again on them.

"Phin is improving by the hour. He is stronger, his wounds are healing so quickly you can almost observe the healing process. His infection is gone. The toxin levels in his blood are nearly undetectable. I suspect by tomorrow morning he will be as strong as he has ever been." He sighed and shook his head. "His brothers are failing. Both Gideon and Daniel have had to be sedated to slow the poisoning effect. Gideon is only slightly stronger than Daniel, and I'm convinced part of that is sheer will power. Daniel is running a fever of one-hundred-six, with accelerated heart rate, low blood-oxygen levels, and toxin poisoning in his blood. He's the worst of the three at the moment."

"Is that all we can do? Sedate them? What about—"

"They refused pharmaceutical mood dampeners." Victor cut him off, raising one had. "Or, I should specify, Gideon spoke on behalf of the Triadic in a moment of lucidity and refused them."

Michael nodded. "I would have expected that decision. I would imagine after having to repress their emotional reactions, even though the acceptance of those emotions causes pain and illness, they would rather have them than not."

"I think it goes deeper than that." Victor waited until Michael met his gaze. "I believe this has a great deal to do with Katrina Bauer." When Michael didn't answer, Victor continued. "You haven't had the chance to observe them since they returned. Katrina has been adamant no harm came to her while she was with them. She has said repeatedly they never threatened her beyond taking her with them, and they were very mindful of her and her needs while in Falls Church."

"She appeared completely unharmed and without fear when we arrived other than her concern for them. Do you not believe her?"

"That's just it," Victor said, tapping the arm of the chair with the tip of his finger. "Everything I've observed supports that fact. She came to the observation room this morning, and the interaction I observed between her and Phin spoke clearly of an emotional connection. She cares a great deal for these men, and I believe it is mutual." Victor shifted forward, assuming his original position with his elbows on his knees. "When they first woke, each of them asked first about her, and then about each other."

"They have placed value on her word. She told me she promised them we would help them," Michael offered.

"It's more than that, my friend." Victor shook his head. "I believe all three of them have developed an intense affection for Katrina."

"You mean they've all fallen in love with her?" Jacqueline asked.

"In a broad sense, yes." Victor's eyebrows rose and he paused. "Or . . . perhaps *one* of them has fallen in love with her, and by means of their connection, they all feel for her. They share the affection of one."

Unable to sit still any longer, Michael leveraged himself forward and held up his hand when Victor moved to leave his chair. He shifted into his familiar gait with the cane as support and crossed the room to the only window. It was late afternoon, and the city was gray. The town center was to be opened tonight to anyone who wished to come, offering a hot meal and provisions, and the invitation to celebrate together as part of the week's events. His father was to speak, and Michael had intended to be there. Pushing aside the random disappointment, he turned and walked back to the bed.

"There are very few emotions that inspire as much of a visceral reaction as love. Few with more power, save perhaps fear." He pivoted on the tip of the shillelagh, a realization shifting over him like a cold breeze. "Phineas."

Victor smiled and nodded. "You have observed them far less than I, but if you can come to that conclusion so quickly I feel better about my own train of thought."

"So, what . . . you keep her away from them?" Jacqueline asked.

Michael looked to Jacqueline and took the single step needed to be within reaching distance. She tipped back her head to look at him, and he welcomed the warm bloom in his chest. He touched her cheek and laid his palm along her jaw. "Whether she is with him, or away from him, if he loves her he will love her. I doubt the device doing this to them deciphers between the rush of endorphins because the woman you love is near, or the variation when she is not and you wish her to be."

"I'm not convinced Phineas is any danger of harm at this point. Just as you said, Michael, she affects him in her presence as well as her absence, and he continues to grow stronger."

A knock at the door drew the attention of all three, and Michael turned to see a young nurse—he believed her name to be Barbara Schroeder—step into the room, an access tablet in her hand. "Doctor, the genetics lab asked me to bring this information to you." She held the tablet toward Victor and smiled at Michael and Jacqueline.

"Thank you, Barbara," Victor stood and crossed the small room to take the tablet from her. "I appreciate your assistance."

She nodded and left, and while Victor reviewed the information on the screen Michael eased himself onto the bed again beside Jacqueline.

He watched his friend's expression shift from slight skepticism to surprise, and waited for Victor to look up, hoping the results might provide answers. Specific answers. He didn't realize he'd reached for Jacqueline's hand until she laced her fingers through his and squeezed gently, covering both their hands with her other.

"Is there something wrong?" she said softly enough it was meant only for Michael.

"Wrong, no. If those results are what I think, they are simply answers."

Victor looked up from the tablet and stepped to Michael, holding it out so the information faced him. "It's the test results you asked for, my friend. I don't know what you wanted, or expected, but there it is."

Michael took it and motioned with a tilt of his chin toward the table beside the bed. Victor retrieved his glasses for him and he slipped them on, scanning the information on the screen. The report results were presented in basic format, with detailed DNA and profile data in connected screens, but the main result page told him what he needed to know.

Subject A: Michael Sean Tanner
Subject B: Gideon Last Name Unknown
Subject C: Daniel Last Name Unknown
Subject D: Phineas Last Name Unknown

Test Result #1
Comparison Subjects B, C, D
100% allele correlation
100% mitochondrial correlation
Result Indication = Identical Siblings

Test Result #2
Comparison Subjects A, B
22% allele correlation
100% mitochondrial correlation
Result Indication = 97% likelihood of familial/sibling relationship with shared maternal DNA

Test Result #3
Comparison Subjects A, C
22% allele correlation
100% mitochondrial correlation
Result Indication = 97% likelihood of familial / sibling relationship with
shared maternal DNA

Test Result #4
Comparison Subjects A, D
22% allele correlation
100% mitochondrial correlation
Result Indication = 97% likelihood of familial / sibling relationship with
shared maternal DNA

"What does all that mean, Michael?"

Michael looked up and to Jacqueline, a strange apprehensive tingling dancing along his skin. He didn't know how to process the knowledge, didn't know what it could mean or what to do with the information. Didn't know if it should or could mean anything at all. More than anything, Michael wanted to talk to his father.

"It means Gideon, Daniel, and Phineas—the three men whom we found on the *Abaddon*—are my half-brothers."

Her eyes widened and her lips parted, and she blinked three times before speaking again. "Not . . . Nick . . ."

Michael shook his head. "No, they claim to also be biological offspring of Kathleen, though not conceived or brought to term in the same manner if the information Victor has gathered is true." He finished the statement by looking to Victor.

"You're likely correct. The records Katrina deciphered imply, though it isn't clearly detailed, the Triadic was created within a laboratory and the bionanetic technology suffused into their biology aided growth and development outside a natural womb." He looked to Jacqueline. "Michael, on the other hand, was conceived and carried through gestation as a normal Human child would and allowed to grow without acceleration."

Jacqueline shook her head and moved to stand. Michael reached for her with his hand not gripping his cane and helped her to her feet. She tugged Michael's sweater over her hips. "Boy, that wacko bitch cannot be dead enough."

Michael clenched his jaw and cupped the back of her head to draw her close and press a kiss to her forehead.

CHAPTER TWENTY-FOUR

10 March 2054, Monday 20:41 hours
Two miles from the Presidential Residence
Alexandria, Seat of Virginia
North American Continent

"*W*e're almost there, sir."

Nick came out of his heavy doze with a jerk, his tired neck muscles protesting when he leveraged his head off the back of the hover seat. He blinked and covered his face with his hands, scrubbing his palms over his cheeks to push aside the tendrils of sleep. A few more blinks and he brought Connor into focus beside him. Mel Briggs sat in the seat facing them.

"Didn't think I was that tired," Nick mumbled, shifting to sit up and look out the window at the passing landscape. They were outside the city, as much of a city as there was, into the rural areas where buildings were further apart and the horizon was dark without electricity to run streetlamps or any other form of illumination.

"It's been a long few days." Connor's trailing voice told Nick more than the shadows of his face in the dim light of the hover interior.

"So, what's up?"

Connor chuckled and Nick caught the shift of his eyes when he looked toward his 2IC before answering. "Good news and bad news, sir."

"Hit me with the bad news first."

"The prisoner we brought back from Falls Church died about twenty minutes ago. They still haven't identified the toxin that killed him, or how he managed to dose himself in the cell. The Alexandria lab is working on it, but we've been advised they're overloaded and can't give a timeframe when they'll have an answer."

Nick nodded and squinted into the darkness. The Xeno had remained stone cold silent about any assassination plans since his arrest in Falls Church, despite Connor's aggressive interrogation. He'd done his fair share of taunting, making threats, and calling names, but nothing useful. Then he'd been found on the floor of his cell, spasming and frothing at the mouth, early that morning. Connor had received word throughout the day on the man's condition, and had passed it on to Nick, but the death wasn't a surprise. Without knowing how to treat him, they had no way of keeping him alive.

"Tell them to keep their focus on the living," he said, the words heavy in his throat. *Focus on the living.* Great advice, since the number of living seemed to be dwindling too fast to keep up with. "What's the good news?"

"Michael's detail reports he and Jackie have been delivered to the residence without issue. The Firebirds have taken up position for the night and will buckle down everything once you're in the house and secure."

Nights like this Nick missed the cabin in Maine with a hard ache in his chest. It had only been a few months since he'd been there with Caitlin, Michael, Jackie, and Nicole. It had only been for a couple days to check on Michael, since he was still recovering from the Bitch's torture, but the fresh air and lush green had revived his resolve. He needed another dose.

Especially after spending the last several hours with the worst victims of the war. A year later, and he felt no closer to recovery than he had after declaring victory against the Sorracchi. Logically, logistically, he knew things were better. Each day another shelter was established, another settlement received a shipment of food, medicine, and necessities, another baby was born without the reign of the Sorracchi, but it wasn't enough.

Nick scrubbed his face again, as much to wake up as to shake off the maudlin wet blanket smothering him.

"Good," he finally said in response to the news. Another thought punched through his tired haze and he jerked up his hand, tapping the air with his fingertip. "Vic got any word on the Triadic?"

"Not that I've been informed, sir."

He nodded and went back to his window. Another quarter mile and they'd be at the residence. The hover had slowed to a more casual speed in preparation for a turn coming up soon. The shift of the power hummed through Nick just like flying a glider. He felt it rather than heard it.

"Sir, there is one thing I'd like to bring up with you before we reach the residence," Connor said, and cleared his throat. "It's a theory we have about who has been leaking information to the Xenos."

That got Nick's attention and he twisted in the seat to better face both Connor and Mel. "We?"

"Captain Briggs and myself. We haven't anything right now other than an educated guess, but I felt you should know before we dig too much deeper—"

"Who," Nick managed to say without biting out the word.

"Sergeant Annalise Nodal," Connor said, a grim twist to his lips. "She fits the profile, first and foremost being female as indicated in the surveillance tapes we've all heard. She has ongoing and nearly unmitigated access to you when she is on detail. She could access files if given the opportunity—"

"Yeah," he snapped, holding up his hand. The reality left a bitter taste in his mouth. He liked Annie. The idea of her being a traitor didn't compute. Didn't make any sense. She was in his home, with his family. She had sworn to protect them to her own death. She . . . she had access to everything, just like Connor said.

Nick shifted forward and rested his elbows on his knees, dropping his head forward with a tired strain across the back of his neck. "How much evidence do you have right now?"

Connor shook his head and pressed his lips together. "Speculation right now. This is a new theory based on what we know and what we suspect. We begin investigating now. We need to keep this between us until we either rule her out or prove our suspicions."

"That means keeping her in the house."

"Do you want her reassigned?"

Nick shook his head and clenched his jaw. "No, we hold the status quo," he hissed through gritted teeth. "We have a better chance if she has no idea we're on to her, *if* there is anything to be on to."

"Understood."

Nick looked to Mel, who had remained silent through the whole conversation. She met his gaze without wavering, then nodded with a sharp jerk of her chin. The hover slowed and stopped in front of the house he called home as long as he held the title of President of the Protectorate. Low lights glowed in the living room window, the oil lamps they used to conserve power. The house was fully powered, but he refused to tap into more energy than necessary when it could be allocated elsewhere.

Connor exited the hover and waited outside the door for first Mel then Nick to exit. The night air was bitter cold, prickling at his skin. His breath curled in front of his face when he exhaled.

"Sergeant Garcia is on duty tonight," Connor said with a tip of his head toward the porch. Garcia was one of three Firebirds, including Annie Nodal, who alternated watching the First Family when Connor and Mel weren't on call. "He'll see you inside."

At least he didn't have to put on his game face tonight. He was too tired. "Come in for a few minutes?" Nick asked, his boots crunching in the snow when he moved toward the stairs.

"No, thanks," Connor answered, the formality of his position dropping momentarily when he slipped into the role of brother-in-law. "We're going to head back and make a plan. Tell my sister I said hi."

Nick nodded and raised a hand in a casual wave before climbing the steps. Garcia opened the door and let him inside, following him. The interior of the house was toasty warm and smelled of burning wood, baked bread, and coffee. A roll of combined laughter came from the sitting room off the foyer, he easily differentiated Jackie, Michael, and Caitlin, and he smiled.

"Nicky, is that you?" his wife called from the other room.

"I sure hope so," he called back, shrugging off his coat to hang it by the door. "Otherwise, a strange man just strolled into the house and is about to go looking for whatever smells so good."

She came into the foyer, arms wide and a smile on her beautiful face before he finished, and he had her in his arms in time to punctuate his promise with a kiss. Caitlin wrapped her arms around his neck and he pressed his cold face into her shoulder, garnering a chuckle and tap on his back when she pulled away.

"Your nose is cold."

Nick chuckled and kissed her again. "How is our boy?"

Caitlin wrapped her arm behind him and they walked together into the sitting room. "He's moving slow, but says the pain is less."

Michael turned and looked at Nick over the back of the couch, Jackie snuggled beside him. "Hey, Dad."

Nick patted his son's shoulder before walking around the couch to take one of the seats facing them. A good fire crackled in the hearth, and Dog was stretched out on his side in front of it. Nicole was nowhere to be seen, so he assumed she had been put to bed at least a couple hours before.

"Sit down and relax." Caitlin smoothed her hand over his hair on her way past to the kitchen. "I'll warm up some dinner for you. Are you a little hungry, or a lot hungry?"

"A lot."

"I'll help you," Jackie said, swinging her legs off the couch. She squeezed Michael's knee before standing, and he watched her walk out of the room, a telling smile on his face.

His son looked happy. There had been a time Nick wasn't sure he'd ever seen his son undeniably happy, especially in the last few weeks. Nick settled into his chair, enjoying the fire warming his left side. Eventually Michael's attention shifted back to him from the kitchen doorway, still smiling.

Nick tipped his chin toward his son. "Doing good?"

Michael nodded and shifted his shillelagh between his knees, twisting it on its tip. "Yes. The treatment worked better this time, the pain is reduced, and I have as much mobility as before." He looked toward the kitchen again when the sound of dishes carried to them. When he looked back, the smile was still there but a tense pinch had appeared around his eyes. "I need to talk to you and Mom when they come back."

"Something I need to worry about?"

Michael shrugged, an action not often seen from his son who tended to live in absolutes, unfamiliar enough to make Nick raise his eyebrows. He shifted forward and set his elbows on his knees, watching Michael for more of a sign of what to expect.

"I haven't decided what my appropriate response should be," Michael finally said, focusing on the head of his cane as he spun it.

"Your appropriate response is your genuine response, Michael."

His son looked up but didn't have a chance to say anything before Jackie and Caitlin came back into the room. Caitlin handed Nick a plate of chicken and rice and a glass of water while Jackie reclaimed her spot on the couch beside Michael. Once Caitlin settled in her chair, Nick took a drink and motioned toward Michael.

"Our boy has something to tell us," he told Caitlin. "If it's to tell us you got your girlfriend pregnant, we already know."

Jackie chuckled, but Michael only tilted his head. Nick waved off the joke, realizing half a second too late his son wouldn't see the humor. Not because he was upset by the comment itself, but because he had no idea why it would be funny. Twenty-five years of living in a hell of Kathleen's creation. Even now, the thought of the slug bitch made Nick's blood pressure spike and his blood heat.

"Never mind. What do you need to tell us?"

The fact Jackie reached for Michael's hand didn't go unnoticed, and Nick mentally braced himself.

"The Triadic wanted me to accompany Connor to the shelter because they were aware of my existence." He looked straight at Nick. "They learned of me from Kathleen after my birth."

"Why?" Nick set aside the dinner, his stomach protesting the idea of food.

Michael's expression never wavered. "They were the first she created." He paused a heartbeat. "They are my brothers."

Nick was on his feet before he actually registered the thought to stand. "How? Everything we've learned said you were the first she—" Nick choked, blinked. "Are they your *full* brothers?"

Michael shifted forward and gained his feet, though slowly. He took the step needed to bring them face-to-face, and only then answered with a shake of his head. "No. The only biological connection we share is through her."

Nick swallowed, not absolutely sure whether he felt relief or regret. "Did you confirm this?"

Michael nodded. "Victor received the results today. There is no margin for question. We are brothers. Gideon, Daniel, Phineas, and myself."

Nick turned away and scrubbed his face with his palms, groaning. He turned back, hands on his hips. "How do you feel about this?" Nick stepped closer and set his hand on Michael's shoulder. "Before you tell me you don't know how you are supposed to feel, I'm going to remind you, whatever you feel is right. Don't try to feel anything except what you feel."

Michael nodded, barely a movement of his head. Nick waited, letting his son find whatever answer he could give. Michael looked past him to where Caitlin sat, then back to Nick. "I honestly don't know how I feel about them being my brothers. But . . ." He stepped back and paced away, leaning heavily on his cane, before turning back. "I am concerned for them, knowing in all likelihood they suffered at her hands. I want to learn more about them." He drew a deep breath. "I want to help them. I want to fix whatever she did to them, just as you did for me."

11 MARCH 2054, WEDNESDAY 07:15 HOURS
VICTORY DAY

"*K*atrina and Karl have spent the better part of the last two days going over every piece of information we have, from medical to technical," Victor explained from the head of the table. Behind him was a display screen and PAC interface, primed and ready for her presentation.

Victor's entire team was here, and even some that weren't part of the team. Michael Tanner, who had never been designated part of the team but was still considered an integral part, sat to Victor's right. Doctors Averill Jones and Agatha Corbin on his left, both the on-staff xenobiologists, Doctor Jones bringing extra-planetary experience because she herself was Areth. Karl sat between Katrina and Michael, and Doctors Lois Maybourne and Richard Anson across from them. Victor's theoretical biologist Corin Lordahl was on his way back from Areth. The final two seated were mechanical engineering and reverse development specialists Njogu Anini of Raxo and Ms. Carmen Ellis. The team had been assembled with the knowledge each of them would have some kind of valuable input whenever dealing with anything foreign or alien, and this case was a prime example.

"At this point we know *everything* we can about physiology, biology, even chemistry and genetic interfacing." He tapped the table with his fingertips. "I don't intend to leave this room until we have a plan."

He motioned toward Katrina, and she nodded, tamping down the nervous clenching of her gut as she stood. Michael offered an encouraging smile as she passed, and Victor patted her shoulder before he sat. Both men knew this was not her strength; in fact, this was one of her greatest fears. She'd practically begged Karl to speak for her, but he insisted—and was right, in the most annoying way possible—she still had more first-hand experience with the three men and was the most qualified to speak.

She cleared her throat and set her PAC on the table, remotely linking it to the screen behind her so her actions would relay for everyone to see. With a tap and slide of her fingertips, the three-dimensional schematic of the neural interface appeared both on her tablet and on the screen behind her, transposed over an x-ray view of Gideon's skull. She touched the screen and a red dot appeared over the interface. She pinched her fingers and opened them, and the image expanded four hundred percent.

"The neural interface device has been implanted at the base of the hypothalamus, with a direct connection into the spinal column," she explained, keeping her focus on the diagram and not all the eyes watching her. "It constantly records and analyzes both chemical and hormonal shifts in the hypothalamus and specific patterns of brain waves, all of which may indicate what . . ." she stuttered over the words, hating to reference the woman in any way, " . . .th-their creator deemed weak, undesirable emotional responses."

She finally looked up, meeting first Michael's compassionate gaze. He wasn't the one she had to convince, she knew he understood what Kathleen—his mother, *their* mother—was capable of. Instead she looked to the others at the table who only had inklings, stories.

"I read in her journals she had all three of them beaten because during a training exercise when they were equivalent to seven-year-old boys the one we call Daniel stumbled and fell and his brothers stopped to help him stand. When physical punishment proved insufficient to train them against such intuitive reactions, she had the neural interface grafted to their skulls."

Some of the team members looked away, some shook their heads, others made small sounds of pity and disapproval. She knew she didn't need to convince them how wrong this was, or that they had to fix it; she wanted to show them who Phin, Gideon, and Daniel were so they realized they weren't working on Sorracchi-created machines. They were men.

Tapping and sliding her fingers again on her screen, she switched the three-dimensional display for a magnified slide of their blood analysis. Even at this magnification, the bionanetics they had found were tiny and difficult to see. On the single image, there were a dozen grafted and linked inseparably from their biology.

"The three of them were created from a single egg but split during the zygote stage into the three personalities who exist now." She shook her head, knowing the unasked question. "We don't know anything about paternal contributions to the process. They were grown in mechanical wombs, each manipulated slightly to develop certain personality traits and to foster certain skills. Part of this was accomplished using bionanetics."

She slid open her pinched fingers and the blood sample magnified again, bringing one of the bionanetic devices into sharper view. It was, even then, little more than a tiny dot, appearing almost like a miniscule tic.

"The bionanetics influenced their cognitive and physical development. Although we have no solid timeframe, we suspect their entire gestation took about eight weeks before they were removed from the mechanical wombs. They were then, most likely, moved into developmental pods—based on data logs and personal observations we've translated—where their physical development was accelerated again to bring them to what she termed a 'trainable' age."

Katrina swallowed hard and engaged a video clip she'd deciphered over the weekend. There was no sound, but sound wasn't necessary. The video showed three young boys, standing in their automatic configuration, dressed in black with hair cropped close to their heads. The golden-flecked hazel of their eyes marked them undeniably as the three men resting down the hall, even at their young age in the video. Their young expressions were set and firm. They moved together in practiced synchronization through several moves designed to train in hand-to-hand combat. One lost his balance, she knew it was Daniel, and the other two faltered. A brunette woman, tall and thin, attractive if one didn't know the darkness of her soul, came into the screen and without pause, backhanded Daniel. Both Gideon and Phin flinched, earning the same for themselves.

Katrina dared a glance toward Michael, who sat silent with a clenched jaw and fisted hand. This was his mother, Kathleen, the same woman who had rained abuse and torture down on him for over two decades, doing the same to three helpless boys.

She swallowed and stopped the video, returning instead to a data graph of the neural output to the bionanetics, various spaghetti string lines in different colors. "The bionanetics were used throughout their development to accelerate growth, and eventually to pause it, to enhance learning skills, to increase intelligence, and to promote accelerated healing, and to either create non-existent psychic abilities— or what we now call Talents—or to enhance what already existed on a genetic level. It is our belief the bionanetics have become integral to their entire biochemical system, just like a portion of the brain dedicated to automated functions like breathing, the heart beating, blood flowing." She paused to take a breath and slid the data away to reveal another chart. "A couple years before they were placed into stasis, the neural interface was implanted to interact directly with the bionanetics to initiate punishment when the previously mentioned emotional impulses were displayed." She swallowed and shifted her gaze around to each person. "The bionanetics make their own body toxic. They attack organs and create symptoms from the inside out, increasing in severity as long as the undesirable reaction is present."

"Can the bionanetics be turned off," Doctor Corbin asked. "There must be a way. Isn't one of them improving in health?"

"It would be like defibrillating a beating heart," Michael added. "The heart was working properly, but a shock used to restart a still heart can stop a natural rhythm. The heart may not know how to beat on its own."

"Is it a greater risk than letting them die slowly?" Doctor Corbin asked.

Katrina looked to Victor and Michael, hoping they would step in and help her explain. She could talk machinery, and theory of reaction, but not the actual toll on their bodies.

"We want to find a better solution. Either we disconnect the neural implant, deactivate it, or find a way to remove it so they can continue as normal men," Victor said, standing. "I am reluctant to trade one evil for another."

"Do we have full detail schematics of dis device?" Njogu asked as he stood and made his way toward the large display screen.

"Uh, yes . . . hang on . . ." Katrina fumbled to open the image again, but rather than putting it on the screen, she engaged the holographic program from her tablet and the enlarged interface appeared two feet above the table in lifelike detail.

She stepped back so Njogu could take a closer look. She felt short around most adults, but Njogu made her feel tiny. He was closer to seven feet tall than six, long limbed, and in comparison to Humans, had disproportionately long fingers. But for the Umani of his sovereign, he was the average. Large obsidian eyes took in the details of the hologram, and he rotated it with flicks and slides of his hands through the air around it.

"How much of dis from Sorracchi record? How much from scans?"

"I found schematics on the computer hard drive from the *Abaddon,* that makes up about eighty percent of what you see. We filled in with detailed scans performed on Gideon exclusively," Katrina explained.

"Have we determined de power source?"

"The body is the power source, completely renewable," Katrina explained. "It takes its energy from the natural charge and conductivity of the Human body."

Njogu fell silent after that, barely blinking as he studied the design. Carmen Ellis joined him and Katrina stepped back further, giving the two reverse engineering specialists room to study.

Doctor Jones also stood and came to the display board to look over the graphics Katrina had displayed. The charts correlated physical reactions to various incidents, from waking from their drug-induced sleep, to her last visit with Phin when the data had been recorded non-stop. She diverted her eyes when Doctor Jones read the explanation of the event and looked her way.

"Can we suppress their emotional responses until we find a solution?" Doctor Jones asked Victor and Michael. "Short of keeping them in near comatose states? Perhaps a mood suppression drug, or a more basic relaxant."

Victor shook his head. "I have mentioned this option to them, and they are against it. Regardless, at this point, Phin seems unaffected since . . ." He trailed off and looked to Michael. "Since he died en route to the hospital and was revived."

Michael nodded, some kind of unspoken communication between

them. Michael arched an eyebrow and Victor inhaled and pushed his hands into his pockets, focusing his attention again on Doctor Jones.

"Understand this is the first time in their entire existence they have been with people who genuinely hold concern for their well-being. People who care for them, and people they can care for other than each other." Victor did smile then. "If I could hypothesize on Kathleen's greatest error when creating these men, I would say it was the fact they are brothers. Had she taken three separate men and tried to mold them into this . . . *fighting machine* . . . she wanted, she might have avoided the inevitable bond held between siblings. They have between them a bond that cannot be broken, and that bond fostered the very Human reactions she sought to smother."

Katrina had to look away and swallow hard against the lump in her throat.

Njogu called out to her with a question, forcing her to focus on the task at hand. For the next three hours they analyzed every piece of data, every diagram, every scan, every x-ray, and idea after idea was presented . . . then excluded from possibility. As noon came and went, the knot in Katrina's stomach twisted tighter and harder. Finally, Victor called for a brief break and everyone filed out of the room. Katrina slumped into a chair and folded herself forward, covering her face with her hands, her forehead on her knees.

Wheels squeaked as someone pulled a chair closer to her, then sank into it. Then a comforting hand stroked across her back. Katrina turned her head, expecting to see her brother, but instead saw Victor. Karl stood past him near the door, undoubtedly waiting for her, but giving her space.

"You did an amazing job on this, Katrina. I wanted to make sure you knew that." He smiled and tilted his head. "Though, I understand the personal motivation."

She smiled back and nodded, sitting up again. "Do you think we're close?"

"I do. We needed to step back from it for a bit. Sometimes the best ideas come when you're not staring right at the problem."

"Maybe that's why I haven't figured it out yet," she said on a long sigh.

"We'll find the solution."

Katrina nodded, unable to think of anything else to say.

Victor patted her arm and stood, turning toward the door. Karl smiled at him with a nod and reached for the door handle to let Victor out. Before he could, the door flew open and Njogu practically leapt into the room.

"I've got it!"

CHAPTER TWENTY-FIVE

*P*hin stood in the space at the foot of his brothers' beds he had claimed hours before when he'd been allowed to leave his own. He situated himself so he could easily stand watch while providing sufficient space for the medical staff to do their work. Neither Gideon nor Daniel had moved, their thoughts silent. He felt their failing life signs, felt them fading away.

For the first time in his life he understood terror.

"His progress is amazing," Doctor Agatha Corbin said from the other side of the room to a colleague Phin had yet to meet.

Her voice was low and she kept her back to him, but with focus her words carried easily. It was in these moments of unknown surveillance Phin hoped to learn the most about the people who now held his brothers' lives in their hands.

"All signs of fever and infection are gone; the incisions from removing the metal appendage ports are nearly completely healed; the bruises forming when he came in are gone; his heart rate, blood-ox levels, and every measurable biological function are at near prime. In just a few hours he has gone from literally *dead* to the most perfect specimen of a Human being I have ever seen. The changes in medical science we could achieve with the technology pumping through his body would be breathtaking."

"If that's the case, why is he improving so fast and his brothers fail just as quickly? All accounts by Connor Montgomery and everyone else present when they got to Falls Church indicate Phineas was the one down and the two brothers were a lot closer to healthy than sick. We no sooner pulled him back and they deteriorated."

"Victor has a theory. Well, I should say Njogu presented the theory and Victor agrees in concept. He's coming down in a bit to explain to Phineas since it'll be up to him."

"Then what?"

"What do you mean," Doctor Corbin asked.

"The theory works, they all live, then what?"

Doctor Corbin shrugged. "Then they figure out what they want to do." She sighed. "I read Katrina Bauer's initial notes on her findings and some of the things they told her while she was with them. Imagine going to sleep a slave, for lack of a better term, and waking up essentially free to do what you want."

"You think they're going to be allowed to just walk away?"

"Why wouldn't they? They're free men. If they want to stay, they can, but after all that has happened there is no way President Tanner would allow anything other than offering them their freedom."

"We have no idea what they are. What if they're actually Sorra—"

"That's enough, Alexa," Doctor Corbin admonished. "Yes, they are no doubt amazing, but they are still men and entitled to their freedom."

All accounts indicated they were indeed more benefactor than master. No one had pressed him for information other than details to assist in his treatment. No one had done anything to him indicative of any intent other than to help. The doctors had spoken freely with him, including Victor. Katrina had assured them he would help, and everything the man had done confirmed her promise. Phin had not seen Michael Tanner, though he understood Michael had been present when they were removed from the slum district, and during the evacuation Michael had been injured and required treatment of his own.

He had no memory of the events leading to his arrival at this hospital. His last clear memory was of fighting a dozen attackers, his brothers at his side. The pain had been excruciating, like nothing he had ever experienced at their mother's hand, but the pain had been inconsequential in comparison to his need to protect Katrina. He remembered the stillness when all the enemy had fallen and turning to assure she was safe. And then nothing until he woke the day before in a hospital bed with his brothers in the beds beside him.

Not until he saw Katrina, even if only through the glass window, did he feel a degree of relief and perhaps acceptance things were just as she had promised. Her people would help.

And they had. Somehow.

His pain was gone, his illness abated, and his strength had returned.

The question still remained why his brothers faltered.

The observation room door opened and Victor entered. He scanned the room, and when he saw Phin he smiled, starting across the space toward him. There was something very open about the man, something that reminded him of Katrina, something he had yet to experience with any other person who had come in and out in the last day and a half. Although his training dictated he hold the man's actions as suspect, his instincts leaned toward taking the man at his word and his commitment to do all he could to help.

Victor shook his head, his smile a contrast to the negative action. "Amazing. Phineas, you are doing great. How do you feel?"

"I am experiencing no lingering effects, Doctor."

"Good to hear." Victor glanced to Gideon's bed, then Daniel's. "Phineas, I and my staff have come up with a plan to help your brothers. We need to speak with you about it, because the treatment isn't without its own set of risks. I know you don't want to leave them, but would you come with me so we can discuss it?"

Phin tilted his head and turned to face Victor. "If you have devised a treatment, why haven't you initiated it?"

Victor paused before answering, and Phin watched him carefully, noting the fact he held Phin's gaze and never flinched. When he spoke his voice never wavered and his words were spoken with confidence, and what Phin determined to be honesty. "Because as their brother, you are their closest living relative and the choice of medical treatment is yours to make, not ours. We can tell you what we think we need to do, but your life—and theirs—is not ours to dictate."

Phin looked away, focusing on Gideon. "My brother did not want to come back here," Phin finally said. "We have never been granted the option to make a decision about our life, or death, or what we are allowed to think or feel."

Victor set his hand on Phin's shoulder, drawing his attention back from Gideon. Phin held no faith in his observations of these people, whether he could determine their thoughts or intents with any accuracy, but he thought perhaps he saw sympathy. Compassion.

"Phineas, you are a victim to the Sorracchi as much as any person on this planet. We are not without our questions. Understand when this is done, you will need to answer to what happened, but you will not be denied any rights given to any citizen of Earth."

"And one of those rights is the choice you speak of."

Victor nodded. "Yes. When possible, we as doctors leave the decision for care to either the patient or the nearest relative to that patient. And what we propose is a major decision."

"Then I will come with you and listen to what you have to say."

Victor smiled and stepped beside Phin so they could walk out side by side. "Good. There will be someone there anxious to see you."

"*A*fter the time you spent with them what do you foresee Phineas' reaction to be to this suggestion?" Michael offered, taking the seat beside Katrina.

His question made her jump. She had been so deep in her own thoughts she hadn't heard most of the people come back into the conference room. After another hour of discussion and deliberation, they had come up with both a plan and a proposal, the idea of which made her chest hurt and her stomach knot. She shook her head, trying to provide an adequate explanation.

"I don't know for sure," she answered truthfully. "It took Phin's near death—" Her voice faltered on the words, a swell of remembered sorrow hitting her. He *had* died. She thought she'd lost him, and since learning he lived all she'd wanted to do was see him—touch him—confirm within her own reality he lived. She attempted a feeble, apologetic smile and cleared her throat. "It took something extreme to convince Gideon to come at all. It wasn't that he didn't care about Phin dying; he didn't want to choose slavery again over death. For any of them."

"You told them that wouldn't happen."

It wasn't a question, but she felt the necessity to nod. "Absolutely. I understand why they would think it—I mean, what else have they known?"

Michael leaned back in his chair, the old mechanisms squeaking under the shift. "It's difficult to believe the word of truth when it's also the word of compassion and all you've known is cruelty and indifference. Our mother used cruelty as a drug, I believe. In our pain she gained the most satisfaction."

Katrina gasped and stared until her eyes burned. She couldn't even . . . her brain shut down completely. Michael's eyebrows edged higher on his forehead.

"They didn't tell you."

She shook her head and finally managed to regain her ability to speak. "No. Are you sure?" He nodded, and she managed to blink. "But, just Kathleen, not . . ."

He shook his head. "Our shared parentage is with her only. Whether they know who their father is, or not, I don't know, but it isn't my father."

She didn't have time to say anything else before the conference room door opened and members of Victor's team filed in, Njogu leading the way. Some of the team looked her way and nodded or smiled, and others spoke to each other. Karl came through the door, scanned the room until he saw her, and came around the table to sit on her other side. Michael pushed his chair back from the conference room table and pushed himself up to stand, his grip on the cane turning his knuckles white. He had to still be in pain, he'd had surgery less than forty-eight hours earlier.

"Guess I finally see the badass who had the balls to kidnap my sister, huh?"

Katrina gasped and stared at Karl. "Karl, don't you dare say or do anything."

He leaned toward her so his words stayed between them. "He's going to answer for what he did. Whether his brothers live or not."

"Don't be so cruel."

"Cruel was dragging you out of this hospital into—"

"Stop it," she hissed through clenched teeth.

"Come in and sit down, Phineas. As soon as everyone is here we'll explain."

Katrina's heart jumped at Victor's voice and she pulled back from Karl. Heat infused her face and neck, but a chill danced up her spine to the base of her skull at the same time. Victor came through the door and stepped to the side, motioning Phin toward an empty chair. Katrina froze, only able to stare.

He looked wonderful.

He wore green standard-issue utility pants and a black sweater with leather patches at the elbows and shoulders. His skin, clean of the ever-present smudges and dust of the abandoned apartment, had lost the sallow paleness and sunken appearance of the last day before they came back. He was clean-shaven, although over nearly a week very little facial stubble had grown on any of them. He walked with strength, as he had those first days in Falls Church. How could he have been so ill just days before; how could he have been *dead*?

He nodded to Victor, acknowledging the instructions, and looked in her direction before gripping the back of a chair. Her breath hitched the moment they made eye contact. Phin stilled and held the contact, a slow smile curling his lips. Katrina smiled back, knowing full well she probably looked like a goof, but she didn't care. She was proud of herself for not running around the table and throwing her arms around him like she wanted to.

Karl moved to stand and Katrina grabbed his arm, forcing herself to look away from Phin. Her brother's stare was hard and cold, his jaw clenched.

"Karl, *please*. Please trust me."

His eyes didn't change but his jaw relaxed, and he nodded, leaning back into the chair. Katrina released a tense breath and nodded, looking back to Victor and Phin.

"Phineas, this is my team." Victor went around the table, introducing each of the doctors and scientists, but once he indicated Michael Tanner Katrina noticed Phin's attention moved no further. When the introductions were complete, Victor cleared his throat and glanced toward Katrina before swiveling in his chair to look at Phin. "We don't mind admitting, Phineas—"

"Phin," he interrupted, glancing toward Katrina. "I prefer Phin."

Victor looked to her and smiled. Heat infused her cheeks again but she smiled wider. "Of course. Phin. I was about to say we were stumped for quite a while as to why you recovered so quickly while your brothers continued to deteriorate. We have a theory, and all our correlating research supports it as viable, but it is highly risky."

"Is it the only option?"

"The only one we have, yes. I don't know if we have time to wait for another."

"Explain."

Victor sighed and linked his hands on the tabletop. "Phin, when we arrived in Falls Church you were failing fast. You were unresponsive, your body burning with fever. Your vitals were dropping by the moment. Your heart stopped two minutes out from the hospital."

Katrina had to clench her hands together under the table and look away, swallowing hard against the lump suddenly choking her at the memory. She wasn't sure she'd even breathed from the moment he flatlined until they took him from the hover, still trying desperately to bring him back. Even though he was alive and well, and just feet from her, she still felt the ache of loss when she thought he was gone.

"We know how long the Human brain can survive without oxygen before brain damage is irreversible and it is pointless to continue lifesaving techniques. We were committed to continue until that point, and your heart restarted just short of four minutes after it stopped.

Based on your medical condition when we arrived, we assumed we would be in for a long fight to keep you alive and fix what was wrong. But . . . that's not what happened."

"The neural transmitter is no longer transmitting to the bionanetics in my system the order to make me ill."

"More than that. The transmitter isn't transmitting *at all*, Phin. It's effectively dead; however, all our study of the device indicates we have no means to shut it off or change its programming. Detailed inspection of the scans and specs say if we tried any means other than original programming to turn off the device it would result in immediate death."

"How is this possible?"

Victor raised a hand and indicated Njogu, and Phin turned his attention to the Umani scientist. Njogu slid a tablet across the table and tapped it active. A three-dimensional image of the neural transmitter projected above the tablet.

"It is our belief dat the device was created wit' a deat' switch, an appropriate name for dis situation. We hypot'esize de creator designed it to shut down upon deat' of de host to prevent detection from de enemy."

Katrina watched the shift of thought move over Phin's features and recognized the moment he understood even though they hadn't said the worst. She held her breath, as much in anticipation of his response as to try to calm her racing heart.

"When you died, Phin, your death shut down the device," Victor clarified. "But because the bionanetics are powered by you, by the electrical currents created within your body, they immediately reengaged when we restarted your heart, thus healing you with speed and efficiency as they were always intended to do."

Phin squared his shoulders and straightened, remaining silent. Then he turned his head and stared at Katrina. She swallowed and held his gaze, hoping as much as he saw the fear in her eyes he might also see her trust in Victor. How she could let him see, she didn't know.

"To save Gideon and Daniel, you must first allow them to die." It was not a question, but a clear statement he understood.

"Allow them to die, no. We can't risk the weakening of their bodies any further," Michael said, and Phin's eyes snapped to his brother.

An electric sensation skittered over Katrina's skin as that reality truly sank in. Brothers. Perhaps not in the sense of brother that existed between Phin, Gideon, and Daniel, but brothers, nonetheless.

"We can induce death," Michael explained. "Stop their hearts and halt their lungs. Because we will be in control, and we will be in control of bringing them back."

"You will kill them—"

"So they can live," Katrina said, rasping over the words.

"We want to do this as quickly as we can, Phin. As Michael said, the sooner we do this the greater our chance of success. It's nothing short of a miracle we were able to bring you back because of how far you'd deteriorated. You were weak and fading, your body ravaged with infection. Your brothers are ill, but they are still better than you were when we reached you."

Victor and the team spent the next several minutes explaining to Phin the exact process they would undertake, how long they intended to allow his brothers to remain technically deceased, and the means they would use to bring them back. Most of it was beyond Katrina's understanding, her knowledge about electrons and transducers, but Phin clearly understood every word and asked questions throughout. When they finished, a silence settled in the room as everyone waited for his response. Phin pushed his chair back from the table and stood, turning his back on them in silence. Victor glanced at Katrina and arched an eyebrow. She shook her head and shrugged one shoulder, not knowing any more than he.

"May I consider your proposal?" he asked, looking over his shoulder to Victor.

"Of course," Victor said, standing and everyone in the room followed suit. Katrina included, although her knees trembled. "I'll come back in a few minutes in case you have any questions."

Katrina was at the far side of the room from the door and waited as each person stood to leave. Karl shoved his chair toward the table hard enough it hit with a bang and rolled back, then he pushed past everyone to get out the door. It would be a long time, she knew, before

Karl could let go of the anger born of his fear. She understood it and couldn't begrudge him for it because she knew it meant he loved her, but she wished she knew how to make him understand nothing was as simple as he wanted to make it. She filed out with the others but kept her eyes on Phin's shoulders. She was the last to reach the door behind Michael and Victor. Michael paused at the door, then turned back to her.

"Wait a moment, Katrina."

She only nodded before Michael diverted around Victor and went to Phin. Katrina took a self-conscious step back to avoid hearing the conversation, but the room was small and Michael's voice carried. He set his hand on Phin's shoulder, leaning on his cane with the other.

"Do not think bringing this choice to you was taken lightly, Phin," Michael said. "We have used all the information available to us, including everything Katrina pulled from Kathleen's files—" Her spine involuntarily tightened at the mention of the woman's—the monster's —name,"—to find another way. In truth, had you not died we might never have known how to save them at all." Michael drew in a slow breath through his nose. "I would very much like to know my brothers, and this is the one thing I know to try to make that happen."

"We thought you dead long ago," Phin said in a voice that made Katrina's skin goosebump, not for its coldness but the weight of the words. "We also would like to know how you survived and who you are."

Michael smiled and patted his hand on Phin's shoulder before moving away from him. He met Victor at the door and looked to Katrina. "Stay with him. I'm sure a familiar face in this would be a comfort."

She nodded and stepped back so Victor could leave and shut the door. Her pulse jumped like a frantic bird and she had to set down her tablet, afraid she'd drop it. As soon as the door closed behind Victor and Michael, Phin turned. Regardless of decorum, or pride, or anything else that might have held her back, Katrina ran to him.

By the time he caught her and wrapped his arms around her, Katrina had given up the fight to hold back tears. He held her so close she had to toe-up to keep her feet on the ground, and she held on as tight as she could. He squeezed her, making it hard to breathe, but she didn't care. She buried her face into the curve of his neck, one cheek on the leather covering his shoulder and the other against his warm skin.

"I thought I lost you," she cried, her voice muffled against his throat. "I saw you die—" She lost her voice in the release, crying this time not because of pain but relief. Phin loosened his hold enough she could stand and she eased back to look into his face, laying her palms on his cheeks. His jaw was damp from her tears. He must have thought she was crazy, the way she cried and laughed and smiled all at once. "You look so good."

His silence made her nervous, and the way his gaze shifted back and forth over her face infused her with heat. Phin's hands pressed firmer into her back and pulled her close to him again. Katrina leaned up again and touched her lips to his cheek, holding there for a long kiss. She wrapped her arms around his neck again and held on.

His hand slid up her spine until his fingers brushed her skin at the base of her neck. A shiver danced up her spine, and she held on tighter. He spoke, but his words were lost in her hair. He brushed his lips against her neck, along her throat, to her hair.

"Wh-what?" she asked, her breath catching. "What did you say?"

He pushed his fingers into her hair and drew back, his cheek smoothing across hers until he could look her in the eyes. "There's no pain," he repeated. "You touch me and there's no pain."

Katrina's heart squeezed and her throat clenched. She blinked, staring at him until she could speak. "Pain?"

He nodded and laid his hand against her face, his thumb brushing her lower lip. "Yes. Always equal measure of pleasure and pain, but not now. It really is gone, Katrina," he said, smiling with a pure sincerity she hadn't seen in his face before, reaching all the way to his hazel eyes. "I'm free."

Phin's gaze lowered to her lips, and something breathtaking bloomed in Katrina's chest. His breathing changed, shifted, nearly as sharp and rapid as hers. In that moment, Katrina knew she could scurry away from the curling warmth in her stomach, let her heartbeat return to normal, get away so she could think . . . or she could . . .

Katrina raised a shaking hand and combed her fingers through his short hair to the back of his head. She licked her dry lips and sucked in a shallow breath before she drew him to her and pressed their lips together. It took less than half a heartbeat for a cold flash to wash over her from head to toe, giving her chills and making her skin flush in the same dizzying moment.

She had a second to draw a breath before Phin took her face in his hands, looked into her eyes, smiled, and kissed her again. His lips opened, kissing her deeper, and Katrina couldn't think past that moment. When his tongue brushed hers, Katrina couldn't help the tiny purr at the base of her throat. Phin's fingertips pressed into her scalp and he tilted her head, deepening the kiss. She'd never kissed a boy like this, never kissed anyone anywhere near this. This was everything every old movie ever said it would be, but more.

Phin rested his forehead against hers, the side of his nose sliding along hers, their rapid breaths mingling in the small space between. "Katrina," was all he said.

She hugged his shoulders, using his strength to stay on her feet. He held her for a while, until her heartbeat resembled normal and she could breathe again. Then he stepped back and leaned his hips against the edge of the table, looking at her. The warmth in his eyes made her blush all over again.

"Thank you," he said.

"For what?"

"You've helped me decide what I need to do."

Katrina scowled and shook her head. "How did kissing help you decide?"

Phin's smile slid, but only to something more serious. "Katrina, my brother resisted returning here because he refused to trade our lives for our freedom. He saw no life if we were slaves again—"

"You're not—"

"I know. *He* needs to know." Phin stood and reached for her hand. "I'm not willing to deny my brothers a chance at a life we have never dared dream could be ours because there are no absolutes. I told Gideon the only surety we faced was death if we remain hidden like spiders in a hole." He pulled her to him and wrapped her hand in both of his, bringing her knuckles to his lips. "I have to choose to let my brothers die in order to give them a chance to live, but if I do nothing, the only surety is death. I have to allow this to happen." He raised his head and looked at her. "Tell me, Katrina. Do you believe this is the right thing to do?"

She nodded, swallowing against the swell of emotion. She doubted he realized the idea of losing Gideon and Daniel made her heart ache perhaps not nearly as much as his, but they meant so much to her. She didn't want them lost for his sake, too. "I believe it's the only thing you can do. It's as right as it can be."

He nodded and turned to the door, drawing her with him. With his hand on the knob, he paused, his head down. Katrina waited, and when he still didn't move, she shifted closer and laid her free hand on his arm, her cheek against his sleeve. His hold on her hand tightened and he turned his head to look at her. "I am unaccustomed to making personal requests."

"What do you want, Phin?"

"Stay with me," he asked. "While I wait to know if my brothers live."

Katrina pressed her lips together and nodded. "Of course," she whispered.

He opened the door and led them into the hall.

CHAPTER TWENTY-SIX

11 MARCH 2054, WEDNESDAY 14:00 HOURS
VICTORY DAY
UNITED EARTH PROTECTORATE, CAPITOL CITY
ALEXANDRIA, SEAT OF VIRGINIA
NORTH AMERICAN CONTINENT

"We won't perform the procedure on both of them at the same time. It's too dangerous."

Victor sat on a couch adjacent to where Phin and Katrina sat in a small room in the surgical wing, Michael Tanner beside him. Both men wore surgical garments and masks hung beneath their chins. Katrina was curled up on the couch beside Phin much like she had on the dirty, worn couch in the apartment they had inhabited for several days, her knees drawn close to her chin and her arms folded between her thighs and chest. She had done as she promised and stayed with him from the moment he made the decision to allow the doctors to proceed.

"We need to focus on one at a time, assure they are through the worst, then move on," Victor continued. "We'll act on Daniel first, as he is in the worst shape of the two. Once Daniel is back with us, we'll prepare Gideon. I'll come back here after each and let you know."

"I'll know," Phin stated, glancing toward Michael. He'd sensed the man, felt the tension in him. Though the sensation and awareness wasn't as acute as with Gideon and Daniel, but it was there all the same. "I will know when they die, and I will know when they come back."

Katrina unfolded her arms and her small hand slid over his, her delicate fingers curling around his. The act seemed so simple for her, so natural. Phin looked down at their joined hands. The absence of punishment accompanying the pleasure of her touch was still new; he anticipated the burn of "correction" with each moment he enjoyed. It never came.

"For that I am sorry," Victor said, shaking his head. "It's likely the event that sent them into their downward spiral was your death, the emotional impact had to be devastating. Especially considering your deep link." Victor stood and offered Michael his hand to pull him to his feet. "In your case, you know they will come back; they had no such warning. We'll do our best to make this as quick as possible."

Phin stood with the men. "I wish to express my appreciation to you and your team for what you have done, Doctor."

Victor patted his hand against Phin's arm. "It's the least we can do."

Victor moved past Michael toward the door, but before Michael left he stepped toward Phin. Michael shifted his weight to his left leg and tucked his cane under his left arm to extend his right hand to Phin. Phin looked down at his extended hand, not sure of Michael's intent.

"In the history of Humanity, two men who wanted to show respect for each other would extend their hands to one another in a gesture of peace," Michael explained. "It's called a handshake, and between friends it is a greeting or a farewell, or a wish for good fortune."

Phin matched Michael's action, and Michael took his hand in a firm grip.

"In three days I will celebrate my birthday for the first time with my father. I look forward to having my brothers there as well."

"I believe I speak for my brothers when I say we look forward to the same," Phin said, tightening his hold.

Michael smiled and nodded, then released Phin's hand and took his cane in hand to follow Victor out the door. As soon as the door closed, Phin sank onto the couch beside Katrina and covered his face with his hands, his elbows on his knees. A knot had twisted in his gut since Victor had explained what needed to be done. He scrubbed his face and shifted again, a crawling tension refusing to let him be still.

"Phin," Katrina said in a low, soft voice that eased some of the edge. He didn't know how a voice could do that, or whether it was just *her* voice, but he welcomed it. Her small hand curled over his shoulder and drew him back into the cushions. She drew her legs up onto the cushions to rest on her knees, sitting close enough she could lean across the back of the couch and touch his head with her fingertips. "Victor and Michael will do absolutely everything in their power to do all they can for Daniel and Gideon."

"I don't doubt their intentions, Katrina." He rolled his head on the back of the cushion to look at her. She looked like she had the night they woke, with rich brown hair in long, spiral curls framing her face, bright brown eyes, no dirt smudging her cheeks.

Beautiful.

He had never looked upon anything, or anyone, and deemed them worthy of the word. It was a Human sentiment, the acknowledgment of beauty a weakness to be suppressed, at least as Kathleen would have them believe. At one time he might have believed her on some level, but when he thought back to what for him felt like only days—perhaps weeks—before, he didn't recognize the man he had been. If he had been a man at all.

"What?" she asked, a smile curving her lips.

Phin raised his hand and touched the pad of his thumb to her lower lip, then ran his knuckles along her cheek. She smiled and turned into his touch. Warmth infused him, so different from the burn of fever he'd felt when the mechanisms inside him abused him for his desire to be near her. He had been overwhelmed by the intensity of his physical reaction to the kiss they'd shared. While Human customs, cultures, and norms had been part of their education, purely so they could understand the weakness of the culture they were intended to subvert, she had taught them such emotions and desires were weaknesses to be suppressed.

Now he realized her indoctrination had been one more way to separate them from their Human inheritance.

"You're beautiful."

Color bloomed in her fair cheeks and she smiled wider. Phin drew in a deep breath, but before he could release it a vicious clenching gripped his chest and he lunged forward off the couch, landing on his knees. A sound tore from his throat, guttural and harsh, and he curled his fist into his sweater in a desperate attempt at easing the pain. His lungs seized, froze, and fought to yield enough so he could take a breath. He fell forward on one arm, clawing at his chest with the other. The pain was excruciating.

Daniel was dying.

"Phin!" Katrina's voice broke through the outer edge of the pain.

Small hands pushed at his shoulders until he fell back to sit on his ankles, her kneeling in front of him. Burning pain radiated from the center of his chest into his arms, his blood on fire. Phin grunted through each new wave, struggling to take a breath. She took his face in her hands, repeating his name until he opened his eyes and looked at her.

"It will be over soon, I promise." Tears ran down her cheeks, and the salty tang on his own lips made him realize he wept as well.

He tried to push past the sudden intensity of death, realizing his mistake too late. He had opened wide his mind and senses from the time he woke, constantly seeking any sign of his brothers' recovery . . . or further deterioration. He should have replaced the walls, should have shielded himself from the unfiltered unity of shared experience. Then the pain snapped, arching his back, and he slumped when it was gone.

Nothing.

Emptiness.

A hollow crater bore through him.

Daniel was dead. All hint of him, the shadow ever present at the edge of his awareness, the hum of his consciousness sharing a mental space with his brothers, was silent.

Empty.

Phin let his head fall back and sucked in air in huge gulps, the urge to scream at the ceiling almost completely overwhelming him. A sound echoed back to him, a throaty cry, and when he sucked in another breath, he realized it was him.

"Phin, please. Come here, look at me. Look at me."

Her voice made it through the noise, and the pounding in his head, and her touch pulled him back from the smothering darkness. Phin blinked, his eyes burning, and focused on her tear-streaked face, gasping to find his breath.

"He's gone," Phin rasped. He sucked in a choking swell of devastation and dropped his chin to his chest. "He's dead. I can't feel him."

"It'll be over soon, I swear," she whispered and kissed his forehead.

"How do you do it?" he begged, shaking his head. "How do you stand the emptiness?"

"He's not gone, Phin." She smoothed her hands over his slick cheeks, nudging his chin until he looked up again. "He's not gone. Just hang on."

Phin dropped his forehead to her shoulder and curled his fingers into her sleeves. "Is this what you felt?" he asked, desperate to find balance. "When you thought I was gone?"

She nodded, but he only felt the motion against his cheek. She stroked his hair and kissed his temple. "But you came back, and so will Daniel and Gideon. Just hang on."

He hung on to her because he had nothing else. Gideon's mind was a whisper lost behind the hollowness, the black emptiness. Phin called out to him but received no response; only his still presence. Perhaps there was some grace in that Gideon would not feel this loss. Not again. Had they been torn apart like this when his heart stopped?

Phin sensed her tension and raised his head to see her glance at the clock on the wall.

Something was wrong. The knot in his stomach curled out and expanded, making him feel ill. He shook his head and pulled back. "No. No. It's been too long."

"They won't wait too long—"

"No." Phin used the couch to gain his feet. She scrambled after him, grabbing his arm before he could reach the door. "No, it's been too long. They need to—" Another cry ripped through him and he dropped again, a completely different—radically opposite—pain shot through him. He stumbled and dropped to his knees.

They were tearing him apart.

Again, another bolt slammed through him. His back arched. Again. Again.

Phin fell forward on his hands and knees, trying desperately to focus enough to close the walls, to give him some distance to breathe. His chest burned, like hot fluid had been injected between his ribs. He choked, gagged, tried to breathe.

Again a surge hit him. He sucked in air. Another jolt. Another.

Then the pain was gone, replaced by a dull, throbbing ache.

The emptiness was gone.

Daniel's presence slipped back into the hollow place.

Phin collapsed forward, his forearms and forehead on the carpet, wracking sobs tearing through him laced with a sudden wave of relief. His heart hurt, but not with the pain of assault, but with the crushing push and pull of loss and gain. Exhaustion dragged at him, different than it had been when he was ill. This was the kind of fatigue that weighed him down after a long, strenuous, exertive training session. Phin sucked in air until his lungs no longer burned and closed his eyes, reaching out again to assure Daniel's presence wasn't a figment of his exhausted mind.

He pushed himself up from the floor, braced on his arms, and looked to Katrina. She knelt a few feet away, dark eyes startlingly wide, her cheeks trailed with tears. Tremors shook her. She pressed her lips together and swallowed. "Is he . . ."

Phin nodded and collapsed back to sit with his aching shoulders against the couch where Victor and Michael had sat. He rubbed his hands over his face and snuffed his nose against the back of his hand. He had never cried, but strangely found the act a relief. He swallowed and licked the salt from his lips.

"Yes," he said, his voice a raspy grate, and nodded. "He's alive."

Katrina hiccupped a small cry and crawled across the floor to him. She came into the space between his raised knees and fell against him, her face pressed to his chest. He wrapped her in his arms and held her until the chaos finally silenced.

"*Y*ou need to go to Gideon. *Now*," Phin demanded, shoving Victor's medical scanner to the side to move past the doctor. "You *must* do this *now*."

Katrina stood on the far side of the small room, her hands tucked behind her back while she leaned against the wall watching. Her stomach still hadn't settled from witnessing the way Daniel's death and resurrection had attacked Phin physically, violently, and emotionally. Her heart hurt at the loss of Daniel, even if only temporarily, but it had been the unadulterated sorrow in Phin's eyes, and the unfiltered pain in his cries, that had torn her apart.

"Phin, we nearly couldn't bring Daniel back. I know you know that. You felt it. I need to make sure he's stable before I shift my focus. And I need to know you can handle this again."

"I can handle it!" Phin shouted, jabbing a pointed finger at the floor. "Daniel can't!"

Katrina flinched. She'd heard him argue with Gideon, but he'd never shouted. Not like this, not with honest rage. He must have caught her involuntary reaction to his anger; his head snapped in her direction and he stepped around Victor to head for her. She held his gaze as he marched to her, having to tip back her head to hold his eyes. He stopped so close their bodies brushed.

"I'm sorry, Katrina. I don't intend to frighten you," he said in a raspy voice spoken low enough she wasn't sure Victor even heard. "He doesn't understand."

"No, he doesn't," she said gently, and tried to offer an encouraging smile. She drew an arm from behind her and laid it on his arm, sliding it down until she could lace her fingers through his and squeeze. He looked down at their joined hands before looking back to her. "But he wants to. He'll listen."

Phin worked his jaw, his lips pressed tight together, then turned enough to look back at Victor. His hand remained with hers. "My brothers and I are always aware of each other. We can share thoughts, sensations, memories, and knowledge. We can also withhold any of those things. Or we can open ourselves completely and act as one, a single unit."

"Like you did in the apartment when the men attacked," Katrina said, understanding now how they had been able to move and act and fight with such beautiful perfection. They had been one machine responding to not just what one brother saw or heard, but what they all provided as input. No wonder they had been so efficient.

He nodded and looked back to her. "When I woke up, I sought out my brothers. When I couldn't find them immediately, I opened my mind and dropped every wall between us in the hopes of hearing them. Even then, Gideon was only a whisper and Daniel a presence, no more." Victor moved closer and Phin spoke to him again. "I should have known to distance myself before you proceeded to stop his heart. Without the walls, I felt everything he felt."

"Everything," she whispered and closed her eyes. No wonder his physical reaction had been so extreme. It would have been like having a heart attack and drowning at the same time, all the pain, all the panic.

"But you can put up those walls before we act on Gideon?" Victor asked.

He nodded again. "I can. Daniel can't. He doesn't know."

Katrina gasped and looked past him to Victor, and thankfully saw understanding in her mentor's eyes. Now that his bionanetics worked to heal him, Daniel could wake up at any time. And he would do the same thing Phin did, he would reach out for his brothers. Phin had a day and a half to build his strength to near full, and the sharing of his brother's death had put him on his knees. What would it do to Daniel?

"Of course," Victor exclaimed and pinched the bridge of his nose. "Of course, yes. I understand."

"That much input could kill him. He isn't strong enough."

Victor nodded. "How long do you need before we can act on Gideon?"

"I've already placed a buffer between myself and Gideon, but I remain open to Daniel. Should he wake I will be able to communicate with him and let him know to close himself to Gideon. But, it would be best if Gideon were recovering himself before Daniel wakes."

"I apologize for being obtuse." He smiled, a strange wry smile, and shook his head. "My wife would be ashamed of me. I should know better." Victor laid his hand on Phin's shoulder and squeezed, offering what Katrina thought to be a comforting smile. He turned to leave the room, bringing his surgical mask over his face as he went.

"Why would his wife be ashamed?" Phin asked as soon as the door closed

"Beverly is an empathic, keenly aware of other people's emotions. It was that ability that allowed her to help Victor."

"When he was a host."

Katrina snorted. "*Host* is too delicate a word. He was stolen from his home hundreds of years ago and a Sorracchi consciousness was shoved in his head." She bounced the heel of her hand off her forehead and walked around him to the couch.

"How is it he survived the overwrite process?"

Katrina shrugged and set her knees on the cushion to kneel, leaning her elbow against the back. "No one is absolutely sure. Like most things it's an educated guess." He sat beside her, sideways to face her, his leg drawn up on the cushion. "Victor has latent Areth DNA, as does most of the Human race by what we understand. And with that DNA he has low-level Talents. So low he had never been aware of them, but their existence was enough to mess up the overwrite process. His original body was cloned several times, and I guess each time the Sorracchi hold on his mind weakened until there was more Victor than Sorracchi."

"Was he aware of this?"

"He doesn't talk about it much. I think it was a really bad time for him, despite Beverly."

"I don't understand."

"Beverly felt the fight between his Sorracchi parasite and his natural mind. She helped him through the toughest fights until he was emancipated." She smiled and sighed. "And that's how they fell in love."

He angled his head, a line digging between his eyes—the expression she'd seen often, especially on him, and especially when he wanted to figure out something. "I don't comprehend the emotion love." Then he winced, closed his eyes, and dipped his head, a strangled sound in his throat. A cold sweat broke out over Katrina's skin, and her heart pounded hard, a sudden panic hitting her he might go through all the pain again.

"Phin?"

He raised his head, a light sheet of perspiration on his brow. His lips twitched as he clearly struggled for control. Another choked groan and his fingers dug into the fabric of the couch cushion. "They have begun with Gideon," he said through clenched teeth.

"I thought you said—"

"It's not as intense." He canted his head with a jerk and closed his eyes for a brief moment. "I am still connected to my brothers. I won't close all the paths. I won't take the chance of leaving Daniel alone."

Katrina laid her hand on his leg, and he immediately gripped it, his hold tight but restrained enough he didn't hurt her. "Can I do anything?"

He trembled visibly now, perspiration running down his nose and temple. He grunted, then all tension drained from his body and he panted. Tears welled in his hazel eyes and anguish pinched his features. Just like before with Daniel, he felt Gideon's death. Katrina shifted closer to him and took his face in her hands, stroking his cheeks.

"It's almost over," she whispered. "Just hang on."

Phin sucked in a breath and closed his eyes, mumbling "No, no . . ."

"What's wrong?"

"Daniel."

Katrina twisted to look at the clock on the wall. Any moment, any second, they'd begin bringing Gideon back. But, if Daniel was waking, even if just his subconscious mind, he'd feel the revival. When she turned back, Phin was silent and still. His eyes were closed, his head down, his breathing steady. She held her breath in the sudden silence of the room, watching him.

Moments later, he jerked like someone had jabbed him, but he never broke his silence. She didn't dare move for fear of distracting him. Tremors shifted through him, then suddenly he arched and his hand slammed into the cushion. He sucked in a sharp breath and his head came up, eyes open. Katrina could only stare until her eyes burned.

Phin finally took a normal breath and scrubbed his hands over his face, his body relaxing. Then he smiled and the knot in Katrina's stomach eased.

"Gideon is alive, and Daniel is waking. He knows all is well, and he can rest."

Katrina smiled and let go her tears of relief. "Phin, look at me." She waited until he looked into her eyes. "I'm going to tell you something. Don't you *ever* think you don't comprehend love." Her final words caught in her throat and she swallowed against the overwhelming swell.

The waiting room door opened and Michael stepped in, his mask only half off his face but enough Katrina saw his smile. "Come with me," he said. "You should be there when they wake."

CHAPTER TWENTY-SEVEN

11 March 2054, Wednesday 15:45 hours
Victory Day
Robert J. Castleton Memorial Building – The Castle
Center for United Protectorate Government
United Earth Protectorate, Capitol City
Alexandria, Seat of Virginia
North American Continent

"*D*oes it say President *anywhere* on my letterhead?"

Nick's voice reached Michael as he opened the door to the secure room where his father waited to give the final speech of the weeklong celebration. He smiled as he closed the door, having no doubt he'd walked in on an argument his father was clearly losing. With his mother.

"Of course it does, Nicky—"

"Then why are you arguing with me about this?"

"I'm not arguing. You are."

Connor and Mel stood outside the range of the argument, and the stern set of Connor's face did nothing to reveal to Michael whether Connor sided with his sister or his boss. If anything, Michael guessed

Connor preferred to be left out of it completely. Jacqueline turned and looked at Michael from her seat on the couch. She smiled and he crossed to her, glancing at his parents before he reached her. He leaned over and she tipped back her head to meet his kiss.

"What are they arguing about?" he asked.

"Your father doesn't want any of us to go on stage with him, and your mother says if we all hide in here we're letting the Xenos win. How did everything go?"

Michael sat on the arm of the couch so he could talk down to her, leaving the spot beside her open when Caitlin decided to sit again. "Both Daniel and Gideon survived the procedure, though we almost didn't bring Daniel back. His entire system was so fatigued, reviving him exceeded our preferred time frame by nearly thirty seconds."

"But he's okay now?"

Michael nodded. "Yes. Both Daniel and Gideon are showing distinct signs of strengthening and recovery. I suspect they will probably wake within the next couple of hours, and then perhaps Phin will get some rest."

"What's wrong with Phin?"

"He experienced physically the process of stopping their hearts. I underestimated the extent of their mental connection."

Sympathy softened her expression and she reached for his hand. "I'm sorry."

Michael squeezed it and leaned over for another kiss.

"Michael, will you talk some sense into your mother?"

He sat up and looked at his parents, smiling. "Dad, I have never seen you win an argument yet with Mom. I doubt you will begin now."

Nick threw his hands in the air and turned away.

UNITED EARTH PROTECTORATE, CAPITOL CITY
ALEXANDRIA, SEAT OF VIRGINIA
NORTH AMERICAN CONTINENT

"*T*he president's speech is about to begin. Do you want to watch it?"

Phin looked up from his spot between his brothers' beds. "Is it significant?"

Katrina nodded and crossed to the vidscreen mounted to the wall opposite the foot of the boys' beds. "I think so. It's his speech wrapping up all the celebrations going on this past week. Today marks one year since the Sorracchi surrendered."

Phin walked toward her while she reached high over her head to turn on the vidscreen, but the mount was too high for her to reach. She popped up on her toes, but still couldn't reach, and silently cursed her mother for every time she said "You're not short, Trini. You're petite. There's nothing wrong with being petite." *Yeah, until you want to reach something!*

Phin's warm hand at her waist startled her, and she stumbled back into his chest. His arm steadied her as he reached over her head to tap the bottom right corner of the screen and turned on the broadcast. As soon as the screen came on, he dropped his hand and stepped back. Katrina tried not to frown too hard. He didn't seem to have any qualms when she reached for him, never backed away, but never held contact long if he was the one reaching.

"Thank you," she said and took a step back so she could actually see the video without snapping her neck at the base of her skull.

The news channel had a camera angle on the stage, and they turned on the broadcast just in time to see President Tanner walk on the stage, holding his wife's hand, and flanked on each side by Firebirds, in this case Lieutenant Commander Connor Montgomery and Captain Mel Briggs. Behind them Michael Tanner and Jackie Anderson came on the stage, also flanked by Firebirds. Security was amped up, clearly. The crowd surrounding the square around the podium numbered in the thousands, and the volume was deafening. Cheers and shouts, chanting "Tanner! Tanner! Tanner!" and "Zeus! Zeus! Zeus!" mingled with whoops and hollers.

"They are insufficiently protected," Phin said, stepping close to her again, his attention fully on the screen. "The enemies of your government had plans to attack your president during these celebrations. Were they intercepted?"

Katrina shook her head, a knot curling in her stomach. "I don't know. Once the men who attacked us were taken into custody my focus was on you. Besides, I'm not anyone they'd tell that kind of stuff to anyway. I honestly don't know what happened."

"Why is Michael with him?"

"Michael and Jackie often attend President Tanner's public appearances. Caitlin, too."

"Is Zeus not a god in your ancient theology?"

Katrina smiled and twisted at the waist to look at him. "I never can guess what you will or won't know about stuff. Yes, Zeus was the Greek god of the sky. When Nick Tanner was in Earth Force, the former version of the military, he was the best pilot on record. He set wormhole flight records no one has ever been able to beat. He was god of the sky."

Phin nodded his understanding and Katrina went back to watching.

President Tanner kissed his wife's cheek and she stepped back to stand with Michael and Jackie while he moved to the podium. It took several moments for the crowd to quiet enough for him to even attempt to speak. He raised his hand in a request for silence, but even that seemed to inspire the crowd to cheer. He planted his hands on either side of the podium stand, leaning forward to the tiny rod holding the microphone. Speakers and sound systems circled the entirety of Alexandria Square to carry his voice to whoever wanted to hear.

"Three hundred sixty-five days," he stated, and silence settled almost instantly. "A lot of things can happen in three hundred sixty-five days. In a single trip around our sun, we the Human race have experienced devastating loss and liberating victory. Our population dropped from ten and a half billion to barely two-point-one billion in a matter of months leading to the war, and in one year we have documented one hundred eighty-nine thousand, four hundred eighteen births." He paused for a moment and smiled. "As of this morning. Welcome to the world, Oliver."

The crowd cheered, and Katrina found herself smiling. President Tanner waited until the crowd settled again.

"Today we celebrate Victory Day. The day our enemy bowed to our tenacity and surrendered to our will not to be repressed or enslaved. One year ago today, the Human race took back what was ours. We took back our birthright. We took back our pride. We took back our future."

Cheers again. Katrina spared a glance to Phin and found his full concentration on the screen. His eyes shifted, seeking, studying, his jaw clenched.

"Is something wrong, Phin?"

"I do not know," he answered simply.

"This week has been a week of acknowledgment and celebration. But fireworks and speeches are just symbols of what we have done, and where we are going. In one year, we have built a military and a government. In one year, we have established safe havens for our citizens and we have found those in need at the far corners of the planet. In one year, we have unified a planet in a way no single nation has ever experienced in recorded history." President Tanner sliced his hand through the air in emphasis.

Cheers. Phin took a step closer.

"This man," he said, pointing to the crowd, and specifically at a man standing at the edge of the crowd as near to the stage the barricades would allow, still fifty feet from the edge of the stage. Middle aged, short gray hair, and a bulky jacket despite the warm break in the weather. "He is one of the ones you call Xenos involved in the conspiracy to attack the president. Your president is in danger."

"We could have followed the predictability of history and fallen into chaos, turned on each other, and watched the infrastructure of our society burn while we held the torches. If the last five decades have taught us anything, if the last few *years* have taught us anything, it's we are filled with uncounted potential, potential far exceeding what is expected of us. We are too strong to be defeated. The Human race is irrepressible."

"Are you sure?" Katrina asked, squinting. She hadn't ever left the apartment, and only saw the men who had attacked them, and even then in a blur. She doubted she could actually identify any of them, except maybe the one she laid out with the fireplace poker.

"There is no doubt, Katrina."

She nodded, ran for the door, and shoved it open. Two armed soldiers stood twenty feet down the hall, having a conversation with a nurse. The bang of the door against the wall grabbed their attention, and the look on her face must have been enough to bring them running. She turned on her heels and bolted back into the recovery room, back to the speech. President Tanner's voice filled the room.

"We are far greater than the sum of our parts. We are more than we ever imagined. We. Are. Alive." President Tanner punctuated each word a solid thud of his fist on the podium.

The door burst open, the two guards running in with weapons raised.

"And we will not be silenced or beaten."

Katrina pointed to the screen. "Come here. Look."

"We will be ignorant no longer to the dangers surrounding us. We will not close our eyes to the wonders and the reality of the universe. We will not blindly follow, but we will lead our own destiny."

"There is a known Xeno terrorist in the crowd at the speech." Katrina pointed at the vidscreen. "That man, there. You need to contact Commander Montgomery *now* and stop them."

"Our unity is not absolute."

The two men looked from her to Phin, and back. "Oh, for goodness' sake, *please*. Just contact Connor Montgomery!"

"Inform him I have knowledge of this man, and will confirm all I know," Phin stated, his voice near-emotionless. "If you do not, your president's death will fall on you."

The weight of his voice gave Katrina chills."

"There are few citizens of the Protectorate who have not been touched by the maliciousness of those amongst us determined to watch us crumble. They declare their mission is to unify, to cleanse, and to cauterize our world of all things not native to this world. They close their arguments to reality that there is no way to purge us of our past, our existence."

"Go. Now. Please," Katrina begged.

One of them released a radio from his shoulder. "This is Captain Beckett, I need a link to Alexandria Square now. We have a Code Crimson alert. Code Crimson P.O.T.U.P alert."

"They are willing to destroy everything they claim to want to save. It is my absolute commitment to you, to the people of Earth, to protect those in my care."

Gooseflesh pebbled Katrina's skin and she crossed her arms over her body, going back to where Phin stood still watching the broadcast. The soldiers spoke between each other and the voiced on the radio, but the pounding in her ears was too hard to let her hear. She stepped beside Phin, and he took her hand, his attention never leaving the screen.

"We hunt them as diligently as they hunt their perceived enemies. We will halt their efforts, and we will show our people the reality of what it is to be Human."

President Tanner's expression had softened, and he'd straightened from his intense lean over the podium, his face turned down. He drew a breath and raised his head. "We are a family of survivors. We are brothers. And sisters. Mothers. And fathers. We hold children not born of our blood, and we mourn the children we have lost. We are husbands and wives, widows and widowers. We are soldiers and doctors and engineers and pilots. Construction workers and teachers. We are the best of what remains of the Human race because we *are* the Human race."

The crowd cheered again. Katrina stared at the man in the crowd who didn't clap, didn't cheer, and barely moved. President Tanner leaned forward again, speaking close to the microphone.

"Three hundred sixty-five days down, the future to go."

The cheers exploded in a cacophony that drowned out anything else. Phin looked toward the door and Katrina following his line of attention. The soldiers spoke between each other, glancing occasionally at them.

"They take too long," Phin said low enough only she would hear. "Without knowledge of who to seek out, they will miss the danger."

"Today, we are not the One World government formed by our predecessors. We are not a world of forgotten nations ruled by outsiders wearing the guise of benefactors. We are the United Protectorate."

"How far away is this place?" Phin asked, tipping his head toward the screen.

Katrina looked to the broadcast. "About a mile, I guess. Maybe less. It's Alexandria Square near the capitol building."

Phin looked past her again, staring at the soldiers. She practically felt them staring back but couldn't look away from the intense determination in his eyes.

"We are a united world, a united people, a united race ruled by our own people and no others. We have allies, but our world is our own. Make no mistake, this world is ours.

"What are you going to do?" she asked, a chill shooting up her spine.

"They have not yet spoken to the Commander Montgomery you named. They do not believe what I say is truth and doubt my trustworthiness."

"How do you know?"

His smile was small, not quite qualifying as an actual smile. "It is who I was created to be. And perhaps who I am created to be can save your president." He looked into her eyes and raised his hand, almost touching her cheek, but he stopped short. "Do you trust me, Katrina?"

"Yes," she said without hesitation.

"Then remain here until this is finished."

"Phin—"

"Promise me you will stay here until it is finished."

Katrina nodded, trying to swallow. He stepped around her and headed for the door, his attention fully on the two soldiers. Katrina held her breath, waiting for them to turn and demand he stop. She stared in amazement, dumbfounded, as he walked right past them, eased open the door, and slipped out of the room. The door clicked quietly as he guided its closing. Even when Captain Beckett finally looked up and jerked in shock, and demanded of her where Phin had gone, she couldn't speak.

"To commemorate and acknowledge our new government, it is my honor today to reveal the new flag of the United Protectorate. We commissioned some of the most talented artists we could find to take the heart and soul of this new world and present a design to represent *us* from this day onward."

The back of Connor's neck itched, and his fingers tingled with the urge to take his gun from his thigh holster. Something wasn't right; he knew it. He glanced across the stage to where Mel stood, her back straight, feet apart, hands tucked behind her hips, eyes forward. She didn't feel it.

"Like the stars and stripes of the nation whose ground we now stand, a flag that inspired patriotism and pride, the flag of the Protectorate must stir within us that same loyalty and trust."

Connor slid a quick look to his sister seated at the back of the stage beside Michael, and Jackie on his other side. She watched Nick with pride and a tear in her eye. Michael took a handkerchief from his pocket and handed it to her. She smiled and wiped her cheeks. Then Michael looked at Connor.

Connor's blood chilled.

Michael felt it too.

His nephew dipped his chin, acknowledging what Connor already knew.

"Of all the designs presented, we are proud to name William Scarborough of the Louisiana region as the artist who captured the essence of what we intend to build."

Nick turned away from the podium to the back of the stage where Mr. Bill Scarborough stood. He was a tall man, standing a good two inches over Nick's six-foot-two frame, with short cropped silver-grey hair and a short moustache and beard also frosted with grey. He met

Nick halfway across the stage with a handshake, and Nick patted his shoulder to lead him to the podium. The crowd clapped enthusiastically. Connor scanned the people, hoping to find the one clue to give him the warning he needed. At the embassy weeks before, it had been the Xeno woman's smug smile. He had almost been too late that day.

Once the men stood side-by-side, Nick turned and angled his arm toward a bare flagpole set at the center of Alexandria square, currently surrounded by hundreds of citizens. Two Firebirds in the crowd, standing at the base of the pole, tugged their thick silk ropes and in one sharp snap the new flag unfurled. The crowd roared. In the center of the flag was a scarlet phoenix, wings spread and stretched across the width of the flag. Talons curled at the bottom of the flag and the Phoenix' open beak screamed into a black, starlit space scene filling the upper portion of the flag. Above the head of the Phoenix was an intricately designed image of Earth in stunning detail, down to the swirl of clouds and revised shape of the continents, changed in the war. Rays of deep blue and verdant green alternated across the bottom of the flag, raining from the spread wings of the firebird.

Nick motioned Mr. Scarborough to the podium.

The big man smiled, but it was nervous and strained, lopsided. He shoved his hands into his pockets, then jerked them free and gripped the podium and cleared his throat. "Thank you, Mr. President." He cleared his throat again, color creeping into his face. "A year ago, President Tanner spoke of the Phoenix as an immortal creature who rises reborn from its own funeral pyre. From the ashes of the fire, the Phoenix rises and begins its life again. President Tanner promised we would rise from the ashes of our funeral pyre, we would be reborn and be stronger than we have ever been.

"That is why the Phoenix is the center of our flag, with wings spread in flight. Above the Phoenix is our Earth wrapped in a blanket of stars. And the ribbons of blue and green the health and life our planet will have again." He stopped with a solid jerk of his head and stepped back, clearly finished with his speech.

The itch became a burn, and Connor scanned the crowd. And in a split second, he saw . . .

A man stood at the edge of the crowd, still and unenthusiastic despite the roar of the throng and the energy saturating the air. Connor slid his hand to his pulse pistol and raised his other hand to tap his ear canal radio. "All Firebirds, alert. Crimson Alert. We have a hostile. P.O.T.U.P two o'clock. Male. Grey hair. Green jacket. Move in."

Mel shifted and looked at him in response to his command.

"I want to thank Bill for his inspiration and his vision," Nick said, keeping his hand on Mr. Scarborough's shoulder so he couldn't move away, which the reserved man clearly wanted to do. "I also want to thank every man and every woman who has stepped up in whatever way they can. Whether that be treating the sick, holding the hands of the frightened, taking into your home the lost, using your mechanical knowledge to fix what's broken, your strength to cut wood to keep others warm, or protecting those who need protecting, you are the reason we are survivors. You are the reason we are unstoppable. You are the reason we are strong. You are the reason we will never be fooled again."

The man in the crowd slid his hand into his jacket. At the same moment, a glint of a reflection from the roofline of a building around the square caught Connor's attention.

Sniper!

"Get down!" Connor shouted and pulled his gun, lunging for Nick.

A combined scream of panic swept through the crowd closest to the podium, and everyone scattered; but the square was packed solid and they only managed to turn into a crush of Humanity, the lone man standing still. Nick was already on the move, heading for his wife, and Connor put himself between his president and the hostile. With one hand, he pushed Nick down and toward Caitlin, and the other he drew his weapon and fired. The hostile dove beneath his line of sight, hidden by the raised stage.

"Sniper on the roof!" he shouted to Mel, who had taken her place shielding Jackie and Michael. Jackie had gotten to the floor, but Michael still stood, staring into the crowd.

Then his head snapped up and he looked to the roofline.

Connor took in everything, in quick succession. The hostile had yet to emerge, Nick had reached Caitlin, Bill Scarborough huddled behind some of the fallen chairs, and Mel protected Jackie. He scanned the area, searching for the gunman, then glanced at the sniper. There was no way his weapon would reach that far, and he only hoped a Firebird would get close enough. One blink, the sniper was alone, preparing to fire, the next blink someone was with him, and in the third blink the sniper fell eight stories to the street below. Connor couldn't help but stare as the unknown person leaped from the roof, landing perfectly on a fire escape landing, and similarly made his way down the side of the building.

Action to his right had him pivot in reaction and the hostile rose over the edge of the podium, weapon in hand. Connor fired, four rapid bursts, but the hostile got off two shots before Connor hit him dead center in the chest, followed by a head shot. He heard a shout from behind him, where Nick and the others tried to get clear of the shooting but couldn't take the moment to look. The hostile flew back, his gun firing wild. A woman fleeing the melee dropped hard with a scream of pain.

Damn it!

"Billy!"

Connor spun, weapon raised, and his heart hit his gut. Nick held Bill Scarborough, the man's back ripped open by the close pulse fire and eased the big man to the floor. Caitlin scrambled from the floor and went to them, kneeling beside Bill as Nick laid him down. The crowd parted, revealing another lone standing man, a smirk on his face and a large rifle in his arms. He met Connor's eyes and raised the long-barreled weapon.

Connor raised his hand, aimed, but before he could pull the trigger the man was gone—dropped to the ground—and in his place stood Phineas.

"What the hell . . ."

Phin picked up the weapon and tossed it, effortlessly, to land on the stage edge.

"Connor!" Nick yelled behind him. "Get medics here now!"

"The perimeter is secure," came a voice through his ear radio. "We've secured three other hostiles, and forces have arrived to manage crowd control."

"Good. When medics arrive, bring two immediately to the stage."

"Is it the president, sir?"

Connor stood straight and looked to his left. Nick was fine, but Bill was not. Blood seeped from his wound to soak the wood of the stage, and he gripped Nick's sleeve with a bloody hand. Connor took another glance around, assuring no other single shooters emerged from the crowd, and came face-to-face with Phineas, who had reached the stage and stepped up without making a sound.

"We're gonna talk," Connor said, pointing to him, then went to Nick and Caitlin.

Michael stood at Bill's feet, leaning on his cane, his face pinched and Jackie held firm against his side. Caitlin tried desperately to staunch the wound that had torn through the man, her hands pressed to his chest, blood soaking her skin, but the wound in his back was worse. There was no way he would live until the medics arrived. Even Connor knew that.

Didn't mean he wouldn't try.

Three Firebirds arrived and he gave them orders to watch the First Family. "I'm going to go hurry the medics," he said and ran for the edge of the stage, leaping free into the cleared square.

"Take it easy, Bill," Nick rasped, holding tight to the man's hand. "Help is coming."

Bill coughed, winced, and smiled, squeezing tighter to Nick's hand. "Tell 'em not to hurry, sir. No need to rush on my account."

Caitlin sucked in a sharp sob and looked from Bill to Nick. "He jumped in the way," she whispered, tears running down her blood-streaked cheeks. "If he hadn't, that Xeno would have killed us."

Nick nodded, not able to force the words "I know" from his tight throat. Caitlin leaned over and pressed trembling lips to Bill's cheek. He closed his eyes and swallowed hard.

"Thank you," Nick finally managed to say.

Bill shook his head. "No thank you necessary, sir. The world needs Nicholas and Caitlin Tanner a whole heck of a lot more than it needs me."

Caitlin wept, her head bowed and her shoulders shaking. Nick wanted to reach for her, hold her, but couldn't let go of the man who would die a hero saving her life. Bill released Nick's hand and slid his arm across his own body until he could touch Caitlin. She raised her head, choking on her sobs and looked at him with glistening eyes.

"Don't cry, ma'am," he said, his own light blue eyes shining. "Don't you worry about me. I know where I'm goin' and I know who's waitin' for me. My lord and my sweetheart."

Caitlin sucked in a breath and pressed her lips together, nodding.

Bill looked to Nick, and Nick envied—just for a moment—the peace he saw in the man's eyes. "You're a good man, Nick," he said, using Nick's name for the first time since they'd met. "I've never prayed so hard as I did in those days followin' the first attacks, and when you came back I knew we'd all be okay. All of us. No matter what, the Human race would be okay."

"You put far too much faith in me," Nick said, shaking his head. They all put too much faith in him. He was just a man.

"Nah," Bill scoffed, then sputtered a cough. "I put faith in the Lord, and He's the one got faith in you." He looked past Nick to Michael and Jackie standing at his feet. "He's got faith in all of you." The last words nearly disappeared in his fading voice, and he blinked heavy, his body becoming dead weight in Nick's arms.

Nick looked up and around the square, and a burst of relief hit his chest when he saw Connor running back toward them with medics and a conveyance stretcher. "Hurry!" he shouted.

Bill sucked in a breath, his eyes popping open. "Sir?"

"Yeah," Nick said, rubbing his cheek against his shoulder. "I'm right here, Bill."

"Do me a favor."

"Anything . . ."

"Get those S.O.Bs and turn them into bantha poodoo."

Nick chuckled and nodded, hearing his son do the same behind him. "I will. I promise." Bill nodded and his eyes slid closed again.

"You're going to be remembered as a hero, Bill. And your legacy will live forever, flying over the Protectorate." Bill didn't open his eyes again, but his beard shifted with his smile. Nick leaned closer and pressed a kiss to the man's forehead. "Say a good word for me when you get there."

One final breath eased from Bill's large frame, and his body relaxed in Nick's hold. His hand slid free from Caitlin's hold to land on the stage with a soft thud. Caitlin cried, folding over herself and Nick reached for her, still holding Bill against his chest. When he touched her she grabbed his hand and held it to her lips. Connor arrived at the stage, but Nick raised his head and looked at his brother-in-law, shaking his head.

CHAPTER TWENTY-EIGHT

Detainment and Interrogation Facility
United Earth Protectorate, Capitol City
Alexandria, Seat of Virginia
North American Continent

"It wasn't your decision to make!" Connor shouted.

"I'm sorry, sir," Captain Beckett stated, at least holding enough of a backbone to stand straight and at attention to take his dressing down. "I was unaware any information from the prisoner should have been considered viable intelligence."

"Who the hell defined Phin as a *prisoner*?"

Rage had simmered beneath his skin since the assassination attempt in the square, coming to a vicious boil when he faced Captain Beckett and Captain Wesley and heard the details of the events at the hospital. Phin's precise identification of the primary assassin; both his and Katrina Bauer's urging to contact Connor and warn him, their ultimate dismissal of the warning, and Phin's as-of-yet-unexplained ability to walk right past them, reach the square over a mile away in what he had calculated to be less than two minutes, and take out at least two Xenos or more before it was all said and done.

301

"The Triadic kidnapped Doctor Bauer, sir. They are held in the secure wing of the hospital. We assumed—"

"That's your problem, Captain!" Connor shouted. "You. Assumed. You were given information regarding a potential danger to your president. I don't care if a duck waddling down the street stops and tells you President Tanner might catch a cold, you *pass on that information*."

"Yes, sir."

"Am I perfectly clear, Captain?"

"Yes, sir," Beckett barked.

Connor turned away, his hands set at his waist, sucking in thick air to find his balance and smother his anger. He bowed his head and closed his eyes, and with one final deep breath, pushed down most of the fury. Connor straightened and twisted back to his officer. "We're not done with this, Captain, but we're done for tonight."

"Yes, sir."

Captain Beckett pivoted on the balls of his feet and quit the room. As soon as the door closed, Connor grabbed the back of the nearest chair and whipped it across the room, the metal legs bending on impact with the wall, leaving a dent in the plaster. He heard the door open again and didn't need to turn to know it was Mel. But, he didn't turn. He wasn't ready yet.

Another one of the chairs in the conference room scraped across the floor before Mel took a seat. Moments later the aroma of coffee and food drifted through the room to reach him, and despite his frustration and anger, his stomach growled in response. She said nothing, just waited for him to let out a gust of air and turn.

Two cups of coffee sat on the table, and two plates with hearty, thick sandwiches. Connor crossed to the chair nearest her and sat, and she pushed one of the plates toward him. He took a swallow of the black coffee and a big bite of the sandwich, curbing the hunger pains, before he was ready to speak.

"What was his excuse?" Mel asked, picking up her own sandwich.

Connor finished chewing and leaned back, wiping his fingers over his mouth. "He thought Phin was a prisoner, so why believe anything he said."

"And how did Phin get past him?"

Connor shrugged. "He doesn't know. Still can't say. He swears Phin was standing beside Katrina watching the speech, he talked with Wesley, looked up and Phin was gone. No sign of him. And Katrina avoided any answer. Moments later, all hell broke loose on the broadcast and they knew they were in deep shit."

Mel leaned forward over her sandwich, picking up half to tap the corner cut against the plate. She looked up, a shallow line across her brow. "Just what is the status of the Triadic? I mean, are they considered criminals? Refugees? Prisoners of War?"

"They're under watch," Connor explained and sat up to take another drink. "Until this afternoon, with two of them incapacitated, the secure wing seemed sufficient until we figured out what to do with them." He shrugged. "Hell, Mel, I swear we've gone from one covert war to another. Four years ago, our enemy was the Areth, some kind of kin to us wearing sheep's clothing. Two years ago, we learned the Areth are really the Sorracchi and they aren't kin, they're *us* and they're not wearing sheep's clothing, they're wearing *us*. Now, we've gotten rid of the Sorracchi—but have we? —and we're fighting each other. Are these three men victims or enemies?"

She smiled. "Feel better to get that off your chest?"

He chuckled, shook his head, and tossed his napkin on the table. "No, not really. Doesn't answer any question, just makes more."

"They were soldiers for the Sorracchi," she stated, and left it hanging.

Connor took two more bites before he responded. "Soldiers, sure. But maybe slaves, too. No choice. Katrina says the records show their life was pretty bad." He held to himself the fact Michael and the three men shared a mother, a bat-shit crazy mother, but a mother. Nick had asked it be kept to family and need to know only. He qualified for both.

"Don't you think she's biased?"

"They took her by force. If she was biased by that, wouldn't it be to convince us not to trust them? She's been on their side since they came back."

"Don't tell me you don't see what's going on there . . ."

"What? That she's likely in love with Phin?"

She nodded and shrugged one shoulder. "People do a lot of things for love."

Connor smiled, licked his lips, and leaned sideways around the table corner. She knew what he wanted, and met him halfway for a deep, coffee-flavored kiss. He sat back, and they finished their sandwiches in near silence. Just as he finished, he reached down the table to grab his PAC. Chewing the last bite, he called up his video program and opened the transferred video from the camera found in the apartment in Falls Church where Katrina had been with the Triadic.

"I want to show you something."

She scooted her chair around to his side of the table while he opened the video. The quality was poor, the picture shaky, but he attributed that to the state of mind of the guy doing the recording. Considering the pile of bodies they had found in the apartment, and the tableau the camera had captured, the guy was probably ready to piss himself.

"This is the camera they found in the apartment," Mel clarified.

Connor nodded. "Based on the short commentary before the action begins, this was intended as documented proof of their attack, and possibly to study the Triadic."

The image froze on a cluster of heads and shoulders, the cameraman amongst the huddle before they burst through the apartment door. When they did, the door slammed open with a resounding crack. As soon as the close cluster of bodies cleared, the cameraman focused on Katrina who had bolted across the room. The fight was chaos, the sound of shouting and fighting cut momentarily by the sizzle of a stunner cutting the air. Katrina screamed and dodged behind a couch. The cameraman then hunkered down in a corner to take in the show.

The first time Connor had watched, his gut had been in his throat. Even though he knew Katrina had come through the attack alive and relatively unharmed, his attention continuously strayed to the back of the room where she huddled—once taking a fire poker to a guy's jaw—while the others fought. The second time he watched he was able to focus more on the Triadic, and now he was able to view the scene with a trained and conscientious eye to see just what the three men were capable of together.

One thing he knew without question: the Protectorate would be a hell of a lot better off with the Triadic on their side, not against them.

While the fight was impressive when only Phineas and Daniel were in the fight, it didn't get really good until Gideon showed up and they became one powerful, fluid, unstoppable unit. Like three perfectly forged cogs, they moved in unison and in response to each other without pause, without hesitation, without so much as a glance to each other. They stood as three points to a triangle, fighting the attackers in hand-to-hand combat, or used each other as leverage and force, using the bodies of their brothers like weapons. There was clearly some Talent use involved, as weapons would fly into their hands—or out, as the case may be—to turn the tide of the fight. Men dropped hard, either by fist or forged weapon, covering the floor, but even then the obstacles they created became part of the machine.

Mel said nothing while she watched. He slid a sideways glance at her and grinned at her wide-eyed, slack-jawed stare.

Then there were none . . . but the one holding the camera. He gained his feet, dropping the hand carrying the camera to his side so the image was now upside down and shot behind him. Connor quickly tapped out the command to flip the image, because the "holy crap" factor was lost unless it was upright. Gideon faced the door, Daniel and Phineas behind him and Gideon turned his head to see the fleeing man. He raised his hand, and from somewhere outside the view of the camera, a long stick flew into view and smacked hard against his hand. Riding the momentum, Gideon turned in a hard three-sixty and released the pole. A sick thud echoed through the room and the cameraman dropped hard, the video device bouncing across the floor.

"Holy crap," Mel mumbled.

"Yeah, that was pretty much my reaction," Connor said.

They finished watching as Phin turned to Katrina Bauer, then dropped to the floor. She begged Gideon to let them get help, begged for Phin's life. Maybe Mel was right, and Katrina's opinion was clouded when it came to these three men, but Connor knew what he saw. There was no fear in her toward any of these men. There was no hesitation on their part to fight and protect her. Whatever had taken her to Falls Church with them, something else brought them back. Connor's *pere* told him often when he was a kid and teenager that the true measure of a man is the man he is when he thinks no one is watching. In the moments after the fight, when they had no idea their actions would be scrutinized by someone they didn't know, Connor saw three honorable men. Misguided, perhaps, but not dishonorable.

He turned off the video and leaned back. "I'm heading back to the hospital now to question all three of them. Victor notified me half an hour ago both Gideon and Daniel are awake and capable of answering questions."

"What's going to happen to them?" she asked and stood to gather the dishes and remains of the meal. The edge of her voice caught his attention.

"Right now, I don't know. We've got to hear what they have to say. And Doctor Bauer, too. We haven't sunk into a complete lack of justice yet."

Mel set down the plates with a thunk and straightened, her lips in a tight line and her eyes shadowed. "They're dangerous, Connor. I don't trust them. If they aren't *actually* Sorracchi, don't you see what the Sorracchi made them to be? Killing machines. They've got a taste of freedom, and they aren't going to want to serve any master."

"Who says they have to *serve* anyone?"

"They can't exactly be a part of regular society," she snapped.

Connor tilted his head, thrown by her visceral reaction. She seemed to realize her over-reaction and waved off anything else with a flip of her hand. "Not my call, I guess. Do you want me to go with you?"

"No," he said without hesitation. "I've got it."

She didn't say anything else, picked up the plates again, and left.

"*Y*ou should eat something. I know damn well you haven't all day."

Katrina looked to her brother, then to the sandwich he set on the desk beside her interface board, and her stomach twisted into a painful, acidic knot. He sighed and walked to the cot she'd slept in the nights following David's waking and before she'd left with the boys. The cot she'd slept in since they came back so she didn't have to leave the hospital, not wanting to be too far away before Gideon and Daniel were out of danger.

They were awake. She'd had only a few minutes to see them before she'd been escorted from the room and asked to wait while Connor and his people "finished their investigation." The words sounded so dooming. Katrina had hoped, perhaps naively, the authorities would see how she had not been hurt, how she held no fear for the three men, and especially after Phin had run to save President Tanner, that all would be forgiven. All would be fine. But she caught a glimpse of Connor Montgomery in the hall on his way to Phin's room, and the grim, hard-set look in his eyes and her hopes had deflated.

"You ready to tell me what happened?"

Katrina looked at him, her vision blurred by tears she didn't realize fogged her eyes, and just as quickly looked away, embarrassed by them.

"Trina, you had to know the Triadic—"

"Don't," she cut him off, then immediately offered an apologetic smile. "I'm sorry. That name is what *she* called them. They're men, not machines."

One eyebrow jerked up toward his hairline, and Karl nodded. "Fair enough."

"They didn't do anything worth punishment, Karl. They were frightened. They didn't know where they were or who *we* were, or if they had woken up in a worse situation than before they went in those damn pods."

"Whoa." Karl chuckled. "You must be serious if you're willing to cuss."

Heat infused her face but she looked her brother in the eye. She took a steeling breath and released it slowly before admitting, "I care about them, Karl. And don't give me a hard time about it. I know they've only been out of the pods for a few days." She involuntarily looked to the three empty, dark pods still sitting on the other side of the room. "I *know* you don't like them because they took me out of the hospital. I know *all* that, but they mean something to me." She looked down at her hands, watching him from the corner of her eye. "I mean something to them."

Karl worked his jaw and ran his tongue along his teeth behind his closed lips, probably trying to choose his words very, very carefully. "Right now, Trina, I'm tryin' *really* hard not to get pissed, and I know you told me I shouldn't worry about what went on in that shelter, but how the hell do you expect me to react to something like that? Do you know what's going through my head right now?"

"Haven't you ever just met someone and felt connected? Not . . ." She shook her head, frustrated. Because, truth be told, she had *never* just met someone and felt connected. Most of her life she'd felt *disconnected* from anyone not family, her parents had made sure of it. In her very early years she'd shown an extreme proficiency for computer technology, and because of her parents' fear for the new world order of "Areth" and Human coalition—and the risks they suspected but had no proof for—they had hidden their children away from prying eyes. She'd been schooled at home, had only a few friends her parents introduced her to, and had fostered her skills in solitude with only her brother as company.

When her parents were killed, her world narrowed to Karl.

In the course of a few weeks, both David Forte and the three brothers had not just come into her life, they had nearly instantly infused themselves into her existence.

Karl waited, though she wondered how patiently. She was tempted to gloss over the full reality, but anything less than full disclosure felt dishonest. Katrina crossed her arms and tucked her hands against her sides. She raised her head and met her brother's unwavering stare.

"I love Gideon and Daniel as much as I love you, Karl. They feel like . . ." She shook her head and shrugged. " . . .brothers. They feel like family. Even David." She smiled, remembering what he'd said the day before when she'd visited him. "He told me he feels like an uncle, like family, to us. That's what I mean about them meaning something to me, and me to them."

Karl drew in a slow, metered breath and chewed on the inside of his cheek. He looked away, then down, then back to her. "What about Phineas?"

A new flash of warmth hit her cheeks, not in embarrassment, but a simple, core reaction to his name. Katrina smiled, feeling liberated in the acceptance. "He's different."

"How different?"

Katrina tipped her head and cleared her throat before she managed to answer. "I don't think of him as anything remotely close to a brother. I think that is clear to everyone. I haven't tried to hide it."

"Do you love him?"

She stared, wide eyed. There it was. The question of all questions. Karl stood, the cot creaking from the shift of weight, and walked to her. He tugged her arms away from her body, taking her hand in his. Katrina tipped back her head to look him in the eyes. He gently squeezed her fingers and asked again.

"Trina, do you love him?"

The realization wasn't a shock; if anything, it was a panacea to her nerves frazzled, frayed and exhausted by the last two weeks. Katrina drew in a breath and relaxed her shoulders as she released it. She nodded and smiled. "Yes."

*I*t was near eleven before Phin and his brothers were able to return to the large room they had been placed in for recovery. Though they tried to hide it, both Gideon and Daniel were weary and worn from the events of the evening and into the night.

Phin understood; the hours following his own waking had been lacking strength and resiliency. By morning, both would be much stronger, but sleep was the best course of treatment. They needed to allow the bionanetics still infused with their systems to heal them.

He waited until they both slept before he left the room with a nod toward the guards in the hall. Commander Montgomery had stated the guards were prevalent throughout the hospital, and they no longer would serve the purpose of retaining the three brothers; though Phin wasn't ready quite yet to presume full compliance by the armed men.

Michael Tanner had come after Commander Montgomery finished his questions. In Michael Phin sensed sincerity, especially when he thanked Phin for his actions at the square. He explained both the president's wife, and the woman Michael held as his partner, were with child; which was why he was at the hospital so late. Although both Caitlin and Jacqueline were unharmed after the events, their physicians had preferred the women be observed to assure the health of the children they carried. Phin was intrigued by the change in his brother's expression, the shift around his eyes, when he spoke of Jacqueline Anderson and his child she carried. His thoughts had gone to Katrina, and he immediately wished Michael would leave so he could find her. He hadn't seen her since he left her alone to go to the square, and he had come to acknowledge the ache in his chest as missing her.

Each hour he learned a new definition for the emotions he was now allowed to experience without retribution or pain.

He had not been beyond the cluster of rooms in the secure wing since they had returned two days before, but as he turned a corner into a separate part of the hospital the surroundings struck him as familiar. Fleeting, lost in the confusion of being newly awake, disconcerted, and afraid, the memories guided him to a closed door with an oblong window. A soft glow to the left of the door illuminated the interior enough he saw three empty, defunct stasis pods and he understood why the hall was familiar. He curled his fingers around the cool metal of the door handle and tried the knob; the door was unlocked and he eased it open.

Disgust tightened his stomach when he looked at the pods. Some of the tentacles and accoutrements that had been infused with their bodies now hung limp and useless on the floor, the tips dark with dried blood from ripping themselves free. Gideon's pod was open, the inside a gaping maw of cold darkness. A chill hit Phin's spine at the memory of waking in the casket, of the bitter bile in his throat when panic slammed hard into him, and the instant relief when his brothers' minds called out in unison.

We are alive. We must be free.

The disgust for the pod turned to disgust for himself when he allowed himself to remember the moment they had seen Katrina come back into the room, and the choice had been made to take her. It hadn't been unanimous as the best course of action, but they all agreed it was the best option available to them. He clenched his jaw in anger at himself, remembering the way she had trembled in his hold, the way her tears had slicked the contact of his hand over her mouth, the frightened sound she made in response to his demands. He had told Commander Montgomery they had no intention of hurting her the night they left here, which was true that night; but his definition of hurt had changed since then and now he accepted the distastefulness of his actions.

Phin stepped into the room and eased the door shut behind him. The glow he had noted was from a bank of computers on a desk facing the pods. He remembered Katrina leaning over them the night they were free, setting a program to run in her absence. Beyond the desk, tucked against the far wall, was a narrow cot. Katrina slept, curled into a tight ball so she barely took up half the length, a blanket tucked beneath her chin. Waves of rich brown hair poked out from the blanket edge to fall across her forehead and lay on the pillow.

How could the cold disgust sitting in his gut like ice change so quickly to a warmth so instant it infused him to the ends of his fingers? Was this the sensation that changed the look in Michael's eyes when he thought of the woman with whom he shared a life?

Phin crossed the room with light steps and crouched beside the cot, studying her in her sleep. She breathed deep, rhythmic, and memories of watching over her while she slept easily pushed aside the darker memories of moments before. He focused on the sensations of lying beside her while fireworks lit up the sky, of her burrowing closer to him for protection. When he saw her that morning—what felt like days before now—for the first time since waking again and she had embraced him.

And kissed him.

Whenever his mind calmed, when nothing else occupied his focus, his thoughts wrapped around the memory of her petite body held against his chest, her fragile arms gripping his shoulders, her delicate fingers in his hair, and her soft, warm lips against his mouth. He had been unprepared for the visceral, intense reaction his body—trained for perfection in control—experienced to the basic contact: lips to lips. Whenever they touched, whenever she drew near to him or reached for him, he felt the solid tug toward her and the desire to remain close, but the kiss had left him not only wanting to keep her near but wanting more. He had no solid definition for what it was he wanted more of, only that it was Katrina, and could only assume that need was the primitive desires his mother had indoctrinated them against. But the vulgar repulsion she had spoken of was so far removed from the pleasure he knew he could not connect the two.

Katrina inhaled deeply, and stretched beneath the blanket, the simple gray material shifting to form over her limbs as she extended her legs. She exhaled on a low, soft moan and something stirred low in Phin's body. Long lashes fluttered and she opened her eyes, blinking, then focused when she saw him crouched beside her. Katrina pulled down the blanket from her face and he saw her smile.

She snaked an arm from beneath the blanket and laid her warm palm against his cheek, her thumb stroked his lip. Heavy lids hooded her dark eyes, and he questioned whether she was fully awake. Regardless, he tipped his face into her touch and inhaled the sweet smell of her warm skin.

"What are you doing here?" she asked.

"I was walking and found you."

His voice seemed to revive her and her eyes popped open, and she gasped. Then she pushed herself up to sit, the blanket dropped to pool in her lap, her eyes wide. "What are you doing here?" she asked again, her voice stronger, more surprised.

Phin smiled. "I just told you. I was walking and found you."

"You're not in the secure wing."

He wasn't sure if it was a question or a statement. "No."

Her eyes widened again. "Does that mean—Did—Did Connor give you clearance to leave? What time is it? What does this mean?"

Phin shifted to rest his weight on one knee, the other parallel to the floor so he could set his arm on his thigh and look up at her. "To your second question, it is near midnight. To your first and third, yes, Commander Montgomery has cleared us from any restriction with the understanding he must also speak with his superiors. He has accepted your word we did you no harm—" The words tasted ashy in his mouth, but her widening smile pushed it aside. "—and our word our loyalties do not lie with your enemies." Phin reached for her hand and held it on top of the rumpled blanket. "It means, for the first time in our existence, we are free men."

Katrina squealed and lunged off the bed, her arms flung wide before she wrapped them around his neck, he went backward, and they both tumbled to the floor. Before he could ask if she was unharmed, though the cot was low and the fall barely constituted as a fall, she took his face in her hands and kissed him. He knew the rush of heat would come, but the knowledge did nothing to prepare him for the overpowering effect.

Every cell came alive, so many reactions slammed into his body at the same moment he couldn't categorize. Couldn't separate or process them. His thoughts fragmented to simple commands fighting for dominance.

Katrina.

Need.

More.

He pulled her over him, her slight body barely a weight on him, but enough to send jolts of pulsing desire through him from hip to throat. Phin nearly lost himself in the overwhelming, overpowering need to touch her more, feel her more, hold her closer, tighter. With a groan born from a pulse in the center of his chest, Phin flipped them as a unit and leveraged himself over her, never breaking the kiss. Her tongue brushed his and he had to clench his fists to keep from gripping her shoulders, knowing he would and could hurt her if he didn't.

Tiny fingers brushed his sides beneath the hem of his thermal shirt, and Phin pressed his face into her throat, his ragged breath hot against her skin, reflecting back to him. The smell of her hair and the skin of her arms filled his senses. Phin inhaled her, finally understanding why he had been warned against Human impulses. This was intoxicating, a drug he needed more of.

Then his name broke through the blood pounding in his ears, and he registered the hands touching him shook, she trembled beneath him. Phin froze and took a split heartbeat to focus his senses on her. Her breath was ragged, rapid, but not as it had been moments before, her hold on him tight but not seeking. Phin pulled back and pushed his weight up off her, balanced on his bent arms so he could look down at her. In the glow of the monitors he registered the deep, dusky blush in her cheeks and down her throat and the glisten in her eyes.

"I'm sorry," he choked, the sick disgust he'd felt for himself when he first arrived returning with a vengeance. He saw in her eyes the same fear he'd seen in the early hours of being in Falls Church. "I've frightened you."

He shifted to move off her, but she gasped and reached for him, lacing her fingers behind his neck to keep him from moving. "No," she blurted and shook her head. "No, you didn't frighten me, Phin. No more than I frightened myself."

"I don't understand . . ."

Katrina swiped her fingers across her cheeks and laughed, but it was a strange sound. Humorless. When she looked at him again, the fear was gone. "I'm not . . . I don't know how to handle this. I don't have any, um, experience with . . ." She laughed again, the sound nervous. "I've never felt like *this* with someone."

Phin swallowed and shifted his weight so he could raise his hand to her cheek and brush away the trail of moisture. Her skin was hot, slick. "Neither have I, Katrina. I believe I may be as overwhelmed by this as you."

CHAPTER TWENTY-NINE

SATURDAY, 14 MARCH 2012
PRESIDENTIAL RESIDENCE
UNITED EARTH PROTECTORATE, CAPITOL CITY
ALEXANDRIA, SEAT OF VIRGINIA
NORTH AMERICAN CONTINENT

"*B*urfday, Daddy? Burfday, Daddy?"

Nicole did her third circuit around the bedroom, squealing gleefully, before she ran straight at Michael and into the space between his knees. Michael laughed, picked her up, and set her on his leg. She had been a bundle of excited toddler energy all day, ecstatically thrilled with the idea of a birthday. It didn't matter it wasn't hers.

"Are you going to help me blow out the candles?"

She nodded, her toothy grin beaming and pigtails bobbing their way free of her hair elastics. She took in a great, deep breath and puffed her cheeks, blowing as hard as she could to show him what she could do. Then she threw her tiny arms around his neck and squeezed as hard as she could, pressed a sloppy kiss to his cheek, and scrambled free to run across the room and out the door. Right past her mother.

Jacqueline laughed, stepping aside just in time not to be bowled over by twenty-seven pounds of pure energy. As the echo of Nicole's little feet hitting the floor at top speed faded away, Jacqueline crossed the bedroom to him. "And this is before cake."

Michael chuckled and reached his hand to her as soon as she was close, to draw her to sit beside him on the edge of the bed. She leaned against his shoulder, reaching for a kiss, and he willingly obliged. She slid her arm between his hand and his side and linked their hands.

"Happy birthday, handsome." Her smile smoothed over his soul like warmth from a fire.

He kissed her again because the fact this year he could was a gift in itself. Two years ago—sometimes he couldn't believe it had only been two years ago—he spent his first birthday free of his prison celebrating with Caitlin in the Phoenix compound buried deep in a Colorado mountain. His father had been jumping wormholes across space to bring them salvation. He had no memory of his birthday a year ago, trapped in a coma and near death after his mother's vicious retribution.

This year he would spend his birthday the way his father told him it should be: surrounded by the people who loved him and cared for him, celebrating life rather than just trying to survive. He had more in this house, on this day, than he could have imagined three years before; in fact, three years before the day would have passed without acknowledgment because he didn't know the date of his birth.

"I love you," he told her, his forehead to hers, his eyes closed so he could feel her and smell her and absorb her. He brought his free hand to her cheek to hold her close and brushed his nose along hers, enjoying the simple contact he craved. He had gone twenty-five years with barely any physical contact other than that intended for pain, or in the days following when Victor would do what he could to heal him. Now, reaching for her was as natural and as necessary as breath. She was food to his soul. "You are the most beautiful gift ever given to me."

She drew back from him enough her dark brown, nearly black, eyes looked into his. "What has gotten into you lately?" Then she smiled, and he smiled in return, unable and unwilling to deny his instant reaction. "I'm not complaining, mind you, but you've been different since I came back."

"How am I different?"

Jacqueline inhaled and released it, not quite a sigh but something close, and canted her head slightly. "I don't know if I can explain without making you feel you've done things wrong, because you haven't."

"Tell me."

Jacqueline laid her hand against his chest, over his heart, and looked down at the point of contact before meeting his gaze again. "Michael, early on I couldn't figure you out. I never quite understood what went on in your brilliant mind." Her smile ticked a little. "But once you made it clear how you felt, I never doubted you."

"Until I left . . ." A ball of dread curled in his stomach.

She brought her finger to his lips and stopped him, shaking her head. "No, not even then. Michael, I won't say it didn't hurt. I couldn't fathom what would make you leave us; but, even in my anger I didn't doubt you loved me."

Michael tipped his head to touch his forehead to hers again. He loved sharing space with her, breathing air with her. "You haven't told me how I am different."

Jacqueline shifted closer to him, close enough she hitched up one leg to drape it across his lap and she sat hip to hip with him. He settled his hand on her stomach, immediately following the curve of their baby.

"You've always made me feel loved, Michael," she said softly, her breath skimming his cheek and ear before she kissed his jaw. "But since I came home, you have made me feel adored." Michael raised his head and looked into her eyes, his heart tightening at the glisten there. She made a small, whispered laugh and smiled, a contrast to the tears. "You have made me feel precious." She laughed more, despite the tears and shook her head. "Stupid pregnancy hormones."

Michael held her beautiful face in his hands and kissed her, tasting the salt on her lips. "You are more than precious, Jacqueline. You are my treasure."

"*H*appy birthday to you!"

      "Burfday you! Burfday you!"

"Happy birthday, dear Michael . . ."

"Daddy!"

"Happy birthday to you!"

"Bwoh! Bwoh!"

Michael laughed and picked up Nicole, holding her against his hip. "Are you ready to help me?"

"Bwoh! Bwoh!" she squealed, huffing in great big cheeks full of air. Michael held her so she wouldn't slip and they both leaned over the cake, twenty-eight candles burning, and together they drew in deep, theatrical breaths. Together he and his daughter blew hard, Nicole more spitting than blowing, but Michael made sure all the candles went out. Nicole cheered and clapped her hands.

"Yay, Daddy! Burfday!"

Michael pressed a kiss to her cheek and she wiggled free, determined to follow Lumpy Caitlin into the kitchen to supervise the cutting and serving. Michael reached beside him, instinctively knowing Jacqueline was there, and drew her to him, turning into her for a kiss. He had fought a lump in his throat since he'd descended the stairs to the gathering of family and friends. Jacqueline was right. He felt the change in himself, and he welcomed it. Somewhere between tormenting himself for hurting her, and forgiveness without condition, Michael had realized he had to stop seeing what was not, what would never change and see the gifts he had been given. He had always known he was a blessed man, blessed far beyond what he knew he deserved, but rather than curse his blessings, he took them and held them as more precious than life.

Jacqueline pressed against him and nuzzled her nose along his jaw to speak softly in his ear. "You okay?"

He nodded and swallowed again. "I have never been happier."

Caitlin came back carrying a tray of plates with cake, and Nicole carried her own piece, holding it just high enough Dog couldn't lick it. There were too many people in the house to sit in the dining room even though the room sat a dozen or more, so everyone ate where they stood, or sat, as the case may be. As Michael finished his cake, and Jacqueline fed a last bite to Nicole, who had managed to get frosting on the tip of her right ear, his father stood and clapped his hands together once to draw everyone's attention.

"I never used to be one for speeches," Nick began, and huffed. "But I've gotten used to it in the last year. This isn't so much a speech as a declaration of thankfulness."

He motioned for Michael to join him in front of the fireplace, and with a squeeze of Jacqueline's hand, Michael made his way between the couch and the coffee table to reach his dad. Nick laid his hand on Michael's shoulder then looked around the room.

"I'm not going to rehash the last couple of years. Everyone here knows the crap we've been through, not as a planet but as a family and as friends. Some lived it right along with us. This is the first time, *ever*, I am spending this day with my son." Nick's voice broke and he looked away, clearing his throat. His hand tightened on Michael's shoulder. "It's been a long time coming." Nick huffed and smiled, looking across the room to where Connor stood. "Bring it in, Connor."

Connor slipped out of the room into the hall, and came back carrying a very old, battered looking wooden instrument case about fifteen inches long, narrow at one end and widening at the base. Despite the fact he was twenty-eight years old, his heart jumped to an excited pounding and he smiled as Connor made his way through the group of friends and family who had pulled in tighter to see. Michael had been attempting to learn to play the violin, but the only instrument he had found was what would have been considered a "cheap" instrument; sufficient but lacking. The sound was tinny and the instrument had been damaged somewhere along the way.

"We've been looking for something decent for months," Nick explained. "By what I've been told, this is a good one."

Michael took the case from Connor, the black stained wood showing spots of age and wear, cracked from years without conditioning he was sure. He crouched at the end of the coffee table and set down the case, releasing the antique latches. The leather hinges creaked with age when he lifted the lid. If the case said anything, what he was about to see was old. Very old. His throat went dry.

He lifted the lid and he couldn't breathe.

The instrument was beautiful. Polished to a rich, red hue it glowed in the firelight. The aroma of spruce, maple, and oil mingled together in a heady, inspiring bouquet. He wanted to rush and take the instrument in hand but forced himself to first inspect and tighten the bow for playing. With reverence, Michael took the violin from the case and stood, resting the lower bout against his chest. The strings were catgut, and showed age, but wherever it had been the instrument had been protected. Michael tipped the body by the neck and squinted to try to read through the f-holes. He saw the label but couldn't quite make it out. Balancing the bow between his fingers, he pulled his glasses from his shirt pocket and slipped them on, trying again. When he made out enough of the label to read, Michael gasped. He looked to his father, wide eyed.

"This is a Domenico Montagnana violin."

Nick raised his eyebrows. "So, that's good?"

Michael had to chuckle. "Yes, that's good. He was one of the most renowned luthiers in history. It's amazing any of his instruments still exist. Even more amazing you found one."

Nick smirked, and Michael had the distinct feeling his father had known all along the value and quality of the instrument he held. "So . . . play it."

"I only hope I can do this instrument justice," he said in apology and set the lower bout against his shoulder, settling his jaw against the chinrest.

The wood felt warm, alive. He tested the strings, and only needed a minor adjustment to the A and the D strings to bring it to standard pitch. Adjusting his chin again, Michael curled his fingers around the neck and drew the bow across the strings. The sound resonated through him, thrumming like a bass in his chest, and he closed his eyes.

*M*ichael Tanner played the violin with such soul it was like listening to life, like setting sound to raw emotion. The notes filled the air, tangible, brushing over Katrina's skin and making the hair at her nape stand on end. She and Karl had slipped into the house as Michael settled the violin against his chin and found a spot in the archway leading from the foyer to listen. Michael played for several minutes, everyone still.

She saw Phin, standing just inside the living room with his back against the wall, his head bowed, and his eyes closed with his hands clasped in front of him. Katrina glanced around quickly to the part of the room she could see, to find Gideon and Daniel. They weren't far away, tucked behind a couch where Beverly and Victor sat. She looked back at Phin and found herself as mesmerized by him as the music. Each time Michael played a particularly powerful harmonization of notes, Phin's response was visibly physical. An angling of his head, a tilt of his shoulder, an intake of air; there was no doubt to her Phin was as lost in the beauty as everyone else.

Michael drew out the final note, his fingers rocking on the string to create a reverberation that hummed over Katrina's senses. As Michael slid the bow, the sound slowly faded, silence settling again on the room. As soon as the note died, everyone clapped their hands together and she wiped tears from her cheeks.

As soon as activity stirred again, Katrina left her brother to slide between bodies until she reached Phin. He still had his head down, his eyes closed. She hesitated touching him, not wanting to pull him from the reverence of the music. When she laid her hand on his arm, he raised his head and looked at her and the emotion in his eyes made her breath catch.

"It's called *Meditation*," Katrina said. "The song he played. From the opera *Thais*. I've never *ever* heard it played that way, that beautifully."

Phin laid his hand over hers where it rested on his arm and looked toward Michael, who worked to put the violin back in the case with the help of his daughter Nicole. Phin shook his head. "I've never heard music, Katrina. It served no purpose and represented mankind's focus on the frivolous and emotionally inspired."

Katrina's throat tightened. "Then I think it's wonderful Michael's talent was the first music you ever heard."

He took her hand from his arm and laid her palm flat against his chest. His heart pounded hard and fast. "Why does my heart beat so fast? Why does it bring tears?"

Katrina swiped her thumb across her cheeks, flicking away some of the tears he asked her to explain. "Because beautiful music is born of emotion, and my mom used to say sometimes the heart gets so filled up with emotion, whatever kind of emotion—sometimes sadness, sometimes anger, sometimes joy, sometimes overwhelming reverence for beauty—and it has to let some go. And that's why we cry." She touched his cheek with her fingertips. "Even you."

Phin inhaled and slid his arm around her waist, drawing her to him. He canted his head, his eyes shifting to study her with an intensity that bloomed heat in her cheeks. "I have missed you," he said with weighted purpose to each word.

"I've missed you too," she whispered, leaning into him, with memories of their heated kiss three days before playing vividly in her head. She'd replayed it again and again, whenever she sat still for a moment or let her mind relax, and she'd wondered what might have happened if neither of them had stopped. That thought alone made her blush deeper.

The party had come to life again, voices mingling around them. She caught random phrases, mostly wishes to Michael or comments on the beauty of his playing, but once Phin held her Katrina didn't hear or care about much else. She had fallen in love with this enigma of a man so fast and so completely she was dizzy, and she had heard plenty from her brother how reckless and naïve she was acting, but she couldn't imagine falling in love could feel any different than this. Phin tilted his head to brush his cheek along her temple, his breath warm on her brow.

"In our past life we were punished for indecisiveness. Our training required immediate and unwavering response, absolute adherence to orders," he said against her hair, his voice skimming across her ear. "We have been engineered to be stronger, faster, more agile, more intelligent than the limitations of our Human genetics."

"And so modest, too," she said with a chuckle.

A chuckle he matched. He brushed his lips across her temple, inhaling before he continued. "She inculcated us with the concept of our superiority, forever reminding us we were still less than the Sorracchi because we would always be Human. She wanted us to see our Human origins as a weakness to be overcome."

Katrina angled back, keeping her body flush against him but back enough she could look at his face. "And?"

"And never before tonight have I understood the extent of her lies." He shook his head, his gaze never leaving her. "Katrina, in a matter of a few days I have experienced more of the *Human weaknesses* she raged against and I . . ."

"You . . . what, Phineas?"

He didn't answer except to lay his hand against her cheek and pull her back to him for a kiss that curled warmth in her stomach like steam vapor. She couldn't help the embarrassing sound fluttering at the base of her throat, but he didn't notice because he deepened the kiss and she had to hold on to his shoulders to keep her feet. When he did answer her question, he spoke against her lips. "I have never felt so ignorant, Katrina. I don't understand any of it. But I know I would rather die than go back to the nothing I was."

Katrina toed up and wrapped her arms around his neck. He embraced her, his hands pressed to her back and his face tucked against the side of her neck. She wanted to tell him he never would have to, but all her words stuck in her throat.

"I'm glad you're here," Michael declared, patting Jace Quinn hard on the back as he embraced him. He moved on to hug

Lilly, pressing a kiss to her cheek. "I know you've come for David but having you here tonight is perfect."

Lilly let him release her for only a moment before she hugged him again and returned the kiss. "We were worried about making it on time." As soon as she let him go again, she smacked his arm. "How can you keep such secrets, Michael Tanner?"

He feigned a flinch but laughed instead. "I'm sorry. I wanted to wait until I could see you to tell you."

"You didn't have to tell us," Jace said, setting his hand on Michael's shoulder. "As soon as we saw Jacqueline, Lilly knew."

"How far along is she?" Lilly asked.

"Four months."

"Oh, I'm so happy for you!" she cried, and threw her arms around him again. "Happy birthday, Michael."

"I have more to tell you, but I want you to meet some people first." Michael glanced past them to take in the room, spotting first Daniel and Gideon together talking with Victor and Beverly. Then he spotted Phin standing alone, his expression intense as he watched the party. "Make your rounds and find me when you're done."

Jace nodded and took Lilly's hand, leading her toward Michael's parents. Michael stopped twice in his attempt to cross the room, thanking people for coming, his attention not straying far from Phin, who had barely moved other than the turn of his head by degrees while he took in the room himself. Michael approached him from the right, and paused a few feet away, to watch his newly discovered brother. Although it was slight, Phin frowned at whatever he saw, though not a frown of obvious annoyance, but perhaps confusion. After a few moments of observing his brother, Michael stepped to him, his cane clicking on the wood floor.

"What do you see?" he asked.

Phin's head snapped in Michael's direction, his hazel eyes shifting by small degrees, then he looked back to the room, sliding his hand through the air to encompass everyone. "They speak of nothing, and yet it seems to be everything. They move from person to person, and the conversations change. The interactions change. One will speak, the other will agree or disagree. They laugh. They smile. They touch. Each element alone meaningless, but together . . ." He shook his head, rubbing his thumb across his chin. "It is music. Like the music you played, Michael. A chorus of voices singing the song of Humanity."

The eloquence of Phin's explanation left Michael silent. And moved. Phin understood in just a few days what had taken Michael months to comprehend: the beauty of Human connection. He swallowed and shifted to stand shoulder-to-shoulder to his brother, taking in the room from the same vantage point.

"Why do you look confused?"

"I am," Phin answered without pause. "I have attempted to break down each relationship by base definition. Parent and child. Siblings. Friends. Lovers. Spouses." He indicated certain people with a subtle point. Jace and Lilly Quinn with Jamie. Katrina and Karl Bauer. Jacqueline talking with Caitlin. Connor Montgomery and Melanie Briggs, an observation Michael found fascinating. Victor and Beverly. "But within each definable relationship there are so many variations I cannot form a solid point of reference."

"You shouldn't try, Phin." His brother looked to him, and Michael drew in a deep breath before he tried to explain, knowing he lacked the same eloquence. "I doubt there was ever a time in Human history the definitions were absolute and without variation, but never more so than now. We look to each other for peace, for sanity, and we find it in any way that peace will come. Sometimes it is with family, sometimes friends, sometimes lovers."

Phin studied him, and Michael wondered if this might have been how his mother and father felt when he was where Phin was now: full of questions and wishing to understand. "I had hoped to seek your counsel on other matters, Michael."

"You can come to me whenever you have questions." Michael rested his hand on Phin's shoulder and smiled. "I understand having questions."

"Then tell me; how does one choose a sexual partner?"

Michael choked on a burst of laughter, trying to hold it back for Phin's sake. Even then, Phin scowled. Michael shook his head. "I apologize. My laughter isn't at your question, but I am beginning to understand the saying 'what goes around comes around,' quite personally." Phin said nothing, waiting. Michael cleared his throat and dared a glance across the room to Katrina. "I assume you are asking because of your attraction to Katrina."

"Is that the proper term?"

"One of many, and unfortunately, there is no perfect answer." He smiled again, remembering Caitlin giving him a similar answer once up on a time. "Opinion on sexuality has changed drastically."

"What is your opinion?"

Michael drew in a breath and scanned the room until he found Jacqueline. She glanced at him and met his gaze and smiled. Warmth curled through him, as it always did. "Some see sexuality as something casual, something to enjoy, I suppose," he explained, watching Jacqueline. "I don't."

"How do you see it?"

Michael hooked his shillelagh over his wrist and pushed his hands into his pockets, smiling. "You challenge me, Phin, in a way I haven't been challenged." His brother, as seemed typical, simply waited. "May I ask you a question?" Phin nodded in answer. "What are your feelings for Katrina?"

Phin shook his head. "I don't know the designations for my emotions."

"That is a fair answer, but whether you know the designation or not, you know how you think and feel for her."

Phin looked across the room to Katrina, and a small smile lightened his expression. "I know I seek her company. I know when she isn't near me or with me, I feel a loss for her presence. I know I crave her nearness, and I enjoy her company regardless of where we are."

"How would you feel if you never saw her again?"

Phin immediately frowned. "I do not wish to consider that possibility."

Michael nodded. "Would you give your life for her?"

Phin snapped his head in Michael's direction. "Of course," he answered with indignation.

"Then you know your answers already, Phin. My simplest answer is to cherish Katrina and accept that she cherishes you in return. I love

Jacqueline. Jacqueline loves me. It is simple and complex at the same time."

He still scowled, but it was more an expression of frustration than annoyance. "I am having difficulty separating what we have been taught, what has been repeated again and again, and what I see and feel," Phin said, shaking his head. "Instinctively, I want to disregard everything she ever said."

"That is probably a very good idea." Michael looked to him. "My advice to you is to learn slowly and be honest with Katrina. Don't be afraid to talk with me if you have questions."

Phin nodded and crossed his arms, staring into the crowd. Near the hearth, Katrina laughed and glanced in their direction, a wide smile bowing her lips and lighting her eyes. Michael glanced at Phin and saw the same light.

"You still have a question," Michael said.

Phin nodded, seeming to mull his thoughts before he spoke again. "She told us marriage was an archaic ritual with no purpose other than to lend credence to propagation, attaching worth to genetic lineage. And yet . . ." He motioned again to the group. "In each instance of marriage in this room, there are drastic variations even in that, except I can observe one single common denominator."

"Love."

Phin nodded, looking to Michael. "If that is the proper designation, yes. Regardless of age or station or situation, the connection is undeniable love."

Michael smiled. "You have full understanding, Phin. Where is your confusion?" In his peripheral, he saw Jace and Lilly coming toward them, hand in hand and motioned for them to come closer.

"You."

He snapped his attention from the Quinns to Phin. "Me."

Jace and Lilly reached them, smiling.

"If love is the primary reason for marriage, why are you not married to Jacqueline?"

"That is a question I would like to hear the answer to myself," Jace said with a chuckle, his hand clamping down on Michael's shoulder.

"Michael has never been one for many words, but I don't think I've ever seen him struck dumb."

Michael blinked and closed his mouth but couldn't shake the hollow feeling where his stomach had once been. Cold realization. He cleared his throat and focused again, managing to motion for Gideon and Daniel to join them. They were near and a few steps brought them into the circle. Michael motioned between Jace, Lilly, and his brothers, his thoughts still tilted. "This is Reverend and Mrs. Jace Quinn, very dear and special friends to me. The little one running around with Nicole is their daughter Jamie."

Jace extended his hand to Gideon, who only paused for a moment before taking it. "Reverend. That is a designation for religious instructors."

"I prefer a guide to faith, but you are correct," Jace said with a wide smile and firm shake.

He shook Daniel's hand as well, and Michael managed to find his thoughts before Jace took Phin's hand. "Jace, Lilly . . . this is Gideon, Daniel, and Phineas. My brothers."

Lilly gasped and Jace grinned, shaking his head. "I suppose I should be surprised, but the good Lord knows I've given up on being surprised by anything. I am, however, very curious to hear the story."

Whatever Phin may have said in response didn't register in Michael's mind. Beyond Lilly, Jacqueline scooted forward to the edge of the couch cushion where she sat, talking with Caitlin as she shifted, preparing to stand. For just a moment, she paused and turned to look at Michael. As soon as she saw him, she smiled with such beauty it made his chest catch. She touched her fingertips to her mouth and turned her fingers toward him, and he read "I love you" on her lips.

In that moment, absolutely everything became clear.

Michael moved between Lilly and Gideon, mumbling an "Excuse Me" and crossed the room, his intent certain. He reached Jacqueline before she could move again to stand and took her hand to help her to her feet. She still smiled, taking in his face.

"What?" she asked. "You look . . . intense."

Michael raised his hand, hovering his fingers near her cheek for a brief moment before he smoothed his fingertips over her soft, warm skin. Jacqueline turned into his touch, her eyes closed, before she looked at him again. "Michael?"

Michael leaned his forehead against hers. He closed his eyes and wrapped her in his arms to hold her close enough he felt her heart beating. It was just as rapid and chaotic as his. "I'm sorry, Jacqueline," he whispered against the side of her throat.

"For what?"

He opened his eyes and drew back only enough he could look her in the eyes. "I have had so much faith in your love, and have loved you so deeply, I failed to honor it."

"I don't understand, Michael—"

"Marry me."

Her eyes widened, and she stared at him for several beats of his pounding heart before she actually blinked. She took his face in her hands, her touch so gentle it made his heart ache.

"Please," he added, holding her hands to his cheeks so he could turn his head and kiss each palm. "Let me be your husband."

Her dark, beautiful eyes glistened with tears. "Michael, do you honestly think I'd say no?"

"I love you," he declared before doing what he'd wanted to do since he crossed the room. He kissed her, deep, until she sighed into his mouth and leaned into him. With enough reluctance to be obvious he didn't want the kiss to end, he drew back and held her against him as he looked around the room. A few had turned their attention to them, but most still talked amongst themselves. He took Jacqueline's hand and drew her back toward where Jace still stood with his brothers, though all now watched him.

"Jace, I need a favor," he said, finding it almost hard to speak with the ferocity of his smile. "Marry us."

"What?" Jace and Jacqueline said together.

Michael turned to Jacqueline. "Marry me now, Jacqueline. We are here with family and friends, and I can't think of any reason to wait."

Her smile brightened and her hold on his hand tightened. He took that as her consent. Michael turned and scanned the room, looking for his parents. They both stood near the hearth, talking with Connor and Mel. "Dad!" Michael shouted across the room. "Mom!"

Both looked up, and the conversations stilled.

"We're getting married."

Caitlin covered her mouth with her hands, and Nick smiled. "Well, about damn time."

"*F*riends and family, we began this evening celebrating Michael's birthday, and we end it celebrating the marriage of Michael and Jacqueline, a permanent joining of the family they have already begun to build." Reverend Jace Quinn stood with his back to the hearth where a low fire burned, with Michael and Jacqueline in front of him. Everyone gathered close, with Nick and Caitlin Tanner the closest, little Nicole in Caitlin's arms.

Katrina had found a nice vantage point where she could see the event without intruding on anyone and held her breath as the ceremony unfolded. She gasped when an arm circled her waist from behind, and Phin's large hand pressed to her stomach, bringing her back against him. She tilted her head back to look at him, and he offered a smile.

"Our world has changed in ways no man could fathom, but throughout that change, one thing has remained consistent; our need for connection to another. It is usually my job to assure two people enter into marriage with a full understanding of their commitment to each other, but if ever in my life have I known two people whose bond is unwavering, it is Michael and Jacqueline. It is also my responsibility to ask of the couple's friends and family if there are any who question the wisdom of their choice, but I seriously doubt *anyone* would stand in their way."

A chuckle rumbled through the gathering.

"Jacqueline Marie Therese Anderson, do you promise to take this man to be your husband; to be his support and his strength when his is gone, to be his comfort and his conscience, to be the food to his soul, to be his and his alone, until death parts you?"

Jackie and Michael hadn't looked away from each other since Reverend Quinn began speaking, and even now their attention never wavered. The way they looked at each other, the way he kissed her fingers and held her hand to his heart, made Katrina's eyes mist and her chest tighten.

"I promise," Jackie answered.

"And in the same way, Michael Sean Tanner, do you promise to take this woman to be your wife; to be her support and her strength when hers is gone, to be her comfort and her conscience, to be the food to her soul, to be hers and hers alone, until death parts you?"

"I promise," Michael whispered, his voice barely carrying to where Katrina stood.

Katrina drew in a shaky breath, and Phin's hold tightened.

"Who blesses this marriage?"

"My wife and I do," Nicholas Tanner said, reaching out to rest his hand on his son's shoulder. "We do without question."

"Then it is time for Michael and Jacqueline to speak their vows."

Michael folded both of Jackie's hands in his and held them between them, holding her so close he spoke to her and only her, despite the gathered standing witnesses. "Jacqueline, in the name of God I give myself to you to be your husband. I loved you long before today, and I promise to you I will love you forever. Nothing will change this promise. Of this I swear."

Jackie lifted her chin to look at Michael. "Michael, in the name of God I give myself to you as your wife. I loved you long before today, and I promise to you I will love you forever. Nothing will change this promise. Of this I swear."

"I stand as witness only to this union," Reverend Quinn said, holding out his arms to encompass Michael, Jacqueline, and all those gathered. "The power of their bond comes from their words, their hearts, their souls, their commitment, and their faith. God consecrates their marriage, and all their days to come. It is by the privilege granted to me through my ordination I happily pronounce this man and this woman now and all days going forward as man and wife."

He never quite got to the "You may kiss your bride . . ." part before Michael had Jacqueline in a kiss that made Katrina's cheeks heat. As the gathering applauded together, Katrina wiped away a tear. She turned enough within Phin's light hold to look up at him and found him watching her.

"I hear you had something to do with this," she said with a smile.

"I simply asked a question."

"It must have been one heck of a question."

He didn't answer, but leaned down and kissed her, too.

CHAPTER THIRTY

EARTH TIME: MONDAY, 16 MARCH 2054
DEFENSE ALLIANCE SHIP STEPPENSCHRAFF
ON APPROACH TO EARTH
ESTIMATED TIME TO EARTH: 4 HOURS

*J*ohn woke to the soft sound of Jenifer going through the single duffle she'd taken from Aretu. After boarding the *Steppenschraff*, she had taken out her clothing and other items and put them in the wardrobe, and then the bag had been placed in the back of the closet. Untouched. Until this morning. He rolled onto his side, propped on his arm, to watch. He barely suppressed a disgusted curl of his lip when he recognized the clothing she set out on the rack leading to the attached bath. Her drab olive utility pants, black standard issue shirt, and Firebird jacket. Her heavy boots already sat on the floor, and her thigh holster already held Damocles, waiting to be strapped on.

"You don't have to look at them with such distaste." Jenifer straightened and dropped the bag on the floor to be packed shortly with the small collection of clothing she'd garnered since leaving Earth weeks before. She turned toward the bed and John took his time enjoying the view. No woman had ever been so appealing wearing nothing but her underclothing. "We both knew this would happen when we went back."

"Doesn't mean I like it."

She smiled, and whatever dread he'd harbored slipped away. It had taken a long time for him to coax a genuine smile from Jenifer Of No Last Name, but once he had he reveled in the ease in which she now gifted him with the beauty a smile bloomed in her eyes. "Good. Remember that when we're in public. I would rather you looked annoyed."

"Frustrated is more like it."

She took the few steps to the bed, and still looking into his eyes, she pushed back the blankets and slipped into the space beside him. He met her with a kiss when she slid her body over his, her legs straddling his hips. "And why is that, John?" she whispered, then teased him with the tip of her tongue.

"Can I help it if I like my hands on you?" he asked, sliding his palms over her thighs to her hips, then traced the bumps of her spine to her shoulders. Lean, powerful muscles flexed and lengthened beneath his touch, the beauty of her strength as sexy to him as the beauty of her form.

Jenifer arched her back under his touch, a husky rumble in her chest, and shifted her weight against him. His body's response was immediate. "Every minute I stand as your body*guard*, know I'm thinking about what I'm going to do to your body when we're alone again," she said against his mouth.

John groaned and took her head in his hands, taking her mouth in an open kiss that curled his toes. He held her there so he could look into her eyes and saw only a fraction of the barriers from early days together. Not all. He wasn't sure he'd ever see past them all. But for now, he had more than he thought he could handle sometimes. John smiled, and she smiled back, her gaze sliding to his mouth.

"Why don't you show me?" he challenged.

"Be careful what you ask for, John," she warned before accepting the challenge.

· · ·

*O*ver an hour later, John walked from the bath into the bedroom, rubbing a towel across his hair, another wrapped around his waist. He paused just inside the room to watch her tighten the final strap of her thigh holster. She sat on the edge of the bed to bend over and lace her boots. "I'm going to the detention cells one more time before we arrive in Alexandria," she said, raising her head to look at him as she tied. Tendrils of hair still damn from her wash curled at her temples and nape. "I don't want to leave anything to chance."

"Give me a few minutes and I'll go with you."

"No," she said with a shake of her head as she stood. "It's time we start the show, Ambassador." If it weren't for the quirk of her lips when she used his title, John might have scowled at the use of it; but, the replacement of his name wasn't the barrier between them it had once been. "I'm your protection, and it's my job to take care of this. Not yours."

John nodded his consent, crossing to the bed where he left his clothing. "I've sent a message ahead to Nick to confirm our arrival. He will have security ready to take her directly from the detention deck to the facility in Alexandria for questionin'."

An immediate glint of annoyance flittered across her eyes and he felt the shift from comfortable to on guard. He knew why and didn't need to ask.

"Nick is keepin' this close to the vest, Jenifer. The only ones who will know of her capture are the ones who need to know, or who he cannot avoid tellin'. Most won't even know we were off planet the last few weeks."

She stepped close to him, not touching him, but close enough he felt her warmth, and tipped back her head the small degree she needed in order to meet his eyes. "I realize what's done is done, but make no mistake, John . . . when I find the person responsible for coming after and hurting the people I care about, I won't give a damn if the Firebirds are handling it, or not. I *will* handle it."

He looked into her hard set, unrelenting eyes. "I know," he finally said.

Jenifer pursed her lips and turned away. "I'll be back." She crossed behind him and he reached for his shirt. Just before she was past arms' length, the she-devil grabbed his towel and yanked, leaving him naked.

"Oy!" He lunged for her, catching only air.

She laughed all the way to the door, tossing the towel back at him before she disappeared.

05:47 HOURS
DETAINMENT AND INTERROGATION FACILITY
COMMAND CENTER AND BRIEFING ROOM
UNITED EARTH PROTECTORATE, CAPITOL CITY
ALEXANDRIA, SEAT OF VIRGINIA
NORTH AMERICAN CONTINENT

"*Have you ever considered Victor isn't what he says?*"

"*What else could he be?*"

"*Think about it . . . he claims he was somehow repressed by some evil Sorracchi consciousness for what, hundreds of years? And suddenly, all the influence is gone and we're supposed to believe he's free and clear and absolutely loyal to the people he helped invade?*"

Connor was yanked from the memory of two days before by the twitter of his comm. He snatched it off the conference table and looked at the screen, confirming it was Nick calling. Connor cleared his throat and opened the line, bringing it to his ear.

"Yes, sir."

"Good morning," Nick mumbled, sounding as tired as Connor felt. The president, however, had some leniency to show it. "Traffic control has confirmed long range communication with the *Steppenschraff*, and they should be docking in about an hour."

"I'm meeting with my team in five to coordinate, sir," Connor said, standing to walk to the bank of windows facing out on the still-dark city. "We'll have a team of three rendezvous with the *Steppenschraff* in orbit and dock on board. John, Jenifer, and Silas will be off the ship before it docks and we'll bring them directly to the secure bay, then to your office after clearance. Another team of three will wait for the *Steppenschraff* to land in the general docking facility, and we will remove the prisoner there, bringing her back here. A general security team will be there to accompany Doctor Cole and Doctor Lordahl off the ship to transport them to the hospital to meet with Victor."

"Good. Which team will you be heading?"

"The one retrieving the Xeno, sir. Unless you prefer—"

"No, that's good. I want no chance of this Xeno escaping." Nick paused to yawn. "Have you found out any more about the subject we discussed?"

Connor sighed. Annie Nodal. She'd jumped to the top of their suspect list as a traitor and spy based almost completely on her sex and her access to information, but since Connor and Mel had brought her name to Nick they hadn't been able to find anything substantial. Mel had pointed out several instances in which Nodal *could* have shared information, but either she was innocent or she was very, very good because they hadn't found anything definitive.

"No, sir," Connor said with regret. Every day that passed without naming the traitor was another day Connor felt the dig of failure. "I'm beginning to suspect we may have jumped the gun based on circumstantial evidence."

"Circumstantial evidence is about all we've got," Nick mumbled. "Come to my office once the Xeno is settled. I want a full briefing with John."

"Yes, sir."

The connection clicked off and Connor clipped the device back to his belt. His thoughts immediately returned to the question Mel had asked at Michael's party, along with her adamant argument after the attempt on Nick's life against offering freedom to the Triadic. Both conversations sent tingles of apprehension up his spine. But why? She was entitled to her opinion, just like everyone else, and he couldn't deny he had questioned things from time to time. It was his job to look past the obvious to determine risk before it became danger. And asking questions had been the instigating event that gave birth to Phoenix to begin with and had the rebellion group not been formed in secret over three decades before the world might today be a very different place.

It wasn't wrong to ask questions.

The briefing room door opened, and Connor viciously shook off his mental play-by-play. Mel led the small group of four Firebirds he'd roused at o'five hundred hours for this meeting. These were his best men, men he would entrust his life and the lives of those he loved without hesitation, men he knew would stand in the line of fire to protect Nick Tanner or anyone else. Men whose loyalty was unwavering.

Mel said something to Jackson and Pruitt as she passed, heading toward Connor.

For the first time in perhaps ever, Connor dreaded a conversation with Melanie Briggs.

He stood, hands at his hips, keeping his face neutral as she approached. She stood a respectable distance from him, but close enough only he would hear her with her back to the men who had accompanied her. Mel crossed her arms and set her feet shoulder-width, meeting his eyes. She was already on the defensive, and he knew he hadn't helped by sleeping alone the last two nights without any explanation beyond he had work.

As much as he had actually slept.

"So, when are you going to share with me what this is all about?"

Connor glanced past her to the four men he'd selected. They talked low amongst themselves, leaving him to impart the information he had held a secret from his second-in-command for weeks. He made sure to keep his features completely neutral so should any of his men look his way, they would see nothing unusual between their commanding officers. When he knew no one was watching too closely, he looked back to her.

"It is very important you do not react to this in any way that might indicate you haven't known this for weeks. Am I clear?"

"Yes, sir," she said with an almost indiscernible nod, her features completely neutral.

"In approximately one hour the Alliance ship *Steppenschraff* will be returning from Aretu," he said, and she nodded subtly. The return of the alliance cruiser was no secret. It was on a regular schedule, with a repeating route between planets. "On that ship will be Ambassador John Smith, his bodyguard Jenifer, his son Silas, and a Xeno assassin who attempted to kill all of them at John's estate. It's likely she was involved, though apparently not directly, with an assassination attempt when they landed on Aretu just over four weeks ago."

Her expression gave away nothing other than a slight cant of her head. "Ambassador Smith has been off planet—"

"Nearly six weeks, yes."

"How long have you known?"

Connor met her eyes, unwavering. "I assisted them in their departure from Alexandria two days after the two of us sent them off in the hover we later found crashed." She opened her mouth, but he shook his head with a tiny jerk. "Don't ask me to tell you how they got back here. I can't."

Her jaw clenched, and she slowly licked her lips, only the slightest hint of color rising in her cheeks. "I see."

"I prefer no one be aware of the fact you didn't know—"

"Since withholding information from your second-in-command might imply a lack of trust." Her voice thrummed with anger, anger he heard because he knew her so well. "And undermine my authority."

Connor took one step toward her, but kept his hands planted firmly at his waist to keep from instinctively reaching for her. It had grown increasingly hard in the last few weeks to keep up the platonic veil. "I was under orders, Mel. We can talk about this later, but for now—"

"No problem, *sir*," she ground out and stepped away from him before she turned.

*A*t just over six feet tall, Connor was taller than the average Human male, but walking between two Umani officers to the detention cells in the lower decks of the *Steppenschraff* made him feel like a child. The two men towered over him by at least a foot. Although he knew the schematics of the Alliance ship, he hadn't been on board; the exaggerated ceiling heights and overall oversized structure made him feel even smaller.

"The prisoner has been aggressive, violent, vulgar, and disruptive," the Umani to Connor's right said, his speech exact and without fluctuation. "She refused to take sustenance on numerous occasions, and in two instances she resorted to physical abuse to her own person. On the first occasion she purposefully ran into the energy field, and on the second she pounded her head against the wall until rendering herself unconscious. She was treated for minor injuries."

"We haven't reviewed the full instance report from Ambassador Smith," Connor explained, "but based on the details we've received, we know her attack on John and Jenifer was violent."

"I guess she doesn't expect to be released for good behavior," Captain Eads said from behind him, a smirk clear in his tone.

Connor chuckled and glanced toward Mel. Her features were set, firm and clearly tense. She didn't look his way. *Yep, still ticked.*

"She is not the most violent prisoner we have held on board, but she is by far, the most disturbing. This way, please," the Umani officer indicated, leading them to a recessed door.

He laid a wide hand, with impossibly long fingers by Human standards, against a scan pad and waited for a blue light to slide beneath his palm. The alarm beeped, and he punched a code into a fifteen-digit keypad. With a hydraulic pop and hiss, the panel divided and opened, allowing them into the detention bay.

Four cells took up the bay, the walls just a shade grayer than white. The bay was bright, lit by ambient light panels in the walls and ceilings. Only the slight shimmer of an energy field indicated the separation of the cell from the walkway between. There was no hiding spot in the cell, with every corner exposed. Each had a narrow bed against the wall with an adequate pillow and blanket, a small table with a single chair, and the "facilities" in the corner behind a half-wall for minimal modesty, but an insufficient space to find refuge.

The Xeno lay on the bed, her back to the energy field. Connor stepped to the barrier, bracketed on each side by Mel and Eads and the two Umani.

"Stand to your feet," one of the Umani ordered.

She didn't move, didn't acknowledge in any way they were there. All Connor could tell was she had dark brown hair, matted and dull looking now, and she wore unbleached linen clothing, loose fitting. It was hard to tell her height the way she was curled, but he'd guess she was slightly taller than average for a woman.

"Prisoner, stand to your feet or be persuaded."

Connor looked to Mel, and this time she met his gaze. He arched an eyebrow in the silent question. *Persuaded?*

The Xeno made a feral sound, starting low while she still had her back to them. As she rolled and swung her feet off the bed, the sound turned into a roar. Wide eyed and wild looking, she launched herself off the bed, but the moment she acknowledged them, she froze, hands curled at her side. Dark eyes shifted back and forth between Connor and Mel.

She looked more animal than woman, rage and fury twisting her features, but Connor knew her immediately and anger curled in his gut.

"You know, Ambassador," Connor said, reaching for the hovercar door handle. "Security would be a hell of a lot easier if you didn't attract every single female within a—"

His words trailed off as one particular woman caught his attention in the crowd of ladies who wanted to have John Smith's alien love child. While the other women blushed and cried, calling out John's name, she stood apart. She was beautiful, with rich brown hair and as far as he could tell, dark eyes. But, it was her expression—the smug calmness—that caught his attention.

"John, get in the car," Connor said in a low, but stern voice. He tapped his earpiece. "On alert," was all he said.

Every Firebird within the perimeter drew their weapons. Connor stepped around John so he stood between the ambassador and his son and the beautiful woman with the cool expression. Connor stared at her through his sunglasses, and she stared right back. Then a small, almost indiscernible smile bowed her lips.

The hairs on the back of Connor's neck stood to attention and he shoved John toward the door just as she took from the pocket of her jacket a small, metallic ball with red lights blinking around the circumference.

"Grenade!"

"You!" she screamed, her voice grating and rough like she'd worn out her vocal cords and ran straight for the energy shield. Arms wide, she hit the barrier and it flashed with power output, a crackling sound making the hairs on Connor's arms stand up.

With a scream of pain, she stumbled back and collapsed on the floor, curled into a ball.

The Umani brought his left hand in front of him and pressed several buttons on the cuff band around his waist. The force shield blinked, then shimmered away, leaving no barrier between them. The two Umani officers went forward first, each taking hold of an arm to lift her to her feet. She immediately struggled against their hold, even though her movements were sluggish and stunned. Her eyes rolled and a line of spittle ran from the corner of her mouth. The officers turned her away from him so he could clip the resistance-coil restraints on her wrists.

"We'll take her from here," he told them and motioned to Eads with a tilt of his head for the Firebird to come forward and grip her other elbow.

Supported between them, Connor propelled her out of the cell and toward the door they had come in, flanked again on each side by the Umani officers. She stumbled along, struggling to keep her feet after the neural numbing shock of the energy field. As they cleared the hull of the ship and crossed the bay toward the transport hover, she shifted from stumbling to resisting, trying to shake off his hold and leaning back to plant her feet in front of her. Each time she leaned back for leverage, he and Eads lifted her by the elbows and set her forward again.

The Umani officers escorted them to the open hatch of their hover.

"We would say it has been a pleasure, but we are thankful to be free of her."

"President Tanner would like you to know he appreciates your efforts in returning her here to face charges." Connor looked at her, and she scowled. "Now that I've seen her face, I believe we'll be adding several accounts of murder and attempted murder to the list of charges."

She screwed her face into an enraged purse and spat at his shoes. "You have no authority to name judgment, you fool. You are nothing. You are—" She cried out in pain, nearly dropping to her knees.

Connor looked at Eads.

"Sorry, sir."

Connor nodded a farewell to the Umani officers and followed Mel into the hover. As soon as the Xeno was inside she resumed her tirade.

"You are all fools!" she shouted, bucking hard against their hold. "You think you are in control? You think you have escaped your masters?" She sniffed the air in Mel's direction and pulled a gruesome face. "Their stench is all over you. You stink like a whore—"

Mel's fist connected with the Xeno's chin, and she slumped in their hold, her knees hitting the floor with a hard thunk. Mel looked at him and shrugged. "I was sick of her mouth."

Connor shook his head. "No problem."

He and Eads dragged her to the restraint chair and dropped her into it while Mel moved to the front of the hover to engage power. Eads moved behind the chair to release the wrist restraints and move her arms to the side chair restraints. Connor crouched in front of her to wrap the restraint around her ankles and across her thighs. As he engaged the last restraint she snapped out of her stupor with a sharp intake of breath. Her head snapped up and she gasped again, looked at Connor with absolute shock and fear.

Such pure, unadulterated terror it froze Connor in his spot.

"*Où suis-je?*" she asked, the entire tone of her voice with a softer, lower sound she hadn't had before. Tears welled in her dark eyes and a tremor shook her. The fact she spoke French startled Connor. "*Où se trouve Adrian?*" She jerked hard against the restraints. "Where is Adrian!"

"*Que est—*"

She screeched, a sound that seemed to come from her soul, and arched against the restraints. Again and again the woman screamed, fighting hard against the bands on her wrists. Connor looked past her flailing head to Mel and nodded. Mel opened a case on the back of the restraint, removed a hyposyringe, and grabbed the woman's head to push it to the side exposing her neck. With a firm jab, she administered the sedative and seconds later the raging woman slumped.

"That was strange," Connor said, standing, the hairs on the back of his neck bristling.

"She'd probably do anything to try to get free," Mel mumbled, moving past him to sit in the chair facing the prisoner.

Connor nodded but didn't fully agree. He didn't voice his thoughts, his gut telling him to keep it to himself until he could pass it on to the president, maybe Victor, and leave the confirmation of fact to them. He glanced toward Mel before moving away and wondered when his gut started telling him *not* to share information with his second-in-command.

CHAPTER THIRTY-ONE

16 MARCH 2054, MONDAY, 09:12 HOURS
ALEXANDRIA HOSPITAL, SECURE WING – INTENSIVE CARE UNIT
UNITED EARTH PROTECTORATE, CAPITOL CITY
ALEXANDRIA, SEAT OF VIRGINIA
NORTH AMERICAN CONTINENT

"*J*'m sorry Victor isn't here to meet with you, Doctor Cole, but if he were here he would tell you we are very thankful to you for coming so far," Michael said as he led Doctor Olivia Cole through the halls of Alexandria Hospital, the click of his cane matching their stride. "As Victor explained, our resources are limited here and even before the war it is doubtful we would have had the technology available to us to help David much more than we already have."

"In truth, Doctor Tanner, with the extent of musculoskeletal degeneration and the amount of time he was in the stasis coffin, I'm amazed you've made as much progress as you have. I've never worked with a patient held in stasis that long. I only hope my trip doesn't prove to be without result."

Michael tilted his head. "I assure you, Doctor Cole, any progress will be worthwhile. David has regained some use of his arms, and with the use of a harness, has managed some movement in his legs, but based on what we know of his training and his past, and men I have known like David, in his mind his inabilities far outweigh what he has accomplished."

"Then we shall endeavor together to find a solution," she said with a delicate smile.

Michael's communicator dinged and he unclipped it from his belt. A message displayed across the screen which both explained Victor's absence and sent a tingle of apprehension down Michael's spine.

VICTOR IS IN MY OFFICE. COME WHEN YOU ARE FREE. WE HAVE A POSSIBLE SITUATION. I'LL EXPLAIN WHEN YOU GET HERE. DAD

There was nothing specific in the message to cause concern, but he felt it all the same. He'd had a strange crawl at the base of his skull all morning and didn't like it. He'd had similar feelings before, just recently before his brothers came back from Falls Church, but this felt different. Wrong. Whatever was coming wasn't good.

"Is there something wrong?" Doctor Cole asked, forcing him to focus again on their destination.

"No," he answered, not knowing any more truthful an answer. "It's a message from my father. Once I have you settled I'll need to go see him."

"Do you need to leave now? We can wait—"

"No, not at all. When we're done is fine."

They walked a bit further down the hallway before she spoke again. "Doctor Tanner, may I ask you a more personal question?"

"Certainly," he said as they reached one of the few working elevators. He pressed the button and leaned against his cane to shift his weight. The pain in his hip was less than it had been the weeks before his fall necessitated an additional surgery, but it was still present.

"I hope you forgive me for pointing out the obvious, but it's clear you have a prominent limp. Might I ask what injury caused it?"

Michael pivoted on the point of the cane to face her. From experience he knew it was difficult to explain without shocking the asker, but short of lying there was no other way to answer. "Extreme torture on a cellular level in an attempt to overwrite and scramble my DNA." As he expected, her eyes rounded.

As a doctor, she probably understood more than most the full extent of his answer without him providing details. "Sorracchi," she clarified.

Michael nodded. "The actual condition is a severe form of osteoporosis. The bones are crumbling." The elevator dinged and the door opened. He motioned for her to enter the car, then followed. "Victor has developed a temporary treatment to cushion the joint, because the cartilage is gone, but has been unable to find a way to slow the deterioration."

Her expression softened, and she laid a warm hand on his arm. "I'm very sorry, Michael." She smiled, the expression immediately comforting him. "Ambassador Smith told us you were a remarkable man. I see now you are exceptional in many ways."

They reached the floor where David had been moved and the elevator doors opened again. Once she exited the elevator car, he followed her into the hall and motioned her toward David's room. It was early, and David wasn't scheduled for physical therapy for another hour, hopefully giving them plenty of time to talk. He led Doctor Cole to David's room and rapped on the door before he pushed it open.

David had been moved to a wheelchair in preparation for taking him to the P.T. room and left to sit by the window until Doctor Ortiz came for him. He looked toward the door when they entered and attempted a smile but the expression lacked any enthusiasm. "Hey, Michael," he said, lifting his hand a small degree from the armrest.

"David, I'd like to introduce you to Doctor Olivia Cole."

She crossed the room to David, holding out her hand. Michael noted she didn't wait for him to reach for her but took his hand as soon as he tried to lift it again. She sat in the chair facing him so they were eye level. "I'm very glad to meet you, David."

"Are you another physical therapist?" he asked, glancing toward Michael. "Because Ortiz works me pretty hard already."

"No, David. I've come to examine you, yes, but I hope to help you beyond physical therapy if there is any way I can."

He smiled, but no humor reached his hazel eyes. "How do you plan to do that?"

Michael stepped behind Doctor Cole so David could see him. "Doctor Cole is the leading Areth physician in cybernetic prosthetics."

David's brow pulled and he stared at Doctor Cole. "You're . . . Areth?"

"Yes, David."

He shook his head and chuckled. "I guess I haven't wrapped my head around this whole concept of aliens *not* being little green men or tapeworm like creatures who take over my mind. Though, that guy Njogu comes close to what was in my head before I woke up here."

"Michael and Victor have told me of your history, what happened to you, and what progress you've made in nearly three weeks."

David snorted. "That couldn't have taken long."

"I realize you don't see your progress the way we do, David, but considering what your body went through, and for how long, quite frankly I am amazed you live. The fact you have gained some use of your hands and progress toward movement with your legs is absolutely astonishing. And encouraging. I will need to take a look at many things, but I believe I can help you regain your life."

David canted his head and squinted. "Cybernetic prosthetics."

Doctor Cole nodded. "My specialty is developing prosthetics designed to integrate with and augment your biological systems as well as strengthen and heal them to the point the prosthetics will eventually no longer be necessary."

"*Cybernetic* prosthetics," he repeated, then shook his head. "I'm not interested in being *upgraded* like some damn Cyberman."

Doctor Cole looked from David to Michael and shook her head. "I don't understand."

Michael moved around to stand beside her chair. "No, it wouldn't be anything like that. More like Steve Austin—"

"You know who Steve Austin is?" David interrupted.

Michael nodded and smiled. "I enjoy vintage science fiction. And perhaps because of that I understand your hesitation. Doctor Cole's prosthetics aren't intended to be permanent. Am I correct?" he asked, looking toward her.

"In ninety-five percent of my patients that is the case. We have had a few instances when I've had to make the prosthetics permanent, but we will only consider permanent integration if a significant period of time has passed without sufficient recovery. We would adjust the prosthetics as you progress, reducing both visibility and obtrusive nature of the devices. Were they to become permanent, we would do our best to make them as inconspicuous as possible."

David struggled to raise his hand, his forearm trembling with the effort by the time he brought his fingers to his mouth and rubbed across his lips. Michael and Doctor Cole waited while he processed what Michael, at least, understood to be a drastic consideration. He drew in a long, heavy breath before shifting his weight back into the chair. "I realize I've been out of things for five decades, but this is a hell of a lot to process."

"I understand, David," Doctor Cole said, leaning forward to touch her hand to his wrist. "I would like to talk with you again, and show you records for the men and women I've treated. Whether we work together or not will ultimately be your choice."

David let his hand drop into his lap. "Before I see anything I want to know if you can get me out of this damn chair."

Doctor Cole smiled. "Your final level of recovery will be determined with time and study, but I can assure you, David, I *will* help you regain your feet again. I promise you that much."

"Then I'll listen."

D o you feel it?

"You seem a million miles away."

Could the procedure have failed? Could the neural implant be reengaging?

"Maybe you are a million miles away."

No. I don't feel ill. I only know something is going to happen.

"Phineas!"

Phin snapped his head up, blinking Katrina into focus. "I apologize. I was speaking with Gideon and Daniel."

She shook her head and looked down at her keyboard interface. "I'm not sure if I'd want Karl to be able to talk to me anytime anywhere. Or . . ." she said, dragging out the word with wide eyes. ". . .knowing what I'm thinking and feeling all the time."

"I can't imagine not having my brothers a single thought away."

Katrina set her arm across the desk in front of her, leaned forward, and tucked a leg under her. He had been sitting with her for the last hour since she arrived at the hospital, satisfied with simply sitting with her while she worked. Housing had been arranged for them until, as Michael said, they "decided where they wanted to be." Phin could imagine no other place than whatever city Katrina called home. He had not yet determined what that meant, and had many questions, but for now he was satisfied with sitting beside her while she worked.

He had requested permission to assist her with her translations and worked alongside her with translating over two petabytes of data retrieved from the *Abaddon*, some of which surrounded their training and development, some covering a variety of other experiments and initiatives the Sorracchi had in process at any given time. Once she returned to her work, Phin sat forward and opened the next file.

"Phin?"

"Yes," he answered, turning his chair to face her. She pulled her lower lip through her teeth, the slightest touch of color in her soft cheeks. As soon as he made eye contact she slid her glance away. "What is it, Katrina?"

She huffed and slid her hands between her knees. "You, Daniel, and Gideon . . . .. you share thoughts and emotions and . . ." Katrina cleared her throat. " . . .everything, right?"

"We were created to act as a single unit during battle. In order to do so, we must experience everything as a unit."

The color deepened in her cheeks, spreading down her throat, and Phin welcomed the spread of heat the demure blush curled in his lower stomach.

He'd recently learned the word "fidget," and Katrina was a prime example of the action. Michael, at the time, had explained the act of fidgeting was a nervous reaction and had used her as the perfect example. He was trained to acknowledge her evasive actions as deception, but with Michael's guidance, he recognized the variation between attempting to deceive and attempting to avoid. Phin dug his heels into the floor and propelled his chair toward hers until he could wrap his fingers around her wrists and draw her hands free. He scooted forward until he could move no closer to her chair and released one hand so he could curl a bit of hair away from her cheek.

"What is it you want to know?"

She took a deep breath and squeezed his hand, a small smile bowing her lips, but she still hesitated. Finally, she looked at him. "Do Gideon and Daniel feel *everything* you feel? All the time?"

Realization hit him, and Phin couldn't help his smile. He leaned in closer until their noses nearly touched, holding her gaze. He took her hand and brought it to his chest. "Do you want to know if they feel my pounding heart, or do you want to know if they feel the reason for my pounding heart?"

"Both, I think," she answered softly.

"Since our creation, my brothers and I have shared nearly every moment, but . . ." He paused when her eyes widened again. "We have complete control over that exchange. I can open my mind to them so they see, hear, even smell everything I do. Or, I can separate myself so only their voices would come to me if needed. It's up to me. Up to us."

"Have you?" Her voice was nearly a whisper.

"Have I shared this?" he asked and she nodded. "No, you are mine and mine alone, Katrina." Phin touched her chin with his thumb and her lips opened. The compulsion to kiss her, and to have her within arm's length, was one he'd given himself over to fully, though he understood the need to temper the nearly instant, always intense, always powerful expectations his body demanded of him. Because his educator had taught of Humanity's primitive, feral sexuality with no consideration of consequence or morality, he chose to view what he acknowledged as a desire to be with her as something to be cherished, simply because it was the exact opposite of what he'd been told. "I wish to keep you to myself as long as I can."

351

She smiled, leaning a fraction closer to him, her gaze sliding down to his mouth and she moved close enough their lips nearly touched. "For someone who has never wooed a girl, you are very good at it, Phin."

"Woo? What is woo?"

"It means telling a girl sweet, romantic things to make her fall in love with you," she said with a pretty smile and a tilt of her head.

A perfect tilt for a kiss. Phin released her hands and laid his palms against her cheeks, drawing her to him the inch needed to touch her lips. She had eaten a sweet roll for breakfast, and shared the iced confection with him, but he preferred the intoxicating taste of it from her lips. He kissed her slowly, taking his time to enjoy each slide of their lips and touch of their tongues, to enjoy the bloom of her taste in his mouth. The Sorracchi race may have held the power of advanced technology at their disposal, but they were ignorant fools to turn their backs on the pleasure of Human contact.

Katrina slid her hand up his chest to his throat, her finger brushing the corner of his mouth. She eased from the kiss and pulled back, licking her lips. The blush in her cheeks made her even more beautiful. She pulled her lower lip through her teeth and smiled.

"I do, you know," she said, her voice low and rough. She paused, swallowed, and took a slow breath. "I love you, Phin."

Phin pressed his hand to his chest, a sudden pressure expanding and pushing out, but wonderful and warm and dizzying. "What is this feeling?" he asked, shaking his head. "I've never felt this—something like it, yes—but—"

"Well . . ." Katrina laid her hand over his. "I guess I should ask if it feels good. Or bad."

"Good," he answered, nodding his head.

She huffed. "Oh, good. I thought for a moment maybe I said too much."

"Why would telling me you love me be too much?" When he said the word love, the feeling bloomed in his chest again and he laughed. "That's it. It's the word. How can a word do so much?"

"It's not the word."

They both jumped and looked to the door of her lab. Michael stood just inside, his hands pushed into his pockets, a smile on his face. Phin eased back and stood. "What is it?"

"It's everything the word encompasses. Some languages have a dozen or more ways to express the intricate nuances of the emotion," Michael said, stepping into the room. "Love for friends. Love for family. Love for . . ." He looked at Katrina and smiled more. " . . .the one person who is capable of making you whole."

Phin looked to Katrina, who still sat in her chair looking up at him. She blushed more than any single Human he had yet to meet, but on her the blush was perfect. "I like that definition."

"I'm very glad to hear that. For both of you," Michael said. "I came by to tell you I am going to my father's office. I'm not sure when I'll be back. Katrina, might I suggest you go visit David? He has a difficult decision to make, and he might need a friend."

"Sure," she said, gaining her feet. "I'll see you later." She kissed Phin's cheek and squeezed his hand before leaving.

"Is there something wrong?" Phin asked once she was gone, once again opening his senses to Gideon and Daniel.

"I believe there is, but I don't know what it may be as of yet."

We will assist in any way possible.

Michael nodded. "Thank you. I appreciate your willingness to help, as will my father."

When David served in Afghanistan in 2003, his convoy had broken down sixty miles outside Al Udeid Air Base where he was stationed. Radio silence limited their ability to call for recovery teams, so he and his team marched twenty hours carrying two-hundred-pound packs through the blistering heat of the day and the bitter cold of night back to the base. By the time they reported in, dropped their cargo, and hit the showers David had been so exhausted he was pretty sure exhausted required a new definition. His CO had cleared them all for twenty-four hours of downtime, excusing them from morning call, and he'd slept straight through. He'd hurt in every muscle and joint for a solid week.

He would have gladly gone through that pain again to be free of the crippling lead in his limbs that refused to let him walk across his room or get dressed on his own. Hell, if he wanted to take a piss he needed help. At least the pain then had been because he'd moved. He'd walked. He'd washed his own hair, damn it.

"I know it hurts, David, but you need to push," his physical therapist, Doctor Phillip Ortiz, encouraged, supporting David in the harness that held him upright.

David clenched his jaw and tried once more to shift his left foot forward a fraction of an inch. The sole of his soft shoe scraped across the floor and he grunted. "It doesn't hurt," he forced through his teeth. "I almost wished it did."

"You've done enough for today. If you push to exhaustion you won't be able to push as hard tomorrow."

David wanted to argue, but he was already near exhaustion and the idea of sitting down was too appealing to resist. Doctor Ortiz dragged a wheelchair to the harness bay and locked it in place behind David. He sank back into the chair with an exhausted sigh and closed his eyes while Doctor Ortiz released the harness connections.

"Are you sleeping on the job?"

David smiled before opening his eyes, then looked toward the door where Katrina stood waiting. "Hey there, Kat. I was beginning to think you'd forgotten about your Uncle Dave."

She smiled and jogged over to him, kissing his cheek before she gave him a firm hug. He knew he should consider it a victory he could lift his arms enough to return the embrace at least partially, but he didn't.

"I'm sorry," she said. "I have no excuse."

"Rumor has it you've got a new boyfriend." David smiled at the bloom of color in her cheeks. "I guess that's a good excuse as any."

She turned his chair and pushed him toward the window. The sun was bright, the sky nearly cloudless, and he'd heard scuttlebutt around the floor that it was gorgeous outside; not that he'd know. Doctor Ortiz went to work cleaning up the mess left from their physical therapy session. Katrina angled his chair so it faced another, then sat and drew her legs up to her chest, her arms wrapped around them. The position made her look tiny, even tinier than usual.

"I saw the end of your session," she said. "I'm very proud of you."

He shrugged. "Everyone keeps telling me how great I'm doing. Doesn't feel it."

"I guess I can understand why you'd feel that way. But, I'm more proud of the fact you haven't stopped. You keep trying."

David glanced outside. He hadn't taken a breath of fresh, outside air since he'd woken. "Is it true this boyfriend of yours is one of those three, what did they call them, the Triadic? The ones who kidnapped you?" He looked back to her.

"His name is Phin," she said, "and I've forgiven them for being scared."

David nodded and clenched his jaw. "Yeah, well, I'll decide if I forgive them or not when I look in his eyes, but that's not why I brought him up."

"Okay . . ."

"I guess I hear a lot of things when they stick me in a corner. I heard these guys—the Triadic—are enhanced." He winced at the word. "Nanogenes. Nanobots. Whatever."

"Bionanetics," she supplied. "I guess enhanced is one way to put it. The woman who created them used the bionanetics to do everything from making them grow super fast to making them stronger, smarter, amping up their psychic abilities. She also used it to control them." The more she talked, the more he heard the disgust in her voice. "She made it so whenever they felt any kind of emotion she didn't like, even compassion for each other, they felt pain and got ill."

"They fixed that, right?"

Katrina nodded, her lips pressed together. "Yes, but they had to die first. Literally."

David nodded. "Does it bother you? The fact they have these *things* in them?"

"Only because they were used to hurt the boys, not because of anything else they do. The bionanetics aren't who they are." She tilted her head and hugged her legs tighter to her chest. "I heard one of the doctors on Victor's team say it would be amazing if we had access to this kind of technology. A lot of people would benefit. They enhance the boys' systems, but also heal them and keep them strong. They could be programmed to help people with injuries and illnesses." Katrina drew in a breath through her nose. "David, what's on your mind?"

He shook his head, not ready to explain until he had a better grip on it himself. He couldn't shake this image of Locutus of Borg with metal and rods and tubes protruding from everywhere on his body. "I'll let you know. Someday."

She nodded. "Okay."

Her attention snapped to the doorway. "Phin . . ."

David twisted enough in his chair to look to the door. A young man stepped inside, the sharp stance of disciplined training keeping his shoulders back and his spine rigid, his arms tucked behind his back. If David didn't know the man's history, he'd have pegged him for a military officer from appearance. Short cut hair, clothing well-kept, body at the ready for action at any second. David wouldn't put him any older than perhaps his late twenties, but if he were one of the Triadic, Michael had told David the men had been "created" just a few years after David had been placed in the damn stasis coffin. Part of him had hoped the men who took Katrina would look the part of kidnappers, and even as he thought the word he practically heard her voice in his head correcting him. She'd said more than once she held no ill will toward them, they had taken care of her, and clearly if she were involved somehow with one she had to trust them. Or maybe she didn't. He'd seen a couple cases of Stockholm Syndrome when he was a cop, but those victims had been traumatized so much he didn't need a psychiatry degree to recognize it. Katrina, if anything, looked happier than he'd ever seen her.

"I apologize for interrupting," he said, crossing the room. "I have heard a great deal about you from Katrina and hoped to meet someone who means so much to her." Phin stopped a few steps from David's wheelchair at a comfortable distance for David to see him without twisting his neck. He canted his head and stared at David for a moment. "I remember seeing you only briefly before we were placed in the stasis pods alongside you."

That was another thing David hadn't quite processed yet; these guys had spent years just feet away from him, suffering the same silent, black torture. And yet this guy looked healthy as a horse while he could barely brush his own teeth. More bionanetic mojo?

"So, this is *the guy*, huh?" David teased, angling his thumb toward Phin.

"David—" Katrina groaned. "You're as bad as Karl."

He chuckled.

"I don't understand," Phin said.

"David is just being an overprotective uncle," she said with a shake of her head, looking between them. "It's tradition for family members . . . to . . ." She paused, but then seemed to shake off whatever thought had grabbed her. "Um . . . sorry. David is showing he cares by being a brat." She grinned again and stuck her tongue out at him.

"Being a brat," Phin repeated. "Original etymology implies being the offspring of a beggar or street dweller, but I believe later meaning infers a person of annoyance. Am I correct?"

Katrina chuckled. "Yes, that's about right. Some people think being a pain is the best way to show you care, except when you're on the receiving end."

"Uncle is a designation provided to siblings of parents. Have you determined you are blood related?"

David let go of some of his prejudice toward the boy, and probably his brothers. He was a foreigner, trying to learn the language. More than that, he was trying to learn an entire culture. Sure, David didn't know how to run half the tech, but he at least had a starting point. This kid had nothing.

"No," Katrina answered, shaking her head. "I kind of adopted David as an uncle. Honorary, I guess." Her voice sounded strange, growing fainter as she talked. Then she folded herself from her chair, still staring between them. "No . . ." she mumbled, stepping toward them. "Maybe. It'd make sense."

"What would make sense?" David asked.

Katrina gripped Phin's arm and pulled him closer to David's chair.

GAIL R. DELANEY

He scowled, not a look of annoyance but more like confusion, and followed her lead. She walked backward, looking between them again. "Holy Hannah . . ."

"What?" David demanded.

"I-I'm not sure." Before either of them could ask her anything else, she dashed from the room.

CHAPTER THIRTY-TWO

16 March 2054, Monday, 9:45 hours
Office of the President
Robert J. Castleton Memorial Building – The Castle
Center for United Protectorate Government
Alexandria, Seat of Virginia
North American Continent

"So, these Urdo Khantan are galactic mercenaries."

John nodded and sat on the edge of the couch in Nick's office, leaning forward to set his elbows on his knees. "Their loyalty lies with whomever pays the most and whomever has what they perceive to be the greatest likelihood of winnin' a war. They do not fear death in battle—in fact, their culture tells them their reward will be greatest in their afterlife if they die with blood on their hands—but they will not follow anyone they don't see as victors. Usually because their employers are as bloodthirsty as they are."

The gathering in Nick's office had grown since they arrived from the *Steppenschraff*. Jenifer had taken up her regular spot in this office, standing near the mantel at the end of the couch where he sat. The three Firebirds who had retrieved them had stayed until Connor

359

Montgomery arrived—alone—and ordered them to take up guard outside the office. Silas was just down the hall, being amused by Nick's secretary, because John didn't want him to hear what they had to discuss. Connor had pulled Nick aside when he arrived, and although neither John nor Jenifer could hear the discussion they had, they both sensed the urgency in the conversation. Within twenty minutes, Victor had arrived. All Nick had said was Michael would be along shortly, and when he arrived they would talk further.

While they waited, he relayed to Nick the information Bryony had given to them before leaving Aretu. It was precious little, but it was enough to make his skin crawl.

"If the Sorracchi have had their asses handed to them all over the galaxy, why would these Urdo Khantan sign up with the losing team?"

John sighed and stood, moving to stand near—but not too near—Jenifer and the hearth. "Most likely out of anger, and the desire for revenge."

"Revenge . . . against us?" Connor asked.

"The Urdo Khantan have been here before, but it was when my people and the Umani were still connected with Earth and the pilgrims who came here. They came here on their own, and were driven out by my ancestors. With no power behind them, they lack a backbone."

"They were here? When?"

"Durin' what you call the Renaissance, I believe. In fact, their presence was documented." He turned to face the hearth, and the screen mounted to the wall over it. With a few taps, the screen came alive and he accessed the data stores as he spoke. "There is a province a day's travel by standard transportation from Devon on the Hill, where my family estate is on Aretu. Kennawick." He found the image he wanted.

"That's the Mona Lisa," Nick said.

John continued, manipulating the photo as he went. "The Davennico family has lived in Kennawick for generations, but when the pilgrims of Aretu and Umani left our side of the galaxy, the youngest Davennico son went with them."

"Are you telling me Leonardo Da Vinci was an Areth?" Nick asked.

"No," John said, turning away from the infamous painting of a smiling woman he had divided, flipped and slid together again to reveal the hidden image.

An Urdo Khantan, the brown leathery flesh of his face stretched over a flattened facial structure, no nose, and slit of a mouth hiding the rows of filed teeth he knew the Urdo Khantan created themselves when they reached the age of maturation. A smooth helmet shielded the alien enemy's head, down over its shoulders, a dart of metal shielding the nasal structure such as it was. A wide, bulging chest plate finished the image. The only thing the image lacked was the array of weaponry an Urdo Khantan soldier would carry.

"He was somewhere between one quarter to one eighth Areth; we aren't sure how many generations descended from the original Davennico he may have been, but there is no doubt he had knowledge of the Urdo Khantan and their presence. Based on this image he embedded in your Mona Lisa."

"Holy crap," Jenifer mumbled beside him.

*C*rossing Alexandria on the way to his father's office, the sense of apprehension Michael had felt for the last few hours turned into a firm, nerve-scraping aggravation. He clenched his jaw and worked his fists, trying to channel away the unexplainable anger. As they passed the detainment and interrogation facility, the pressure in his chest became so intense he couldn't take a breath until the building was behind them again. He closed his eyes, sucking in several breaths to ease the burn, and whispered a short prayer of peace Jace had instructed him in while he was in Florida. The aggravation had eased to the underlying apprehension he'd battled all day.

The Firebird piloting the small, personal hover stopped it outside the private entrance to the capitol building tucked away from view of the general public. Two Firebirds waited on each side of the door, and opened it to allow him entrance. He would apologize later for his lack of greeting, but the pressure had him distracted. He had accepted his precognitive sense of events to come was real, it had been too much of a coincidence in the past to be denied, but this feeling was different. It wasn't an anxiousness to know what was to come, but a desire to avoid it at all cost, whatever it was. Outside his father's office, two other Firebirds stood guard and one opened the door for him after four sharp knocks on the door.

The moment he stepped into the room, the sense of foreshadowing slipped away, taken over by his pleasure at seeing John once again, healthy and alive. Michael crossed the room and met his friend in a firm embrace, patting John's back.

"It is good to see you, my friend," he said, stepping back, holding John's shoulders. "I was thankful to hear you had made it safely to Aretu, but I'll admit I'm glad to see you back."

"By what I hear, we have a great deal to catch up on," John said with a wide smile.

"We'll do that over dinner tonight," Nick said, drawing everyone's attention. "Right now, though, we might have a different problem." He looked to Connor and nodded.

Michael turned to face the room, his back to the massive hearth. "What's going on?"

Connor took two steps forward, his arms crossed over his chest. "We had an incident when we went to the *Steppenschraff* to pick up John's friend. The Umani officers who guarded her during the trip told us she was very disruptive, violent, even vulgar. She looked . . ." He curled a hand around his face, " . . .almost feral. She screamed and ran into the force shield when she saw us. Once we cuffed her, she fought us the whole way to the hover."

"I'm no' that surprised," John said. "She wasn't exactly calm when she broke into the house and tried to kill us."

"I'm not talking pissed off. *C'est un truc de ouf*," he said, lapsing into French as he twirled his finger near his temple "But here's the kicker. When we were trying to get her into the hover, she was knocked unconscious." He slid a look to Nick. "Don't ask. Anyway, we carried her into the hover and while we were strapping her into the restraints she woke up." Connor paused. "I don't think it was the same woman."

A crawl moved up the back of Michael's neck. John shifted and stood straighter.

"She spoke, but her voice was different. She'd gone from having a deeper, husky for a woman kind of voice to a softer, much more feminine voice. With an accent. Southern European. She said *Où suis-je.*"

"Where am I," Michael translated. "French."

Connor nodded. "The French surprised me. Then she asked for someone named Adrian. She looked . . . terrified. The kind of fear a person can't fake, ya know?" Connor shook his head and swallowed. "Then she screamed and thrashed against the restraints, crazy again. Mel sedated her until we got her into an actual detention cell downtown."

"You believe she's a Sorracchi," Victor said. He rose from the couch where he sat to move toward Connor. "Did she revert to her initial personality?"

"She was still unconscious when I left the detainment facility. Mel and Eads stayed there."

Michael rolled his neck and pushed his hands into his pockets, remembering with dread the twist in his gut and the anger he'd felt when passing the same facility. At least he had the source of the feeling, but he had yet to determine the connection. The cause. What made *him* feel the pull, yet the wish to avoid?

"Did either of them witness this?" Nick asked.

"Eads had moved to the front of the hover by then, so it was just Mel and me. She commented she thought the Xeno was just trying to get free."

John looked to Michael. "What's wrong?"

Michael shook his head. "I don't know yet."

"We've always assumed we didn't catch them all when they surrendered," Nick said. "We knew eventually they'd surface, but the idea the Sorracchi have infiltrated the Xenos . . ." He let the idea hang. "So, now what? We examine her and determine if we can perform an emancipation?"

Victor nodded. "If the former Human identity is breaking through, there is a much better chance we can achieve a successful separation."

"There's something else you should know," Connor said. "Not that it will matter if we split the slug from the true identity, but this woman is the same woman who attacked John at the embassy a few weeks back. The one who nearly blinded me and killed four Firebirds and three civilians; forget everyone left injured."

"So, this probably isn't a new overwrite. She is deep enough into the Xeno infrastructure to take on big jobs. Unless, of course, the original host is also a Xeno," Nick said.

"We won't know that until we separate them," John pointed out. He shook his head. "I have felt the battle of a conflicting mind, just as I did with you, Victor, when we first met. But, I felt nothing like that from this woman."

"I think I might have," Jenifer said, speaking for the first time since he'd arrived.

John spun to face her. She shook her head.

"Not like you felt Victor, at least not like you told me. Maybe I didn't feel the conflict like you talk about, but I felt *her*. In the house. I knew she was there before I heard her."

"You may have sensed her intent," John explained. "Your focus was so honed in on protecting all of us, your Talents found her as a threat."

"Talents?" Michael asked, leaning around so he could see Jenifer past John's shoulder.

"Yeah," Jenifer said, sarcasm dripping from her tone like venom. She'd apparently not gotten past her dislike of him. "You're not the only Obi Wan around here anymore."

"We can either bring in a Sensitive to determine whether she is acting, mentally disturbed, or conflicted, or we can do a full brain scan. It's most effective if she's awake and fully conscious to see if we can identify two individual brain patterns, but if she's as violent as Connor reports, that type of exam may be a challenge," Victor said.

"I want to see her first," Michael said before anyone offered another option. His father looked to him, and Michael met his gaze. "I sense something, much like Jenifer. I have since this morning. I want to see if this woman is the reason why."

Nick nodded. "Good enough. You don't need me for this, so I'll let you head to the detention center with Connor and see what's going on."

With that statement, everyone responded in unison and headed toward the door.

"*I* guess you're the only people around here who can give me any kind of real knowledge about what might have gone down on that ship," David Forte said, twisting only slightly at the waist. Katrina had told them of the man's paralysis, but seeing his struggle made Phin feel what he suspected might be both empathy and compassion for the man.

What might he and his brothers have been in a few more years? Even with the bionanetics to keep their bodies strong?

Phin canted his head. "Gone down. In this scenario, you are asking what may have happened aboard the *Abaddon*. Am I correct?"

David nodded, and Phin smiled. Conversation by conversation, he gained a stronger hold on the nuances of the language. "May I sit?" he asked, motioning toward the chair Katrina had recently occupied. Having no knowledge of where she had gone, he had the choice to either return to the lab, go looking for her, or speak with the man he had come to meet.

"Sure," David said. "No matter what Katrina says about me, I'm not going to give you a hard time. A few days ago I wanted to kick your ass for taking her, but she has been pretty damn convincing about your intentions."

Phin sat and faced Mr. Forte. "I am appreciative of Katrina's willingness and persistence in defending our actions, but in all truth, the regret I feel for any fear she experienced or harm she suffered for our actions is likely to be with me for a very long time. We acted instinctively, and have learned in the days since our instincts were flawed by our indoctrination."

Mr. Forte stared at him for several moments, then nodded and sat

365

back in his chair. "Okay, fair enough. I'd be worried more if you and she are as close as I'm hearing and you *didn't* feel regret for what happened." He squinted and looked at Phin from the corners of his eyes. "So, are those rumors true, too? That you and she . . ."

Phin drew in a breath before answering.

Yes, that is an answer we all would like to hear.

I cannot withhold an answer I do not know.

"I have not yet learned all the many ways Humans seem to define relationships with one another," he answered as best he could. "I do not know the term for what we are, but I understand enough to know I love her."

We have been denied the existence of love since the day of our creation. How can you, after a handful of days, understand it?

Gideon's question wasn't without foundation, but Katrina had helped him understand love was not one emotion for one person. It was felt in many ways and for many people. At the core was the realization that person's life meant more than his own.

Mr. Forte chuckled. "Well, guess you've figured out enough."

Is this the man found with us?

Yes, Daniel.

We are curious about him and his origins.

"If it is acceptable to you, Mr. Forte, my brothers would also like to be of assistance with answering your questions. We are curious about you as well."

Mr. Forte squinted, his brow pulling between his eyes. "Yeah, sure. And call me David."

Phin nodded and opened himself more to Gideon and Daniel to guide them to the room. "We aren't confident we have much information to provide. Although we were aware of your existence on the ship, we were restricted from the area you inhabited."

"I guess I want to know more about this woman everyone keeps talking about. Kathleen right?"

"That was the name she used, yes."

David shifted in the chair, and Phin tamped back the instinct to stand and assist the man, but he hesitated not knowing if the act would be seen as condescending.

"I've picked up a few things. I know she was apparently one crazy bitch, excuse my French." Phin must have expressed his confusion in his face because David waved off what he said. "Sorry. I'll try not to use too much slang."

"She was a violent woman," Phin provided, understanding at least part of David's statement. "She was unbending in her discipline, showing no mercy for error."

David raised a hand, with what Phin interpreted as a great deal of effort, and rubbed the pad of his thumb across his lower lip. "And . . . she was your mother."

"Yes," came Gideon's voice from the room doorway. David turned to look, his eyes widening. "We were unaware of her maternal contribution to our existence until Daniel inadvertently discovered the data."

Gideon and Daniel came into the room to stand near Phin's chair. David looked between them, and eventually smiled. "Katrina said you were brothers. She failed to point out the obvious, that you were triplets."

Phin indicated first one brother, then the other. "This is Gideon, and Daniel." Each nodded in turn.

"The most accurate definition of our existence is clone," Daniel provided. "We were created from a single zygote, divided into three identical embryos, then manipulated on a genetic level to create our variations."

David arched his eyebrows and looked up at Daniel. "Okay, then." He cleared his throat, and released a long yawn, rubbing his forehead. "And I heard this woman is Michael's mother, too. So, you're all brothers."

"Yes, sir."

David shook his head. "And she's the woman who tortured him to the point of nearly crippling him. The more I hear about this woman, and the Sorracchi, I think we came damn close to the Nazis all over again."

"I have read of the ones you speak of," Gideon said. "They aspired to cleanse mankind and create a super race. At the expense of anyone they deemed inferior. In that, the Sorracchi are very much alike."

367

"You know, I once saw this documentary that said the Nazis may have been allies with aliens. I always thought it was crazy, but you don't suppose—"

Katrina burst through the door, bright eyed and flushed cheeks, sliding to a stop.

Phin gained his feet and moved around Daniel to go to her. "Katrina, what's wrong?"

Her silence concerned him more than the shine in her eyes and her rapid breath. She trembled visibly, gripping the sleeves of his sweater as she looked past him to his brothers and to David Forte. Then a slow, unreadable smile bowed her flushed lips.

David dropped his hands over the side of the chair, and with a strength Phin had yet to see demonstrated from him, twisted the wheels to turn the chair toward her and move forward. "Kat, if you don't spit it out—"

"I figured out who their father is," she blurted out, then looked up at Phin. "I found out who your father is. I don't know why none of us thought to check, I mean, it makes so much sense now," she rambled, shaking her head. "I didn't—I mean, when I saw you it's so obvious. You have the same eyes."

"I don't understand, Katrina."

She took his hand and led him back to his brothers, stopping near David's chair. "I don't know if I'm the one who should tell you, but, I don't think I can wait until someone comes back. I checked and I checked and I *checked* to make sure."

David looked to Phin. "I've gotten pretty good at following Kat-ramble, but I'm lost here. Do you know what she's talking about?"

"She wants to tell us she has determined you are our father," Gideon said at the same moment the realization spread between them.

"What?" David said, staring at Gideon. He turned and looked to Katrina and Phin. "What?" he said louder. "You mean she was in my junk?"

Detainment and Interrogation Facility
United Earth Protectorate, Capitol City
Alexandria, Seat of Virginia
North American Continent

ichael followed Connor and Victor into the detainment facility, swallowing hard against the wave of nausea he'd been fighting since they stopped outside the building. John and Jenifer followed; John saying he was curious to confirm whether the woman was indeed a Sorracchi and a conflicting personality. Michael, while anxious to help the woman who might have fallen victim to the Sorracchi, also was anxious to determine the source of his apprehension.

Connor led the way to the detainment cell hallway. "Either she's calmed down or she hasn't come to yet." They stopped at the last security door before the cells, and Connor entered his code. "I'm kind of hoping for still unconscious because a woman like *that* being quiet can be more dangerous."

The lock disengaged with several clicks and Connor pushed open the door. They stepped into the hall and a force as solid as a punch hit Michael in the chest. He stumbled back, struggling to keep his feet. John caught him from behind, keeping him upright.

"Easy, Michael. You a'right?"

At John's question, Connor and Victor turned back. "What's wrong?" Victor asked, coming back to them.

"It's her," Jenifer answered, looking down the hall. "Geez, even I feel it. It's like you can taste her special brand of crazy."

"I'm fine," Michael insisted, straightening. He swallowed hard and pushed back against the wave. "Now that I can identify it, I can resist it."

Connor nodded, jaw clenched, and motioned them around a corner.

Mel Briggs stood in the hallway outside a cell, her back to them as they approached. At the sound of their steps, she turned.

"Sir," she said, acknowledging Connor. "She woke up not long ago, but has been uncommunicative."

"Thank you. We'll take it from here."

Michael found it curious Connor would dismiss his 2IC, especially since Michael had strong yet unconfirmed suspicions the two of them were lovers, and had been since before he returned from Florida. She slid a scathing look toward Connor, but nodded her assent and walked through them, weaving around Connor and through John and Jenifer back the way they came.

"She still makes me twitch," Michael heard Jenifer whisper to John once Mel was gone.

"Hey," Connor shouted, banging his hands against the bars. "Wake up, sleepy head. You've got visitors."

From the back of the cell Michael heard a shuffle. "Going to let your little bitch knock me around some more?" The voice was rough, raspy, like she'd spent her life screaming.

Not the words, not the voice, but something about the woman poured acid down Michael's spine and realization choked him. As much as his mind, his instincts, the fear and anger engrained practically into his DNA knew the truth, he didn't want to accept it.

"Dear God, how can this demon from hell still be on this earth," he whispered.

"Michael—" Victor said, turning to face him.

In his eyes, Michael saw the truth. Victor knew it, too. He hadn't suffered under her hand, but he had seen it, he had brought Michael through it, he had spent hundreds of years smothered in the stench of her evil. He knew it, too.

Michael raised his hand and laid it against his friend's chest, moving past him. Victor matched the contact, but to stop him. "We know. That's all. Don't—"

"No," Michael said, shaking his head. "I refuse to cower. She may have risen from the dead, but I'm alive and she will know it."

Victor pressed his lips together but lowered his hand and let Michael pass. When he stepped into her view, she turned with a look ready to lay out her venom to him as she had been Connor. She was different, of course, the shell he'd known as Mother crushed and long since rotten on the floor of the ship in which she'd held him over a year before where she had broken his body, but he'd refused to allow her to break his soul. This woman was more feminine in build than the body his mother had once wished to possess, and her features were more exotic, her skin slightly darker in tone. Her hair was long and dark, perhaps with a curly wave when not matted and dirty.

Even though the eyes were different color, the cold hardness he knew as his mother still tainted them. When those eyes connected with him, the cold distance snapped into an unadulterated rage. She flew at the bars, slamming hard into them, reaching through the bars for him.

Michael didn't flinch, didn't move, just stared back. When she paused to breathe, Michael smiled. "Hello, Mother."

CHAPTER THIRTY-THREE

16 March 2054, Monday, 13:10 hours
Office of the President
Robert J. Castleton Memorial Building – The Castle
Center for United Protectorate Government
Alexandria, Seat of Virginia
North American Continent

"*N*icky! Nicky, stop!"
"Nick!"

Nick heard every voice calling after him, but hot, blinding rage had deafened him to everything but murder. Never had he wanted to choke the life out of a Human being, to watch their eyes bulge and their face turn red while they struggled to be free; but then again, *she* wasn't Human. She was a demon spawned from hell, and he was her exorcist.

He yanked open his office door and turned on the nearest Firebird standing guard. As soon as he came out of the office the guard snapped to attention. Nick thrust out his hand. "Give me your sidearm."

The soldier's eyes widened. "Sir?"

"Give. Me. Your. Damn sidearm!" he shouted, the soldier slapping the grip into his palm by the time the last words of the order echoed back off the hallway walls.

Caitlin stepped in front of him, blocking his path. Nick stopped short, not so far gone he would push past his wife to find retribution. Tears streaked her cheeks and she raised a trembling hand to touch his chest.

"Nicky, don't do this. Think about this," she whispered, her voice barely audible through the waver of her chin.

"How can you ask me to stop?" Nick asked, pressing his eyes closed. He brought the back of his wrist to his forehead, the lingering smell of ion clinging to the barrel of the weapon he held in his hand and tingling in his nose. "She *killed* Michael, Caitlin. She tortured him, and then brutalized him, and she *killed* him!"

"Michael isn't dead, Nicky,"

"Not because she didn't try," he hissed through clenched teeth. He didn't want her to have his anger, but it pumped so viciously through him it overflowed onto everything and everyone.

She flinched from him, but didn't step away. "I know," she whispered, reaching up to stroke her fingers across his cheeks, the contact hot and slick with his tears.

Nick sniffed and swallowed the lump in his throat. "She took him from me, Caitlin," he choked out. "She stole twenty-five years with him. She robbed him of a *life*. She—"

"Dad . . ."

Nick spun around, facing his son. His chest ached, just like the day Caitlin had come to him in Parson's Point and told him his boy was alive. He'd lived so long numb and hollow, his heart had come back to life that day and it had nearly killed him. Nick pressed his lips together until his jaw hurt and he shook his head. Michael crossed the hall to him, the tip of his cane a dull thump on the worn carpets.

"I'm here, Dad," he said, reaching Nick. "After everything she did, I'm still here."

Nick dropped the pulse pistol with a clunk and clatter across the floor, and embraced his son. He knew someone somewhere would tell him the President of the World had no place crying in the halls of the capitol, but he didn't give a damn. He sucked in a hard breath and pulled back, taking his boy's head in his hands.

"I know all that, Michael," he said, speaking only to his son despite the gathering of people around them. "But she needs to pay. She *deserves* to die."

"She does," Michael said with a nod within Nick's hold. "But does that woman whose life she stole deserve to die too?"

Nick flinched and looked away, snuffing his thumb against his nose. "Sure, apply logic."

Michael smiled and laid his hand on Nick's shoulder. "She deserves to face justice for *all* the things she has done, she should face *all* the people she has hurt, not just the Tanners. But, I won't seek justice at the cost of her newest victim."

"However," Victor said from behind them near the office door, "I personally am not opposed to some 'in your face' revenge. I saw how enraged she was to come face-to-face with Michael. Imagine how much it'd irritate her to see a whole party. Michael. You, Nick." Victor looked to Michael. "And perhaps a set of triplets she once left to die."

Michael nodded. "They deserve to know she lives. Katrina told them she was dead, and although she spoke in good faith, they should know reality." He looked to Nick. "I'd like to go tell them."

"Is that your way of asking if I'm going to go homicidal again while you're gone?" Michael only smiled and Nick chuckled, the blinding, red rage dissipating enough he could again see. He reached out and Caitlin's hand slid into his, squeezing it with both of hers. "I'm fine. I can wait until we have a nice little family reunion."

"There's something you should know before you speak to them," Victor added. "I received a message from Katrina just as we were leaving the facility, and didn't have a chance to pass it on. She figured out—and has confirmed—who Kathleen used as a paternal genetic donor for Gideon, Daniel, and Phineas."

"Who?" Nick asked. "And how the hell did she figure it out?"

Victor smiled. "David Forte. Makes sense once you know. He was placed in stasis before they were created; she probably chose him and kept him for a reason." Victor shrugged and smiled again. "Katrina said it was their eyes. Once she saw David with 'the boys'—her words, not mine—she said it was clear as day to her."

"And they know?" Michael asked.

"Yes. I didn't make her wait until I returned. She said there was absolutely no doubt, and confirmed the analysis half a dozen times to be sure. I think she might have exploded if she had to wait, especially considering my delay in returning."

"Thank you for telling me," Michael said. He looked back to Nick. "I'm happy to know while we share the worst of mothers, we all have good fathers. David is a good man."

Nick nodded and sniffed one last time, letting go of the final vestiges of anger. "I'm not sure who might be luckier. Fathers. Or sons."

"Two," Gideon said, followed by Daniel's "Three."

David nodded and counted five cards off the deck, sliding two across the table to Gideon and three to Daniel. It wasn't easy for him, Katrina saw, but she was proud of him because for the last half hour David had laughed, smiled, and barely focused on how hard it was for him to do simple things. Shuffling the cards was out of the question, but he'd told Phin how while he taught his sons the rules of Poker.

She smiled, and shifted in her position on the edge of the seat between Phin's legs, sitting together in one of the armless chairs in the common room. When the realization had hit her that the three men could be, at least on a biological level, David's sons she hadn't known how any of them would react. The boys certainly didn't have positive thoughts about the concept of a "parent," but that had been one sided. David had already had so much thrown at him, and taken away from him; how much more should he be expected to process?

After the initial shock, and some disbelief, David had shaken his head and laughed and made a joke about back child support. Katrina explained the concept, but the joke was still lost on the boys. Now, they sat around a table in the common room playing poker, nothing about any of them saying these three men were genetically engineered super soldiers, or the man teaching them was not only their father, but had spent the last five decades in prolonged stasis.

"Yo, Kat."

Katrina jumped and looked down at her hand. "One, please."

David arched an eyebrow. "You sure."

"Yes, just one."

He shrugged one shoulder and slid a card across the table to her. Katrina picked it up and added it to the four matching numeric cards in her hand.

"Phineas?"

"Four," Phin said, leaning forward to slide his cards across the table toward David, his chest brushing her back.

That earned a double eyebrow arch from David, but he dealt out the cards. "Just because you're sharing a chair doesn't mean you get to combine hands."

Katrina stuck her tongue out at David and fanned the cards in her hand, careful to hold them close to her chest so Phin couldn't see. He laughed and shook his head. "Do you think I'll cheat?" he asked.

"Oh, please," she said, rolling her eyes. "I know full well all you have to do is blink and tell both of them what I have in my hand." Katrina tipped her head toward Gideon and Daniel. "And besides, what makes you think I don't intend to beat you, too?"

He wrapped his free hand around her waist, his hand splaying against her stomach to draw her more securely into the chair, his laughter rumbling against her back. It was a good thing she'd been dealt a great hand from the beginning, because she was having a hard time focusing otherwise. Squeezing into the chair with Phin had seemed completely harmless at the time, and she'd done it more to see what his reaction would be, but now she was rethinking her strategy. He'd looked down at her, but it hadn't been shock or confusion she'd seen in his eyes. Even now, thinking of the way her stomach had tumbled then made her cheeks warm right to the tips of her ears.

They went around the table a few times, until Daniel folded, and eventually so did Phin. It was down to Gideon, David, and her and the pile of toothpicks in the middle of the table had become a haystack. The bidding continued, and eventually David tossed his cards into the discard pile and she faced Gideon across the table.

"Are you sure you haven't played poker before?" David asked, relaxing back in his wheelchair.

She glanced at him, then back to her cards. "Did I say that?"

Phin chuckled and she glanced over her shoulder at him. He smiled and warmth infused her again. He had changed so much in the few weeks since they had woken from the pods. Falls Church seemed unreal now. A dream, but one she'd awoken from with a new life.

"Are you playing poker or making googly-eyes at your boyfriend?" David teased.

Katrina set her elbows on the table. "Okay, fine." She purposefully made a confused face. "Four of a kind is a good thing, right?"

Gideon groaned and chucked his cards on the table as Katrina splayed her cards in front of her and reached across to drag the pile of toothpicks toward her. She bounced on her little edge of the chair, giggling, until Phin's hands came to rest on her hips, holding her in place. The door to the common room opened and Karl came in, immediately grinning.

"It's a good thing you're playing with toothpicks, or she'd have your piggy bank empty by now," Karl said, crossing the room.

David looked between him and Katrina. "So you *do* know how to play?"

She said nothing, but gathered up the cards into a neat stack and looked at her brother. Karl laughed, tipping back his head.

"How do you think we taught her to count?"

David chuckled too. "Damn, Kat. You've got the best poker face I've ever seen."

She grinned again and winked, split the deck, twisted her hand, and turned the cards into a perfectly formed waterfall shuffle. The cards hissed and slid through her fingers, arching and flipping until she bundled them again and slammed the edge down on the table to align them again. "Anyone for Five-Card Stud?"

Katrina began the deal, but before she got around the table a second time, all three of the boys tensed and sat up, looking toward the door. Phin stood, swinging his leg over the back of the chair so she didn't need to move, and stood near Gideon when the door opened and Michael came in, a look on his face grim enough to make Katrina's pulse jump. She looked from Michael to Phin, then to David, who himself had an expression of confusion and concern.

"What is it? What's wrong?" she asked, leaving the cards on the table.

"Our brother bears bad news," Daniel said, standing as well.

Probably without thinking, they had taken up their familiar positions with Gideon standing forward center, Phin and Daniel a step behind and angled behind him. The triangle, the Triadic. Was it so engrained they couldn't help it, or was it instinctive in response to whatever Michael came to tell them?

Michael crossed the room, waiting until he reached them before he said anything. "Daniel is right," he said, but smiled. "First, however, Victor informed me of Katrina's discovery. I can only hope you found the news as good as I did." He looked between the boys and David. "David, you are a good man, and you are a man I know they will be proud to call father."

David cleared his throat and rubbed a hand across his mouth, looking toward the three men he had so recently learned were biologically equivalent to his sons. "Yeah, well, I'm still trying to process the whole thing," he said, twirling a hand slowly in the air. "Not sure how it happened, exactly, but I guess if a man is going to find out after being frozen for fifty years he's got kids, I made out pretty good. We're . . . getting to know each other."

"Good." Michael nodded and smiled, the expression strained but genuine. "It would seem we are all in a continuous stage of adjustment." Then the smile slipped away, and Michael paused with his jaw set as he took a breath. "Ambassador John Smith of Aretu returned to Earth today with a woman we believed to be a Xeno assassin sent to Aretu to kill either him, his son, or both. When Connor retrieved her from the *Steppenschraff*, he began to suspect she may actually be a Sorracchi but with a conflictive personality."

"What the hell does that mean?" David asked, rolling the wheelchair back from the table, with a twist so he faced the four men.

Katrina stood and came around the back of the table to stand beside David. "The Sorracchi no longer have bodies of their own. They steal people and hijack their bodies. Most of the time they overwrite the person's identity so fully all trace of the original personality is gone; but sometimes it doesn't work all the way. It's kind of like having multiple personality disorder, but instead of two sides of the same person it's the original person fighting with the Sorracchi consciousness who wants to be in control."

"Damn," David mumbled.

Michael looked to David. "After the Sorracchi surrendered, we took all the stolen hosts we could find, and if we could determine there was *any* trace of the original Human personality—no matter how dormant —we eradicated the Sorracchi and emancipated the Human victim. Our success rate . . . varies."

"There is more to this situation," Gideon said, and Michael nodded.

"I went with Victor and others to the detainment facility with the intent of examining her prior to attempting the eradication process." Michael paused, and pressed his lips together. The grip on his cane whitened his knuckles. "It's her."

Katrina gasped, but the boys showed no outward sign of a response beyond the subtle curling of their hands and a tightening along their jaw.

"Her? Her who?" David demanded.

Katrina stepped to the side and laid her hand on David's shoulder, unsure whether she could keep her feet otherwise. *Dear God! She was supposed to be dead!*

"K-Kathleen," she managed to stutter. "Their mother. The woman who placed them, and you, in the stasis pods." Her insides trembled, making her feel sick. "The woman who . . ." She swallowed hard and crossed her arms over her body. "Her list of crimes is endless."

"We were told she was dead," Gideon nearly growled through clenched teeth, his stare shifting to settle on Katrina.

"When Katrina told you that, we all believed it to be the truth. No one more than I," Michael said, taking a step forward, drawing Gideon's attention again. "We don't know how she survived, how she found a new body, or how long she has been involved in the Xeno uprising. We only know she is here, now, and we have every intention of assuring justice."

"By her death?"

Katrina looked to Daniel. It surprised her he would suggest death so quickly. Not Daniel. His soul was somehow gentler than the others, but right now, the anger was just as dark in his eyes.

"Her ultimate judgment isn't decided, but nothing will happen until we free the woman she has taken." Michael looked from his brothers to David, glancing briefly to Katrina before he turned back to them. "We do believe, however, she should be forced to face those she has wronged. All of us."

"She will be enraged," Gideon said.

Michael nodded. "Yes, quite likely, based on her initial reaction at seeing me."

"Will your father be there as well?" Daniel asked.

"Yes," Michael answered. "My father has not had the . . . *opportunity* . . . to confront her since he learned of her deception. I worry he may give in to his own rage, but he has committed to suspend judgment until this woman is free."

The three of them exchanged looks, and she knew they were talking amongst each other. They all faced forward again, and Phin smirked. "Regardless of what face she may wear now, and regardless of the final outcome, we are reluctant to admit how we would very much enjoy witnessing her first sight of Nicholas Tanner."

Michael nodded, a small tip of his chin. "We intend to revisit the detention and interrogation center at five this evening, and will come for you at four-thirty."

"We will be ready," they said in unison, sending chills up Katrina's spine.

Detainment and Interrogation Facility
United Earth Protectorate, Capitol City

"Why are you keeping me out of the loop?"

Connor looked up, a dread-induced headache pounding at his temples. Mel stood in the doorway of the small office he'd claimed when he worked at the facility, her arms crossed over her body, her shoulder to the jamb, her expression far less than happy.

"Mel, this isn't personal."

"Sure feels it, Connor."

He released a long breath and leaned back, motioning for her to come into the room and close the door. At the core of any strong leadership structure was trust in each other, and for years Connor had placed his absolute trust in Melanie Briggs. He hated now the niggling sense that made him doubt her, especially since he couldn't pinpoint any one comment, any one action, or any one opinion that was so far to the left to justify his hesitation. She shut the door and sat in the chair on the other side of the desk from him, her arms crossed defensively.

"So talk to me."

Connor shook his head and tapped his fingers on the scarred and worn wood of the desk. "President Tanner wanted information about John and Jenifer kept between only those of us who absolutely needed to know."

She groaned and rolled her head. "Yes, of course. *President Tanner* spoke and you came running."

Connor shot forward and slammed his hand on the desk. "Damn right, and if he ordered *you* to do something, and not tell me, I'd damn well expect you to do just that. His word—"

"He's not God, Connor," she snapped. "Half the planet loves him, and half the planet hates him. But you . . . you idolize him."

"Don't take your anger at me and turn it into something it isn't, Mel." Connor sat forward, clenching his jaw against the wave of anger. Blowing up wouldn't make his point, and wouldn't fix the problem. "Bottom line, I was ordered to keep you on the outside of this, and I did. We are still a military structure, a military chain of command, and he's the top of the chain."

"What if he shouldn't be," she demanded, leaning forward, speaking in a hissed whisper. "Connor, haven't you ever wondered— even if just for a moment—if Nick Tanner is the right man to lead us? What makes him qualified? What authority does he wield to decide how we should interact with the rest of the galaxy?"

"What would qualify *any* of us?"

"Exactly, Connor. Just because he brought the Umani and the Areth here? That makes him think he has the right to govern us all?"

Connor shook his head and launched from his chair, walking to the window. A full gathering of people would be here in two hours, and he'd been sitting here trying to figure out how to get Mel out of the building without causing another fight. He hadn't even mentioned the gathering yet, or her need to leave without telling her about it, and his gut was already in a knot.

"That's just the thing, Mel. He doesn't think he should be governing us," he said, quieter, forcing himself to be calm. "Personally, I think that makes him the best leader we could have."

"You're blind. Just like most of this—"

"Don't," he snapped, twisting back to her. "Mel, I recommend you stop talking before you say something that makes me question your loyalties."

She stood, her jaw clenched, and walked around the table to him. Mel stepped into his space, and despite his frustration, his body responded to the closeness of his lover. She leaned close, her breasts almost brushing against him, and tipped back her head to look into his eyes.

"My loyalties always have been, and always will be, with you, Connor." Her lips whispered over his, not a kiss, but a promise. "Before there was a Protectorate. Before anyone knew Nick Tanner's name. It was you and me."

Connor closed his eyes. "And I want it to stay that way, Mel. You just need to trust me, even if that means not questioning what I can't tell you."

She sighed and stepped back.

Connor opened his eyes and looked at her. Just as beautiful as ever, she stirred him. He wished he could forget his concerns and questions.

"Go back to the Nest," he said, raising his hand to touch her cheek, hoping to ease the tension. "I have to stay here for a while, but I'll be back tonight."

She pressed her lips together and nodded, taking another step backward. "Sure, Connor. I'll see you when you get back."

Mel crossed the office, opened the door, and closed it behind her without looking back. As soon as the door closed behind her, Connor released a long sigh, the air in the room already easier to breathe. He scrubbed his hand over his face, and sank hard into his chair.

CHAPTER THIRTY-FOUR

16 MARCH 2054, MONDAY, 15:55 HOURS
ALEXANDRIA HOSPITAL, SECURE WING – INTENSIVE CARE UNIT
UNITED EARTH PROTECTORATE, CAPITOL CITY
ALEXANDRIA, SEAT OF VIRGINIA
NORTH AMERICAN CONTINENT

"*I* don't have nearly the whole story, do I?"

David waited, wondering if Katrina had even heard him. She had been sitting curled up in a chair in the corner of his room for twenty minutes, staring out the window, silent. He had wondered a couple times if she'd turned to stone. Gideon, Daniel, and Phineas had excused themselves, leaving her alone with him, and she had been mostly silent since.

"Kat . . ."

She drew in a long breath through her nose, and released it as she turned her head to look at him. Her dark eyes shined and a single tear track marked her cheek. "The only ones who know the whole story are the three of them. I know more than I think I want to at times, and I know my knowledge only scratches the surface."

"That bad?"

"Worse." She shifted enough to put her back mostly against the cushion of the chair so she could look at him. "The three of them were created. They weren't born. They were grown and manipulated and abused in an attempt to make them emotionless but massively powered super soldiers for the Sorracchi. I think if the experiment had worked, we would be facing armies of men just like them."

"What is 'just like them'?"

"Have you heard people use the word Talents?"

"Yeah." He nodded. "We used to just call them psychic abilities. Telekinesis. Supposedly mind reading, precognition. Most people figured it was hokum."

She pulled a face at 'hokum,' but didn't ask. Katrina sat up and drew her knees to her chest, hugging her bent legs. "I guess I don't know what you know, so if I'm repeating something just say so. You must know the Sorracchi came here fifty years ago, but called themselves the Areth."

David nodded. "Last I knew before waking up, they were already beginning to infiltrate the government, saying they were our brethren and we were their descendants. Just before I was caught and . . . *frozen* . . . I heard enough to know that was a lie."

"Years after they arrived, a group of Humans founded an underground rebellion group they called Phoenix. That group functioned for years just beneath the surface of everything, and it was Phoenix that ultimately discovered the truth, forced it into the light, and began the war against the Sorracchi a year ago. We didn't know until just a few years ago they weren't the Areth at all, but they were using a stolen name." Katrina shook her head and sighed. "There's just so much to tell, I don't know—"

"Stay with the boys. Tell me about them."

The weight of his voice seemed to ground her and she nodded. "Kathleen's plan was to create super soldiers from us as stock. She used her own DNA, and now we know yours, to create them."

"Daniel told me they were created. Split at the zygote level and manipulated."

"They were known as the Triadic. Alpha, Beta, and Omega." Katrina shook her head. "David, I've never seen anything like them. Never even imagined it. When we were in Falls Church and the Xenos attacked, they were . . . beautiful. They can combine their thoughts, their actions, even their sensations and emotions so they function as one mind, practically one body. They're strong, they're fast, they are intensely intelligent, they have abilities that blow my mind."

"You said Alpha, Beta, and Omega . . ."

"Gideon is Alpha. He was designed to be the leader, but they have explained to me they still take action and make decisions more as a three-part unit rather than a single commander. Daniel is Beta. Phin is Omega. When I was first with them, they barely spoke at all, everything was in their heads. I could tell they were talking because they would look between each other, as if having a regular conversation, just their lips weren't moving. Eventually I got them to talk, though they still do it sometimes. They did it today when Michael was here. They only knew their designations, nothing more."

"So, where did the names come from?"

Katrina smiled and curled some hair behind her ear. "I named them. I told them they deserved to be more than designations."

David studied the gleam in her eyes when she talked about them. If he had any lingering doubt about what had happened when they had been gone, it disappeared. In her eyes he saw true affection. "They mean a lot to you."

She smiled. "Daniel and Gideon are as much brothers to me as Karl."

"And Phineas . . ."

"I love him," she said without pause, and smiled. "I don't know what that means. He's still trying to figure out his world—"

"I wouldn't worry about it," David said with a grin, one he hoped looked reassuring. "I'm pretty sure he feels the same, even if he doesn't know what to call it."

She sighed. "I hope so, but I guess it's because I care about them so much I get so furious with that woman. Ugh! I don't even like calling her that; it's too humanizing. She's evil incarnate. Do you know—really know—what she did?" she demanded, a sudden burst of fire in her eyes.

"No. That's why I asked."

She held up her hand and began ticking off gruesome details. "Point One. She put those bionanetic things in them from early development and accelerated their growth exponentially. They completed infancy and early childhood in a matter of weeks, and came out walking and talking. This was so she could begin their physical and cognitive education immediately, but forcing their bodies to grow so quickly caused the excruciating pain. Point Two. As young men— physically—if they showed *any* sign of compassion, even toward each other, they were punished. Beaten." Her eyes welled but she kept talking. "Point Three. Because the first growth spurt wasn't enough, she did it again to bring them to adulthood. They are in pain *all* the time, David. *All the time.* But they don't show it. Imagine the worst aching joint you've ever had, and put it in every joint of your body."

A slow burn kindled in David's chest, and he began to intimately understand her anger.

"Point Four. As adults, their indoctrination was even worse. I've lost count of how many times she brought one, or all, of them to near death as punishment for something she deemed wrong. She made them brothers, but she expected them to be machines." Tears rolled from her eyes now, but she kept going. "Point Five. The entire experiment came into question, and so the Sorracchi hierarchy decided they needed to try something new. She was ordered to seduce and trick Nick Tanner into marriage and fathering a child with her, then they faked her death at childbirth and she took Michael away to make him into a new lab rat. Michael was as abused and tortured as them, but he didn't have bionanetics to help him recover."

Her chin trembled now, and she held up her second hand to start fresh. "Point Six. When she returned to them to continue their training, they said she was filled with rage. In their early years she was determined, now she was angry. She was so determined they would never show the weakness of Human emotion, even though they *are* Human, she drilled into their heads and implanted a device to punish them." Her last words were so weak, he barely heard her and she had to stop.

David swallowed against the hard lump in his throat.

"Whenever they showed any sign of compassion, affection,

rebellion, anything normal and natural, that *thing* in their heads would turn their own bodies against them. The bionanetics designed to heal them, hurt them. But, it didn't stop them." Katrina swiped at her cheeks and looked out the window. "I read the account that led to their placement in the stasis pods. They were ordered to kill an entire village of conquered aliens. Women and children. And they refused. As a unit, a single heart, they refused. They were placed in stasis until she got around to either 'fixing' them or killing them."

Katrina looked at him again. "When they came out of the pods, they had no idea where they were, who had them, or what would happen to them. They took me with them in desperation, but not once, not ever did they threaten me. They took care of me. And David, they wanted to learn. So much. They just wanted to learn." A small sob shook her and she sucked back a hard breath. "Phin was getting sicker and sicker, because of me. All three of them were sick, but Phin was the worst." Her voice was a lost whisper. "He died on the way back to Alexandria."

David wished he could stand from his chair and go to her, and ground his jaw in frustration because he couldn't. He did manage to wheel the chair toward her, close enough he could reach out a hand to squeeze hers. "He's here now, you have to remember that."

Katrina nodded. "They had to all die to be free," she told him. "That was the only way to effectively turn off the neural implant killing them. When their hearts stopped, the device failsafe shut it down, then they were brought back." She swallowed hard. "Phin experienced their deaths with them, just to make sure they came back, and if they woke up so they would know it was okay."

He didn't have anything he could say. "I'm sorry" seemed so inadequate.

"Do you understand now?" she asked.

David nodded and rolled back. "Yeah. I understand something else, too. We have as much a right to look this bitch in the eye as any of them. Those are my boys." The tightening choke in his throat surprised him, but he refused to deny it. "I guess paternal instinct has kicked in full force. Kat, go find them. We're going with them."

She nodded, unfolded herself from the chair, and ran from the room.

*A*s soon as Michael told them the news, Phin and his brothers understood the niggling apprehension that had been at them since that morning. It had been the return of their torturer, their educator, their master . . . their mother. They had been so engrained with the idea she ruled over them, their attuned psyches had felt her return to the city. Believing she was dead had excluded the probability from their thoughts, until Michael's revelation. Now, the anticipation of dread had been replaced with another, very different sense of anticipation.

Anticipation of closure.

They arrived at the detainment facility in several armored vehicles, President Tanner leading the procession with his wife, Michael, and Michael's wife. In the second vehicle rode Vice President Surimoto and Victor, Ambassador John Smith, and his companion Jenifer, as well as Reverend and Mrs. Jace Quinn. Phin had learned recently the reverend had been held captive and tortured by her so severely he had lost all recollection of his wife and his life. It had taken months for him to regain his memory and his strength.

They had once believed the three of them—and in later years, Michael—were her sole torturous focus. To learn she had wrecked so many lives brought both a feeling of camaraderie and conflict; though they could commiserate with each person riding to face their torturer, their desire would be that no others had endured her particular form of amusement. Although their connection was not one to be desired, for the first time Phin believed himself to be part of something extending beyond the Triadic and the limited world they had always known.

Phin and his brothers rode in the final vehicle, along with Katrina, and their newly discovered father. Katrina and David's insistence on attending had surprised them, though they understood why of the two David would want to face Kathleen. She had stolen from him everything he knew of his life, including his strength. She had wronged him as much as any of them, though in the most impersonal of ways. She'd left him to die, and ultimately left him broken.

But David had told them it wasn't about what Kathleen had done to him, but what she had done to *them* and whether Kathleen ever intended either him or them to know of his contribution to their existence, he was for all intents and purposes their father. He didn't take the realization lightly, nor would he belittle the significance, by staying behind.

Katrina had said much the same by telling them she loved them all, and she hated Kathleen for what she had done to them. Katrina had suffered no direct harm from her, and yet she had been the one to come to them with tears to ask if they might go. Now she sat beside him in silence, her small hand squeezing tight to his as the hover stopped in front of the facility. They waited until Commander Connor Montgomery exited the building and greeted President Tanner. Then with a nod from Michael to indicate it was time, each hover emptied. Gideon and Daniel assisted in removing their father from the hover, and Gideon—without a word—took care of pushing the chair as they followed Montgomery into the building.

The air is heavy with her rage.

Phin looked to Daniel, who glanced at him as he projected the thought. Phin nodded. Her presence was like a stench, cloying and clinging to everything, filling their lungs and fouling their skin.

"Other than the Firebirds who brought you, no one knows all of you are here," Commander Montgomery said, leading them through a large, open room toward a hallway leading to the back of the facility. "If she is connected to the Xenos, and they assume we're holding one of their own as a prisoner, having the entire high echelon of government and high profile individuals here at the same time would be a risk."

"No one else is in the building?" President Tanner asked.

"No," Montgomery answered, his voice edged. "Just me."

President Tanner nodded, but said nothing more.

"Before I dismissed the guards, we moved her to our larger interrogation room. She's restrained, but I figured I would leave it up to you if you want her gagged."

President Tanner snorted. Montgomery stopped outside a metal door with a small, metal mesh enforced window, and turned back to them. "The cameras and recording devices in this room have been disengaged. Not because I expect anyone to do anything incriminating —hell, I'd be surprised if you didn't—but after discussing it with Nick and John, we want no documented evidence we know who this woman really is. Her Xeno buddies will want her out, but if others learn she's Sorracchi, it might be just has hard to keep them at bay. I'd rather deal with one frenzied group at a time."

Reverend Quinn separated from the group and joined Connor, standing shoulder to shoulder. "I'm not going to preach, and I know Michael made this point already; please remember the face you see in there is yet another victim. Kathleen inhabits the body of an innocent woman. You may want to hurt her in some fraction of the way she has hurt every one of us, but the woman she holds hostage doesn't deserve our anger. She deserves our compassion, something Kathleen would never give."

"Phin," Katrina whispered beside him. He looked down into her wide eyes; her skin was pale, her hand cold in his. "I don't like how it feels here." She shook her head and leaned closer into him.

He released his hand to lay his arm across her shoulder and bring her against him. "You shouldn't go inside," he said, pressing his lips to her forehead. "She may wear a different face, but her soul is still the same. I would rather you not see what type of monster created me." She tilted her head back with a sudden jerk, but he laid his finger on her open lips before she argued against him. "I want to protect you from this. Please, Katrina. Stay out here."

She reached for him and laid her small, cool hands against his cheeks, drawing him down to her for a steady, firm kiss. "I love you," she whispered between them.

Phin closed his eyes, absorbing the warmth her touch and her words spread through him. So much more than the temperature of the

Human body, she filled him with life. He sought her lips again, holding her head in his hands to give all he could to the kiss. This act of connection was still foreign, and whether he failed at expressing his intent through the kiss or not he didn't know, but it was more an edict than a choice. Her small hands curled around his forearms, holding on to him until he knew he had to let her go. Phin wrapped her in his arms and held her to him harder and tighter than he knew he should, unable to give less.

"I love you, Katrina," he whispered against her ear and her hold on him tightened.

"Let's get this done," President Tanner ordered.

Phin released Katrina, and she stepped back from the crowd, doing what he asked by staying behind. Montgomery turned to the door and entered a code into the electronic keypad. The lock disengaged with a metallic clank, and Connor opened the door. Immediately the sound of foul language rolled into the hall.

"Good to see you too, sunshine," Connor said. "I've got some visitors for you."

We could crush her with a thought.

Phin glanced at Gideon and shook his head. *We could, but you know this woman does not deserve our wrath.*

Then how do we find justice?

We live, Daniel. Phin looked at Katrina once more before following his brothers into the room. *We live, despite her.*

<PRESIDENTIAL RESIDENCE>
ALEXANDRIA, SEAT OF VIRGINIA
UNITED EARTH PROTECTORATE, CAPITOL CITY
ALEXANDRIA, SEAT OF VIRGINIA
NORTH AMERICAN CONTINENT

*T*hey had been back at the house twenty minutes before Jackie realized Michael had slipped away from the main room. No one had said they would return to the residence, but after an emotionally exhausting hour of each of them facing their shared demon, the convoy to the house had seemed natural, although subdued.

Kathleen had been vicious, bloodthirsty, relentless, and without mercy. She had torn at every weak spot she knew, some she probably imagined, some she helped to create. Regardless, each of them had stood strong, shoulder-to-shoulder, sometimes hand-in-hand, and looked into the eyes of their nightmare. Sometimes with declarations, and sometimes with absolute silence, each had declared their victory over her.

No matter what took them into the room, or how they left, tonight they needed to be together. Except Michael wasn't anywhere to be seen. Jackie made a quick circuit through the downstairs, not finding either Michael or Nicole in any of the rooms. Nicole had been crying when they came through the door, and had scrambled free from the arms of the poor, haggard Firebird left in charge of the children: Nicole, Jamie Quinn, and Silas Smith. Jackie wouldn't be surprised if the little girl somehow sensed the tension and sadness from the people she loved.

But now, the house was silent of her cries, and Jackie followed her instincts to where she might find father and daughter.

She slipped away, seen only by Caitlin who offered a soft smile and nod in acknowledgment, and went up the stairs to their daughter's bedroom. Jackie stood at the door, her ear pressed to the wood, listening. When she heard no crying she eased open the door on the dark room. Nicole's bed was positioned so she would be seen as soon as the door opened, but the bed was empty, and Jackie wondered if she had been wrong. She opened the door further and looked to her left.

And saw them.

Michael was on the floor, his back to the wall, his cane beside him, and Nicole curled asleep against his chest. Jackie slipped into the room and shut the door, silencing the subdued noise from downstairs. He didn't say anything as she crossed the dark room and eased herself down to the spot beside him with her shoulder to the wall so she could see Nicole's face against his heart. A small, shuddered breath rustled through her, at peace in her Daddy's arms.

Jackie kissed her daughter's crown and smoothed her hair, then ran her fingers through her husband's hair and leaned forward to kiss his temple. She tasted the salt on his skin and closed her eyes. He sucked in a sharp breath, smothered behind his pressed lips to keep from waking Nicole. Jackie swallowed her own tears and wrapped her arm around his shoulder and embraced him to her.

He had informed the monster who had sworn to take his life that he not only lived, but he lived abundantly. She may have tried to destroy him, and she had left him damaged, but far from broken. He had been strong, unwavering, and proud. But in the dark, he couldn't hide his wounds. In the dark, with Jackie, he didn't have to.

*N*ick stood in the hall outside Nicole's room, his head bowed and his eyes closed. He had to focus to hear past the sound of conversation downstairs, but past the talking and the cooking in the kitchen, he heard the heart-wrenching sound of Michael's pain.

"He needs to let go," Caitlin said beside him, her hand slipping into his. "I know it sounds strange, but maybe Kathleen being alive was the best thing for him. He was able to do something he never could have otherwise. He faced her on his terms."

Nick nodded, struggling to do much else. His voice was strangled, rough, when he managed to speak. "I've thought many times in the last few years what I would do if I had the chance. I didn't realize until today how much the idea of killing her had become a part of me." He snuffed at his nose with his free hand and swallowed. "I'm ashamed to admit I still wanted to choke the life out of her, I didn't care whose face I saw, because I know she was inside."

Caitlin stepped in front of him, close enough her pregnant belly brushed against him, and despite the rolling rage he'd fought for hours, a warm peace pushed it aside. Nick laid his hands on her sides, stroking her stomach with his thumbs, and smiled when a gentle nudge pushed against his hand. His wife raised her arms and pressed her palms to his jaw, urging him to look at her. Her eyes shined, but more than the tears he saw her love.

"You are such a good man, Nicholas. Such a good man," she whispered.

Nick leaned into her touch and kissed her.

Today was the first time David had left the hospital since he'd woken, and he found some satisfaction in the fact the world was not so radically different than the one he'd left behind. He looked around the room, to all the people who had gone to face down this woman who had wronged them, and wondered if they had any other common thread.

"May I speak with you for a moment?"

David looked up, not knowing which of the three young men he would see. It still took him a moment to determine whether it was Gideon or Daniel, quickly excluding Phin for lack of the small scar on his upper lip. The differences were subtle, but he differentiated Gideon from Daniel by the tension around their eyes. Gideon carried more weight on his shoulders, whether it was self-imposed or mandatory.

"Yeah, sure." David glanced around, but there was no place to offer for Gideon to sit. He motioned toward the coffee table in front of him. Gideon did sit, bringing him relatively eye-level with David. "What's on your mind?"

"I had hoped to speak with you regarding Katrina's discovery." Gideon met his eyes, and if Katrina Bauer had a great poker face, Gideon's was amazing. There was nothing there for David to gauge to get even the slightest read on his son.

His son.

When he thought about it—really thought about it—something in the back of his mind told him he should be flipping out over waking up fifty years removed from his life to be told he has three sons who were created without his knowledge or consent. He had no idea if Davey or Anthony lived, let alone where they were or if they remembered him, and now this.

"Look," David said, "I realize you probably never expected to know who your father was—hell, I don't know if I qualify as a father—so this is one hell of a shock."

"May I admit something to you?" Gideon asked. David nodded, motioning him to continue. "Although I cannot speak for my brothers in this instance, their responses are their own, but I have harbored jealousy toward Michael Tanner since we have come to this place and learned of the life he has formed since gaining his freedom, the smallest of which not being his relationship with the man who fathered him." Gideon paused, unwavering as he met David's eyes. "In this revelation, I now understand Michael's pride in his father. It is of great solace to me to know we have come, even if in part, from a man of honor."

David shook his head. "You don't know me, Gideon. Not yet. I'm not sure I deserve that kind of respect."

Gideon drew in a breath and looked around the room, then back to David. "My brothers and I agree that much we were taught now rings false, from the nature of mankind to the perceived detrimental nature of inherent Human frailties; however, we were also trained to not only observe but interpret the intentions of others. When strength is found, we are trained to find a way to weaken it. Where there is weakness, we were taught to prostitute that weakness and use it to our greatest advantage. In all that, we were trained to feel and interpret character and intent." Gideon nodded his head, a slow and smooth movement. "You are a man of honor."

David swallowed and looked down at his near-useless hands. "Yeah, well, I'm not exactly up to tossing around the football these days," he mumbled, intensely affected by Gideon's confession. It left an ache in his chest he didn't yet want to define.

Gideon shifted forward, leaning his elbows on his knees. David looked up again, meeting his son's intense eyes. Yeah, eyes the same color of his own. "In this I speak for my brothers: we will assist you in any way within our power. Her crimes were against all of us, and as Michael told her today, we will all continue to live despite her because we do it together."

"You sure as hell have a way with words. Anyone ever told you that?"

Gideon smiled. "Katrina spent several days instructing us to use our words. Perhaps I am too successful a student?"

"She has a way of being convincing," he agreed with a nod.

"As Phineas will attest, it is difficult to refuse her request. Whatever it may be."

David laughed. "Yeah, but that's not because she demands it. You ever notice that?" Gideon tilted his head, possibly seeking more clarification. "You don't do what she asks because she demands it, you do it just because it's what she wants and you want to give it to her. Am I right?"

Gideon nodded his agreement. "Yes, I understand."

Apparently sensing a conversation about her, Katrina stepped into the living room from the connected kitchen, glanced around, and spotted them. "Gideon, can you come help me?"

Gideon looked to David and smiled. "As you said . . ." He rose and worked his way through the room toward her. When he was near enough, she took his hand and led him out of sight.

David chuckled, watching the eldest of the three—supposedly the Alpha, and the leader of the triad—led about by a little sprite of a girl. Although Phin held her heart, David wondered if each of them hadn't fallen in love with her in some small way.

"Jace Quinn."

David looked first at the hand extended to him, then to the man crouched to the side of the chair he occupied near the fire. Clenching his jaw against the effort, David raised his hand from his lap. The man met him half way, gripping his hand firmly in a solid shake. Apparently David was the go-to guy for conversation that evening. Perhaps because he was, without a doubt, a captive audience.

"You're the reverend, right?" The guy nodded. "David."

Jace stood from the crouch and sat on the edge of the coffee table near David's knees where Gideon had just vacated. "I've heard a lot about you, David. In fact, you're kind of why I'm back here in Alexandria."

David chuckled. "Someone send you to save my soul, Rev? Hate to tell you but I'm Catholic . . ." He paused, tilted his head. "Is there such a thing as Catholic anymore?"

"If you're asking if there is a formal entity known as the Catholic church, then no. The concept of denominational faith has all but disappeared. But, faith itself still exists. The Sorracchi spent a great deal of effort trying to convince us having faith was archaic and foolish, but they didn't succeed. But, my occupation isn't why Michael and Victor asked me to come."

David shifted as best he could and cleared his throat. "Okay. Why?"

"Because I understand what you're going through."

He looked at the healthy, strong, young man in front of him and nearly laughed. They might appear the same age, but David was—strangely—probably fifty years Jace Quinn's senior. "Reverend, you might know what I'm going through, but I doubt you could understand."

Quinn arched an eyebrow and tilted his head. "Do you know why I wanted to go to that cell today and face that woman?"

David shook his head. "I have no idea."

"Over three years ago, during the mission to rescue Michael and dozens of other Humans held in captivity, I was taken prisoner by the Sorracchi. The woman in that cell tortured me for the next nine months." He pointed across the room to the fierce, dangerous looking woman who stood with Ambassador John Smith. David had seen her in news stories, and had no doubt she wasn't someone he wanted to tick off. "That woman and Jackie Anderson—" He paused and grinned. "Excuse me, Jackie Tanner, found me and brought me home. But by then I was emaciated, unable to walk, barely able to lift my arms, and I had no memory of the last five years of my life." He looked across the room to where his wife sat talking with Caitlin Tanner. "Or my wife." He turned back to David.

"Damn," David mumbled.

Jace nodded. "I wasn't always a reverend, David. Until last year, I was Lieutenant Jace Quinn of Phoenix, formerly Earth Force. I was a soldier and a pilot, and when all those memories came back to me I was angry. Angry because I couldn't get out of a chair on my own. Angry because when my wife collapsed, I couldn't catch her. Angry I couldn't hold my newborn daughter—a daughter I didn't even know about or experience watching her grow inside my wife—because my arms were too weak." He leaned forward and patted his hand on David's arm. "David, I don't know what can or will be done for you physically, but I know there isn't a medically minded person in this room who won't do everything in their power to give you back your body. What I do know is how it feels to have to rely on them to do it."

FIREBIRD COMMAND BARRACKS—FORMER HOTEL DISTRICT
"THE NEST"
UNITED EARTH PROTECTORATE, CAPITAL CITY
ALEXANDRIA, SEAT OF VIRGINIA
NORTH AMERICAN CONTINENT

Connor opened the door to his room, not knowing even at that moment if he wanted Mel to be in the room waiting for him, or not. The room was dark and quiet, and he released what he realized was a sigh of relief. Not because he didn't want to see her, but because he didn't know yet how to set things right between them. Her words earlier that day had made his instincts stand on edge, and he hoped he had misinterpreted her intent.

The question that chewed at his gut was . . . what if he hadn't misinterpreted anything?

He loved her, but he couldn't keep her as his 2IC if her loyalty was in question.

Connor turned on the light and went to the small table against the wall to remove his gun holster. He toed off his boots and dropped into one of the chairs. The bed called and looked so damn comfortable, but his mind was going in too many directions to allow sleep for a long time. Instead, he opened his tabletop access system and logged in. Several messages populated his communication program, mostly shift reports and remote aid sites, but at the top was a message from Mel. Marked private. Connor swallowed hard and opened the message.

I meant what I said today, Connor, when I told you my loyalty always has been and always will be with you. I have watched the pain you went through when your family was killed in the Sorracchi attacks on Paris, I know how much you hate what the aliens have done to our world, and I have wanted to do something to help you for so long.

I know you believe Nick Tanner is some kind of savior for us, but you're wrong. We both joined Phoenix years ago to take back our world, and just because Phoenix no longer exists in its previous evolution doesn't mean this world doesn't still need help. Just like those first rebels who came together in secret to fight what they knew was wrong, there are citizens now doing the same. And I'm one of them.

I have to go. I have a job to do. We all have jobs to do, and we all have sacrifices to make. I only hope that someday you will understand. And you will see where you need to be.

I love you, Connor.

Connor's blood ran cold and he snatched up his closed-line communicator to the detention facility, connecting to Lieutenant Resen who commanded the shift for the night. It only took moments for the lieutenant to open the line. "Yes, sir."

"How is everything there," Connor asked, trying to keep his voice calm.

"All is quiet, sir. Lieutenant Briggs just came through to check on things, too."

"Briggs is there?"

"Yes, sir. She's doing a walk through now."

Connor leaned over and dragged his boots to him. "Listen to me, Resen. *Do not* allow Lieutenant Briggs to leave the facility. I will be there in ten minutes."

"Is there a problem, sir?"

Connor stood and reached for his holster with his empty hand. With the weapon balanced in his hand, he closed his eyes and swallowed his dread. "We have a situation," he finally admitted. "Code Crimson." Resen cursed, and Connor knew exactly how he felt. *Please, Mel, please* . . . He wasn't sure what he begged her for, but hoped the universe heard.

He ran for the door, slapping the internal alarm that opened all communication channels within the Nest and every vehicle and duty city within the city and ten miles of Alexandria proper. "All Firebird Alert! All Firebird Alert! Code Crimson!" The announcement overrode any and all active connections and called all on duty and off duty Firebirds to action. "All Division One and Division Two units to the residence. Repeat, all Division One and Division Two units to the residence. All other units to designated locations. This is not a drill. Repeat. This is *not* a drill!"

CHAPTER THIRTY-FIVE

Detainment and Interrogation Facility
United Earth Protectorate, Capital City
Alexandria, Seat of Virginia
North American Continent

The metallic tang of blood and gore, and the ionized singe of charred flesh, churned Connor's stomach and burned his eyes. He couldn't breathe, didn't want to pull into his body the raw, fresh smell of death. Pain shot up his body when he dropped to his knees on the hard, concrete floor of the cell, Blood—still warm—soaked the heavy denier of his pants. He thought his guts were going to turn inside out, and black spots danced in his vision.

Mel's dark, unevenly dilated eyes stared at nothing, her beautiful brunette hair matted and slick with the pool of blood congealing beneath her head, tilted at a bad angle. Connor held shaking hands over her, needing to touch her but sick at the thought. He tamped down the choking sorrow and laid his hand at the base of her throat as running footfalls came down the hall toward him. Her skin was warm, a small, out-of-rhythm pulse thumped against his fingertips. Connor bowed his head and closed his eyes.

"Oh, baby," he whispered, unable to find any other words.

"Commander!" someone shouted, their boots scraping across the floor as they skidded to a stop. "Damn."

Connor swallowed and raised his head to look at his men. "Get the medic back here as soon as they get here. She still has a pulse."

One of them turned and ran, leaving the other standing in the door of the cell. Connor couldn't process their faces enough to give them names, even though they were his men. He dragged his touch away from her warm skin and braced his hands on the floor to force himself to his feet, more blood slicking his skin. Connor stumbled, grabbing the bars of the cell to stand.

"What happened, sir?" the one in the doorway asked. "Geez, what the hell happened?"

Resen and Esposito were dead; Connor had stumbled over their bodies on his way to the cell. Hobbes was unconscious with a bad gash across the back of his head, probably pistol whipped. Resen and Esposito had been shot with a pulse weapon, likely the one missing from Mel's holster, but not Mel. Her head had been pounded against the floor until it cracked and her spine snapped.

Vicious and merciless.

"The Xeno prisoner has escaped, that's all we know for sure," Connor said, the words hurting his throat. His chest hurt like his heart wanted to burst through is ribcage. He didn't have the luxury for the sorrow of loss, even though the woman he loved lay near death on the floor behind him. "The president is going to be her priority target." He sucked in a hard breath, forcing his grief aside until his job was done. "The president and vice president are both at the residence, along with a hell of a lot of other people the Xenos might like to see dead, including Ambassador Smith." He shook his head, trying to think past the moment. The smell. The stifling thickness of the air. "Children. There are children."

"All units are deployed. We'll find her, sir."

Connor stepped into the hall, unable to look back at Mel. "She won't be alone."

The Firebird nodded and left Connor alone, running back down the hall. The medics would be here any moment. There was nothing else he could do here, not for her, not for any of his fallen men, but he'd be damned if that bitch claimed another life without a fight.

*E*motion permeated the interior of the house like a fog, thick and heavy, saturating Phin's lungs with each breath and pressing down at the base of his skull. The three of them felt it, and for once, understood it. It was a heady concoction of relief, release, and heartache. Every person in the house had been injured by the woman they had faced together, some physically, some emotionally, some because they had to watch the pain inflicted on someone they loved.

He had met many of them at Michael's birthday, which tonight felt like weeks before rather than just two days, and those he hadn't met then he had come to know today. With the introductions he had learned their stories.

Some had suffered and survived her unique tastes in torture, some had been forced to stand by without the ability to stop it, some hadn't felt physical pain but hurt physically for those they loved who had. But every person in this home had faced their own form of demon when they stared down the monster who bore the name Kathleen.

Katrina came into the room from the hall, scanned the space, then saw him and smiled. She crossed the room, weaving past furniture and people to reach him. She knelt on the floor by his feet, setting her folded hands on his thigh so she looked up at him. "I'm not sure if we should all cry or sigh in relief," she said, looking around the room. Conversation was subdued, lacking the rambunctious enthusiasm from Saturday's celebration. "I feel like everyone is in mourning. Shouldn't this be a celebration?"

"Everyone here believed this nightmare was over," he said, laying his hand over hers. "In a few hours they learned what they believed to be truth to be wrong, and faced down an evil they believed gone."

Katrina shifted to sit and laid her head on his lap. Phin inhaled and released, smoothing his hand over her hair. He never would have suspected contact with another person could soothe rage, sorrow, or fear, but she had proven it was possible. He wondered if this was one more element of love.

Danger, a prickling harsh sensation, slammed into the base of his skull. He looked up as Gideon and Daniel marched into the room, making eye contact with him across the space. Katrina raised her head, looking between them.

"What is it?" she asked. "Phin, what's wrong?"

There is danger. To everyone here.

Gideon and Daniel looked toward the door as Phin stood. He cupped her elbow to draw Katrina up with him. Her eyes already rounded with fear. She had to sense it from him or see it in his expression.

Firebirds approach. I cannot sense the source of the concern, but they are here on a mission. Daniel, Phin, be prepared.

"Katrina," Phin said, leaning down to speak to her low enough only she would hear. For now. "No matter what happens, you stay with me or you do as I say. Do you understand?"

"What's wrong?"

"Promise me, Katrina."

She nodded. "Of course, but what is *wrong*?"

Before he could answer, the front door to the house crashed open and a dozen Firebirds ran in, immediately disbursing, and President Tanner ran down the stairs, his wife two steps behind. At the burst of activity, the inhabitants of the house stood or came from other rooms. Phin wrapped his arm around Katrina and brought her to his side.

"What's going on?" Vice President Surimoto asked, crossing the room to the president, her husband with her.

Behind the president, Michael descended stairs at a slower pace, his wife at his side carrying their sleeping daughter.

"Connor is on his way here," President Tanner said, his lips pulled tight into thin lines. "Kathleen escaped the detention facility." His expression twisted into tight anger. "Someone *broke* her out."

A collective mix of gasps and curses rolled through the room. Katrina tensed in his embrace, her fingers curling into his sweater.

"Two Firebirds are already dead," Nick said through a clenched jaw. "Two critically injured. Her whereabouts are unknown, but we all know damn well where she's headed. Here."

"Dear God . . ."

Phin didn't know who whispered the benediction, but if any hope could be demanded from the deity they called their God, he hoped their deity listened.

*T*he residence was lit up like a prison, with massive security lights from the edges of the cleared property lighting every inch within fifty yards of any side of the house. No one could approach the house without detection. Every room in the house was now occupied by a minimum of one Firebird, with most rooms on the main floor manned at every window. The property was already mined with motion detection equipment programmed to allow through only those wearing properly encrypted transmission devices to identify them.

"We have thirty Firebirds surrounding the perimeter of the building, and several teams watching all the ways out of the city. Another two-dozen are in close proximity to the house, and two dozen within the house. She'd have to come here with a small army to get through," Connor explained, standing in the foyer of the residence.

He would have preferred to have the conversation in Nick's office, but there was too much risk in separating everyone; this way, he had eyes on just about every person in the house. He'd tried to get Nick to at least take shelter with triple set of guards, but exactly as he expected before he actually made the suggestion, Nick shook his head and refused. To the world, he was the most important person in this house, but to him there was not one person he could stand to lose and he'd be damned if he sat protected while they were in danger.

"I wouldn't rule out anything," Nick practically growled. "We don't know how deep into the Xeno ranks she had gotten, or how much power she held. Damn it." Nick looked around the house, taking in everyone in the room hanging on their conversation. He closed his eyes and inhaled before His stern gaze leveled on Connor. "How did she get out?"

Connor huffed a hard breath, refusing to hide the tinge of shame. He played a part in this, he knew it, and no doubt so did Nick. "Mel," he answered, simply. Anything more would sound too much like an excuse, but he doubted he was capable of saying much more.

Nick's angry scan of the room stopped abruptly when he looked at Connor. He set his hand on Connor's shoulder, nodded, and looked around the room. "We take no chances, Connor."

"No, sir."

He stepped away from his commander-in-chief and into the archway leading to the large living room where everyone waited. His chest tightened when he looked past John Smith, Jace Quinn, and Michael Tanner, each with their child in their arms. This was the worst-case scenario of all worst-case scenarios.

"The only thing we can do right now," he said, speaking loud enough his voice would carry to everyone, "is prepare as best we can for what *might* happen. Everyone here knows what this woman is capable of one-on-one, but I seriously doubt she would come here alone looking for a fight. She's going to gather supporters and attack in force. Chances are, since she's been functioning under the guise of a Xeno, those supporters are also Xenos. They aren't going to come here thinking they're following a Sorracchi war criminal, but under the pretense of zealous anarchy. I don't know what's worse.

"We have Firebirds in the house, around the house, and around the property, but frankly, I am not one to refuse help. I know in this house we have some of the most powerful minds in the Protectorate and the Coalition." He turned his focus on Gideon, Daniel, and Phin. "I'm also not opposed to turning her own weapons back on her."

Gideon tilted his head in a single action of acknowledgment. Connor would take it.

"Jenifer and I will move upstairs and watch from the windows," John said, shifting his son in his hold. The boy was seven, but he still looked young and frightened in his father's arms. "Once we have visual contact, we can disarm or incapacitate the attackers."

Connor nodded. Jenifer had made a comment earlier that day in Nick's office implying she also had developed some sorts of Talents while off world; this would certainly prove to be a test he hoped she would pass.

Michael agreed to a similar action, but positioned in one of the downstairs rooms on the side of the house Connor suspected as the most likely angle of attack. He then turned to the Triadic. "Do you have to stay together to be effective?" he asked.

"No," Gideon answered. "Unless we are in a close proximity battle, then we are strongest as a unit."

"I hope as hell it doesn't come to that." Connor scrubbed his hands over his face and took a moment to scan the room. "We need to separate the children to keep them out of harm's way, especially if we have weapons fire." On the edge of his peripheral vision, he saw his sister lean into Nick, her hand over her mouth and tears in her eyes. He hated knowing she was afraid, hated all of this. "Gideon, take them into the basement. There is an enforced room in the east corner. I'll send two Firebirds with you, but I need you to defend that room."

"Above all else," Gideon said with a sharp nod.

"You made me promise to stay with you," Katrina whispered, holding hard to Phin with her cheek pressed over his heart.

Strong hands smoothed across her shoulders to her base of her neck, and he rubbed his cheek against her hair. "I also asked you to promise me you would do as I said." His voice was firm, but gentle, and he kissed her temple. "Katrina, I need you to be safe. Commander Montgomery has asked Gideon to watch over the children, and they need you. Gideon is the only one I would trust more than myself to keep you safe."

"I'm afraid," she admitted, wishing she could hide against his chest until this night was over, and at the same time, hating herself for being so pathetic. She was a computer tech, she was a mouse who hid in her lab! She'd survived the war by luck—or chance—or providence—not by any great skill of her own. Guns frightened her, fighting made her feel ill, and the idea the people she loved and cared about could be hurt made her body ache.

"So am I." His thumb brushed her chin and tipped back her head so she looked up at him. "I am afraid for you, but I can do more to protect you, by protecting this house and everyone in it, if I know you are safe and under Gideon's protection."

Katrina blinked, freeing tears to run from the corners of her eyes. Phin slid his palm up her cheek and pushed his fingers into her hair, stroking away the tear with the rough pad of his thumb. She could never doubt him when he looked at her with such honesty. "Tell me it will be okay, and I'll believe you," she whispered.

Phin smiled, but it held no spark of humor or happiness. A smile of reconciliation, maybe. He smoothed his thumb over her lip. "I can only tell you we will do everything in our power to see it is; that you can believe."

"Then tell me you love me, and I'll believe it."

His smile changed; his entire expression changed. "I do love you." Phin wrapped his arm behind her shoulder to pull her against him and lowered his head to kiss her. The gentle pressure of his thumb on her chin pulled her lips apart, and Katrina's stomach fluttered when his tongue slipped into her mouth.

Every kiss had been a new experience, from the first kiss that had been a surprise to both of them, to a kiss of comfort when he struggled through the deaths and resurrections of his brothers, to the kiss that left them both breathless and wanting more. This kiss made her want to weep, hold on to him, and never let go. It made her desperate. She raised her arms around his neck, not letting him leave her. When the cry in her throat was too much to let her hold the kiss, she toed up and held him tighter. Phin wrapped his arms around her so tight her feet nearly left the floor. She buried her face into the warmth of his neck, biting her lip in a futile attempt not to be weak enough to weep.

"I'm sorry," she whispered. "I don't know how to do this."

Phin jerked his head back and looked up seconds before a whistling sound made every hair on her body stand on end. He bundled her up and dropped to one knee, bringing her down with him to cover her a split moment before the house shook. The children screamed, and she thought she might have too, but the sound was lost in the rumble.

As soon as the shaking stopped, Phin stood and hauled her to her feet, practically lifting her to take her to the door. He handed her off to Gideon, who shuttled her into the room with two other Firebirds and the three children.

"Phin!" she called out, and he stopped at the door. She didn't know what else to say.

"Stay safe," he begged, then turned to Gideon. "You know what you protect."

Gideon nodded, and she heard no more as he shut the door, closing them in.

Katrina dropped to the floor, immediately gathering Silas and Jamie to her. Her insides shook so violent she thought she'd either be sick or pass out, but she forced herself to smile and take a deep breath. "Come here," she rasped out, settling Jamie in her lap. Silas curled against her side as close as he could be.

"I'm scared, Miss Katrina."

Katrina stroked Silas' wiry curls and hugged him close. Jamie cried through shaky sobs for Mama and Daddy. One of the Firebirds assigned to guard them, a woman Katrina didn't know, held Nicole Tanner who had cried herself dry. The thick walls of the safe room muffled the terrifying sounds overhead, but it wasn't drowned out completely. The walls vibrated against her back.

"I know you are, sweetheart," she soothed. "It's going to be okay."

"Miss Jenifer is with Papa," he told her, nodding with surety. "Miss Jenifer won't never let anything happen to Papa, and Papa won't never let anything happen to Miss Jenifer. And they won't never let anything happen to me. They told me."

"Of course they won't. That's what papa's do," she promised and closed her eyes.

*H*umans were no better than sheep. Where she led, they followed, to their death if she so commanded it and convinced them it would benefit their cause. Even now, they attacked facing hopeless odds against dozens upon dozens of the most highly trained and skilled soldiers this pathetic race had to offer. She didn't care if every one of them were left to rot in the morning sun, as long as Nick Tanner was dead, that spawn of his flesh she'd been forced to birth was dead, anyone else she could send to the Human's hell with them were dead, and the next phase of her plan was set into motion.

*T*he Xenos were frenzied in their attacks, falling like timber as they stormed the house, scavenged weapons waved in the air. One by one they were taken down, but more came from the darkness, screaming like they were possessed. Few reached the house, and those who did never made it past the front door.

The worst attacks came from SSM and GGM volleys, attacks launched from locations possibly a mile from the residence. After the first attack, Connor had called an order to access the satellite systems and track the firing points. Once pinpointed, units were disbursed to stop the source of the fire, but until they reached their destination the house-shaking waves of artillery didn't stop. The only thing that kept the house from falling under the massive firepower was the group of six people standing together, hand-in-hand, in the center foyer of the first floor. If Connor had been spared a moment to pause, he would have stood in awe of the massive display of power.

President Nicholas Tanner, Ambassador John Smith, Jenifer, Michael Tanner, Phin, and Daniel could have been mistaken for congregants of Jace Quinn's church, heads bowed, eyes closed, lips still; but if what they did constituted as prayer it was a prayer of the faithful because it was that prayer that kept every one of them alive. He didn't pretend to understand the awesome power of their combined wills, or exactly what it was they did, he only knew each blast intended for this house never made impact. The walls shook, the sound rumbled, and with each blast the six of them swayed, but their combined thoughts had created an impenetrable shield to hold back death.

Then the air attacks lulled.

Connor's communicator sounded an alarm before the voice of Captain Kate Stanic reported "Commander, three surface-to-surface launching stations have been neutralized. Long range scans indicate these are the only locations firing."

"Understood, Captain. Secure all hostiles."

"Yes, sir."

Connor wouldn't allow himself to be fooled by the temporary reprieve. He took the opportunity to shout out commands and take stock of their personnel. They had lost two Firebirds within the house, and no one could give him a solid count around the exterior of the house and perimeter of the property. In the respite, Connor made a quick run through the main floor, redistributing his manpower and confirming the safety of his charges.

"We have reports the SSM launch sites have been neutralized," Connor said, stepping into the hall and the circle of friends. "But I still have active scans going to inform us if anything else goes airborne."

Each of them raised their heads, fatigue clearly playing off their features. John Smith turned to Jenifer and touched her face. "You were amazin'," Connor heard him tell her in a hushed tone that dug at him, and he violently shoved aside all thoughts of Mel and similarly whispered words.

"What's happening," Nick asked.

"They're probably regrouping," Connor said, huffing his breath. "I've got more troops coming in from standard divisions to approach from outside the attack, hopefully to close them in and shut this down. I doubt this pause will last long."

Nick nodded. "We still have everyone?"

"In the house, two Firebirds are down. I'm waiting for external reports to come in. But all protected souls are accounted for."

"Commander!" shouted a voice from the dining room. "Incoming!"

Connor ran to the nearest window, and swore. Xenos swarmed from the darkness, six to eight deep, on all sides running straight for the house. "Open fire now!"

hin and Daniel stepped clear of the circle and moved to parallel windows at the front of the house. With the threat of air attack suspected over—for now—they shifted their focus to the zealots storming the residence. At one time, he might have been able to simply kill each of the attacking horde—snap their necks easily enough —but despite their murderous intent, Phin resisted the engrained urge. Instead, he assured each of them would be unconscious and immobile for hours, giving the Firebirds time to gather up the war criminals and dole out Human justice. Whatever that justice entailed.

These Xenos are too frenzied for a normal horde.

Phin spared only a glance at his brother. *It is possible she has somehow twisted their thoughts and motivations, controlling them in ways we have not yet surmised.*

Between the Firebirds on the house perimeter and along the outer edges, and the Firebirds and defenders within the house, the onslaught of Xenos were debilitated or shot down, or those left standing turned and ran back into the darkness. Most pursued by Firebirds to apprehend them. With the exclusion of a few pulse weapon fires from the darkness, accompanied by flashes of light, a tense lull of silence settled over the residence.

Commander Montgomery came from the hall into the room, his shoes crunching on the broken glass littering the hardwood floors. "We're still fighting off a few along the back of the house, but other than that, their fight seems to be going out of them," he said, stopping with his hands at his waist.

"Do they have her?" President Tanner asked, coming in behind him.

Phin and Daniel, confident the threat within their sight was neutralized, turned to face the commander. Commander Montgomery's face told more than anything he could have said. He shook his head, his lips pressed together, and President Tanner cursed before he turned and marched away to the portion of the house where his wife was being guarded, along with Michael's wife Jacqueline. Both women had resented being tucked away, but ultimately hadn't argued for the sake of the children they carried.

"We may be able to assist in tracking her whereabouts once the immediate danger has passed and everyone is secure," Daniel said, passing on the offer for both of them.

"I appreciate that," Connor said, nodding toward them. "Any help we can get."

The flash hit them like a wave, jolting a new, fresh, powerful surge of adrenaline through them. Phin bolted first, closest to the hall, and knew Daniel would remain behind long enough to explain before he followed. The intense tug led him to the cellar stairs, and his heart pounded harder with every step.

Pain.

Intense pain ripped through him and Phin staggered at the top of the stairs, but propelled himself forward. *No! No!* Daniel's desperate thoughts chased him. Phin was bombarded by Gideon's pain—and desperation—and Daniel's grief, slamming hard and vicious against his own. He yanked open the cellar stairway door and propelled himself toward the sound of multiple pulse weapon fire and the flash of intense light trapped in the closed, underground space. Katrina's scream and the wail of children made him leap from the second step to land semi-crouched at the bottom of the stairs.

Phin drew in every ounce of power he had and lashed out, fighting instinctively with only his own eyes—his own senses—to guide him.

414

He felt blind. Flashes of pulse weapons and the crack of projectile guns echoed off the walls, and he deflected them all, sucking in the power to fuel his outthrust. Through his assault, Katrina's desperate scream—shouting Gideon's name—drove him on.

Daniel reached his side, with several Firebirds running behind. In seconds, every invading enemy lay dead on the floor. Phin dropped his arms, sucked in a hard breath, and turned, both dreading and needing to see what waited for him.

Shouting from the Firebirds was useless, garbled chatter. He knew they ran back up the stairs and out through the now destroyed hatch tucked against one wall where the attackers had blasted their way inside, the noise likely muffled by the frenzied attack. Phin took a step forward, and reality popped back into focus.

Katrina was on the floor, sobbing. The side of her face was red, already showing the bloom of a vicious bruise, blood trailing from a split above her eye. She sobbed, rocking on her knees, trying desperately to hold Gideon's body off the floor and against her. His brother's chest had been torn apart—viciously—and blood covered her hands and blouse. The other Firebirds he'd left with Gideon lay dead on the floor. A huddled mass of weeping children curled in the darkness of the far corner of the safe room. Through the miasma, Phin acknowledged Silas Smith shouting for his father.

Phin stumbled forward. He dropped all walls, opened all pathways between him and his brothers, begging in the silence for a response. Somewhere someone screamed for a medic. Someone else screamed, "She's gone!"

Gideon! Gideon!

Silence answered Phin's cries.

Alpha!

Daniel fell forward, scrambling across the floor to lay his hands on Gideon's chest. Katrina released him to Daniel, her body trembling violently, but he couldn't move. Daniel bowed his head, a bellow of grief ripped from him, from his soul and Phin's, and he collapsed against Gideon's destroyed body.

Something inside Phin broke, leaving behind a blackness that overwhelmed him.

"I'm so sorry," Katrina cried. She folded, doubling herself over, and wept.

Phin dropped hard to his knees at his fallen brother's side.

"*E*veryone, go now! Go! Go! Go! We don't stop until we have her!"

Connor's shouting from the front of the house made Nick look up and toward the door. The activity in the house was suddenly amped up, Firebirds running through the halls and out the doors to the property beyond. He thought for a moment about not standing, or going to see what was wrong; exhaustion dragged hard at him after the combined efforts of the night to hold back the attacks. Frankly, he hadn't known he was capable of that kind of thing, but Michael had been adamant and had brought him into the circle with the others. While in the circle, the power rippling through the six of them had been like a drug, but as soon as it was over he'd been left with one hell of a headache and heavy limbs.

"What's happening?" Caitlin asked from beside him on the couch.

"I don't know. Sounds like they're going to look for the bitch." He pushed his fingers through his hair and forced himself to stand. "I'm going to check on bringing up the kids." He glanced to Jacqueline. She was curled in a chair, as anxious as them, waiting for it to be over once and for all.

She nodded and smiled. "Thank you."

Nick crossed the office to the door and opened it.

And came face-to-face with the end of a pulse pistol.

"No!" Caitlin screamed.

Dozens of weapon blasts and footfalls clashed, and Nick dropped hard to the floor, agonizing, burning pain ripping through his chest.

"Nick!"

He only saw Caitlin's face for a moment before blackness overwhelmed him.

CHAPTER THIRTY-SIX

20 March 2054
Office of the President
Robert J. Castleton Memorial Building – The Castle
Center for United Protectorate Government
Alexandria, Seat of Virginia
North American Continent

"This breaks my heart, Victor."

Victor crossed his wife's office to where she stood at the window, and wrapped his arms around her to draw her to his chest. She laid her arms over his and leaned into him, releasing a long, shuddering sigh. She had barely slept in days, not since they walked away from the shattered remains of the presidential residence, and in the small hours of the night he had held her while she wept.

One of her first duties in Nick Tanner's stead should not have been planning a mass funeral to honor all who lost their lives; it would be a memorial service with full military honors, and deserved exceptional attention. Sadly, due to the chaos that had ensued so quickly after the assassination attempt on Victory Day the week before, the funeral services for William Scarborough who had died protecting Caitlin and Jacqueline had been postponed and now, he would be honored with all the fallen.

There was so much pain.

"Tell me what you need, *Cusbibil*."

She turned her head enough to look at him. "Can you change what happened?"

"No," he answered, "I wish I could."

"Then, you are doing all you can and all I need."

Victor kissed her cheek, and wrapped her tighter in his arms. When they married he had no misconceptions of how hard it would be to be married to the second most powerful person on Earth, and they had both accepted the knowledge her position would come with risk, but acceptance and knowledge didn't lessen the heartache on days like this.

He held her as long as he could, until the time came when he had to go to let her continue in her duties as acting head of state. Victor walked the painfully quiet halls of the building, nodding with grim acknowledgment to the Firebirds standing on duty. None smiled. None tried to hide the pain of loss. They were the elite, the few, the best, and they were now fewer than they had been.

His trip across the city to the hospital wasn't nearly long enough to prepare him for the heavy shadow hanging over the building. It would take time, and for some, the end was nowhere in sight. His heart hurt for Michael in a way he could never comprehend, could only imagine, and even then the imagining was almost too much to stand. Victor greeted doctors and nurses with a nod as he navigated the halls, traversing what had become his normal route. He knocked on David Forte's door and waited for a response before opening it.

David was out of his bed and seated in his wheelchair near the window. He had attacked his physical therapy in the last few days with a vengeance born of grief, and in a matter of days had steadied his hands and managed three steps before his weakened legs gave out on him. Considering the fact Victor once wondered if the man would ever have use of anything below his shoulders, the improvement was mindboggling, were it not for the reason for his drive.

David looked up when Victor entered, but didn't smile. Victor crossed the room and sat in the chair opposite him. They sat in silence for several minutes, as they had the last couple of mornings. Finally, David drew in a long breath through his nose and let go.

"Tell Doctor Cole I want to do it."

"Your decision shouldn't be made out of—"

"Out of what, Victor?" David snapped. "Guilt? Anger? Well, it's going to be a hell of a long time before I do *anything* not driven by guilt and anger. I want out of this chair," he shouted, slamming his hand on the chair's arm, "as soon as possible."

Victor nodded. "I'm sorry. The response was automatic. I will tell her, but I want to be sure you understand what this entails."

David nodded and looked out the window again. "I get it. I'm going to be more cyborg than man, but at least I won't be a man who lays helpless on the floor while his son—" His voice choked and he swallowed hard. "While his son dies." He snapped his head hard to look at Victor, his jaw set and his eyes shining. "And don't you dare explain to me how he wasn't a son, just a product of my DNA soup."

Victor sat forward, holding David's gaze. "I would never dare, David."

David sniffed and looked away again, his knuckles white with his clenched fists. He nodded, but that was all the response he provided. Victor stood and stepped to the side of David's chair, resting his hand on David's shoulder before he headed for the door.

"Vic," David called just before he reached for the door handle.

Victor looked back as David maneuvered the chair to face him. "Yes?"

"I don't know who to talk to about the funeral . . ."

"My wife is handling the arrangements. Gideon will receive full military honors."

David nodded, his lips pressed hard together. "I need her to do something for me."

"Anything you want."

"Give him my name. On the marker, or whatever you do for him. Please. Let him be known as Gideon Forte."

Victor nodded. "Of course. We'll see to it. I promise you."

David looked away, and Victor left him to his sorrow. As he closed the door behind him, he flicked away the moisture on his own cheek. From one man in pain, he moved on mentally to the next. As much as Victor wished he could go to his friend and offer some solace, there was none to give and Michael had not come to the hospital since Monday, not even for visitations. He was too far into denial, and had buried himself deep in the search. Victor doubted Michael would find rest until his family was somehow whole again.

Victor had known Michael since almost his infancy, watched him grow and become a man of integrity and strength despite a brutalized childhood; but, in the coming days, Victor instinctively feared what his friend might become. As much as Michael had become a man who loved fiercely and without reservation, that love tore him apart now. Victor had never seen such fury in any man hidden just below the surface of his constant calm, and it was the calm that frightened Victor the most. He understood it. Michael refused to allow his own pain to shadow the pain Jacqueline suffered, and as much as he was capable, he comforted her, and refused comfort in return. Victor worried how long his friend could withstand the pressure before he no longer bent, but snapped.

"Doctor!"

Victor turned toward the frantic call to see one of the nurses in the secure wing running toward him. His gut dropped. "What is it?"

"He's awake, sir. He's demanding to see someone. Anyone."

Victor nodded and took off in a dead run for the secure wing of the hospital. Firebirds tensed at his approach, but let him pass until he reached the right room. He paused at the door, sucked in a couple quick breaths, then opened it and stepped inside. President Nick Tanner was half way out of the bed, his legs swung over the side, with two nurses trying to hold him back.

"Damn it, get the hell out of my way!"

"Nick," Victor said, doing his best to keep his voice calm as he crossed the room. "You need to stay in bed. You won't get ten feet down the hall, trust me."

Nick already looked blanched, and he reluctantly slumped back on the reclined headrest. Victor nodded to the nurses who immediately went to work on reattaching the electrodes and IVs he'd tried to yank away, sending the machines into loud shrills of alarm. Victor moved to the side of the bed and helped. He leaned toward one of the nurses and whispered calmly.

"Please notify obstetrics the president is awake and arrange transport."

"Yes, sir."

"Tell me what the hell is going on!" Nick's voice bounced off the walls, and his newly reattached heart monitor jolted.

Victor laid his hand on Nick's chest, forcing him to recline. "I will, I promise you, but you need to relax or I *will* sedate you until you can calm down. You have a severe chest wound that required extensive surgery. A fraction of an inch and there would have been nothing I could have done, so I will do what I have to in order to assure you don't undo all my hard work."

Nick practically growled and visibly relaxed. "What day is it?"

"Friday the twentieth. You have been unconscious four days."

"Where are Caitlin and Michael?"

"Caitlin is currently in obstetrics under observation—" He brought up his hand, silencing Nick before he could make any more demands. "She *and* the baby are fine. We've kept her just to be sure because her stress levels were understandably elevated. She has been here daily. I suspect the nurse will have her here in the next few minutes." Victor drew a breath. "Michael is not here, but he is physically fine. Once he hears you are awake, I'm sure he'll come." He wasn't sure at all. "Jacqueline is fine physically."

"Was anyone else hurt?"

Victor gripped the side rail of the bed and bowed his head, gathering his courage before he answered. The next bit of news was likely to throw Nick over the edge. "Many Firebirds were lost, but of those of us in the house . . ." Victor huffed. "Gideon is dead."

Nick cursed and covered his face with his hands. "Damn."

"Nick—"

"Just tell me, Victor, is she dead? Please tell me someone killed that bitch."

Victor shook his head. "Dead, no. Recaptured, yes, and incapable of running ever again." Nick's raised eyebrow asked the question for him. "Mel Briggs was left alive but effectively brain dead after Kathleen attacked her. Although her body was being kept alive by machines, there was no hope of her mind ever coming back. We made the decision to attempt a transfer of Kathleen's consciousness from the host she'd stolen into Mel Briggs' body, and it was successful. She is conscious, alive, within the body but Mel's spinal cord was partially severed and she is paralyzed from the neck down."

"I suppose I should find some solace in that, but I don't."

"We needed to keep her alive, Nick. She may be the only chance we have to—" Victor looked up and away, the reality slamming into him again. He shared no blood, no name, no connection other than a deep love for the Tanner family and the words alone tore him apart.

"What?"

Victor looked to his friend again, not seeing a president or a military leader. But a father. A husband. A grandfather. "Nick, Gideon died defending the children—"

"Dear God—"

"Jamie Quinn and Silas Smith are fine but . . . Nick, whoever killed Gideon took Nicole. They escaped in the chaos."

*N*o one bothered to check on her other than the required rounds, no one asked if she wanted a drink or needed anything. No one cared. Not a person in all of Alexandria Hospital cared if this patient lived or died, except that they needed her alive.

Michael waited in the dark shadows of the room, and knew she had woken before her eyes ever flittered open. That was about all she could do besides chew, swallow, and talk. Or curse and spew venom, which was closer to reality. Some had said they had a hard time separating the face of Mel Briggs from the mind now inhabiting her body, but Michael had no such shortcoming. Whatever body this monster occupied, she twisted their very soul until the evil and malice tainted their eyes. Mel Briggs had been the traitor, the one who set her free to tear apart his world once again. His brother was dead. His father could have been.

His daughter was gone.

He had no problem hating *this* face as much as the one his mother had worn for decades.

She stirred, just a small shift of her head since she could do no more, and opened her eyes. Michael waited while she took in her assumed solitude, and when she believed herself alone, he moved out of the darkness enough to reveal his presence.

"Who is that?" she demanded. "Go ahead. Hide like a coward."

He waited, shoving his rage into the darkest places of his soul. Each day Nicole wasn't home the darkness grew, and one day she would feel the extent of it, but not today. Not yet.

"Hello, Mother," he said barely stronger than a whisper.

She tried to see him, tried to twist, but couldn't. He felt her fear, and he smiled. He imagined all the times she had strapped him down in her torture chamber, held him useless and powerless, and pulled screams from him while she smiled. There was no pleasure in the moment, only satisfaction at the transfer of roles.

"Come to kill me?" she asked. "Seeking your final vengeance?"

Michael stepped into her line of sight, her once-familiar eyes snapping to look at him. Michael tilted his head and studied her like some oddity. "No," he finally answered. "I believe that is what you want. You are hopeless. Powerless. Humiliated. Death would be an escape from your disgrace and indignity."

"You're too much of a coward to kill me," she spat. "You tried once and failed. I bet you wet yourself from the guilt of it. Am I right? You and your sanctimonious Human sensibilities and moralities probably ate at you for months over killing me." She puckered her lips and spit, only succeeding in drooling on her own chin.

Michael stared, silent. His refusal to rise to her insults would fire her rage more than anything he could say. In the times when he could push past the pain and remain silent, refusing to give her the screams she wanted, she had been most infuriated, and now his refusal to be goaded was fuel to her fire.

"How's *Daddy*," she hissed, smirking.

"Do you mean to ask if you succeeded in killing him?" he asked, taking a step toward the bed. Her eyes widened a small degree. "You didn't. Add it to your list of failures."

She clenched her jaw and tipped back her head, growling until it turned into a scream. All she could do was thrash her head against the pillow, and Michael watched. He had told the nurses he would be here, to stay away no matter what, and they had nodded without question. They wouldn't come now. Michael walked to the side of the bed, his hands pushed into his pockets because he still held some doubt in his own ability to keep from choking the life from her. He could do it without every laying a hand on her, but somehow the thought of killing her so impersonally held no appeal.

"What was your goal that night?" he asked. "Kill him? Kill me? Kill as many of us as you could, whether it was by your hand or not? It must have been an insult to your pride to face down all those people you had sought to crush and failed. No wonder Warrick had demanded your punishment. That's what I was, right? Your punishment for failing with Gideon, Daniel, and Phineas." Her eyes twitched in confusion, but he refused to grant her an explanation. Not when it had been like choking on acid just to say Gideon's name.

"If I were you, Mother, I would fear the retribution each of those you wronged might seek. Death will be welcome, just to escape."

"Why let them have the pleasure?" she hissed. "Do it yourself. Kill me."

"No, I won't be selfish," he said taking a step closer. "But I might be persuaded to grant you mercy."

Her gaze flicked toward him. "Why? What do you want?"

Michael leaned over her until their noses were just inches apart. "Tell me where they have taken Nicole and I will do as you want. I'll kill you. I might even do it quickly."

She laughed, a slow rumble that began in her chest until it gurgled free. "What does it matter now? They took her at *my* command, and only *I* can save her. You are such fools! Sheep to be led to slaughter, or to kill, at the whim of a stronger shepherd."

"What do you want with her? Other than to hurt me."

"To pick up where I left off with you," she hissed, her eyes wide. "You carry too much of *his* DNA, you were tainted from the beginning. But his DNA still holds value, and your child—"

His hand was at her throat before he could even think to draw back. Her eyes bulged and she gasped for air. "She isn't mine!" he screamed in her face.

Her eyes widened and he yanked himself back, stumbling away from the bed. Michael covered his face, gasping for control, and when he finally had it he turned back. She still fought to breathe, terror in her eyes. "I am not her father. She carries no part of me—" *Other than my love.*

"Then there is no use for her."

"So, what do you think?"

Daniel turned away from the window in one of the rooms previously assigned to him and his brothers until housing could be found for them, or they decided if they intended to stay in Alexandria at all. The lack of sparkle in Daniel's eyes—usually the joker, the funny man—made Katrina's heart ache.

"Have you discussed this with Phin?" he asked.

Katrina shook her head and walked toward him. "I actually haven't been able to find him. I wanted to talk to both of you, but . . ." She shrugged. "I'd hoped he was here with you."

Daniel lowered his head and turned away again. "What is Karl's opinion of the prospect of us residing with you? He hasn't had a positive opinion of us since we returned with you."

"It was actually his idea." Daniel looked at her over his shoulder, one eyebrow cocked. Katrina smiled, and immediately regretted it. The bonded skin above her eye still pulled with certain expressions, and the ache in her jaw from the impact of a Xeno rifle butt across her chin hadn't quite gone away. "I know. It kind of surprised me, too. Karl understands, and he knows how much I care about you." Her throat caught for a second, and she paused to clear it. "We can put in for a larger space, and we can probably get a three-bedroom eventually; but, until then, we'll make it work."

"I doubt Phin would have any qualms about the situation," Daniel said, just the slightest touch of a grin on his lips. Katrina pulled her lower lip through her teeth, waiting for his answer. "I admit, Katrina, I have considered leaving Alexandria, but I have lost one brother—I can't fathom the idea of losing another." He turned fully to her, a true smile now. "Leaving you is not an option for Phin, although right now he sees nothing clearly."

"I don't want to lose either one of you, Daniel."

Daniel crossed the remainder of the space between them, and stopped in front of her. He raised his hand and ran his knuckle across her cheek. "We have all thrived in the affection you bestowed on us, and your acceptance has made us better men, but Phin is by far the luckiest of us." Then he sighed and stepped back. "My answer is yes."

Katrina didn't let him get far. She opened her arms and wrapped them around his neck, holding on as tight as she could. He returned the embrace, and held on just a little tighter before he released her.

"Now if I can just find Phin . . ."

His eyes darkened again. "Go to where you gave him his name."

Spring had a tentative but tenacious hold on March. All the snow in Falls Church had melted, leaving the streets slick and wet and water running freely into the gutters. Within the hover she could appreciate the bright sunlight and the blue sky, the way the wet stone of the buildings glistened like diamonds. Once Karl stopped the hover and she opened the door, the beauty was smothered by the stench of spring thaw. Sins frozen during the winter came back in full force. Mud and sewage, and the tinge of death somewhere nearby.

"I can't let you go in there," Karl said, swinging out of his side of the hover. "Katrina, the building is condemned."

"I'll be fine. I know where I'm going and I know it's okay."

"No," he said with a slam of the hover door. "I'm sorry, but I can't. I'm walking you inside."

She wanted to argue, but he had been so frightened after the attack she couldn't cause him more worry. Not again. Not so soon. Katrina nodded and stepped back while he locked down the hover and engaged the security protocol to assure it was still here when they came back. Katrina walked the familiar alleyway along the side of the apartment complex until it emptied into the courtyard. This might have been a lovely place to live once upon a time. Karl followed her wordlessly through the lobby doors, now shattered. Bits of broken glass crunched beneath their feet into the faded, frayed rug. She glanced only briefly to the spot where she had held Phin and begged Michael for help.

Her legs burned by the time they reached the fourth floor, and Karl huffed out of breath. Katrina stopped at the end of the hall and turned back to him. "Will you wait here? Please? If he's not here, I'll be right back. You can see me right until I go inside."

Karl pressed his lips together, but nodded.

It felt surreal to enter the apartment again. It looked so different from when they had stayed here. The furniture was knocked over, splintered, things broken on the floor from the fight, dark stains penetrated the wood. Dust made her nose twitch and her eyes water. The main room was empty, and she turned left down the hall to the bedroom. As she suspected, she found Phin, but finding him broke her heart.

He sat on the floor with his knees drawn up, his back to the wall beside the window, and his head resting on his folded arms; the smothered sound of his grief echoed too loud and too painful in the empty room. Katrina ran to him, leaping over the pile of blankets they'd left behind and dropped to her knees beside him, wrapping him in her arms. Phin turned hard into her, burying his head against her stomach, his arms around her so tight she couldn't have moved away from him even if the thought dared cross her mind. His entire body shook with his sobs, the violence of the grief too overwhelming—she knew—to hold in.

She had lived her entire life knowing, understanding, and controlling the whirlwind of emotions people learned to exist with each day, and on the day her parents had died it had torn her apart. How devastating it had to be to be overwhelmed with grief with no filter, no temperance, no way to understand and absorb the grief before it lashed out again.

It had to be so much worse for them, for him and Daniel. They didn't just lose their brother, they *felt* him die. He was connected to them, and then he was ripped away without mercy. This time there was no reprieve, no doctors working diligently to bring him back, no hope for Phin the pain would end. She had held Gideon as he died, but they had died, in part, with him.

Katrina folded herself around him, rocking him as best she could, and whispered again and again she loved him.

"*N*urse! Bring me a sedative, now!"

Victor struggled to get a hold on the patient, her flailing arms ripping cables and wires from her monitors. An IV ripped free of her arm, sending a spray of blood across the white sheets. She screamed and tried to shove away his hands.

"Hey, hey, hey," he kept repeating, trying to catch her frantic attention. "You're okay. You're with friends." He managed to get her head in his hands, and held her firm. Wild golden brown eyes rolled frantically in her eye sockets, looking everywhere but at nothing. Tears rolled down her temples to her hair.

Two nurses came to the bedside, each restraining an arm and one injected the sedative. Almost immediately, the woman relaxed if at least by a small degree. She panted, trying to free herself from his hold.

"Come on, look at me. Right here."

Finally, her wild eyes shifted to look at him, widening in instant fear.

"No, it's okay. We're not going to hurt you. You're in a hospital."

"*Où suis-je?*" she asked, her voice softer, lilting, just as Connor had described when she slipped through Kathleen's dominant personality. "*Où suis-je?*"

"You are in Alexandria. *Vous parlez l'anglais?*" She nodded, though didn't answer. "Do you know where Alexandria is?"

"Egypt?"

He shook his head. "Alexandria, Virginia. The capitol."

She gasped, and struggled again, but the sedative had taken away her strength. Victor's heart broke for her. He tried to smile, but knew it was unconvincing. "Tell me, sweetheart. What is your name? *Comment vous appelez-vous?*"

She stared at him, wide eyed, her bruised lips gaping. New tears welled in her eyes.

Victor stroked her brow to try to soothe. "It's okay. We'll help you, but we need to know your name."

Her eyelids slid heavily over her eyes as the sedative calmed her. He didn't want to put her into too deep a sleep, but she needed to be calm enough not to hurt herself. "Hey, hey," he said again until she opened her eyes again. "Tell me your name, then you can go back to sleep."

"I do not know . . ." she answered, finally in English, before the sedatives took over and she slipped back into a calm sleep.

When she slept again, Victor released his hold on her and stepped back, scrubbing his face with his hands. They had removed Kathleen from this woman's body as quickly as the idea to transfer her to Melanie Briggs' useless shell was proposed in an attempt—though the odds were slim—to gather information to find Nicole Tanner. There was a chance, also slim, the woman might wake with some of Kathleen's memories. Enough perhaps to give them a direction, give them *something* to lead them to the child.

All he knew was she spoke fluent French and she had at one time asked for someone named Adrian. If her memory loss remained consistent, she didn't even know her name. Examination of her after bringing her to the hospital had revealed a startling truth. The woman had given birth approximately six months previous. Precious little to rebuild a life on, and nothing to bring back Nicole.

CONTINUED IN
PHOENIX RISING BOOK THREE: STASIS

PLEASE ENJOY THE FOLLOWING PREVIEW

Lt. Cmdr. Connor Montgomery's trust in his own judgment is gone, wiped out with the betrayal of someone he once trusted with his life. His failure to see the wolf in their midst has cost the people he loves more than they can afford to lose. His niece Nicole has been taken by the Xenos, by order of the most heinous and evil leaders of the Sorracchi race, and Connor will do whatever it takes to find her and bring her home safe.

In the hours and days following the war, the Sorracchi fled and hid however they could, including snatching people out of their lives to create new husks and hide behind unknown faces. Evelyn woke in a world she didn't recognize, with no memory beyond her name. They call her an "Emancipated", a human freed from the possession of a Sorracchi conscience, but the people in charge of her care will tell her little else.

When the memories come, they are dark and sickening, and she can only pray they are not her own. To save the life of a stolen child, Evelyn must face the crimes her hands committed and gain the trust of a man with no trust left. Not even for himself.

PLEASE ENJOY THE FOLLOWING SAMPLE CHAPTER OF

PHOENIX RISING BOOK THREE: STASIS

STASIS: CHAPTER ONE

3 June 2054, Wednesday
Alexandria Hospital, Secure Wing – Surgical
United Earth Protectorate, Capitol City
Alexandria, Seat of Virginia
North American Continent

"I can't promise you this won't be painful, Michael." Doctor Olivia Cole moved from the computer workstation in the corner of the treatment room to his bedside, standing on his left with Jacqueline on his right. "The bionanetics will be using your own body to regenerate the cells they need to form. They will use your own bones, your own cartilage, your own nerves and muscles to clone and reform what has been lost."

"I understand the science of it, Doctor," Michael said, trying to keep his tone level, despite the frustration clawing at him.

The pain in his lower body was a dull, distant ping; a reprieve due to the spinal anesthetic Victor had injected an hour earlier. It left him numb, feeling detached, and he despised it, but the pain of the initial injection would far exceed anything he had endured to that point. He knew it, but he still detested the drugging effect. Jacqueline had asked him, sometimes begged him to take the pain medication Victor had provided, and only when tears shined in her eyes did he give in. The drugs didn't just numb the pain but numbed his thoughts.

He never wanted the ache of loss to be lessened, because sometimes in those moments of intoxicated reprieve he forgot—even if just for a second—his little girl was gone.

"I know," Doctor Cole said with a small smile and sigh. "I suppose it makes me feel better to say it, just to be sure. Not all doctors have patients with a greater expanse of knowledge than their own."

"Well, I'm not half as smart as either of you, so can you explain for my benefit?" Jacqueline asked.

Michael reached for her hand, and she let him take it, but didn't look away from Doctor Cole. He hated every moment of the last three months, hated the strain it had put on her, hated the moments they had been robbed of, and most of all hated he could do nothing to change it. Invalided. Impotent to fix her heartbreak. Torn.

"Of course," Doctor Cole said, looking at his wife. "I've been researching the concept of nanotechnology for several years, but as of yet haven't found a practical use in my field as most of the wounded I work with are either dealing with weakened bodies, or adaptation to prosthetics. Michael's case presented as a unique situation where the bionanetics would be of use because their programming to rebuild and repair. Michael's bone deterioration cannot be fixed by my usual means of treatment; in fact, my usual approach would more than likely cause more damage." She glanced over her shoulder to the monitor mounted on the wall where a magnification of the bionanetics danced on the screen like living blood cells.

"Has this ever been done before?" Jacqueline demanded.

"Yes, actually," Doctor Cole said, turning back. "In those three young men you found a few months back." For a moment, her eyes saddened. "Two now, of course. Michael's half-brothers. This technology was used to accelerate their maturity then halt their aging, enhance them, and heal them. And of course, as we all know, in sadistic manipulation. But the core theory is sound. Program the bionanetics to join with the precise DNA of the host, so the machines can not only identity damage, but repair it, as needed." She canted her head and shrugged, pushing her hands into the pockets of her lab coat.

"They are so detailed in their programming they can only work within the body of an exact DNA match; if that weren't the case we could have transferred the technology in part from either Phin or Daniel. It's a necessary coding, but it will assure the best possible chance at success."

"But it's never been done by someone other than a sadistic bitch?"

Michael tugged on her hand enough to silently request she move closer to him, and when she did, he raised her hand to his mouth and kissed her knuckles. Doctor Cole met his gaze for a moment before looking again to Jacqueline.

"Not in any experiment the Areth or Coalition medical communities are aware of, no."

"Is there any risk—"

"Jacqueline—" Michael said gently. She ignored him.

"No," Doctor Cole answered with a smile and a shake of her head. "The worst possible outcome will be that Michael's body rejects the bionanetics outright, with no progress made. As bad as his current situation may be, it will not be made worse by this and there is no risk to his life."

"Jacqueline," Michael said again, drawing her hand until she looked down at him. "I have read every word of her research, and I worked with her in the lab as we perfected the coding. I believe in this."

"She said you'll still be in pain. Can it be worse? Michael, it kills me to watch you go through that."

"Yes, it will be painful. But the pain will be finite."

Jacqueline lowered her head and closed her eyes, but not before he saw the tears. Michael laid his hand on her belly, the cotton of her tee shirt stretched over their child growing within her. She was nearly seven months, the baby growing cumbersome and fidgety. Even now the baby responded to his touch and pushed against him. Jacqueline laid her hand over his and tried to hide her sniff.

"Jacqueline, I have accepted this has the potential not to work. I need to be able to—" Bitter anger hit the back of his throat and he swallowed hard.

"I know," she said softly, giving him reprieve from having to explain anything more.

A rapid three knocks at the door preceded Victor's entrance. "Are we ready?"

"Yes," Doctor Cole affirmed, stepping aside so Victor could come to the side of the bed. "We were going over some last-minute questions Mrs. Tanner needed to know."

Victor nodded and winked at Jacqueline. "Don't worry, Jackie. We've been refining this for weeks. It's as flawless as possible."

As he spoke, Doctor Cole went to the computer terminal and opened the imaging program. A light over the bed switched on, casting a glow over Michael's torso, pelvis, and upper thighs. A holographic image appeared above the foot of his bed representing his musculoskeletal structure, the areas of damage and erosion showing grayer and less substantial than the rest. He had lost nearly a quarter of an inch in height on his worst side, the image clearly showing the lack of cartilage and bone. His body had been either absorbing the fragmented dust, or as of late, he had found bits erupting through his skin in painful rashes.

"We will be injecting the bionanetic serum as close to the damage as possible to allow immediate integration and initiation," Doctor Cole explained.

She and Victor both retrieved sanitary masks, placing on their own as they handed one to both Michael and Jacqueline. For a procedure such as this, Michael did not need to be anesthetized; he preferred to be conscious to observe. Even the local anesthetic might slow the process, but a deep anesthetic could delay the onset for hours. He didn't even want that much delay. Victor lowered the head of the bed to recline him flat, and Jacqueline shifted her position to stay close to his head, her grip tight on his hand. When Victor moved aside the blankets to expose the sanitized skin over his hip, coated in a plastic sheet for protection, she looked away and focused on Michael while Victor pulled away the seal.

"I love you," she whispered, her voice muffled by the mask.

"I love you, too."

"I'm going to inject the bionanetics," Victor said, his unsaid "This will hurt" unnecessary.

Despite the anesthetic that numbed him from mid-chest

downward, the pain was vicious, burning, acidic, and spreading. They had done all they could to reduce the pain, he knew that, but this was a new microorganism, though part mechanical, being introduced to a body already ravaged by torture and experimentation. There was no way to make it easy.

Michael clamped shut his eyes and grit his teeth through the pain, willing himself not to move. He couldn't hold back the deep, ripping groan in his chest. He forced himself to release Jacqueline's hand to avoid hurting her. He had to find focus, had to find something other than the pain.

An image of a blond-haired, blue-eyed girl filled his thoughts, her toothy grin, her lopsided ponytails, and her tiny hand in his.

"It will ease soon, my friend. I swear to you," Victor's voice carried from beyond the red haze.

He didn't care. All he cared about was the final result.

When he had his feet again, he would find his daughter.

And God help those who took her.

ALEXANDRIA HOSPITAL REHABILITATION ANNEX
FACILITY FOR LIFE INTEGRATION
UNITED EARTH PROTECTORATE, CAPITOL CITY
ALEXANDRIA, SEAT OF VIRGINIA .
NORTH AMERICAN CONTINENT

"You're agitated today, Evelyn."

Evelyn clenched her jaw to keep from snapping a sharp retort, trying to focus on the scene of green trees and blooming flowers outside the private conference room window. Outside was calm, a sharp contrast to the simmering frustration curling in her chest like smoke from a fire. She wrapped her arms around her body, gripping her own sides in a concerted effort not to march another circumference of the room.

"What has you on edge?"

She turned away from the idyllic setting to focus on Damian Ali seated in the chair across from her; an attractive man with wide shoulders, thick chest and arms, and a bald, rich brown head that practically shined beneath the overhead lights. His voice was like the rumble of thunder rolling in over the valley where the hospital sat, low and deep but calming, his Trinidadian accent softening his words further. He canted his head a few degrees and smiled, his white teeth a slash across his face.

The smile was likely an effort to calm her nerves, but it only made them prickle.

The hallway walls were dark, not from paint or lack of light, but a dank saturation that left the air thick and musty. It scratched her throat and left a taste like algae at the back of her tongue. Indignation at the necessity to subject herself to such squalor crawled under her skin like the sand fleas of Giz'Karnak.

"Evelyn . . ."

She sucked in a sharp breath and took several steps away from the window. "Yes, I'm agitated," she finally said, barely tempering the evidence in her voice.

"Why?"

Evelyn laughed, humorless and rough, tipping back her head to look at the ceiling. "Why am I agitated? Oh, I can't imagine what could possibly agitate me." Arms still wrapped around herself to keep from waving them in frustration, Evelyn looked to Damian again. "I'm this . . . *husk* . . . of a woman with no past, no present, and as such *no* future, barely a name . . . Should I continue?"

Damian braced his hands on the arms of his chair and rose, a fluid motion indicative of his subtle strength. He may be her therapist of sorts now, but it was evident in every movement and every limb he had once been a soldier. Whether he intended to intimidate, or not, everything about the man declared his power.

"Don't call yourself a husk, Evelyn. That is a word used by the ones who took your past from you."

"That's what everyone tells me, Damian, but that's all I have. What people tell me about me, about *us*." She lost her struggle, and swept her arm away from her side, taking in the window and the view—the whole world—beyond. "I wake up in this world I don't know, I'm told this fantastical tale, and I don't even remember going to sleep!"

"You have every right to your frustration—"

"Thank you for your permission," she snapped, and immediately closed her eyes and pressed her lips together, taking in a long breath through her nose as she sensed his approach. She released air through pursed lips before opening her eyes to look up at him, standing an arm's length away. "I'm sorry, Damian. You don't deserve my anger. I haven't been sleeping well, and I'm overtired."

"I believe it's more than that," Damian led. "Evelyn, answer me truthfully. Are you experiencing memories?"

She drew in a long breath and eased it out her nose, only allowing herself a brief glance toward the window before she focused on Damian. A male voice, one she knew but didn't have a name for, whispered in her mind. "Always look people in the eye, Evie. Even when you don't know what you're talking about, they think you do." Was he a father, a grandfather? Unlike the thought of the hallway of moments before, the revisiting of this voice offering life advice left her with no unease; yet frustration squirreled under her skin; she wanted to scream to release it.

"Randomly, for no reason I can tell," she admitted, crossing again to the window to look out on the bright afternoon. "They've woken me in the middle of the night, they've come to me sitting in the dining hall. At least three since we came in here. How am I to know if they are mine?" She glanced over her shoulder at him.

"I can't answer that. None of us can," Damian said with a shake of his head. "You are only slightly more a mystery to us than you are to yourself."

Evelyn sighed and leaned her shoulder into the window frame, touching her forehead to the cool glass. "Your guidance is without measure, Damian Ali."

Three months earlier she had woken from a nightmare; the best and only way she had to describe it. It had taken five weeks for the name Evelyn to break the surface, but there were days when she wasn't convinced at all the name was hers. Some days it felt natural, perfect, and correct, then there were days like today when Evelyn was a stranger. No one could or would tell her anything other than she was now one of the Emancipated. She knew of the Emancipated, but the explanation felt more like a fairytale or urban legend. She didn't know the Sorracchi, and only an engrained understanding of the Areth, but her understanding conflicted with what she had been told. Even now it confused her. The Areth were not the Areth, but the Sorracchi who stole the name of the Areth. There had been a war, a devastating near-apocalypse that had left the world wounded and changed everything. They told her the Emancipated were Humans who had been stolen by the Sorracchi, their bodies hijacked by an alien conscience, but had been freed through a reverse process to give them back their own lives.

Damian had confided in her that he himself had once been one of those stolen souls and was now an Emancipated. He had awoken as if from a dream, with only fragments of his experience flittering behind his own life. He was one of the lucky ones.

It didn't always work.

She had seen the worst-case scenarios wandering the hallway of the facility, blank shells struggling to learn the basics of eating food and maintaining personal hygiene. Some thought the worst case was death during division, but to her being left as a blank shell would be a fate worse than death.

"I've lost you."

Damian's voice pulled her back from her contemplations. She sighed and looked at him. "*Je suis désolé*, Damian. I don't have the mind for this today." Even as the words were out of her mouth, she wondered where she'd learned French, and why it came to her nearly as easily as English.

"Days like these are normal, Evelyn, and now that fragments are breaking through they are likely to occur more often. Don't doubt your progress for it."

Evelyn nodded and turned away from the window, offering a final smile. Damian curled his large hand around her upper arm and smiled back. Never once had she seen anything less than absolute honesty and concern in his dark eyes. There had been moments when she saw reservation in the eyes of the facility staff, and perhaps at times outright hostility. It was then she wondered who she had been, whether by her own will or not.

"They won't listen until someone dies!"

Evelyn gasped and swayed, caught from falling by Damian's firm grip on her elbows. She stared at him several moments before his face registered through the shock. The words, however, continued to echo in her head. *"They won't listen until someone dies!"* The voice was hers, but it was wrong. Harsher, deeper, lacking the accent she knew she had but hadn't yet identified.

But it was the smothering, choking hatred she suddenly drowned in that made her ill. Hatred so visceral it burned. Hatred so intense it was psychopathic. She didn't just sense it, she *felt* it.

"Evelyn, what is it?"

The tears hit her in a drowning rush; she nearly choked on them trying to breathe.

"Mon Dieu, Damian. What was I? What *am* I?"

END OF SAMPLE

ABOUT THE AUTHOR

 Gail R. Delaney is a multi-published, award-winning author of romance in multiple sub-genres, including contemporary romance, romantic suspense, and epic science fiction romance. She always wrote stories as a kid through her teens, but didn't decide to write 'for publication' until her early twenties after the death of her mother. While helping her father go through her mother's papers, she found a box her mother kept with everything Gail had ever written—from book reports to short stories. It was then she realized her mother saw her as a writer, and it was time to live up to her mother's vision.

You can find out more about Gail R. Delaney's body of work at:

http://www.GailDelaney.com

ALSO BY GAIL R. DELANEY

Baker Street Legacy

Baker Street Legacy is a romantic suspense series with a Sherlock Holmes bloodline.

Book One: My Dear Branson

Book Two: The Empty Chair

Book Three: Indefinite Doubt

Coming Soon

Contemporary Romance

Something Better

Precious Things

Feel My Love

Fools Rush In

A Love at First Sight novella

Made in the USA
Columbia, SC
24 September 2022

67894873R00276